REDEMOLISHED

ALFRED BESTER

ibooks
new york
www.ibooksinc.com

DISTRIBUTED BY SIMON & SCHUSTER

An Original Publication of ibooks, inc.

An ibooks, inc. Book

Distributed by Simon & Schuster, Inc.
1230 Avenue of the Americas, New York, NY 10020

ibooks, inc.
24 West 25th Street
New York, NY 10010

The ibooks World Wide Web Site Address is:
http://www.ibooks.net

ISBN 0-7434-8679-X
First ibooks trade paperback printing December 2000
First ibooks mass market paperback printing September 2004
10 9 8 7 6 5 4 3 2 1

CONTENTS

Introduction

Alfred Bester (1913-1987) was a legendary author. Most notable for two major science fiction novels written in the 1950s, *The Demolished Man* and *The Stars My Destination*, Bester also wrote several great short stories, interesting later novels, and many fascinating articles and essays during his long career. Bester contributed to science fiction an intelligent cinematic style it was lacking, and applied his healthy curiosity about the sciences and human interactions to create truly unique works.

Born and raised in New York, he was educated at the University of Pennsylvania (where he majored in several subjects, joined the Philomathean Society, and tried his best to be a "Renaissance Man") and Columbia (where he studied law briefly).

After college, Bester drifted into SF and comics at the same time in the 1940s (see the essays "Science Fiction and the Renaissance Man" and "My Affair with Science Fiction"), working on SF stories like "The Probable Man,""The Push of a Finger" and "Hell is Forever."

In the comics field, Bester wrote for *Superman* and the original Golden Age *Green Lantern* (and not only came up with the Green Lantern oath that still survives to this day, but also developed notable villains like Vandal Savage and Solomon Grundy) for National Comics (now DC).

Note how Bester learned quickly; the nominal "Probable Man" story is nearly raw pulp, with only a few of Bester's brilliancies showing through under a welter of cliches; only a year later he was able to write the mature "Push of a Finger," where the breezy style and cinematic virtuosity pushes the pulp elements nearly aside.

Bester segued into radio/TV in the early 1950s, working on detective/mystery programs and variety/quiz shows, while continuing to write great experimental SF, novels like *The Demolished Man* (see the restored 1952 prologue in this volume), and stories such as "The Roller Coaster."

He also attempted to break out of SF with a mainstream psychological thriller about the TV world, *Who He?* (a.k.a. *The Rat Race*), 1953. This novel met with limited success, but was one of only two Bester books to be reviewed by *The New York Times*, and the movie option sale gave Bester the funds to go to Europe for a time to write *The Stars My Destination*.

By the late fifties, after producing *The Stars My Destination* and a wide range of dazzling short stories, Bester felt he had had it with SF (summing his feelings up in the essay "Science Fiction and the Renaissance Man," 1957), and took steps to divorce himself from the field, but hard.

In a revealing series of columns in *The Magazine of Fantasy & Science Fiction* in the early 1960s, Bester waded in and punched SF in the nose, in the guise of *F&SF's* book reviewer. During his 18-month tenure he would twit and censure the authors of the books he was reviewing; even going so far as to drop the books from one column as being entirely too bad to review, and replacing the reviews with "A Diatribe

Against Science Fiction" (February 1961) that went right for the throat.

He back-pedaled swiftly the next month with his review of the great SF authors of the current time, ("The Perfect Composite Science Fiction Author," 1961), showing that not all SF sucked.

At the same time as his SF-writing meltdown (starting circa 1959 and continuing throughout the 1960s), Bester was struggling with the demands of a heavy writing load. This period included TV scriptwriting, a column for *Rogue* magazine, plus the start of a long stint as an interviewer (and later Senior Editor) for *Holiday*. Bester was convinced that his talents lay in the mainstream writing field, though he would not make much headway beyond a series of remarkable interviews for *Holiday* (several, written between 1957–1969, are included in this collection). A psychological thriller apparently written in this period, *Tender Loving Rage*, went unpublished in Bester's lifetime, and was finally released in a hardback edition in 1991 by Tafford Press.

The stories from this time include trenchant pieces he managed to produce for his *Rogue* column ("Bester's World," generally a mix of celebrity gossip, commentary about the entertainment field, and nonfiction articles about life in New York), such as "I Will Never Celebrate New Year's Again" (1963) and "The Lost Child" (1964).

Even in his SF exile, Bester kept ties with the field. His collection *The Dark Side of the Earth* appeared in 1964. It was a collection of 1950s stories from *F&SF* that have been collected elsewhere (*Virtual Unrealities*), except for "Out Of This World" (1964), a short alternate-universe piece that reads like a reworked *Twilight Zone* episode.

Out of SF, Bester's restless nature led to a series of remarkable interviews and articles for *Holiday* magazine. As early as 1960 he was trying to dovetail his SF knowledge into entertaining articles for the *Holiday* crowd (see "Gourmet Cooking in Outer Space," which reads like a chapter of Bester's "missing" 1960 SF novel), and throughout his tenure at that magazine he was able to put his scientific knowledge and restless curiousity to work in articles like "The Sun" (1969) and "The Moon" (1969).

But the interviews are the real prizes from this time period. Bester was working for a major publication, and could go anywhere and interview almost anybody. The support was fantastic (as Bester himself tells it in the introduction to the Interviews section), and he took full advantage. The interviews were well-produced in *Holiday*'s very handsome large format, with photographs by some of the best in the business (Diane Arbus, Phillipe Halsman, Bruce Davidson, Hans Namuth, Arnold Newman, and others).

The bottom fell out of *Holiday* in 1970 (the magazine was sold, reverted to a standard format, and moved its editorial offices to Kansas City), and Bester was left high and dry. He was still in communication with *F&SF*, and queried them about a long fantasy story he'd written, "The Animal Fair" (1972). They were receptive, printing the story (and giving Bester a special cover line), and welcomed him back to the field. Bester was back in gear by the early 1970s.

Bester concentrated exclusively on SF from this point on, even as his health began to fail. This material included a pair of SF-related interviews for *Publishers Weekly* ("Isaac Asimov" and "Robert Heinlein," both 1973). In this time he also produced essays and satires on the SF field ("Writing and *The Demolished Man*," 1972; "My Affair with SF," 1973), and saw his earlier stories collected in the omnibus collection *Starlight* (1976).

During the 1970s and into the 1980s Bester still had a lot of writing potential, and produced a series of remarkable stories (like "Something Up There Likes Me," 1973 and "The Four Hour Fugue," 1974, included in this collection) and novels, including *The Computer Connection* (1973), *Golem*^{100} (1980), and *The Deceivers* (1981).

Even though his novels of the '70s and '80s were well received (for the most part), and his earlier novels *The Demolished Man* and *The Stars My Destination* were almost never out of print (indeed, *The Demolished Man* appeared in a deluxe Easton Press edition in 1986, with an introduction by Kurt Vonnegut Jr.), by 1987 Bester's reputation (and net worth) was at a low ebb. The later novels were out of print, and his last story collection had appeared in 1976. Though he was recognized as a Grand Master by the SFWA in 1987 (and knew about the award), he still wound up dying unnoticed in a critical care facility at the age of seventy-three (although as Julie Schwartz tells it, Harlan Ellison tried to ease Bester's transit by calling the hospital, pretending to be a reporter from *USA Today*, and haranguing them into giving Bester the best care).

After his death, Bester's reputation rose, as is the unfortunate way. To quote Herman Melville, no stranger to this process:

"All ambitious authors should have ghosts capable of revisiting the world, to snuff up the steam of adulation, which begins to rise straightway as the Sexton throws his last shovelful on him. Down goes his body & up flies his name." (1849)

In 1979, Byron Preiss and Howard Chaykin, working with Bester, produced the first part of a striking graphical version of *The Stars My Destinantion*. It was one of the first full-scale graphic novel attempts, and, unfortunately, events occurred that left the second part out of print until 1992, when a complete edition was published by Epic Comics, as produced by Byron Preiss Visual Publications.

Preiss's interest in Bester's work led directly to its early 1990s renaissance, as new editions of *The Demolished Man* (introduced by Harry Harrison) and *The Stars My Destination* (complied and edited by Alex and Phyllis Eisenstein, and introduced by Neil Gaiman) appeared, as well as a new short fiction collection, *Virtual Unrealities* (edited by Robert Silverberg, Byron Preiss and Keith R. A. Candido), and a new novel, *Psychoshop* (a posthumous collaboration with Roger Zelazny).

Continuing through 2000, other reissues include *The Deceivers* (with an afterward by Julius Schwartz), and *The Computer Connection* (introduced by Harlan Ellison), and this new collection, *Redemolished*.

Redemolished makes up the best source for Bester's uncollected short fiction, essays, articles, and miscellaneous writings, including the deleted prologue to *The Demolished Man*. It gives you full access to the range of Bester's extraordinary five decades as a writer, and lets Bester speak for himself as you follow his restless mind across any subject he could ferret out with his amazing curiosity, drive, and exemplary writing talent.

Richard Raucci
San Francisco, 2000

The Probable Man

I

The black car drew alongside, then swerved in front of their roadster. Brakes squealed. David Conn kicked the door open, shouldered the heavy rucksack and grabbed Hilda's wrist.

"Come on!" he said.

The gloom of late afternoon lowered as they ran panting across the fields. Conn saw the grass alongside whip, and a fraction of a second later heard the crack of a gun sounding from behind. Hilda gasped.

"They mean business," Conn said.

He twisted his head as they ran. Shapes followed them through the dusk. Five-six-seven. If only he could find cover. But they were running across a broad open lawn that looked like a fairway. Two hundred yards to the left he saw the jet outline of bunkers; a green topped by a fluttering flag.

"This way!" Conn grunted.

Shots sounded again, sharp and clear in the April evening as they tumbled over the edge of the bunker down into a soft sandpit. Conn got the rucksack off his shoulder, turned and squirmed up the side of the pit, facing their pursuers. He slid his gun out and fired at a dim shape. Hilda came up alongside to watch.

"Get down," said Conn. "They want you."

"Alive," said Hilda, "not dead. I won't be any good to them dead."

"I will," said Conn.

He tried to catch his breath. Beyond pistol range the seven black figures closed to a tight group and consulted. Conn counted cartridges. Two clips. Twelve. It wouldn't be enough. They would wait until it grew a little darker and then rush. He couldn't afford to lose time. He had to get to the machine by eight—and that gave him less than an hour to fight and win an impossible battle.

"Save a bullet for me," said Hilda.

Conn looked at her quickly. The soft blond hair and blue eyes. This, he thought, is downright weird. I fall in love with a girl who died a thousand years before I was born. I look at her full lovely mouth and I want to kiss it, and all the time I know her mouth has been dust and ashes for a thousand years.

"That's stupid talk," Conn said. "You don't know what I can do."

"Maybe you don't know what Nazis can do," Hilda answered. "They'll take me back to Holland. They'll use me for political blackmail. They'll keep me locked up—like Leopold of Belgium. Save a bullet."

The seven forms were still consulting. Conn knew what their big problem was. They were wondering how to avoid killing Hilda in the attack. It was getting black rapidly. Conn sent two slugs their way just to let them know. Then he stole another glance at Hilda. She smiled tremulously.

"I'm thinking that you're beautiful," Conn said.

"You're thinking how sorry you are you ever got mixed up with a refugee," Hilda answered. "You're wishing Prime Minister Pietjen never had a daughter—"

"No," Conn said. He was beginning to lose control of himself at the thought of anyone wanting to hurt Hilda. "It just occurred to me that a thousand years ago our name might have been Cohen. It makes me want to shoot straight."

"A thousand years?" Hilda stared.

"Listen," Conn said. "I haven't had the heart to tell you. I was waiting until the last minute—until I reached the place I'm headed for, up the side of that slope there. Can you guess what I meant when I said—a thousand years?"

"No," Hilda shook her head. "It sounds crazy to me. All I know is that you were in a hurry to get some place when they cut us off. You told me last month you were a reporter from the West Coast—"

"Reporter is right, but not from the coast—" Conn fingered the revolver nervously "Maybe you won't believe this—"

Hilda nudged his elbow. The forms had separated. He could barely see them. Through the hush of nightfall he heard the faint squeaks of shoes on dewy grass. Conn waited while his heart thumped.

They would rush from all sides, he thought, and in the night he might get one or two at the most. Then the rest would pick up Helga. She'd be bound and gagged, and in a month she'd be back in Holland. She wouldn't be Hilda any more. She'd be Hilda Pietjen, daughter of the prime minister, just another chip in the Nazi poker game. And he'd be dead in the bunker, a thousand years before he'd been born.

A spike of red flame flared and cracked. Conn fired at the flash. It had been a signal. Feet thumped on the turf. Conn thought: What have I got to lose? He got to his knees and scrambled to the lip of the trap, exposing himself. He fired the last shots carefully at the looming shapes, and as the echoes boomed, he rolled down into the pit, fingers groping for the last clip. It seemed to him that floodlights were sparking around him.

A black figure hurtled over the bunker and came down at him. Conn dropped the clip and smashed his empty gun in the man's face. At that moment a second caught him on the flank and bore him down. Grit seared Conn's cheek. He rolled with flailing arms and drove an elbow into the man's neck.

He tried to get to his feet in the shifting sand. The man kicked him heavily in the belly. Conn fell forward, fists pumping toward the jaw. Cartilage squished and the man groaned and slumped. Then Conn's right drove against the jaw. Everything was still.

"No more?" Conn croaked. Hilda helped him up, her eyes distended with fright. Conn repeated: "No more? There ought to be. I couldn't have killed five men with two shots." He examined the surrounding fairway closely. In the glow of the rising moon he saw nothing. The turf looked torn.

"No more," Hilda said. "Oh, darling, I—"

Conn took her in his arms and kissed her. This, he thought, should be the last paragraph. Nothing else comes after this but "They lived happily ever after" and then "The End." He nestled his bruised cheek against her silky hair and tried to memorize its scent. At last he pushed Hilda gently away.

"I've got to go now," Conn said. "It's nearing night.

This is goodby, Hilda, for a long time. Maybe forever—"

Even in the darkness he could sense the way Hilda stiffened. She stepped back a little, her hand raised to her lips.

"Oh," she said.

Conn said: "It's not what you think, darling. I love you, but—" Too overwrought to continue, he hunted shakily for his revolver and clip, found them at last and tried to brush out the sand.

"I think we'd better go back to the car," Hilda said.

"No, I'll walk the rest of the way," said Conn. "It's not far

to where I'm going—in a sense." He shouldered the heavy rucksack, paused for an instant. Suddenly he grasped Hilda's arms and shook her a little. "You've got to understand," he said. "This is something I must do. I'm not a free agent—I've got a tremendous responsibility."

"Don't talk," Hilda said. "Excuses don't make it any easier to understand."

"You're not making it any easier," Conn said.

Hilda broke away from him and tried to struggle up the side of the sandpit. Conn helped her up. They stood on the open fairway, feeling the night breeze cool their faces.

"Listen to me a moment," Conn said. He pulled out the keys of his roadster and handed them to her. "This is for the car. It's yours now. I won't be needing it, ever again. Hilda, this isn't the way I wanted to say goodby. I thought we'd drive to the place and I'd explain there. The apparatus would have made understanding easier for you. Maybe this way is better after all. We'll part here. You'll drive back to the city, hating me. Pretty soon you'll forget—"

She took the keys in silence, eyeing him contemptuously. Suddenly Hilda slapped his face. The blow stung. Conn grinned wryly.

"All right," he said. "Goodby—"

He started toward the hill where the machine was cased. After a dozen steps he turned his head and dimly saw Hilda standing there in the night. After a dozen more he heard her cry: "David!" And then again in an altered, almost joyous tone: "David!" He thought that a wind brushed past him, like the ghost of himself returning to Hilda.

He wanted to go back to her more than anything else. He thought: To hell with Dunbar and my responsibility to him. To hell with the machine—let it rot forever. To hell with everything but Hilda—But it was twenty minutes to eight and the discipline was bred strong in him. He pushed into the high weeds at the foot of the hill and began to mount the slope.

Every step pushed this pleasant land farther into the past. His own day loomed before him—the day a thousand years to come. The same earth, but a place of towering cities, of giant laboratories; of vast engines that reshaped the land and thundering rocketships that pierced the skies.

Conn thought of the ordered existence to which he was returning and sighed. It was tailored. Life was too smooth and easy. There was too little work, no excitement; too little adventure, no danger. In this crude earth of the past which he was leaving he had found all the breathlessness for which he'd yearned. He'd found and left a girl crying out for him, a girl whose cries had died away a thousand years ago.

Conn reached the crest of the hill. The core was of solid granite, as old as eternity; Dunbar had made sure of that. Conn probed carefully in the turf until he found the soft spot. He dug energetically until he uncovered the bank of studs. He pressed them in combination and stood up.

Slowly a yard-wide circle of turf slipped downward, carrying him with it. Fifty feet it lowered until a narrow steel door set flush in the side of the shaft slipped up before Conn. He thrust it open, stepped inside and pressed a button placed high on the jamb. The circle of turf ascended again.

Conn shut the door behind him and switched on the lights. The apparatus glittered before him, a maze of solenoids and selenium generators, as gleaming and new as though Dunbar had assembled it half an hour before. He glanced at his wristwatch. Five minutes to eight. Dunbar had given him strict instructions to return within a year at the utmost. Power had drained off from the banks of accumulators through sheer inactivity. This way there was just enough left. Another day's delay might make return impossible.

Hastily Conn inspected the written records and samples he had packed into the rucksack. Underneath these were the tinned reels of motion pictures he had shot. He shouldered the sack, checked instruments, and at last stepped up on the small platform in the center of the apparatus. He reached out for the giant knife-switch.

He thought: I'm a fool. Here's where I belong. Hilda needs me. Just because we've fought off one group of Nazi agents doesn't mean she'll be safe forever.

He thought: What am I getting excited about Nazis for? This is all past and forgotten. Democracy will survive. The last vestiges of Fascism died out in 1945. That will be four years from this moment. Hilda will be older. Maybe she'll be married with children and a PTA candidate. Maybe sometimes she'll think about the "reporter" she met New Year's Eve 1941. Maybe she'll think of the way he ditched her.

He thought: I don't belong in the dead world of the past. Why don't I cheer up? I'm going back to my own family and friends. I belong in 2941. Dunbar's waiting for me to make my report.

It was eight o'clock. He yanked down the switch, and as the machine roared he said: "Damn!"

II

A thousand years through time took less than five seconds. Conn stood impatiently on the platform, waiting for the last emanations to die away from the tube. The solenoids still whined in dying sighs like the final whispers of a siren. Some of the contacts sputtered and violet light played in the slow turning generators. That was all. All that was left of the surge of power that had thrust him a thousand years forward through the Time Stream.

Conn stepped down and glanced at the accumulator index. The needle hung over the red exhaustion mark. He'd had barely enough power. He walked wearily to the door and yanked the heavy steel plate open.

Conn pressed the stud again and presently the circular plate dropped down. He could make out the crescent of pale light aloft. That would be old Dunbar's laboratory, built at the crest of this century-old granite outcropping. Dunbar would probably be there, pacing the marbelite floor in anxiety. He'd been pacing maybe five minutes since the time Conn had started out. Conn remembered the vastness of the laboratory. The gleaming walls and lofty ceiling.

He would say hello to Dunbar first. Then, before anything else, he would step out on the balcony and look east to where the golf course had been, and farther to where the Merrick Highway had wound its silver thread toward New York. Now there would be nothing but the inane regularity of masses of mile-high buildings. No—there was no more green land and forest in his time. Only mile after endless mile of towering steel and marble buildings, and perhaps, here and there, a carefully planned little garden.

The disk shuddered to a halt before him. Conn stepped forward, then gasped. It was not topped with the gleaming gray marbelite of Dunbar's lab floor. It was covered with a brown rubble. Rubble chinked with dirt; and in that brown moist earth grew sparse blades of grass. Conn looked up, bewildered. The light from overhead was still pale. In that circle he saw a sprinkling of stars.

He started the disk and arose in an agony of wonder. In choked tones he called: "Dunbar?" and then: "Dunbar! This is Conn!" There was no answer. Only the creaking whisper of the lift mechanism.

It was not too dark. A full moon rode overhead. To the north there was a heavy black forest. East and south were rolling hills showing patches of naked rock and moon glints on a vast broad river. West stretched shimmering wheat fields, and a mile beyond them Conn discerned the silhouette of towering battlements pierced with amber lights.

What had happened to his world?

Conn fingered the sack of records. He thought: There can't be any mistake. Dunbar tested and retested the apparatus. It was set for April, 2941, and if it was set that way, then that's the time I'm in. What's happened to my world?

Ten feet to one side of him, a boulder jerked silently into the air and settled in a cloud of dust. Conn swivelled and stared, oblivious of the hail of cutting particles that slashed his face. As a second rock, a little closer, leaped up, he threw himself down and shielded his head. This time the fragments bit through his clothes like small knives.

Below him, completely encircling the hill, he saw the minute flashes of explosions. It was as though the hill were ringed with enormous fireflies. But these weren't explosions. There was no sound. He could feel the slight concussions and dimly he made out the craters that opened up magically under the flashes, but there was no sound.

Conn squinted through the dark. A silent battle seemed to be raging around the foot of the hill. As his eyes accommodated to the gloom, he saw below him two figures partially concealed in a mass of boulders. They were big men encased in plate armor that gleamed in the moonlight. Lying prone, they held ten-foot lances to their shoulders, like rifles. Behind them, lying quietly, were two horses. Conn heard them snort softly and clash their bits.

Surrounding the besieged men was a flitting horde of animal-like figures. They were men, but they looked more like enormous furry rabbits. They, too, carried the lances, and Conn saw them continually drop to one knee, throw up the lances and fire. Evidently these were the weapons that were producing the flickering silent explosions.

The horde of rabbitmen milled around the besieged pair with lightning speed, never advancing closer than fifty yards. Conn felt his pulse quicken for the gallant stand those two men were making. He watched breathlessly as they coolly waited for the attackers to come in, then raised slightly and fired. He heard no reports, but he saw the quick hail of craters.

A high whistle sounded. The attackers paused. Conn knew it was the preamble to a final assault, and he knew the men in armor would surely be borne under. With quick fingers he shook the final particles of sand from his revolver and slipped in the last clip.

A second whistle sounded as he hurled himself down the hill, rucksack banging against his hips. He gathered momentum and sprinted as the rabbitmen came forward toward the boulders in a solid wave. He had a glimpse of the armored men standing upright pumping their lances, then he had steadied himself and began to fire.

At the first shot a rabbitman screamed and dropped. The others skidded to a halt and Conn saw white flashes as they turned their faces toward the sound of his gunfire. He shouted in exultation and the hills boomed back as his gun spat twice. Two more rabbitmen slumped. Conn heard their lances clatter on the stones.

"Go on, big boys, I'm with you!" Conn shouted. But the two men stood, paralyzed by the sight. Conn fired three times, slowly, deliberately. At each shot another figure fell. By the third, the rabbitmen screamed in terror and fled. Conn jogged down the slope. When he had reached the men in armor, the attackers had faded into the darkness.

"Lucky for you I happened by," Conn said. Through the milky gloom he saw they were dead ringers for the Knights of the Round Table. Only they had removed the steel visors from the helmets and replaced them with heavy crystal.

"Lucky for you," Conn repeated. He was annoyed at the way they kept their lances trained on him. "What's the matter, boys, didn't I do enough for you?"

One laughed abruptly. It sounded hoarse and a little harsh to Conn. "Drop your lance, Schiller," he said. "The man is no Reader."

"Then where is his armor?" the man named Schiller demanded. He kept his strong, heavy face on Conn. "Are you a Swast?" he asked.

"Look, friend," Conn said. "I'm a stranger here. I don't know anything about Swasts or Readers. I just happened by and helped you out. The least I expect is a thank you."

"Of course," said the first man. He laughed again. "We are all suspicious these days, but Schiller here carries it too far. My thanks go to any man who would kill six of the Reader rats." He thrust forth a gaunt-leted hand. "Give you thanks, stranger. My name is Horst."

"The name is David Conn." Conn took the proffered hand and shook it. Horst jogged his companion's elbow.

"Come, come Schiller," he said. "No words for a man who saved you from being flayed alive?"

"Aye, my thanks," Schiller said gruffly. He did not offer his hand. Instead he turned and brought the two horses to their feet. Conn watched him doubtfully as the man mounted and turned his horse toward the castle beyond the wheat fields.

Horst took his horse's reins over his arm and walked alongside Conn as they started after Schiller. They trudged along a narrow dirt road that snaked through the high wheat.

"Schiller," said Horst, "is nervous. The Readers have been pressing us hard—very hard. He's anxious to get back to the castle. That's the only place where a Swast can feel safe these days."

"That so?" Conn said.

"They're like rats, those Readers," Horst went on. "They swarm everywhere. Now they've even begun threatening the castle. If that falls, I don't know what we'll do." He shook his head. "It's the last stronghold."

Conn said: "That's tough." His mind was churning in bewilderment. Now that the first excitement of the fight was over he had begun to wonder again. He put the empty gun back in his pocket and tried to puzzle things out. What had happened to his earth? Who were these Swasts and Readers?

"Every man counts, these days," said Horst. "The castle could ill afford to lose two fighting men, and we're glad to get another volunteer. You're the first Swast to get through to us in three years. I don't think there are any more left in America."

"I guess not," Conn said. Who were the Swasts? Why weren't there any more left in America?

"What kind of lance did you use back there?" It was Schiller up ahead. He had suddenly turned on his horse and was eying Conn again. "Never saw a lance that made so much noise."

"It wasn't a lance," Conn answered. "It's a gun."

"Gun!" exclaimed Horst eagerly. "You mean the old kind? The ancient explosion kind? Where did you get it. Let's see it!"

Conn thought for a moment. He stared at the high wheat around them and wondered how much he could tell these men. He thought he'd best look around a little before he showed his hand.

"I'll show you when we get to the castle," he said.

Schiller reined in his horse so abruptly that the bit cut the animal's mouth.

"Why so anxious to get to the castle?" he demanded.

"I'm not," said Conn. "I'd just like to get there and—"

"You see?" Schiller shot at Horst. The latter paused and nodded.

"Maybe we'd better look him over," he said. His voice regained its harsh quality. "I'd like to see that gun. And I'd like to look into that sack on your shoulder. The Readers are cunning. They could well afford to sacrifice six men to get a spy into the castle."

Conn looked at them. Schiller had already taken his lance from its boot. It was lying across his saddle, muzzle pointed at him. Conn took out the empty revolver.

"Here," he said. "Look it over."

Horst examined the revolver curiously, then slipped it into his saddle bag. He reached out hands for the rucksack. Without removing the strap from his shoulder, Conn held up the bag with flap turned back to reveal the contents.

"This is a hell of a thing," he said angrily. "How

many men do I have to kill for a passport? I'm no spy. No Reader."

"Books!" Horst snarled. He held up a small bound volume of Conn's records for Schiller to see. "Books! The swine's a Reader!"

Schiller cursed and raised his lance. Conn snatched the volume out of Horst's hands and with the same sweep smacked it sharply against the neck of Schiller's horse. The animal reared, snorting with pain. Schiller's shot blasted a silent crater down the road. He cursed again and yanked at the reins.

Conn swerved from under the horse's hoofs and brought his knee up into Horst's stomach. The armor bruised him, but Horst grunted and doubled over. Conn clutched the rucksack in both arms and sprinted off the road into the wheat. Schiller shouted. Abruptly a flare of light appeared in the wheat alongside Conn. A crater opened out like a flower and the night was filled with flying razor particles.

Behind him he heard the clopping thunder of hoofs as Schiller and Horst followed him. He bent low and prayed the high stems would conceal him. Pushing through the wheat was like running through molasses. His breath came in heaves.

He veered and doubled his tracks. The horses were charging up on him swiftly. Conn was filled with a sickening sense of dismay. As the silent explosions continued to flare around him he felt like a blind man running in the unknown.

Horst shouted: "There he goes!" and his voice was dangerously close.

Conn prayed as he ran.

A cross-fire of explosions burst at his toes. As Conn threw his hands up to seared eyes and plunged forward, the ground underneath him gave way. He shot under and crashed in a mass of wheat stems and earth. Dazed, he struggled up from the debris and was horribly aware of furry figures around him, closing in. A multitude of hands seized him.

A voice said: "One sound out of you—"

Conn nodded.

III

The searchers continued to shout. As their horses milled, Conn felt the concussion of hoofs on the earth. Little driblets of dirt trickled down. In the dark he heard the tense breathing of the men around him.

"Too close to the surface!" one whispered. "I warned you. There was less than five feet between the apex of the shaft and the surface."

"Shoring," came the answer. "It would have been all right if we could have got the timbers in place. Not enough time!"

"Anyway," whispered a third, "Who'd have thought the damned Swasts would go blasting in their wheat fields? 'Twas the blast that broke through. The blast and this!" He shook Conn.

Dirt trickled down Conn's neck. He was afraid to brush it away. Then someone gasped, and the grip on his arm tightened. Hoofs were punching the ground above them, and cascades of earth and stones began to thud down.

He could even hear the heavy panting of the animals and the creak of leather harness. Conn heard Schiller cursing his horse. If one of those horses fell through—

"We've got to get back!" came a whisper. "We can't

just stand here and wait for hell to break! We'll be crushed—"

Conn stared. Overhead was the four-foot hole the explosion had made and through which he'd fallen. It looked as though he was standing at the pit of a fifteen-foot crater with a narrow mouth. Like an upside-down funnel. On either side of him what had been the shaft was choked solid with earth. More was still dropping, packing still more tightly around them.

"How are we going to get back?" The speaker gazed up anxiously. "Once the Swasts sight us they can shoot us down like rats. We haven't even got lances to make a fight of it."

"Get back? We'll dig, of course."

"Through the debris? It'll take hours."

"Not through the debris!" The speaker tapped the hard floor impatiently. "We'll dig under. Three-level-twenty crosses under here. Less than three feet down. Dig, man, dig!"

The man who had spoken yanked Conn to one side. The other two immediately began to sink their picks into the earth. The hard surface turned over slowly. At last the softer earth began to come up. They dropped their picks and shoveled furiously.

Overhead Conn heard Schiller growl in the distance: "Gone back to one of his rat holes. Keep your eyes on the ground, Horst. Maybe we can spot the entrance."

Horst cursed faintly. "I'm a fool!" he said. "I might have suspected. But who could know they'd kill six men for the sake of a ruse? Dismount, Schiller. We can beat through on foot!"

One of the diggers exclaimed. "Timber!" he whispered. "I've struck the overhead beams—"

"Dig to one side, then, and make it fast!"

The earth flew. Conn saw a small hole widen. He could hear the sounds of earth dropping down to the lower tunnel. Then the tools were tumbled through. They clanked as they landed.

"Big enough!" gasped the digger. "Let's go!"

He dropped his legs and squirmed until his torso slipped under. A moment later he landed. The second man disappeared. The man who held him pushed Conn toward the hole. As Conn squirmed down, he bruised his hip on the timber alongside. He gripped the timber and dropped.

Schiller's voice was close. He yelled: "Horst! Here! Down in this pit!"

As Conn landed, hands yanked him out of the way. A pair of legs spurted through the tunnel head. Horst and Schiller were shouting. The men alongside him seized the legs and pulled down violently. The earth trembled and there was a flare of light as Horst and Schiller began firing. More earth began to drop. Timbers creaked ominously.

"Quick!" said the third man. "They've blasted this shaft, too. It won't hold up another second."

The tunnel was black. It was narrow, Conn felt, and just high enough for a man to crouch and run. As they sprinted down its length, Conn blundered against the heavy beams set in the walls. The concussion dazed him. He reeled and the man behind him stumbled on his heels. There was a whispered curse and the party halted.

"No use," said the man who was evidently the leader. "*He* don't know the tunnel. We'll have to carry him. Lay down!"

Conn stretched out on the shaft floor. Instantly his

ankles and shoulders were gripped and he felt himself being lifted.

"Now!" whispered the leader.

They started off again. Conn swayed like a hammock. He clutched his rucksack with both arms and sickened at the headlong flight through darkness. He winced at each sway, anticipating another violent collision with the wan beams. Far behind them he felt rather than heard the thundering fall of earth. That, he thought, would be the cave-in caused by the Swasts' shots.

Suddenly there was light. The party stopped and dumped Conn down. He got to his feet painfully and saw they were at a fork in the tunnel. Two branches were before them, both broad and high. Spaced at ten-foot intervals overhead were tiny spots of luminescence.

"Right or left?" asked the man who carried the tools.

"Left," the leader said. "We've got to take this fella to Rollins and make our report. Besides, something has to be done about the cave-in."

They hustled Conn down the left tunnel at a brisk pace. Gradually it dipped lower, widened, and deepened until it was an enormous thoroughfare. Other tunnels continually entered it. Conn felt like a blood corpuscle taking a sightseeing trip through a venous system.

After another half mile, they came abruptly upon a vast bulkhead set across the tunnel. It was of heavy wrought iron, set in granite and it looked as solid as Gibraltar. The leader hastened up and knocked, then peered through a small grille that opened. After a few words a small panel slid aside and Conn ducked through with the others.

He was so astonished he halted in his tracks and stared. A breeze struck his face, warm and perfumed. Before him stretched a vast arcade. At least a hundred feet high, twice as wide, it stretched far down like a blazing underground station. It was entirely floored with white sparkling sand, and checkered with small white cottages. The roofs were of tile in scarlet, green and blue. Palms clustered around the cottages, throwing a light shade.

Yes, there was shade. Conn stared up at the roof of the arcade and blinked. It was a solid sheet of luminescence that blazed and bathed him with warmth. There were small crowds of people, all wearing bathing suits, and all looked tanned and healthy. It was an underground beach resort, Conn thought. It looked like a subway version of Miami Beach.

"Nice, eh?" a voice grunted alongside.

Conn turned. The three men who had brought him were shucking the heavy furs that had given them the rabbity appearance. Their leader stood alongside him in sandals and trunks. He, too, was tanned, and his muscles were impressive.

He took Conn down the arcade. As they passed through the crowds Conn gaped at the well-built men and women. The girls, he thought dazedly, looked as though they assembled for a beauty contest, and their scant suits left nothing to the imagination. Not that he objected.

Conn was embarrassed at the way the crowd stared at his clothes and rucksack. He was relieved when he was taken into a large stucco building of two stories and rushed upstairs. By now he was so dizzy that everything seemed to whirl in white blazes before his eyes. He was conscious of marble steps and a broad door. Then he was in a room standing before a table. There were men seated at the table, some young, mostly old. They wore official-looking tunics and all had a keenness, almost a harshness, about them that was frightening.

"Well, Bradley?" The man at the head of the table spoke. He was iron-gray. His face was gray under its slight tan, and his eyes had gray lights in them. The lines on his face looked like the creases formed when iron is bent.

"Look what I've got, Rollins," Bradley began without preamble. "It fell into the new shaft we were working at three-level-fifteen—" He jerked a thumb at Conn.

"Fell in!" exclaimed Rollins. The others looked agitated. "Is he a Swast?"

"Certainly he's a Swast," burst forth one of the younger Men. He leaped up excitedly and pounded the table. "That's the man that shot down six of us an hour ago, you know. I told you the story. He used some kind of new percussion gun."

Wearily Conn thought: I'm crazy. We're all crazy. I go back to my world and find King Arthur aloft and Miami Beach below. The Swasts call me Reader and the Readers call me Swast. And who in hell cares—

He said: "I'm not a Swast."

"He's lying!" the young man shouted. He turned to Rollins. "It'll be a great pleasure, Peter, if you'll let me supervise the execution."

"I'm not lying," Conn said. He squared his shoulders. This was going to be tough to explain. "I admit killing six of your men. But it…it was a misunderstanding."

"Misunderstanding!" Bradley snorted.

"Yes, just that. I've got a long story to tell, but maybe I'm not going to live long enough to tell it. Here's the tail-end, anyway. I came to the top of that hill. I saw two men attacked by twenty. I didn't know who was fighting whom for what, and I didn't care. I just pitched in on the short side. That was the way I was brought up to do things."

"You were brought up to do things impetuously," said Rollins softly, but iron bit through his words. "Sometimes it pays to stop and think of what may lie under appearances."

Conn said: "Yeah. The two babies I helped out turned on me half an hour later. For some peculiar reason or other—"

"To hell with his story," the violent young man blurted. "He's a Swast. He's killed six of our men. The tunnel's caved in at three-eleven-fifteen and God knows what'll happen when the Swasts at the castle find that out—"

"They've found out by now," put in Bradley.

"Oh, my heavens!" groaned the young man. "Rollins, this is no time for—"

"One moment!" Rollins said. He eyed Conn curiously. "This man wears strange clothing. You say he used a strange weapon. He says the Swasts turned on him for a peculiar reason. I'd like to know that reason."

"The reason," Conn said, "was books."

There was an appalled silence. In it Conn watched the table, faces and room begin to whirl around his head.

"You said books?" Rollins inquired softly.

"I said books!" Conn shouted. He swung the rucksack off his shoulder and hurled the contents fluttering in the faces of the men. They squawked as the volumes clattered over the table and dove for them. "I said books!" Conn roared, "and what's more I mean books. Books, books, books!"

He turned on Bradley and planted his fist just under the ear. Bradley went down with a groan. Conn dove across the table and pistoned his fists into the violent young man's middle. He took four punches and then folded up with a surprised look on his face. Conn twisted and prepared to charge out through the door. Then the white floor leaped up and smote him full in the face.

IV

Rollins said: "Sorry we had to lay you out."

Conn rolled over and sat up. He was at the edge of a small cot. Around him were myriads of shelves and bottles. Sinks, oil lamps, candles, lots of glittering glass and stoneware. There was no one else around but Rollins.

"This is my lab," Rollins said.

"You mean padded cell," Conn groaned. He stared out the window at the brilliant sparkle and felt hot and feverish. "Listen," he said, "either you're crazy or I'm crazy. If I am, you can go ahead and lock me up. But before you do I've got to tell you something because if I don't get my story out I'm going to tear things apart again—"

"Go ahead," Rollins said quietly. He pointed to the

pile of books and canned film lying alongside the rucksack. "I figure you've got quite a story to tell."

"What's the year?" Conn asked.

"2941."

"It is, eh? Oh—Well, all right, Rollins, see if you can work this out. I'm a stranger, see? My name is David Conn. To the best of my knowledge I've neither seen nor heard of Readers, Swasts or any other phase of the life You people seem to live. Now here's the hitch. In the Year 2941, *I* lived on earth. My earth was a highly civilized and mechanized society. It was a planet entirely covered by one gigantic city. There wasn't a green field, a river or a forest anywhere. Half the ocean beds had been filled in to make room for the city of man—"

"You said earth?" Rollins interrupted. "Our earth?"

"Our earth, our moon, our sun, our stars—the very same. We had already solved the problem of rocket flight and were in contact with the other planets. We had controlled atomic energy. We had even investigated the mechanics of Time, and one of us, a man by the name of Dunbar, had solved the problem."

"Time—" Rollins nodded slowly. "Time travel. I might have known."

"Yes, that's it—" Conn paused and felt a wave of helplessness rush over him. "Yes, Dunbar solved time travel; I was his assistant. In April, 2941, Dunbar and I set up the apparatus in the heart of a granite outcropping—the same hill where I unfortunately killed six of your men. As Dunbar's assistant, I was the first to use the machine. He sent me back a thousand years as a kind of journalist in Time. I had plenty of money, equipment and so forth. I was instructed to return within a year to April, 2941, return to a moment but a few minutes later than that in which I'd left. When I did return—I was here."

"I see," Rollins said. He paced a little and fingered one of Conn's books. The bright light flooded his features and softened them. "And you want me to explain, eh? Well, I'd best begin by saying that theoretically you don't exist here."

Conn reached out a hand and gripped Rollin's arm firmly. "What's this," he inquired, "ghosts?"

"I said 'theoretically.' You and I are cousins, Conn, or better still, step-brothers. I see that your race was strong on the mechanical side—you could build time machines. We couldn't do that, but we have our strength, too. Theory. And I'm afraid you people were weak there."

"I don't like the way you use the past tense," Conn said. "It makes me feel that my world is dead."

"The only correct tense," Rollins answered, "hasn't been invented yet. It would have to be the alternative tense. Sit back a little and let me explain. You're real, don't worry about that. You and your world were always real. In 2941 when you started your journey through Time, you were a reality. In 1941 you were a reality. But now, back in 2941, you're an alternative reality existing in the wrong alternate. That's why I said theoretically you don't exist here."

"Alternative?" Conn said. He felt in his pockets for cigarettes. That was the second wonderful habit he'd acquired in the twentieth century. The first was loving Hilda.

"It's like this," Rollins went on. "The future can never affect the past without becoming part of the past—and thus destroying itself."

"As for instance?"

"Well," said Rollins, "take this set-up. A man enters a house and wonders whether to go upstairs or downstairs. He doesn't know it, but if he goes up he'll meet a girl whom he'll marry and if he goes down he'll meet a man who'll murder him. Now at the moment he enters the house and wonders which to do, there are two alternatively possible futures awaiting him—murder or marriage. His choice decides which of those futures he shall enter and make real for himself, although in theory each alternative future may coexist and be real unto itself."

Conn said: "Ouch!"

"And by the time this man makes up his mind," Rollins continued inexorably, "and starts either up or down—that same choice becomes part of the past—the very same past which affects and controls the future. You couldn't have a future of marriage without a past of choosing to walk upstairs. See?"

"I think so," said Conn.

"Now then, suppose at the moment of choice, the skies suddenly cleaved apart and a head appeared, saying: 'John Smith, this is your grandson speaking to you from the future. Unless you walk upstairs, you will not meet Dorris Doe, you won't get married, and I'll never exist. Therefore I command you to walk upstairs.'"

Conn laughed.

"In theory," Rollins smiled, "this could happen, because there would be the possibility of such a grandson. However he would never say those words because the past for him—which would be John Smith's future—would of necessity have been Smith's walking upstairs. He would take that for granted. But here's the twist which your Dunbar neglected. If the grandson did appear and in some way affected John Smith's choice so as to send him upstairs, the grandson could never again return to his own present, in other words, to the future."

"Why not?"

"Because the future is controlled and molded by the past. The future in which the grandson existed depended on John Smith standing alone and deciding to go upstairs. Having once appeared to John Smith and influenced him to go upstairs, he has so altered the past that his future no longer exists for him. He will have to return to another future."

"Wait a minute," Conn groaned. "We're weak in theory, same like you said. Put it in simple terms."

"Let's try it with symbols," said Rollins. He picked up a slate and pencil. "Take this equation: SUM OF THE PAST=THE FUTURE. Let ABC represent the past. Then ABC=abc, the future. You see that abc is the only possible logical result of ABC. If the past had been BCA, then the future would be bca. I think you'll see, moreover, that at the moment of present when factors A, B, and C exist, there are six alternatively possible futures: abc, bac, cab and so on."

"I've got that," Conn said.

"Hold on to it, then," Rollins chuckled, "because I'm almost finished. Here's the joker Dunbar neglected. Suppose that in the equation ABC=abc, factor b of alternative future abc traveled back through Time, past the equal sign to visit ABC. Then b becomes a member of the group ABC, and by that very act makes it impossible for him to return, although his own present may continue to exist, it can never again exist for him."

"Why not?"

"Because the past for him will now contain the factors ABC plus b. In other words, ABC+b can never equal abc. That time equation wouldn't balance. So, although b can reverse his time machine and go back to his own date, he will never find the reality of the present he left. He will always land in another of the infinite number of alternate futures coexisting. ABC+b may result in abcb, abbc, babc and so on—but never in abc!"

"I get it," Conn said. "You're trying to say that by traveling back into my past, I've switched over to a different track so that I couldn't move forward again on my original track."

"I'm trying to say more than that," Rollins broke in. "I'm saying that you'll never be able to move forward on the same track twice. In other words, that time travel is impossible in the sense that a man can take a journey to the past and return to his starting present.

"You see, you could continue to shuttle back and forth between 1941 and 2941, but although for obvious reasons you'd find the same present in 1941, you'd never find the same in 2941. There are an infinite number of alternative coexistent futures. Each time you made a round trip you'd create another infinitude of alternates. Representing each trip as an equation, here's the mathematical proof of why, once you'd traveled back in Time you could never return to your starting point—"

Rollins wrote swiftly:

(1) ABC=abc

(2) ABC+b=abc+b

(3) ABC+2b=abc+2b

(4) ABC+3b=abc+3b...

(5) ABC+n (b)=abc+n (b)

Conn's fingers shook, but he finally managed to get the cigarette lit. The flaring match looked dull in the bright light. Conn held the match until it seared his fingers.

He dragged on the cigarette. He thought: This is a lovely mess. It serves me right—leaving Hilda and dithering about duty to a man, to an existence I'll never see again. Maybe Dunbar will send someone else back to look for me. Maybe hell send back dozens, wondering why none return. Maybe he'll figure out what Rollins here calls the joker.

And all that while he was filled with a bitter sense of futility, the nostalgia of a man lost to everything. He wasn't even a man, he thought, he was only an alternative—a mere probability that coexisted with an infinitude of other probabilities. All the probable Conns should get together, he thought grimly, and kick him.

At last he said wearily: "What about the Swasts—and the Readers—and the fighting. This tunnel system; the castle and all that?"

Rollins smiled. "I'd have to give you a thousand years of history. This is it briefly. About nine hundred years ago, America was invaded and conquered by a horde of Nagees. Their credo was the superiority of brute strength over reason. Their symbol was the swastika from which comes their present name—"

"Nagee," Conn said, "or Nazi. Of course. I should have realized. But according to history Nazism never reached America. It was defeated in Europe around 1945—"

"I said this was the history of our alternate," Rollins answered. "At any rate, the few Americans who held out and fought a guerilla war became known as Readers because of their respect for learning. That's why the mere possession of books got you into trouble with the Swasts you unfortunately aided, and why they got you out of a tight spot with us. Your books and records will be invaluable for us; but I should like to ask about the cans of celluloid pictures—"

"Motion pictures," Conn said. "My notes will show you how to build a projector. They'll do more for you than all the books. What about that castle?"

"It's the last stronghold of the Swasts in America. They took possession of that building centuries ago. Originally it had been used for something important by the Readers, but unfortunately our records don't say—"

There was a sharp knock on the door and Bradley almost shot through. Nevertheless he clamped down his impatience and waited for a chance to speak.

"Listen," Conn said, "don't think I'm ungrateful, but I'd like to get out of your world. You seem to have it nicely worked out. It's a beautiful place down here, but I'd rather not stay. I'd...I'd like to—"

He had to stop. The memory of Hilda choked him. When he realized how near she was, how swiftly the machine in the hill could return him to her, he trembled with eagerness.

"I'd like to recharge my batteries," Conn said. "I'd like to go back into the past and stay there. You said I'd find it the same?"

"The same." Rollins nodded. "It takes time, lots of time before the alternate futures split off and differentiate. You'll find the same 1941 you left—but I'm afraid I don't know what you mean by 'recharge.'"

"Batteries," Conn repeated. He smothered a growing

sense of panic. "Accumulators—you know, generators, electricity, batteries—"

Rollins shook his head sadly. "We've been trying to recapture the lost art of electrical engineering for generations," he said. "So far it's evaded us."

"Then we'll work it out together," Conn snapped. "In my records you'll find the material necessary to recapture your lost art. In a month I'll have this place electrified, and in two months I'll be going back to—"

He broke off. Rollins' face had dissolved into an expression of incredulity mixed with childish delight. He gripped Conn's shoulders and stared, eyes filling. Then stepped forward.

"In a month" Bradley said, "there won't be anything to electrify."

"What's that?" Rollins started.

"I said there won't be anything left," Bradley answered in a queer, harsh voice. "There won't be any underground—any Readers—anything. The Swasts have returned to three-level-fifteen. They're following the lead and blasting every tunnel wide open with their lances. They'll reach the city in an hour. It's all up."

Conn finally realized what Bradley meant.

"Nothing's all up," he growled. "I'm getting back to 1941 if I have to win your war for you." He slapped Bradley and Rollins smartly on the shoulders. "Pick up your faces, Readers, I've brought a few tricks with me from a thousand years ago that're going to make a hell of a lot of difference in this future. Let's go to the council room!"

V

Faces looked up from the table as they entered. Dismayed faces. Rollins rapped his knuckles on the table.

"In the emergency," he said, "David Conn will supervise defensive tactics. Please!" He held up his hand. "I understand that Conn has come to us under highly embarrassing circumstances. I have heard his story and I assure you that I have full confidence in him. I think you will, too, when you've had time to hear his explanations. For the moment I think it would be wise to have faith in his leadership."

Rollins escorted Conn to the head of the table and seated himself alongside. There were grumbles from the others and a low whistle of surprise. Eventually they all nodded.

"The first thing," Conn said swiftly, "is arms. What have you?"

"Just the lances," Bradley answered. "That's all."

"What's the mechanism of those lances—the silent explosions?"

The hot-headed young man spoke up. Rollins leaned toward Conn. "Name is Wilder," he answered. "Chief technician. Be nice to him. He didn't relish those punches."

"We really don't know," Wilder was saying. "Actually the lances are no more than self-coiling spring guns. They shoot a radioactive pellet—Uranium 237. The same isotope gives us light and heat in the form of slow radiation. We treat minute particles to disintegrate on violent contact and they induce subsidiary disintegration in the surrounding area."

"I get it," Conn said. "You use spring propulsion for gradual acceleration. If you shot the particles out too hard, they'd explode at the moment of initial impulse and blow up gun and shooter."

Wilder glowered. "That's what I was about to say."

"What's the range of your lances?"

"Thirty or forty yards."

"What about explosives. Guncotton? TNT?"

All looked blank. Conn realized that this was another lost art for the Readers. He turned quickly to Bradley.

"Just what are the Swasts doing? Coming down through the tunnels after us?"

"Hell, no!" Bradley looked furious. "They won't come into the tunnels yet, not until they're too deep for blasting. Right now they're opening up the small capillaries from the surface. Sort of plowing them open with their lances—"

He caught himself, raised his head and stared into space. Conn, too, had sensed the vibrations. Seconds later, it seemed he heard a mutter. The sound boulders make when they rumble down the slope of a distant valley.

Bradley whispered: "No! Not yet!" He leaped to his feet and tore out of the room, Conn hard on his heels. The others followed.

Outside, under the glittering cavern ceiling, the Readers were dashing about in fright. Bradley had paused with ear cocked toward the cavern entrance. Again came the muttering rumble as the earth underneath them shook. Squads of Readers, bearing lances, were sprinting down toward the entrance. Men were herding the women and children back toward the recesses. Bradley stopped one.

"What is it?" he demanded.

The man looked weary. "Swasts!" he said. He had

a kid under his arm, a two-year-old that was crying lustily. "The Swasts have come down through the tunnel—all of them. Hundreds. They're outside the gate now, trying to blast through."

As he started off with the child, Conn stopped him. "Going out the back way?" he asked, pointing toward the recesses of the arcade.

The man shook his head. "There isn't any back way," he said. "We just hide in the depths—"

"In three hundred years," Bradley said apathetically, "the Swasts have never dared to attack us at our gates. There was never any need for more than one exit—"

Conn grabbed Bradley's arm and shook the man until he appeared to waken. "How long can you hold the gate?" Conn asked. He repeated the question until Bradley answered.

"Twelve hours, maybe. The gate's strong, but not enough—"

"Twelve hours is enough time for me!" Conn shook Bradley again. "Snap out of it. I got you into this mess and I'll get you out. You're my lieutenant, understand? Go down and see to the gates. I'll be along—"

Bradley nodded mutely. Life began to flow back into his eyes. Conn gave him a push and he galloped down the cavern toward the gate.

"Rollins!" snapped Conn. "I've got to work fast. I'll need the help of every technician you can spare—plus a squad of diggers."

"You'll have them."

"Get the diggers first. I want a shaft sent up from the cavern to the surface. You can drill, blast, dig or scratch with your fingernails—I don't care how, so long as it's done in six hours."

"You're mad," Wilder snarled. "Even granting it could be done."

"It can," interrupted a young man with a snub nose. "The rock overhead and through this entire sector is honeycombed with passages and faults. It'll be dangerous—but we can do it."

"Granting that," snapped Wilder, "there's no sense creating another hazard for us and another vantage point for the Swasts. We're trying to hold them off from one entrance. You're planning another."

"That so?" Conn eyed Wilder and wanted to punch him again. "Maybe it hasn't occurred to you that we're trapped down here. If we don't do something but quick, it won't matter how many holes the cavern's got in it. We won't be alive to know the difference."

Rollins had given the order for the diggers. The snubnosed young man ran off to supervise. Conn took Rollins and the rest of the technicians back to the lab. The same glittering light pouring through the windows gave him the impression that less than a few moments had elapsed since he'd first sat up on the cot. It was peculiar not to have a sun that moved. Phony.

Conn glanced at the lab, then at the nervous men around him. He thought: It's all my fault. If I don't use my head and figure something out, then there won't be any more phony sun, any more Readers or cavern. It's a thousand years from 1941, but I still hate the Nazis and their children's children. I hate everything they stand for. I hate the thought of what'll happen to those strong, clean people and children, those pretty girls—

He couldn't think about that. It brought Hilda to his mind again. Conn shivered and tried to concentrate on the job ahead. He had to figure something out.

"Rollins," he said, "you don't know what I mean, but we need munitions. Explosives. Could you build up big pellets of Uranium 237—sort of bombs?"

Rollins shook his head. "Impossible," he answered. "They'd burn the men to crisps before they could get near them. There's no known insulation—"

Conn said: "Yeah." He tapped his teeth with the slate pencil and stared around the laboratory, gazing abstractedly at the bottles. They were of heavy glass—so heavy they wouldn't break if you dropped them. Conn looked at the reagents. The Readers had evidently lost the art of chemical notation, but maybe they'd rediscovered the essential ingredients of what he needed. Maybe—

"Potassium nitrate?" Conn said. "Got it? Also known as—"

"Plenty," answered Rollins.

"How about sulphur? Yes? Fine. Charcoal and wax? Yes?" Conn went into action. He lined up the technicians before him. "From now on, you boys are just cooks. Is that understood? You're to follow my instructions to the letter. Make this up. Potassium nitrate, sixty-five percent. Sulphur, two percent. Charcoal, twenty percent. Plain wax to make up the rest."

Pencils squeaked on slates. Heads nodded.

"When you've compounded this I want it packed carefully into heavy pint-sized bottles," Conn went on. He picked up a specimen. "Like this. I want the mouths corked tight. Through the corks, well into the compound, and extending at least a foot outside, I want you to run a heavy candle wick. Got that?"

He started to leave while they were still nodding. At the door he paused. "One last word, boys. Treat this mixture extra gentle, please. And if you value your lives, don't let a spark of flame come near it."

He vaulted down the stairs and set off for the cavern gate. The cavern itself was deserted. All the noncombatants had withdrawn to the deep recesses. As Conn approached the gate he passed the scattered signs of hasty flight. Children's toys, a sandal, a handful of grapes, and a little portrait painted on wood. Conn wondered if the owner would live to pick it up.

The gate itself was shuddering with palsy. The muttering rumbles continued without pause now, and Conn understood that the Swasts were blasting it continually on the other side. There were no more than a hundred and fifty Readers marshaled with lances, and for the first time Conn realized how appalling the odds were. He located Bradley.

"How goes it?" he asked.

"It could be better," Bradley said. "Thank heavens there's solid rock around that gate. It'll hold for a time. These lances can't blast through rock very quickly—only earth."

"You haven't got many men," Conn said.

Bradley looked over the little army. "We've got twenty more," he answered, "but they're busy digging to the surface. What's the general idea?"

"It's old where I come from," Conn said. "When the enemy attacks and you're fighting a losing battle, the only way to make him draw off is to counterattack him where it hurts. That's what we're going to do. Any idea where it'll hurt?"

Bradley stared. "The castle?" he gasped.

"That's it," said Conn grimly.

VI

It was two hundred feet to the surface. The shaft had been started from a side of the cavern and thrust upward a zigzag course that took advantage of every rock fault and slide. Conn tugged experimentally at the rope ladder that hung down from the open mouth of the shaft above him. The ladder still quivered from the heels of the last Reader to mount.

"That's a hundred," Bradley said. He strapped his lance across his back and looked at Conn. "Now what?"

"Go on up yourself," Conn said tensely. "Keep your men under cover up there and wait for me. I'll be along in no time to speak of."

Bradley nodded and started up the ropes. In a few seconds his mounting legs disappeared in the dark shaft mouth. Conn picked up his bulging rucksack and slung it gingerly over his shoulder. In it were twenty-five pints of destruction. He didn't relish the idea of carrying it up through the narrow, twisting shaft. That was why he wanted his little army to be in the clear in case of accidents.

The snub-nosed mine technician placed a hand on Conn's shoulder. "Be careful going up," he said. "You're not acquainted with our terrain. This is all loose granite rock. It's honeycombed with flaws and faults, and our tunnels haven't done much to strengthen it. Too much of a jar might start a slide that would result in the settling of all the rock for miles around. This cavern—everything—would be crushed."

Conn said: "Thanks for the bedtime story." He tried to make it sound funny. To Rollins he said: "Here are your orders. Hold the gate with your skeleton crew at all costs. Only send your women and children up this ladder as a last result. The Swasts would slaughter them in open country. Don't worry. I'll get you out of this mess. I swear it!"

He started up the ladder. It quivered and shook, and his rucksack thumped slightly against his back. It was pitch black in the shaft, but the Readers had coated one strand of the rope ladder with uranium. It glowed before him like a never-ending worm.

The ladder arose for seventy feet, and Conn bruised elbows and knees against the rough shaft wall. Then be came to a small shelf. He crawled over and followed the rope along the gutter of a narrow mounting tube that had razor sides. He could hear his clothing shred, and the rucksack caught on the projections and tugged at him. The glass clinked.

A rock slipped under him and he heard it go thundering down the tube. A dull muttering began and then a creak and a whisper. He thought it must be the echo of the fall, but it sounded more like the scream of rock under pressure. Conn swallowed hard and tried to climb faster. If the shifting layers of granite cut the ladder above him—

The tube ended and the ladder mounted again. Conn climbed through open space, swinging like a pendulum. He had no idea how long he struggled. He lost count of rungs. In the black nothingness he was cut off from time altogether. But at last his groping hand touched rock and he wormed his way between two flat masses of stone barely three feet apart.

They were like two vast palms. Giant palms waiting to press slowly together and mash him to butter. Conn pulled himself upward with fingernails, not daring to listen to the whisper and mutter of the trembling rock. The trembling tamed into a shake and the sound grew. He could sense the heavy palms pressing gently together. He groaned and struggled feverishly. It would be a very slow death, very gentle and very horrible.

Then hands gripped him and pulled upward. Bradley whispered: "Sh-h-h-h—" and Conn was blissfully aware of night wind on his face, stars overhead and the comforting nearness of a hundred fighting men. He lay a while until he caught his breath.

It would be about three or four in the morning, Conn thought. The moon had passed the zenith and was a small silver apple dropping to the west. He got to his feet and peered cautiously around. A mile across the fields towered the castle. About a quarter of a mile to one side was a large black smudge that made quiet noises.

"Horses," Bradley said. "The Swasts have got them picketed there under a small guard. Have to give'em a wide berth."

Conn nodded. In a single file they started out, bending low to get all the cover the wheat afforded. There was hardly any sound. The Readers, after hundreds of years of skulking, knew how to move quietly.

They approached the hill and swiftly passed it. Conn thought: Time is peculiar. I always knew it was, but it never affected me personally. If this ruse works, we'll wipe out the Swasts. Maybe in a month or two I'll be able to build enough equipment to recharge my batteries and get back to Hilda. Maybe I'll get back to the day after I left her—She'll have missed me only a day, and yet I'll have missed her for ten weeks—

The thought came to him that he might take Rollins back through Time with him. Rollins could gather up every clue he needed to recreate an advanced civilization in his own time. Then Conn shrugged. He'd forgotten. Rollins would make it ABC+3b. He could never return to his own alternate. Rollins, too, would become a probable man. No, there was nothing more Conn could do for these people. They had his records. That would be enough.

Bradley caught his arm.

"This is it," he whispered. "Probably the Swasts left a guard. We'd better be careful."

The castle loomed before them. It was a high square building with a tower at each corner. Around the building the Swasts had constructed a heavy rubble wall at least twenty feet high. It would be impossible to climb it. The Swasts could shoot them down as they came over the crest.

Conn lit a cigarette. He brought the rucksack around under his arm and opened the flap so that be could dip in quickly and grab a bottle. The Readers formed a wedge behind him and they advanced cautiously, with Conn at the apex.

Suddenly lights flared and a gong began to bang. It was so deep-toned it had no sound. It just pressed on the ears, beat—beat—beat. From the towers giant torches flared, spraying ruddy light over the surrounding terrain, flooding the grounds with brightness. There were shouts from the castle and flaming craters began to appear before them.

"Alarm!" Bradley shouted above the roar of the torches. "They've given the alarm!"

Conn growled: "Keep moving!" He sprinted.

He cradled the rucksack in his arms and wondered if a lance blast would reach him. The craters were coming dangerously close. If he was hit, he and his little army would go up in an explosion that would sing the end of the Readers. He didn't want to lose this last battle with the Nazis. The Battle of America.

Conn pulled out a bottle and touched the fuse tip to his glowing cigarette ember. It fizzed and flamed. Still on the run, he yanked back his arm, striking Bradley across the shoulder. He almost dropped the bomb, but managed to let it fly. It exploded as it reached the wall, and the bang hurt his ears. But when the dense smoke drifted, he saw that part of the rubble had disappeared.

Bradley exclaimed hoarsely and there were terrified yelps from the Readers.

Conn lit another fuse and sent the bottle toward the breach. This time a rumble of clattering stones followed the explosion and the wall came down for a space of twenty feet.

They reached the wall and huddled under its cover just to one side of the breach. It was cold there after the heat from the giant torches. Conn watched the haze of craters exploding silently in the breach. He thought: They're covering it. Anyone trying to get through there will go up in a puff.

"The noise!" Bradley screamed. "It'll bring the other Swasts back!"

"That was the general idea," Conn said.

He lit a third fuse and heaved the bottle far down the length of the wall. It exploded with a boom, and rubble forty feet away clattered. As it did, he had already lit a fourth fuse. It was a long chance, but he had to take it. Maybe the Swasts in the castle would cover the site of the fresh explosion. They ought to be bewildered.

Conn jerked to his feet and stepped around into the open breach. A black arch showed in the side of the castle, just before him. He let fly toward it and dove back to cover as the bomb blasted. When he crawled back to look, he saw a great jagged rent where the arch had been. Light shone through twisted window frames. He had blasted in a row of castle windows. It was crazy, but he noted that they were Gothic. High and pointed.

"Bradley," Conn said, "take half your men and go to the second breach I made. You'll wait until you hear two more bombs land—then make a dash to get into the castle."

Bradley nodded and vanished. Fifty men, lances poised in their hands, drifted off into the darkness.

Conn peered around the corner of the breach and heaved two bombs in quick succession. The first had too short a fuse. It exploded while it was still rolling. He heard the whine of glass fragments. Conn cursed Wilder. The second plunged into the castle and went off with a muffled bang. Screams sounded.

He puffed his cigarette and barked: "Come on!" and then they were swerving around the breach and legging it for the hole. The craters flared and men began to drop with choked grunts. To one side Conn saw Bradley's men hurdling rock fragments and charging down the second breach. A dozen disappeared in silent flowers of light while they were jumping. The rest converged toward the rent windows.

Conn lit a fuse on the run and hurled it before him.

By the time the bomb exploded, he had already entered the castle. What he could see of the room he entered was a shambles. It had evidently been some kind of vast hall. Now the flagged flooring was shattered. The walls toppled and the ceiling overhead sagged. Splotches of ghastly blood and flesh pasted pieces of mail armor to the stone.

Hoarse bellows came from above, and then from behind. Craters leaped and flared. Conn saw the Swasts were firing down through the gaps in the ceiling. Before him was the broken remnant of a broad stairway. The shouting Readers behind him went sprinting up.

Conn pulled to a halt. He grabbed Bradley as the man hurtled by and brought him to one side.

"Listen," shouted Conn. Bradley looked around wildly. He licked his lips.

"We've broken them!" Bradley panted. He looked exultant. "The last stronghold's fallen. We can mop up in here inside of an hour." He turned to follow his men. Conn could hear the shouting and crashes of falling stone as the Readers blasted through the floors above.

"Listen," Conn repeated. "We've only done a quarter of the job. The rest of the Swasts will be back any minute. Keep half of your men for mopping up. Send down the rest to me to hold the Swasts."

Bradley nodded and ran. Conn counted bombs. Twenty left. He stared around the broken hall, wondering what it could have been. There were broken marble pillars and fragments of what looked like sarcophagae. Could the Swasts have buried their men inside this hall? A graveyard? There were the tapestries, too. Great hangings, now torn and spattered. Most confusing of all was the giant Sphinx at the head of the stairs. It had a ruined face and it looked incredibly old. Maybe the Swasts were collectors of art. That didn't seem to jibe with what Rollins had said.

Twenty Readers came vaulting down the stairs. They were torn and looked blood-drunk. Conn lined them up and tried to shake sense into them, but they muttered to themselves incessantly and fingered their lances. It was impossible to shake a thousand years of hatred out of their veins all at once.

They trotted out on the double and Conn spaced them along the crest of the wall. He had barely returned to his mm position when his ears caught the thunder of hoofs. He lit another cigarette and watched the far fringes of the blood-red floodlit area. Dim shapes galloping there. There was the ruby glint of light on metal and the long streaks that were lances. Craters began to flame again. Along the wall the Readers yelled.

Conn heaved a bomb. It exploded far short, but the whirling fragments of glass whistled around a horse and rider. The horse reared and screamed. Conn didn't like that. The rider went jerking to the ground. Conn saw him get to his feet and run back to the cover of darkness. The Swasts continued to circle and fire.

Bradley ran out with a small squad, yelling for Conn.

Conn shouted, "Here!"

"This is no good," Bradley panted. "They can keep us besieged and still attack the cavern. What are you going to do?"

"I don't know," Conn spat. "I'd counted on getting

out of the castle before they returned and ambushing them."

Bradley said, "We might be able to pick them off better from up above. We've got to make a helluva fight of it here and now. Otherwise we'll be worse off than before."

VII

Conn ordered ten of Bradley's men to the walls. The rest followed him and Bradley went back into the castle. They clattered up the stairway and rounded the Sphinx. Bradley led Conn through a low hall racked on all sides with arms. The middle was aisled with shattered crystal cases. Within the cases were tumbled heaps of armor.

"Storeroom," Bradley grunted.

But it didn't look one to Conn. He could understand the Swasts getting their armor here, but it still didn't look like a storeroom. As they ran through with their little squad, his mind struggled with the problem.

Bradley led him briskly past a hall filled with paintings and statuary, up another flight of stairs and into a large room that was the entire width of the tower. Conn gaped and skittered to a halt.

"Come on," Bradley snapped. "Don't let this place scare you, I don't know what it is, but it's nothing to worry about."

Only Conn knew. Suddenly he understood. He looked at the scale models on the walls; at the tiny helicopter hanging from the ceiling; and lastly at the giant tractor within the crystal case. Suddenly he realized that the Swasts had appropriated a museum, of all places, for their last stronghold.

"Wait a minute," he said to Bradley's excited yells. He walked to the case within which stood the tractor. It was a dump machine with a vast steel bin in the rear that had evidently been used to cart tons of earth or stone. Probably, he thought, it was a twenty-first-century model, for it was better than anything 1940 had seen, and it was Diesel powered. That was what gave him the idea. He'd fight a 1940 war in 2941 with a harmless 2040 machine. Abruptly he seized a lance from one of the Readers and shattered the crystal case.

A cloud of gas, so pungent it almost knocked him over, whiffed around him as he stepped through the naked case frame. That was a good sign. Whoever had set up this tractor exhibit had taken pains to make sure it would remain in good condition.

It seemed to be a new machine. The steel gleamed and the rivet heads were solid. Conn went over it. Cylinder heads; crankshaft; exhaust manifold, the fuel feed pump—everything was in brand-new condition.

"Bradley!" he said curtly. "How do the Swasts get those big torches in the towers. Oil?"

Bradley nodded.

Then take all these men and get up to the towers. Locate the oil-feed and bring down all the oil you can carry. Make it fast!"

Bradley gaped and flared into action. He drove the squad before him up toward the towers. Conn carefully hid his rucksack of bombs in a corner, ferreted out a small oil lamp and began heating the cylinders. Diesels had to be plenty hot before they started.

The Readers began to hurry back for containers. Conn dumped mineral exhibits on the floor and gave them the metal bins. He ripped his shirt off and improvised a cloth filter. From the Diesel came the strong odor of heating metal.

They were able to collect a total of fifteen gallons. As Conn refiltered it and waited for the Diesel to heat, he reflected that that would be enough to drive him to California and back. He improvised a funnel and poured the oil into the fuel tank. The fuel-system filter, he saw, was of the waste type. The cotton wadding was fresh and white.

The Diesel was fitted with an electric starter. The batteries were dry and Conn sent Bradley for water and filled them. They'd still have to be charged, and although Conn noted a five-hundred-watt generator connected to them, the generator wouldn't charge them until the Diesel was turning. He'd have to start the Diesel by hand.

They ran a loop of heavy rope around the fly wheel and Conn got a good running start and yanked. The wheel turned crustily. He kept yanking until he was exhausted. Then Bradley took over. He was prodigiously muscled, Conn remembered. Now the muscles cracked and strained. Abruptly the tractor coughed and bellowed. Bradley had the rope burned through his palms. He spit on them, yowling with pain.

But the tractor was rattling and bellowing furiously, and Conn knew the war was more than half won.

"Sorry, Brad!" Conn yelled. He shouldered his sack of bombs and vaulted into the driver's seat. "Get your men into the back."

The Readers gathered up their lances and helped Bradley into the vast steel bin behind. Conn threw in the clutch. The tractor coughed again and calmly shuddered through a pair of cases before he could get it turned. He drove it shakily down the stairs while the men bounced and murmured in the bin and Bradley cursed fiendishly at his raw palms.

In the armor room, Conn rammed through half a dozen exhibits as an experiment. This tractor, he thought, was almost as deadly as the best Panzer tank. He swerved around the giant Sphinx and charged down the broken stairway, fragments of stone and steel crackling under the treads.

The rent windows were a little too narrow. The treads kicked out space for themselves and left crumbling stone behind. Conn drove up to the breach in the wall and yelled for the Readers. A score of them mustered enough courage to vault into the bin. They could conceal themselves, Conn figured, and fire out at the Swasts. The steel would protect them. He was the only one exposed, but he'd have to take the chance.

He thundered through the breach in the rubble wall. The Swasts were still galloping around the castle. Squads of them were poised on the flanks waiting to rush in. Conn fumbled at the dashboard and tried the light switch. The forward search-lights flickered and eddied out long brilliant streamers. It was astonishing how quickly the batteries charged—astonishing how efficient this machine was.

Craters sent earth and stone banging against the steel walls of the tractor bin. Conn could just hear them clank over the interminable roar of the engine. He braked a tread and sent the tractor in a long course through the wheat fields. It would make riding tougher for the Swasts.

They galloped on all sides, like swarms of furies. The horses were frightened at the horrible sound, and still the Swasts managed to dart in, fire their lances at the bin, and then pivot and gallop away. The Readers in the bin were firing rapidly. Swasts were vanishing from their saddles in blinding flares of light. The night was filled with roars.

Conn thought: Oh, hell, let's get it over with fast. Hilda's waiting. He drove his heels down to steady himself in the jiggling driver's seat, managed to get another cigarette lit and began heaving bombs. They sounded like empty thumps in the open, but the flames they set off were real, and the dry wheat began to run with rivulets of fire.

He felt utterly dispassionate about it. He had the illusion that he was watching a stranger light the glass bottles of wholesale death and throw them. It seemed that these little groups of armed riders that were torn into screaming bloody bits were toy figures. It seemed that someone was hammering on his back.

Someone was—Bradley. His face was contorted with pain, but he continued to bang Conn's back. Conn shouted: "Is it all over?" and set his ears to Bradley's mouth.

"We've cleaned 'em out," Bradley screamed, "but that's not it. You've got to stop throwing bombs. You've started a landslip."

Conn stared around. There were no more Swasts in sight He threw the clutch and let the Diesel idle. He listened and stared. Then he caught it. The growling shake of earth underneath. It made him feel sick.

"That snub-nose warned me," he said. "The mining chief. He said this area is one big honeycombed fault. And I don't suppose your tunneling did anything to strengthen it."

First Conn thought of the cavern and felt nauseous.

There were hundreds of Readers down there, but he remembered Rollins and Wilder and the other technicians. They'd realize in time. They'd get everyone out. Besides, all the land was theirs now. They could build anew in the sun and open air.

He knew he was trying to put the hill in the back of his mind. The fear was gripping him. The hill was a granite out-cropping. It would be the first to crash away under the strain. There wouldn't be any more time machine. He would never see Hilda again.

Bradley screamed: "The cavern might hold and it might not. We've got to get there!"

Conn gritted: "No!" He threw in the clutch again. The Diesel howled and he turned the machine in starts and drove headlong for the hill. Wheat swished and the tractor banged into hollows and mounted the rolling rises. Behind him, Conn heard Bradley curse and bellow questions. He ignored him.

As the hill came into sight, Conn sensed heat on his back. He turned and suddenly realized what Bradley had been cursing about. Acres of dry wheat were aflame. A curtain of red-orange, topped by a thick, oily smoke cloud was marching after them. Then the jerk of the tractor as it began to mount the hill recalled his attention. He eased it up to the crest and let the motor idle again. The Readers leaped out of the bin.

"What the hell, Conn!" yelled Bradley. "Are you mad?"

Conn paid no attention. He bent and uncovered the stud bank. The earth was shuddering underfoot. Fire and earthquake and a war, that's what he was going through for Hilda. But it was worth it.

"Are you mad?" Bradley repeated.

"No," Conn said. "Look, Brad, I've got to recharge my batteries and get back in time before this landslip crushes the machine. Will you help me?"

"I don't know what you're talking about."

Conn said: "I explained all that to Rollins. Listen, Brad, this means life to me. I couldn't be happy in your world. I've got to get back to where I belong. Just help me for ten minutes. That's all I ask."

Bradley said: "Ten minutes. That's all I can spare. Conn. We'll be needed in the cavern."

"Fine." Conn pointed to the tractor. "Get her jacked up on boulders or something and smash off the treads—"

He pressed the studs in combination. The disk of rubble sank down, carrying him with it. The walls of the shaft were ominously cracked, and as he neared the chamber entrance he could hear the steel squealing.

He thrust open the door. The batteries were exhausted so he could get no light. Conn fumbled in the spare-parts cabinet and withdrew a coil of insulated wire. He made quick connections to the battery terminals, unreeled the wire and started the disk upward, playing out the wire as he arose.

Bradley and his men had gotten the tractor up on boulders and were hammering off the treads. Conn removed his belt, squirmed under the machine, and belted the forward drive axle to the generator. This way, he figured, he'd get double the power in half the time. The generator might burn out. Then again it might not. This was a terrific tractor. Conn yanked the generator leads off the storage batteries and connected them to the wires from his own batteries.

He threw in the clutch. The Diesel roared and set

the axle into a spinning whine. Conn prayed the vibrations wouldn't throw the tractor over on her side before his batteries were charged. He leaped to the disk and sent it down.

The accumulator needle had already drifted away from the red exhaustion point and was creeping along the dial. Overhead Conn heard Bradley shout. He stepped out on the disk and looked up. Bradley's head was a black dot in the shaft mouth.

"Fire's almost reached us, Conn!" he shouted.

Conn felt the earth rumble again. Suddenly he realized that Bradley had his own troubles, too.

"O.K., Brad," he called. "Don't need you any more. Get about your own business. My regards to Rollins and the rest. Good luck—"

"Good luck, Conn!" Yet Bradley lingered.

"Go on," Conn laughed, "get out of this. Oh, and by the way—I left my sack of bombs up there. Fair exchange. Heave me down one of those lances, will you? Nineteen forty-one could use them—"

The lance slithered down. Conn managed to cradle it in his arms. He looked up at Bradley and had a mighty desire to shake hands with the man—with his whole fighting generation. But there was a fifty-foot gap between them; a thousand-year gap between them.

Conn said: "Will you get out of here!"

"All right," Bradley said. "So long. I wish you'd stay with us. We could use your guts—"

Then he was gone. Conn brought the lance inside and placed it on the platform. He set the controls for April, 1941. Then he looked at the accumulator dial. The needle had crept far up. It wouldn't take long now.

Maybe a thousand watts or so were pouring into his batteries. Maybe more. Whether or not he got back to Hilda would depend on how long it took before the fire reached the tractor and fused everything, or how long it took before this hill settled down a few feet and washed him flat. He listened to the far-off drone of the Diesel and prayed. He listened to the creak and groan of rock on steel and prayed.

A whiff of smoke reached his nostrils. Conn stood at the door, waiting until the last minute before he would be forced to send the disk up. He was quivering with fear. He tried to think of anything to distract himself. He thought: Those Readers. With Uranium 237 they've stumbled closer to atomic power than we did in all the glory of our mechanized society.

He thought: America can use these blast lances. That'll be another factor added to the past from the future—and it'll create still another infinity of alternative futures.

Conn coughed and realized that the shaft was heavy with smoke. Above him he heard a rumble, as though a heavy machine was starting to roll down the hill. As if by magic, the ends of the wire sputtered away from the terminals and whipped up the shaft, carried away by the tractor. He sent the disk up after them, thinking stupidly: That's the way a fishing line looks to a fish. He shut the door.

Conn stepped up on the platform, afraid to look at the accumulator dial. He might have as much or twice as much power as he'd need, but he'd have to push back through Time, no matter what. If he fell short of'41 in this track, he'd come out into the Dark Ages again, and be stuck for eternity. There'd be neither electricity nor the chance to create any.

He picked up the lance and reached for the knife switch. It was, he thought, like jumping blindfolded into an unknown vastly more terrifying than mere infinity.

He yanked down the switch.

VIII

The silver-apple moon had slipped back toward the eastern horizon when Conn at last came to the surface. It was blood-red and vast. The sky around it was steel-blue. He leaned on the lance he had brought with him and felt sick and weary.

The distant crack of a shot made him prick his ears, Conn stamped the thick turf carefully over the stud bank and went loping down the side of the hill. All this seemed like a bad dream he'd had once before—but he had an idea, a most peculiar idea.

He pushed through the high weeds at the foot of the bill and found himself at the edge of a lush fairway. A hundred yards before him, Conn saw the slight mound of a green. A flag whipped above it. Far beyond the mound he saw a small group of figures. Seven figures. They split up and began to creep in his direction. Suddenly Conn understood.

He got to all fours and began worming forward through the turf. A spike of red flame flared and cracked. From the sand pit, just before the green, came an answering shot. The seven figures poised and began to run. At the sand pit the dark form of a man clambered up. He fired twice and then dove back into the cover. The figures continued to sprint forward.

Conn murmured: "Take it easy, Probable Conn. I'm with you—"

He got to one knee, threw up the lance, and pressed the firing stud. There were five silent flares of light. Craters appeared in the grass—and only two of the Nazi attackers were left.

Conn sighed and walked over to the edge of the green. He lay down easily and prepared to wait. It would only take a few minutes, he knew. The Probable Conn would lay out the two last Nazis, kiss Hilda, get slapped and say goodby. He might even see him walking away through the gloom.

He would walk up to the time machine, Conn thought, and surge forward into still another alternative future. Maybe he'd be happy there—maybe not. Maybe he'd try to come back, too. There was no telling. There was no sense wondering what he had in store for him because Time was too infinite for the human mind to comprehend. There would be a lot to explain to Hilda, Conn thought.

Why he'd left her? Why he'd returned so quickly? How he came to have his clothes torn to shreds? Where he got this lance? All this and more. But it wasn't important. Hilda was the only thing that was important and she'd understand.

A figure walked past him, trodding sadly through the moist turf; the figure of a Probable Conn with a rucksack on his shoulder. Conn wanted to get up and say: "Hi!" and maybe go over and shake hands; but the figure passed after a lingering look back, and, anyway, Conn heard Hilda cry: "David!"

That was his cue. He got to his feet and ran toward her. When she saw him she cried out again in a joyous tone: "David!"

Conn took Hilda in his arms and kissed her. He kept murmuring: "It's all right, darling, it's all right."

And the thought came to him that this was the last paragraph for real. Nothing else came after this but "They lived happily ever after" and "The End." He nestled his bruised cheek against her silky hair and felt sorry for all the infinity of Probable Conns. He wondered how many of them knew what they were missing.

Astounding, July 1941

Hell Is Forever

Round and round the shutter'd Square
I stroll'd with the Devil's arm in mine,
No sound but the scrape of his hoofs was there
And the ring of his laughter and mine.
We had drunk black wine.

I screamed, "I will race you, Master!"
"What matter," he shrieked, "tonight
Which of us runs the faster?
There is nothing to fear tonight
In the foul moon's light!"

Then I look'd him in the eyes,
And I laughed full shrill at the lie he told
And the gnawing fear he would fain disguise.
It was true, what I'd time and again been told:
He was old—old.

—from "Fungoids," by Enoch Soames

There were six of them and they had tried everything.

They began with drinking and drank until they had exhausted the sense of taste. Wines—Amontillado, Beaune, Kirschwasser, Bordeaux, Hock, Burgundy, Medoc and Chambertin; whisky, Scotch, Irish, Usquebaugh and Schnapps; brandy, gin and rum. They drank them separately and together; they mixed the tan alcohols and flavors into stupendous punches, into a thousand symphonies of taste; they experimented, created, invented, destroyed—and finally they were bored.

Drugs followed. The milder first, then the more potent. Crisp brown licorice-like opium, toasted and rolled into pellets for smoking in long ivory pipes; thick green absinthe sipped bitter and strong, without sugar or water; heroin and cocaine in rustling snow crystals; marijuana rolled loosely into brown-paper cigarettes; hashish in milk-white curds to be eaten, or tarry plugs of Bhang that were chewed and stained the lips a deep tan—and again they were bored.

Their search for sensation became frantic with so much of their senses already dissipated. They enlarged their parties and turned them into festivals of horror. Exotic dancers and esoteric half-human creatures crowded the broad, low room and filled it with their incredible performances. Pain, fear, desire, love and hatred were torn apart and exhibited to the least quivering detail like so many laboratory specimens.

The cloying odor of perfume mingled with the knife-sharp sweat of excited bodies; the anguished screams of tortured creatures merely interrupted their swift, never-ceasing talk and so in time this, too, palled. They reduced their parties to the original six and returned each week to sit, bored and still hungry for new sensations. Now, languidly and without enthusiasm, they were toying with the occult; turning the party room into a necromancer's chamber.

Offhand you would not have thought it was a bomb

shelter. The room was large and square, the walls paneled with imitation-grained soundproofing, the ceiling low-beamed. To the right was an inset door, heavy and bolted with an enormous wrought-iron lock. There were no windows, but the air-conditioning inlets were shaped like the arched slits of a Gothic monastery. Lady Sutton had paned them with stained glass and set small electric bulbs behind them. They threw showers of sullen color across the room.

The flooring was of ancient walnut, high-polished and gleaming like metal. Across it were spread a score of lustrous Oriental scatter rugs. One enormous divan, covered with Indian batik, ran the width of the shelter against a wall. Above were tiers of bookshelves, and before it was a long trestle table piled with banquet remains. The rest of the shelter was furnished with deep, seductive chairs, soft, quilted, and inviting.

Centuries ago this had been the deepest dungeon of Sutton Castle, hundreds of feet beneath the earth. Now—drained, warmed, air-conditioned and refurnished, it was the scene of Lady Sutton's sensation parties. More—it was the official meeting place of the Society of Six. The Six Decadents, they called themselves.

"We are the last spiritual descendants of Nero—the last of the gloriously evil aristocrats," Lady Sutton would say. "We were born centuries too late, my friends. In a world that is no longer ours we have nothing to live for but ourselves. We are a race apart—we six."

And when unprecedented bombings shook England so catastrophically that the shudders even penetrated to the Sutton shelter, she would glance up and laugh: "Let them slaughter each other, those pigs. This is no war of ours. We go our own way, always, eh? Think, my friends, what a joy it would be to emerge from our shelter one bright morning and find all London dead—all the world dead—" And then she laughed again with her deep, hoarse bellow.

She was bellowing now, her enormous fat body sprawled half across the divan like a decorated toad, laughing at the program that Digby Finchley had just handed her. It had been etched by Finchley himself—an exquisite design of devils and angels in grotesque amorous combat encircling the cabalistic lettering that read:

THE SIX PRESENT
ASTAROTH WAS A LADY
By Christian Braugh

Cast
(In order of appearance)

A Necromancer	Christian Braugh
A Black Cat	Merlin
(*By courtesy of Lady Sutton*)	
Astaroth	Theone Dubedat
Nebiros, an Assistant Demon	
Costumes	Digby Finchley
Special Effects	Robert Peel
Music	Sidra Peel

Finchley said: "A little comedy is a change, isn't it?"

Lady Sutton shook with uncontrolled laughter.

"Astaroth was a lady! Are you sure you wrote it, Chris?"

There was no answer from Braugh, only the buzz of preparations from the far end of the room, where a small stage had been erected and curtained off.

She bellowed in her broken bass: "Hey, Chris! Hey, there—"

The curtain split and Christian Braugh thrust his albino head through. His face was partially made up with red eyebrows and beard and dark-blue shadows around the eyes. He said: "Beg pardon, Lady Sutton?"

At the sight of his face she rolled over the divan like a mountain of jelly. Across her helpless body, Finchley smiled to Braugh, his lips unfolding in a cat's grin. Braugh moved his white head in imperceptible answer.

"I said, did you really write this, Chris...or have you hired a ghost again?"

Braugh looked angry, then disappeared behind the curtain.

"Oh, my hat!" gurgled Lady Sutton. "This is better than a gallon of champagne. And, speaking of same...who's nearest the bubbly? Bob? Pour some more. Bob! Bob Peel!"

The man slumped in the chair alongside the ice buckets never moved. He was lying on the nape of his neck, feet thrust out in a V before him, his dress shirt buckled under his bearded chin. Finchley went across the room and looked down at him.

"Passed out," he said.

"So early? Well, no matter. Fetch me a glass, Dig, there's a good lad."

Finchley filled a prismed champagne glass and brought it to Lady Sutton. From a small cameo-faced vial she added three drops of laudanum, swirled the sparkling mixture once and then sipped while she read the program.

"A Necromancer...that's you, eh, Dig?"

He nodded.

"And what's a Necromancer?"

"A kind of magician, Lady Sutton."

"Magician? Oh, that's good...that's very good!" She spilled champagne on her vast blotchy bosom and dabbed ineffectually with the program.

Finchley lifted a hand to restrain her and said, "You ought to be careful with that program, Lady Sutton. I made only one print and then destroyed the plate. It's unique and liable to be valuable."

"Collector's item, eh? Your work, of course, Dig?"

"Yes."

"Not much of a change from the usual pornography, hey?" She burst into another thunder of laughter that degenerated into a fit of hacking coughs. She dropped the glass altogether. Finchley flushed, then retrieved the glass and returned it to the buffet, stepping carefully over Peel's legs.

"And who's this Astaroth?" Lady Sutton went on.

From behind the curtain, Theone Dubedat called: "Me! I! *Ich!Moi*!" Her voice was husky. It had a quality of gray smoke.

"Darling, I know it's you, but *what* are you?"

"A devil, I think."

Finchley said: "Astaroth is some sort of legendary archdemon—a top-ranking devil, so to speak."

"Theone a devil? No doubt of it—" Exhausted with rapture, Lady Sutton lay quiescent and musing on the patterned divan. At last she raised an enormous arm and examined her watch. The flesh hung from her elbows in elephantine creases, and at the gesture it shook and a little shower of torn sequins glittered down from her sleeve.

"You'd best get on with it, Dig. I've got to leave at midnight."

"Leave?"

"You heard me."

Finchley's face contorted. He bent over her, tense with suppressed emotion, his bleak eyes examining her. "What's up? What's wrong?"

"Nothing."

"Then—"

"A few things have changed, that's all."

"What's changed?"

Her face turned harsh as she returned his stare. The bulging features seemed to stiffen into obsidian. "Too soon to tell you...but you'll find out quick enough. Now I don't want any more pestering from you, Dig, m'lad!"

Finchley's scarecrow features regained a measure of control. He started to speak, but before he could utter a word Sidra Peel suddenly popped her head out of the alcove alongside the stage, where the organ had been placed. She called: "*Ro*-bert!"

In a constricted voice, Finchley said, "Bob's passed, out again, Sidra."

She emerged from the alcove, walked jerkily across the room and stood looking down in her husband's face. Sidra Peel was short, slender, and dark. Her body was like an electric high-tension wire, alive with too much current, yet coruscated, stained and rusted from too much exposure to passion. The deep black sockets of her eyes were frigid coals with gleaming white points. As she gazed at her husband, her long fingers writhed; then, suddenly, her hand lashed out and struck the inert face.

"Swine!" she hissed.

Lady Sutton laughed and coughed all at once. Sidra Peel shot her a venomous glance and stepped toward the divan, the sharp crack of her heel on the walnut sounding like a pistol shot. Finchley gestured a quick warning that stopped her. She hesitated, then returned to the alcove and said: "The music's ready."

"And so am I," said Lady Sutton. "On with the show and all that, eh?" She spread herself across the divan like a crawling tumor the while Finchley propped scarlet pillows under her head. "It's really nice of you to play this little comedy for me, Dig. Too bad there're only six of us here tonight. Ought to have an audience, eh?"

"You're the only audience we want, Lady Sutton."

"All! Keep it all in the family?"

"So to speak."

"The Six—Happy Family of Hatred."

"That's not so, Lady Sutton."

"Don't be an ass, Dig. We're all hateful. We glory in it. I ought to know. I'm the Bookkeeper of Disgust. Someday I'll let you all see the entries. Someday soon."

"What sort of entries?"

"Curious already, eh? Oh, nothing spectacular. Just the way Sidra's been trying to kill her husband—and Bob's been torturing her by holding on. And you making a fortune out of filthy pictures...and eating your rotten heart out for that frigid devil, Theone—"

"Please, Lady Sutton!"

"And Theone," she went on with relish, "using that icy body of hers like an executioner's scalpel to torture...and Chris...How many of his books d'you think he's stolen from those poor Grub Street devils?"

"I couldn't say."

"I know. All of them. A fortune on other men's brains. Oh, we're a beautifully loathsome lot, Dig. It's the only thing we have to be proud of—the only thing that sets us off from the billion blundering moralistic idiots that have inherited our earth. That's why we've got to stay a happy family of mutual hatred."

"I should call it mutual admiration," Finchley murmured.

He bowed courteously and went to the curtains, looking more like a scarecrow than ever in the black dinner clothes. He was extremely tall—three inches over six feet—and extremely thin. The pipestem arms and legs looked like warped dowel sticks, and his horsy flat features seemed to have been painted on a pasty pillow.

Finchley pulled the curtains together behind him. A moment after he disappeared there was a whispered cue and the lights dimmed. In the vast low room there was no sound except Lady Sutton's croupy breathing. Peel, still slumped in his deep chair, was motionless and invisible, except for the limp angle of his legs.

From infinite distances came a slight vibration—almost a shudder. It seemed at first to be a sinister reminder of the hell that was bursting across England, hundreds of feet over their heads. Then the shuddering quickened and by imperceptible stages swelled into the deepest tones of the organ. Above the background of the throbbing diapasons, a weird tremolo of fourths, empty and spine-chilling, cascaded down the keyboard in chromatic steps.

Lady Sutton chuckled faintly. "My word," she said, "that's really horrid, Sidra. Ghastly."

The grim background of music choked her. It filled the shelter with chilling tendrils of sound that were more than tone. The curtains slipped apart slowly, revealing Christian Braugh garbed in black, his face a hideous, twisted mass of red and purple-blue that contrasted starkly to the near-albino white hair. Braugh stood at the center of the stage surrounded by spider-legged tables piled high with Necromancer's apparatus. Prominent was Merlin, Lady Sutton's black cat, majestically poised atop an ironbound volume.

Braugh lifted a piece of black chalk from a table and drew a circle on the floor twelve feet around himself. He inscribed the circumference with cabalistic characters and pentacles. Then he lifted a wafer and exhibited it with a flirt of his wrist.

"This," he declared in sepulchral tones, "is a sacred wafer stolen from a church at midnight."

Lady Sutton applauded satirically, but stopped almost at once. The music seemed to upset her. She moved uneasily on the divan and looked about her with little uncertain glances.

Muttering blasphemous imprecations, Braugh raised an iron dagger and plunged it through the wafer. Then he arranged a copper chafing dish over a blue alcohol flame and began to stir in powders and crystals of bright colors. He lifted a vial filled with purple liquid and poured the contents into a porcelain bowl. There was a faint detonation and a thick cloud of vapor lifted to the ceiling.

The organ surged. Braugh muttered incantations under his breath and performed oddly suggestive gestures. The shelter swam with scents and mists, violet clouds and deep fogs. Lady Sutton glanced toward the chair across from her "Splendid, Bob," she called. "Wonderful effects—really." She tried to make her voice cheerful, but it came out in a sickly croak. Peel never moved.

With a savage motion Braugh pulled three black hairs from the cat's tail. Merlin uttered a yowl of rage and sprang at the same time from the book to the top of an inlaid cabinet in the background. Through the mists and vapors his giant yellow eyes gleamed balefully. The hairs went into the chafing dish, and a new aroma filled the room. In quick succession the claws of an owl, the powder of vipers and a human-shaped mandrake root followed.

"Now!" cried Braugh.

He cast the wafer, transfixed by the dagger, into the porcelain bowl containing the purple fluid, and then poured the whole mixture into the copper chafing dish.

There was a violent explosion.

A jet-black cloud filled the stage and swirled out into the shelter. Slowly it cleared away, faintly revealing the tall form of a naked devil; the body exquisitely formed, the head a frightful mask. Braugh had disappeared.

Through the drifting clouds, in the husky tones of Theone Dubedat, the devil spoke: "Greetings, Lady Sutton—"

She stepped forward out of the vapor. In the pulsating light that shot down to the stage, her body shone with a shimmering nacreous glow of its own—the toes and fingers were long and graceful. Color slashed across the rounded torso. Yet that whole perfect body was cold and lifeless—as unreal as the grotesque papier-mache that covered her head.

Theone repeated. "Greetings—"

"Hi, old thing!" Lady Sutton interrupted. "How's everything in hell?"

There was a giggle from the alcove where Sidra Peel was playing softly. Theone posed statuesquely and lifted her head a little higher to speak. "I bring you—"

"Darling!" shrieked Lady Sutton, "why didn't you let me know it was going to be like this? I'd have sold tickets!"

Theone raised a gleaming arm imperiously. Again she began: "I bring you the thanks of the five who—" And then abruptly she stopped.

For the space of five heartbeats there was a gasping pause while the organ murmured and the last of the black smoke filtered away, mushrooming against the ceiling. In the silence Theone's rapid, choked breathing mounted hysterically—then came a ghastly, piercing scream.

The others darted from behind the stage, exclaiming in astonishment—Braugh, Necromancer's costume thrown over his arm, his makeup removed; Finchley like a pair of animated scissors in black habit and cowl, a script in his hand. The organ stuttered, then stopped with a crash, and Sidra Peel burst out of the alcove.

Theone tried to scream, again, but her voice caught and broke. In the appalled silence Lady Sutton cried: "What is it? Something wrong?"

Theone uttered a moaning sound and pointed to the center of the stage. "Look—There—" The words came off the top of her throat like the squeal of nails on slate. She cowered back against a table, upsetting the apparatus. It clashed and tinkled.

"What is it? For the love of—"

"It worked—" Theone moaned. "The r-ritual—It worked!"

They stared through the gloom, then started. An enormous sable Thing was slowly rising in the center of the Necromancer's circle—a vague, amorphous form towering high, emitting a dull, hissing sound like the whisper of a caldron.

"What is that?" Lady Sutton shouted.

The Thing pushed forward like some sickly extrusion. When it reached the edge of the black circle it halted. The seething sound swelled ominously.

"Is it one of us?" Lady Sutton cried. "Is this a stupid trick? Finchley...Braugh—"

They shot her startled glances, bleak with terror.

"Sidra...Robert...Theone...No, you're all here. Then who is that? How did it get in here?"

"It's impossible," Braugh whispered, backing away. His legs knocked against the edge of the divan and he sprawled clumsily.

Lady Sutton beat at him with helpless hands and cried: "Do something! Do something—"

Finchley tried to control his voice. He stuttered: "W-We're safe so long as the circle isn't broken. It can't get out—"

On the stage, Theone was sobbing, making pushing motions with her hands. Suddenly she crumpled to the floor. One outflung arm rubbed away a segment of the black chalk circle. The Thing moved swiftly, stepped through the break in the circle and descended from the platform like a black fluid. Finchley and Sidra Peel reeled back with terrified shrieks. There was a growing thickness pervading the shelter atmosphere. Little gusts of vapor twisted around the head of the Thing as it moved slowly toward the divan.

"You're all joking!" Lady Sutton screamed. "This isn't real. It can't be!" She heaved up from the divan and tottered to her feet. Her face blanched as she counted the take of her guests again. One—two—and four made six—and the shape made seven. But there should only be six.

She backed away, then began to run. The Thing was following her when she reached the door. Lady Sutton pulled at the door handle, but the iron bolt was locked. Quickly, for all her vast bulk, she ran around the edge of the shelter, smashing over the tables. As the Thing expanded in the darkness and filled the room with its sibilant hissing, she snatched at her purse and tore it open, groping for the key. Her shaking hands scattered the purse contents over the room.

A deep bellow pierced the blackness. Lady Sutton jerked and stared around desperately, making little animal noises. As the Thing threatened to engulf her in its infinite black depths, a cry tore up through her body and she sank heavily to the floor.

Silence.

Smoke drifted in shaded clouds.

The china clock ticked off a sequence of delicate periods.

"Well—" Finchley said in conversational tones. "That's that."

He went to the inert figure on the floor. He knelt over it for a moment, probing and testing, his face flickering with savage hunger. Then he looked up and grinned. "She's dead, all right. Just the way we figured. Heart failure. She was too fat."

He remained on his knees, drinking in the moment of death. The others clustered around the toadlike body, staring with distended nostrils. The moment hardly lasted; then the languor of infinite boredom again shaded across their features.

The black Thing waved its arms a few times. The costume split at last to reveal a complicated framework and the sweating, bearded face of Robert Peel. He dropped the costume around him, stepped out of it, and went to the figure in the chair.

"The dummy idea was perfect," he said. His bright little eyes glittered momentarily. He looked like a sadistic miniature of Edward VII. "She'd never have believed it if we hadn't arranged for a seventh unknown to enter the scene." He glanced at his wife. "That slap was a stroke of genius, Sidra. Wonderful realism—"

"I meant it."

"I know you did, dearly beloved, but thanks nevertheless."

Theone Dubedat had risen and gotten into a white dressing gown. She stepped down and walked over to the body, removing the hideous devil's mask. It revealed a beautifully chiseled face, frigid and lovely. Her blonde hair gleamed in the darkness.

Braugh said: "Your acting was superb, Theone—" He bobbed his white albino head appreciatively.

For a time she didn't answer. She stood staring down at the shapeless mound of flesh, an expression of hopeless longing on her face; but there was nothing more to her gazing than the impersonal curiosity of a bystander watching a window chef. Less.

At last Theone sighed. She said: "So it wasn't worth it, after all."

"What?" Braugh groped for a cigarette.

"The acting—the whole performance. We've been let down again, Chris."

Braugh scratched a match. The orange flame flared, flickering across their disappointed faces. He lit his cigarette, then held the flame high and looked at them. The illumination twisted their features into caricatures, emphasizing their weariness, their infinite boredom. Braugh said, "My—my—"

"It's no use, Chris. This whole murder was a bust. It was about as exciting as a glass of water."

Finchley hunched his shoulders and paced up and back like a bundle of stilts. He said, "I got a bit of a kick when I thought she suspected. It didn't last long, though."

"You ought to be grateful for even that."

"I am."

Peel clucked his tongue in exasperation, then knelt like a bearded Humpty-Dumpty, his bald head gleaming, and raked in the contents of Lady Sutton's scattered purse. The bank-notes he folded and put in his pocket. He took the fat dead hand and lifted it toward Theone. "You always admired her sapphire, Theone. Want it?"

"You couldn't get it off, Bob."

"I think I could," he said, pulling strenuously.

"Oh, to hell with the sapphire."

"No—It's coming."

The ring slipped forward, then caught in the folds of flesh at the knuckle. Peel took a fresh grip and tugged and twisted. There was a sucking, yielding sound, and the entire finger tore away from the hand.

The dull odor of putrefaction struck their nostrils as they looked on with curiosity.

Peel shrugged and dropped the finger. He arose, dusting his hands slightly. "She rots fast," he said. "Peculiar—"

Braugh wrinkled his nose and said, "She was too fat."

Theone turned away in frantic desperation, her hands clasping her elbows. "What are we to do?" she cried.

"What? Isn't there a sensation left on Earth we haven't tried?"

With a dry whir, the china clock began quick chimes. Midnight.

Finchley said, "We might go back to drugs."

"They're as futile as this paltry murder."

"But there are other sensations. New ones."

"Name one!" Theone said in exasperation. "Only one."

"I could name several—if you'll have a seat and permit me—"

Suddenly Theone interrupted. "That's you speaking, isn't it, Dig?"

In a peculiar voice, Finchley answered, "N-no. I thought it was Chris."

Braugh said, "Wasn't me."

"You, Bob?"

"No."

"Th-then—"

The small voice said, "If the ladies and gentlemen would be kind enough to—"

It came from the stage. There was something there—something that spoke in that quiet, gentle voice; for Merlin was stalking back and forth, arching his high black back against an invisible leg.

"—to sit down," the voice continued persuasively.

Braugh had the most courage. He moved to the stage with slow, steady steps, the cigarette hanging firmly from his lips. He leaned across the apron and peered. For a while his eyes examined the stage; then he let a spume of smoke jet from his nostrils and called, "There's nothing here."

And at that moment the blue smoke swirled under the lights and swept around a figure of emptiness. It was no more than a glimpse of an outline-of a negative, but it was enough to make Braugh cry out and leap back. The others turned sick, too, and staggered to chairs.

"So sorry," said the quiet voice. "It won't happen again."

Peel gathered himself and said, "Merely for the sake of—"

"Yes?"

He tried to freeze his jerking features. "Merely for the sake of s-scientific curiosity, it—"

"Calm yourself, my friend."

"The ritual...It did work?"

"Of course not—My friends, there is no need to call us with such fantastic ceremony. If you really want us, we come."

"And you?"

"I? Oh...I know you have been thinking of me for some time. Tonight you wanted me—really wanted me, and I came."

The last of the cigarette smoke convulsed as that terrible figure of emptiness seemed to stoop and seat itself casually at the edge of the stage. The cat hesitated and then began rolling its head with little mews of pleasure as something fondled it.

Still striving desperately to control himself, Peel said, "But all those ceremonies and rituals that have been handed down—"

"Merely symbolic, Mr. Peel." Peel started at the sound of his name. "You have read, no doubt, that we do not appear unless a certain ritual is performed, and only if it is letter-perfect. That is not true, of course. We appear if the invitation is sincere—and only then—with or without ceremony—"

Sick and verging on hysteria, Sidra whispered, "I'm getting out of here." She tried to rise.

The gentle voice said, "One moment, please—"

"No!"

"I will help you get rid of your husband, Mrs. Peel."

Sidra blinked, then sank back into her chair. Peel clenched his fists and opened his mouth to speak. Before he could begin, the gentle voice continued. "And yet you will not lose your wife, if you really want to keep her, Mr. Peel. I guarantee that."

The cat was lifted into the air and then settled comfortably in space a few feet from the floor—They could see the thick fur on the back smooth and resmooth from the gentle petting.

At length Braugh asked, "What do you offer us?"

"I offer each of you his own heart's desire."

"And that is?"

"A new sensation—all new sensations—"

"What new sensations?"

"The sensation of reality."

Braugh laughed. "Hardly anyone's hearts desire."

"This will be, for I offer you five different realities—realities which you may fashion, each for himself.

I offer you worlds of your own making wherein Mrs. Peel may happily murder her husband in hers—and yet Mr. Peel may keep his wife in his own. To Mr. Braugh I offer the dreamworld of the writer, and to Mr. Finchley the creation of the artist—"

Theone said, "These are dreams, and dreams are cheap. We all possess them."

"But you all awaken from your dreams and you pay the bitter price of that realization. I offer you an awakening from the present into a future reality which you may shape to your own desires-a reality which will never end."

Peel said: "Five simultaneous realities is a contradiction in terms. It's a paradox—impossible."

"Then I offer you the impossible."

"And the price?"

"I beg your pardon?"

"The price," Peel repeated with growing courage. "We're not altogether naive. We know there's always a price."

There was a long pause; then the voice said reproachfully, "I'm afraid there are many misconceptions and many things you fail to understand. Just now I cannot explain, but believe me when I say there is no price."

"Ridiculous. Nothing is ever given for nothing."

"Very well, Mr. Peel, if we must use the terminology of the marketplace, let me say that we never appear unless the price for our service is paid in advance. Yours has already been paid."

"Paid?" They shot involuntary glances at the rotting body on the shelter floor.

"In full."

"Then?"

"You're willing, I see. Very well—"

The cat was again lifted in the air and deposited on the floor with a last gentle pat. The remnants of mist clinging to the shelter ceiling weaved and churned as the invisible donor advanced. Instinctively the five arose and waited, tense and fearful, yet with a mounting sense of fulfillment.

A key darted up from the floor and sailed through midair toward the door. It paused before the lock an instant, then inserted itself and turned. The heavy wrought-iron bolt lifted and the door swung wide. Beyond should have been the dungeon passage leading to the upper levels of Sutton Castle—a low, narrow corridor, paved with flagstones and lined with limestone blocks. Now a few inches beyond the door jamb, there hung a veil of flame.

Pale, incredibly beautiful, it was a tapestry of flickering fire, the warp and weft an intermesh of rainbow colors. Those pastel strands of color locked and interlocked, swam, threaded and spun like so many individual life lines. They were an infinity of flames, emotions, the silken countenance of time, the swirling skin of space—They were all things to all men, and above all else, they were beautiful.

"For you," the quiet voice said, "your old reality ends in this room—"

"As simply as this?"

"Quite."

"But—"

"Here you stand," interrupted the voice, "In the last kernel, the last nucleus so to speak, of what once was real for you. Pass the door—pass through the veil, and you enter the reality I promised."

"What will we find beyond the veil?"

"What each of you desires. Nothing lies beyond that veil now. There is nothing there—nothing but time and space waiting for the molding. There is nothing and the potential of everything."

In a low voice, Peel said, "One time and one space? Will that be enough for all different realities?"

"All time, all space, my friend," the quiet voice answered. "Pass through and you will find the matrix of dreams."

They had been clustered together, standing close to each other in a kind of strained companionship. Now, in the silence that followed, they separated slightly as though each had marked out for himself a reality all his own—a life entirely divorced from the past and the companions of old times. It was a gesture of utter isolation.

Mutually impulsed, yet independently motivated, they moved toward the glittering veil—

II

I am an artist, Digby Finchley thought, and an artist is a creator. To create is to be godlike, and so shall I be. I shall be god of my world, and from nothing I shall create all—and my all will be beauty.

He was the first to reach the veil and the first to pass through. Across his face the riot of color flicked like a cool spray. He blinked his eyes momentarily as the brilliant scarlets and purples blinded him. When he opened them again, he had left the veil a step behind and stood in the darkness.

But not darkness.

It was the blank jet-black of infinite emptiness. It smote his eyes like a heavy hand and seemed to press the eyeballs back into his skull like leaden weights. He was terrified and jerked his head about, staring into the impenetrable nothingness, mistaking the ephemeral flashes of retinal light for reality.

Nor was he standing.

For he took one hasty stride and it was as though he was suspended out of all contact with mass and matter. His terror was tinged with horror as he became aware that he was utterly alone; that there was nothing to see, nothing to hear, nothing to touch. A bitter loneliness assailed him and in that instant he understood how truthfully the voice in the shelter had spoken, and how terribly real his new reality was.

That instant, too, was his salvation. "For," Finchley murmured with a wry smile to the blankness, "it is of the essence of godhood to be alone—to be unique."

Then he was quite calm and hung quiescent in time and space while he mustered his thoughts for the creation.

"First," Finchley said at length, "I must have a heavenly throne that befits a god. Too, I must have a heavenly kingdom and angelic retainers; for no god is altogether complete without an entourage."

He hesitated while his mind rapidly sorted over the various heavenly kingdoms he had known from art and letters. There was no need, he thought, to be especially original with this sort of thing.

Originality would play an important role in the creation of his universe. Just now the only essential thing was to insure himself a reasonable degree of dignity and luxury—and for that the secondhand furnishing of ancient Yahweh would do.

Raising one hand in a self-conscious gesture, he commanded. Instantly the blackness was riven with light, and before him a flight of gold-veined marble steps rose to a glittering throne. The throne was high and cushioned. Arms, legs and back were of glowing silver, and the cushions were imperial purple. And yet—the whole was hideous. The legs were too long and thin, the arms were rickety, the back narrow and sickly.

Finchley said, "Owww!" and tried to remodel. Yet no matter how he altered the proportions, the throne remained horrible. And for that matter, the steps, too, were disgusting for by some freak of creation the gold veins twisted and curved through the marble to form obscene designs too reminiscent of the erotic pictures Finchley had drawn in his past existence.

He gave it up at last, mounted the steps, and settled himself uneasily on the throne. It felt as though he was sitting on the lap of a corpse with dead arms poised to enfold him in a ghastly embrace. He shuddered slightly and said: "Oh, hell, I was never a furniture designer—"

Finchley glanced around, then raised his hand again. The jet clouds that had crowded around the throne rolled back to reveal high columns of crystal and a soaring roof arched and paved with smooth blocks. The hall stretched back for thousands of yards like some never-ending cathedral, and all that length was filled with rank on rank of his retainers.

Foremost were the angels; slender, winged creatures, white-robed, with blonde, shining heads, sapphire-blue eyes, and scarlet, smiling mouths. Behind the angels knelt the order of Cherubim; giant winged bulls with tawny hides and hoofs of beaten metal. Their Assyrian heads were heavily bearded with gleaming jet curls. Third were the Seraphim;

ranks of huge six-winged serpents whose jeweled scales glittered with a silent flame.

As Finchley sat and stared at them with admiration for his handiwork, they chanted in soft unison: "Glory to god. Glory to the Lord Finchley, the All-Highest,...Glory to the Lord Finchley—"

He sat and gazed and it was as though his eyes were slowly acquiring the distortion of astigmatism, for he realized that this was more a cathedral of evil than of heaven. The columns were carved with revolting grotesques at the capitals and bases, and as the hall stretched into dimness, it seemed peopled with cavorting shadows that grimaced and danced.

And in the far reaches of those columned lengths, covert little scenes were playing that amazed him. Even as they chanted, the angels gazed sidelong with their glistening blue eyes at the Cherubim; and behind a column he saw one winged creature reach out and seize a lovely blonde angel of lust to crush her to him.

In sheer desperation Finchley raised his hand again, and once more the blackness swirled around him.

"So much," he said, "for Heavenly Kingdoms—"

He pondered for another ineffable period as he drifted in emptiness, grappling with the most stupendous artistic problem he had ever attacked.

Up to now, Finchley thought with a shudder for the horror he had wrought, I have been merely playing—feeling my strength—warming up, so to speak, the way an artist will toy with pastel and a block of grained paper. Now it's time for me to go to work.

Solemnly, as he thought would befit a god, he conducted a laborious conference with himself in space.

What, he asked himself, has creation been in the past?

One might call it nature.

Very well, we shall call it nature. Now, what are the objections to nature's creation?

Why—nature was never an artist. Nature merely blundered into things in an experimental sort of way. Whatever beauty existed was merely a by-product. The difference betw—

The difference, he interrupted himself, between the old nature and the new god Finchley shall be order. Mine will be an ordered cosmos devoid of waste and devoted to beauty. There will be nothing haphazard. There will be no blundering.

First, the canvas.

"There shall be infinite space!" Finchley cried.

In the nothingness, his voice roared through the bony structure of his skull and echoed in his ears with a flat, sour sound; but on the instant of command, the opaque blackness was filtered into a limpid jet. Finchley could still see nothing, but he felt the change.

He thought: Now, in the old cosmos there were simply stars and nebulae and vast, fiery bodies scattered through the realms of the sky. No one knew their purpose—no one knew their origin or destination.

In mine there shall be purpose, for each body shall serve to support a race of creatures whose sole function shall be to serve me—

He cried: "Let there be universes to the number of one hundred, filling space. One thousand galaxies shall make up each universe, and one million suns shall be the sum of each galaxy. Ten planets shall circle each sun, and two moons each planet. Let all revolve around their creator! Let all this come to pass. Now!"

Finchley screamed as light burst in a soundless cataclysm around him. Stars, close and hot as suns, distant and cold as pinpricks—separately, by twos and in vast smudgy clouds—Blazing crimson—yellow—deep green and violet—The sum of their brilliance was a welter of light that constricted his heart and filled him with a devouring fear of the latent power within him.

"This," Finchley whimpered, "is enough cosmic creation for the time being—"

He closed his eyes determinedly and exerted his will once more. There was a sensation of solidity under his feet and when he opened his eyes cautiously he was standing on one of his earths with blue sky and a blue-white sun lowering swiftly toward the western horizon.

It was a bare, brown earth—Finchley had seen to that—it was a vast sphere of inchoate matter waiting for his molding, for he had decided that first above all other creation he would form a good green earth for himself—a planet of beauty where Finchley, God of all Creation, would reside in his Eden.

All through that waning afternoon he worked, swiftly and with artistic finesse. A vast ocean, green and with sparkling white foam, swept over half the globe; alternating hundreds of miles of watery space with clusters of warm islands. The single continent he divided in half with a backbone of jagged mountains that stretched from pole to snowy pole.

With infinite care he worked. Using oils, watercolors, charcoal, and plumbago sketches, he planned and executed his entire world. Mountains, valleys, plains; crags, precipices and mere boulders were all designed in a fluent congruence of beautifully balanced masses.

All his spirit of artistry went into the clever scattering of lakes like so many sparkling jewels; and into the cunning arabesques of winding rivers that traced intricate designs over the face of the planet. He devoted himself to the selection of colors; gray gravels, pink, white and black sands, good earths, brown, umber and sepia, mottled shales, glistening micas and silica stones—and when the sun at last vanished on the first day of his labor, his Eden was a paradise of stone, earth, and metal, ready for life.

As the sky darkened overhead, a pale gibbous moon with a face of death was revealed riding in the vault of the sky; and even as Finchley watched it uneasily, a second moon with a blood-red disk lifted its ravaged countenance above the eastern horizon and began a ghastly march across the heavens. Finchley tore his eyes away from them and stared out at the twinkling stars.

There was much satisfaction to be gained from the contemplation. "I know exactly how many there are," he thought complacently. "You multiply one hundred by a thousand by a million and there's your answer—and that happens to be my idea of order!"

He lay back on a patch of warm, soft soil and placed palms under the back of his head, looking up. "And I know exactly what all of them are there for—to support human lives—the countless billions upon billions of lives which I shall design and create solely to serve and worship the Lord Finchley—that's purpose for you!"

And he knew where each of those blue and red and

indigo sparks was going, for even in the vasty reaches of space they were thundering in a circular course, the pivot of which was that point in the skies he had just left. Someday he would return to that place and there build his heavenly castle. Then he would sit through all eternity watching the wheeling flight of his worlds.

There was a peculiar splotch of red in the zenith of the sky. Finchley watched it absently at first, then with guarded attention as it seemed to burgeon. It spread slowly like an ink stain, and as the moments fled by, became tinged with orange and then the purest white. And for the first time Finchley was uncomfortably aware of a sensation of heat.

An hour passed and then two and three. The fist of red-white spread across the sky until it was a fiery nebulous cloud. A thin, tenuous edge approached a star gently, then touched. Instantly there was a blinding blaze of radiance and Finchley was flooded with searing light that illuminated the landscape with the eerie glow of flaring magnesium. The sensation of heat grew in intensity and tiny beads of perspiration prickled across his skin.

With midnight, the unaccountable inferno filled half the sky, and the gleaming stars, one after another, were bursting into silent explosions. The right was blinding white and the heat suffocating. Finchley tottered to his feet and began to run, searching vainly for shade or water. It was only then that he realized his universe was running amuck.

"No!" he cried desperately. "No!"

Heat bludgeoned him. He fell and rolled across cutting rocks that tore at him and anchored him back with his face up-thrust. Past his shielding hands, past his tight-shut eyelids, the intolerable light and heat pressed.

"Why should it go wrong?" Finchley screamed. "There was plenty of room for everything! Why should it—"

In heat-borne delirium he felt a thunderous rocking as though his Eden were beginning to split asunder.

He cried, "Stop! Stop! Everything stop!" He beat at his temples with futile fists and at last whispered, "All right...if I've made another mistake, then—all right—" He waved his hand feebly.

And again the skies were black and blank. Only the two scabrous moons rode overhead, beginning the long downward journey to the west. And in the east a faint glow hinted at the rising sun.

"So," Finchley murmured, "one must be more a mathematician and physicist to run a cosmos. Very well, I can learn that later. I'm an artist and I never pretended to know all that. But...I *am* an artist, and there is still my good green earth to people—Tomorrow—We shall see...tomorrow—"

And so presently he slept.

The sun was high when he awoke, and its evil eye filled him with unrest. Glancing at the landscape he had fashioned the day previous, he was even more uncertain, for there was some subtle distortion in everything. Valley floors looked unclean with the pale sheen of lepers' scales. The mountain crags formed curious shapes suggestive of terror. Even the lakes contained the hint of horror under their smooth, innocent surfaces.

Not, he noticed, when he stared directly at these creations, but only when his glance was sidelong. Viewed full-eyed and steadfastly, everything seemed to be right. Proportion was good, line was excellent, coloring perfection. And yet—he shrugged and decided he would have to put in some practice at drafting. No doubt there was some subtle error of design in his work.

He walked to a tiny stream and from the bank scooped out a mass of moist red clay. He kneaded it smooth, wet it down to a thin mud, and strained it. After it had dried under the sun slightly, he arranged a heavy block of stone as a pedestal and set to work. His hands were still practiced and certain. With sure fingers he shaped his concept of a large furred rabbit. Body, legs and head; exquisitely etched features-it crouched on the stone ready, it seemed, to leap off at a moment's notice. Finchley smiled affectionately at his work, his confidence at last restored. He tapped it once on the rounded head and said, "Live, my friend—"

There was a second's indecision while life invaded the clay form; then it arched its back with a clumsy motion and attempted to leap. It moved to the edge of the pedestal where it hung crazily for an instant before it dropped heavily to the ground. As it lumbered on a halting course, it uttered horrible little grunting sounds and turned once to gaze at Finchley. On that animal face was an expression of malevolence.

Finchley's smile froze. He frowned, hesitated, then scooped up another chunk of clay and set it on the stone. For the space of an hour he worked, shaping a graceful Irish setter. At last he tapped this, too, and said, "Live—"

Instantly the dog collapsed. It mewled helplessly and then struggled to shaking feet like some enormous spider, eyes distended and glassy. It tottered to the edge of the pedestal, leaped off, and collided with Finchley's leg. There was a low growl, and the beast tore sharp fangs into Finchley's skin. He leaped back with a cry and kicked the animal furiously. Mewling and howling, the setter went gangling across the fields like a crippled monster.

With furious intent, Finchley returned to his work. Shape after shape he modeled and endowed with life, and each—ape, monkey, fox, weasel, rat, lizard and toad—fish, long and short, stout and slender—birds by the score—each was a grotesque monstrosity that swam, shambled or fluttered off like some nightmare. Finchley was bewildered and exhausted. He sat himself down on the pedestal and began to sob while his tired fingers still twitched and prodded at a lump of clay.

He thought: "I'm still an artist—what's gone wrong? What turns everything I do into horrible freak shows?"

His fingers turned and twisted, and a head began to form in the clay.

He thought, "I made a fortune with my art once. Everyone couldn't have been crazy. They bought my work for many reasons—but an important one was that it was beautiful."

He noticed the lump of clay in his hands. It had been partially formed into a woman's head. He examined it closely for the first time in many hours; he smiled.

"Why, of course!" he exclaimed. "I'm no shaper of animals. Let's see how well I do with a human figure—"

Swiftly, with heavy chunks of clay, he built up the

under-structure of his figure. Legs, arms, torso, and head were formed. He hummed under his breath as he worked. He thought, She'll be the loveliest Eve ever created—and more—her children shall truly be the children of a god!

With loving hands he turned the full, swelling calves and thighs, and cunningly joined slender ankles to graceful feet. The hips were rounded had girdled a flat, slightly mounded belly. As he set the strong shoulders, he suddenly stopped and stepped back a pace.

Is it possible? he wondered.

He walked slowly around the half-completed figure.

Yes—

Force of habit, perhaps?

Perhaps that—and maybe the love he had borne for so many empty years.

He returned to the figure and redoubled his efforts. With a sense of growing elation, he completed arms, neck and head. There was a certainty within him that told him it was impossible to fail. He had modeled this figure too often not to know it down to the finest detail. And when he was finished, Theone Dubedat, magnificently sculpted in clay, stood atop the stone pedestal.

Finchley was content. Wearily he sat down with his back to a boulder, produced a cigarette from space, and lit it. For perhaps a minute he sat, dragging in the smoke to quiet his excitement. At last with a sense of chaotic anticipation he said, "Woman—"

He choked and stopped. Then he began again.

"Be alive—Theone!"

The second of life came and passed. The nude figure moved slightly, then began to tremble. Magnetically drawn, Finchley arose and stepped toward her, arms outstretched in mute appeal. There was a hoarse gasp of indrawn breath and slowly the great eyes opened and examined him.

The living girl straightened and screamed. Before Finchley could touch her she beat at his face, her long nails ripping his skin. She fell backward off the pedestal, leaped to her feet and began running off across the fields like all the others—running like a crazy crippled creature while she screamed and howled. The low sun dappled her body and the shadow she cast was monstrous.

Long after she disappeared, Finchley continued to gaze in her direction while within him all that futile, bitter love surged and burned in an acid tide. At length he turned again to the pedestal and with icy impassivity set once more to work. Nor did he stop until the fifth in a succession of lurid creatures ran screaming out into the night—Then and only then did he stop and stand for a long time gazing alternately at his hands and the crazy moons that careered overhead.

There was a tap on his shoulder and he was not too surprised to see Lady Sutton standing beside him. She still wore the sequined evening gown, and in the double moonlight her face was as coarse and masculine as ever.

Finchley said: "Oh...it's you."

"How are you, Dig, m'lad?"

He thought it over, trying to bring some reason to the ludicrous insanity that pervaded his cosmos. At last he said, "Not very well, Lady Sutton."

"Trouble?"

"Yes—" He broke off and stared at her. "I say, Lady Sutton, how the devil did you get here?"

She laughed. "I'm dead, Dig. You ought to know."

"Dead? Oh…I—" He floundered in embarrassment.

"No hard feelings, though. I'd have done the same m'self, y'know."

"You would?"

"Anything for a new sensation. That was always our motto, eh?" She nodded complacently and grinned at him. It was that same old grin of pure deviltry.

Finchley said, "What are you doing here? I mean, how did—"

"I said I was dead," Lady Sutton interrupted. "There's lots you don't understand about this business of dying."

"But this is my own personal private reality. I own it."

"And I'm still dead, Dig. I can get into any bloody damned reality I choose. Wait—you'll find out."

He said: "I won't—ever—that is, I can't. Because I won't ever die."

"Oh-ho?"

"No, I won't. I'm a god."

"You are, eh? How d'you like it?"

"I…I don't." He faltered for words. "I…that is, someone promised me a reality I could shape for myself, but I can't, Lady Sutton, I can't."

"And why not?"

"I don't know. I'm a god, and yet every time I try to shape something beautiful it turns out hateful."

"As how, for instance?"

He showed her the twisted mountains and plains, the evil lakes and rivers, the distorted grunting creatures he had created. All this Lady Sutton examined carefully and with close attention. At last she pursed her lips and thought for a moment; then she gazed keenly at Finchley and said, "Odd that you've never made a mirror, Dig."

"A mirror?" he echoed. "No, I haven't—I never needed one—"

"Go ahead. Make one now."

He gave her a perplexed look and waved a hand in the air. A square of silvered glass was in his fingers and he held it toward her.

"No," Lady Sutton said, "it's for you. Look in it."

Wondering, he raised the mirror and gazed into it. He uttered a hoarse cry and peered closer. Leering back at him out of the dim night was the evil face of a gargoyle. In the small, slant-set eyes, the splayed nose, the broken yellow teeth, the twisted ruin of a face, he saw everything he had seen in his ugly cosmos.

He saw the obscene cathedral of heaven and all its unholy hierarchy of ribald retainers; the spinning chaos of crashing stars and suns; the lurid landscape of his Eden; each howling, ghastly creature he had created; every horror that his brain had spawned. He hurled the mirror spinning and turned to confront Lady Sutton.

"What?" he demanded. "What is this?"

"Why, you're a god, Dig," Lady Sutton laughed, "and you ought to know that a god can create only in his own image. Yes—the answer's as simple as that. It's a grand joke, ain't it?"

"Joke?" The import of all the eons to come thundered down over his head. An eternity of living with his hideous self, upon himself, inside himself—over and over—repeated in every sun and star, every living and dead thing, every creature, every everlasting moment. A monstrous god feeding upon himself and slowly, inexorably going mad.

"Joke!" he screamed.

He flung out his hand and he floated once more, suspended out of all contact with mass and matter. Once more he was utterly alone, with nothing to see, nothing to hear, nothing to touch. And as he pondered for another ineffable period on the inevitable futility of his next attempt, he heard quite distinctly, the deep bellow of familiar laughter.

Of such was the Kingdom of Finchley's Heaven.

III

"Give me the strength! Oh, give me the strength!"

She went through the veil sharp on Finchley's heels, that short, slender, dark woman, and she found herself in the dungeon passage of Sutton Castle. For a moment she was startled out of her prayer, half-disappointed at not finding a land of mists and dreams. Then, with a bitter smile, she recalled the reality she wanted.

Before her stood a suit of armor; a strong, graceful figure of polished metal edged with sweeping flutings. She went to it. Dully from the gleaming steel cuirass, a slightly distorted reflection stared back. It showed the drawn, high-strung face, and the coal-black eyes, the coal-black hair dipping down over the brow in a sharp widow's peak. It said: This is Sidra Peel. This is a woman whose past has been fettered to a dull-witted creature that called itself her husband. She will break that chain this day if only she finds the strength—

"Break the chain!" she repeated fiercely, "and this day repay him for a life's worth of agony. God—if there be a god in my world—help me balance the account in full! Help me—"

Sidra froze while her pulse beat wildly. Someone had come down the lonesome passage and stood behind her. She could feel the heat—the aura of a presence—the almost imperceptible pressure of a body against hers. Mistily in the mirror of the armor she made out a face peering over her shoulder.

She spun around, crying, "Ahhh!"

"So sorry," he said. "Thought you were expecting me."

Her eyes riveted to his face. He was smiling slightly in an affable manner, and yet the streaked blond hair, the hollows and mounds, the pulsing veins and shadows of his features, were a lurid landscape of raw emotions.

"Calm yourself," he said while she teetered crazily and fought down the screams that were tearing through her.

"But wh—who—" She broke off and tried to swallow.

"I thought you were expecting me," he repeated.

"I...expecting you?"

He nodded and took her hands. Against his, her palms felt chilled and moist. "We had an engagement."

She opened her mouth slightly and shook her head.

"At twelve-forty—" He released one of her hands to look at his watch. "And here I am, on the dot."

"No," she said, yanking herself away. "No, this is

impossible. We have no engagement. I don't know you."

"You don't recognize me, Sidra? Well—that's odd, but I think you'll recollect who I am before long."

"But who are you?"

"I shan't tell you. You'll have to remember yourself."

A little calmer, she inspected his features closely.

With the rush of a waterfall, a blended sensation of attraction and repulsion surged over her. This man alarmed and fascinated her. She was filled with fear at his mere presence, yet intrigued and drawn.

At last she shook her head and said: "I still don't understand. I never called for you, Mr. Whoever-you-are, And we had no engagement."

"You most certainly did."

"I most certainly did not!" she flared, outraged by his insolent assurance. "I wanted my old world. The same old world I'd always known—"

"But with one exception?"

"Y-yes—" Her furious glance wavered and the rage drained out of her. "Yes, with one exception."

"And you prayed for the strength to produce that exception."

She nodded.

He grinned and took her arm— "Well, Sidra, then you did call for me and we did have an engagement—I'm the answer to your prayer."

She suffered herself to be led through the narrow, steep-mounting passages, unable to break free from that magnetic leash. His touch on her arm was a frightening thing. Everything in her cried out against the bewilderment—and yet another something in her welcomed it eagerly.

As they passed through the cloudy light of infrequent lamps, she watched him covertly. He was tall and magnificently built. Thick cords strained in his muscular neck at the slightest turn of his arrogant head. He was dressed in tweeds that had the texture of sandstone and gave off a pungent, peaty scent. His shirt was open at the collar, and where his chest showed it was thickly matted.

There were no servants about on the ground floor of the castle. The man escorted her quietly through the graceful rooms to the foyer, where he removed her coat from the closet and placed it around her shoulders. Then he pressed his hard hands against her arms.

She tore herself away at last, one of the old rages sweeping over her. In the quiet gloom of the foyer she could see that he was still smiling, and it added fuel to her fury.

"Ah!" she cried. "What a fool I am…to take you so for granted. 'I prayed for you,' you say—'I know you'— What kind of booby do you think I am? Keep your hands off me!"

She glared at him, breathing heavily, and he made no answer. His expression remained unchanged. It's like those snakes, she thought, those snakes with the hypnotic eyes. They coil in their impassive beauty and you can't escape the deadly fascination. It's like soaring towers that make you want to leap to earth—Like keen, glittering razors that invite the tender flesh of your throat. You can't escape!

"Go on!" she cried in a last desperate effort. "Get out of here! This is my world. It's all mine to do with as I choose. I want no part of your kind of rotten, arrogant swine!"

Swiftly, silently, he gripped her shoulders and brought her close to him. While he kissed her she struggled against the hard talons of his fingers and tried to force her mouth away from his. And yet she knew that if he had released her, she could not have torn herself away from that savage kiss.

She was sobbing when he relaxed his grip and let her head drop back. Still in the affable tones of a casual conversation, he said, "You want one thing in this world of yours, Sidra, and you must have me to help you."

"In Heaven's name, who are you?"

"I'm the strength you prayed for. Now come along."

Outside, the night was pitch black, and after they had gotten into Sidra's two-seater and started for London, the road was impossible to follow. As she edged the car cautiously along, Sidra was able at last to make out the limed white line that bisected the road, and the lighter velvet of the sky against the jet of the horizon. Overhead the Milky Way was a long smudge of powder.

The wind on her face was, good to feel. Passionate, reckless, and headstrong as ever, she pressed her foot on the accelerator and sent the car roaring down the dangerous dark road, eager for more of the cool breeze against her cheeks and brow. The wind tugged at her hair and sent it streaming back. The wind gusted over the top of the glass shield and around it, like a solid stream of cold water. It whipped up her courage and confidence. Best of all, it renewed her sense of humor.

Without turning, she called, "What's your name?"

And dimly through the noisy breeze came his answer; "Does it matter?"

"It certainly does. Am I supposed to call you; 'Hey!' or 'I say, there—' or 'Dear sir—'"

"Very well, Sidra. Call me Ardis."

"Ardis? That's not English, is it?"

"Does it matter?"

"Don't be so mysterious. Of course it matters. I'm trying to place you."

"I see."

"D'you know Lady Sutton?"

Receiving no answer she glanced at him and received a slight chill. He did look mysterious with his head silhouetted against the star-filled sky. He looked out of place in an open roadster.

"D'you know Lady Sutton?" she repeated.

He nodded and she turned her attention back to the road. They had left the open country and were boring through the London suburbs. The little squat houses, all alike, all flat faced and muddy-colored, whisked past with a muffled *whump-whump-whump*, echoing back the sound of their passage.

Still gay, she asked, "Where are you stopping?"

"In London."

"Where, in London?"

"Chelsea Square."

"The Square? That's odd. What number?"

"One hundred and forty-nine."

She burst into laughter. "Your impudence is too wonderful," she gasped, glancing at him again. "That happens to be my address."

He nodded. "I know that, Sidra."

Her laughter froze—not at the words, for she hardly heard them. Barely suppressing another cry, she turned and stared through the windshield, her hands trembling on the wheel; for the man sat there in the midst of that turmoil of wind, and not a hair of his head was moving.

Merciful Heaven! she cried in her heart. What kind of a mess did I—who is this monster, this—Our Father who art in Heaven, hallowed be thy—get rid of him! I don't want him. If I've asked for him, consciously or not, I don't want him now. I want my world changed. Right now! I want him out of it!

"It's no use, Sidra," he said.

Her lips twitched and still she prayed: Get him out of here! Change everything—anything—only take him away. Let him vanish. Let the darkness and the void devour him. Let him dwindle, fade—

"Sidra," he shouted, "stop that!" He poked her sharply. "You can't get rid of me that way—it's too late!"

She stopped praying as panic overtook her and congealed her brain.

"Once you've decided on your world," Ardis explained carefully as though to a child, "you're committed to it. There's no changing your mind and making alterations. Weren't you told?"

"No," she whispered, "we weren't told.

"Well, now you know."

She was mute, numb and wooden. Not so much wooden as putty. She followed his directions without a word, drove to the little park of trees that was behind her house, and parked there. Ardis explained that they would have to enter the house through the servants' door.

"You don't," he said, "walk openly to murder. Only clever criminals in storybooks do that. We, in real life, find it best to be cautious."

Real life! she thought hysterically as they got out of the car. Reality! That Thing in the shelter—

Aloud, she said, "You sound experienced."

"Through the park," he answered, touching her lightly on the arm. "We shan't be seen."

The path through the trees was narrow, and the grass and prickly shrubs on either side were high. Ardis stepped back and then followed her as she passed the iron gate and entered. He strode a few paces behind her.

"As to experience," he said, "yes—I've had plenty. But then, you ought to know, Sidra."

She didn't know. She didn't answer. Trees, brush and grass were thick around her, and although she had traversed this park a hundred times, they were alien and grotesque. They were not alive—no, thank God for that. She was not yet imagining things, but for the first time she realized how skeletal and haunted they looked; almost as if each had participated in some sordid murder or suicide through the years.

Deeper into the park, a dank mist made her cough and, behind her, Ardis patted her back sympathetically. She quivered like a length of supple steel under his touch, and when she had stopped coughing and the hand still remained on her shoulder, she knew what he would attempt here in the darkness.

She quickened her stride. The hand left her shoulder and hooked at her arm. She yanked her arm free and ran down the path, stumbling on her stilt heels. There was a muffled exclamation from Ardis, and she heard the swift pound of his feet as he pursued her. The path led down a slight depression and past a marshy little pond. The earth turned moist and sucked at her feet. In the warmth of the night her skin began to prickle and perspire, but the sound of his panting was close behind her.

Her breath was coming in gasps, and when the path veered and began to mount, she felt her lungs would burst. Her legs were aching and it seemed that at the next instant she would flounder to the ground. Dimly through the trees, she made out the iron gate at the other side of the park, and with the little strength left to her, she redoubled her efforts to reach it.

But what, she wondered dizzily, what after that? He'll overtake me in the street—Perhaps before the street—I should have turned for the car—I could have driven—I—

He clutched at her shoulder as she passed the gate and she would have surrendered at that moment. Then she heard voices and saw figures on the street across from her. She cried, "Hello, there!" and ran to them, her shoes clattering on the pavement. As she came close, still free for the moment, they turned.

"So sorry," she babbled. "Thought I recognized you...Was walking through the par—"

She stopped short. Staring at her were Finchley, Braugh, and Lady Sutton.

"Sidra, darling! What the devil are you doing here?" Lady Sutton demanded. She cocked her gross head forward to examine Sidra's face, then nudged at Braugh. and Finchley with her elbows. "The girl's been running through the park. Mark my words, Chris, she's touched."

"Looks like she's been chivvied," Braugh answered. He stepped to one side and peered past Sidra's shoulder, his white head gleaming in the starlight.

Sidra caught her breath at last and looked about.

Ardis stood alongside her, calm and affable as ever. There was, she thought helplessly, no use trying to explain. No one would believe her. No one would help. She said: "Just a bit of exercise. It was such a lovely night."

"Exercise!" Lady Sutton snorted. "Now I know you're cracked."

Finchley said, "Why'd you pop off like that, Sidra? Bob was furious. We've just been driving him home."

"I—" It was too insane. She'd seen Finchley vanish through the veil of fire less than an hour ago—vanish into a world of his own choosing. Yet here he was asking questions.

Ardis murmured, "Finchley was in your world, too. He's still here."

"But that's impossible!" Sidra exclaimed. "There can't be two Finchleys."

"Two Finchleys?" Lady Sutton echoed. "Now I know where you've been and gone, my girl! You're drunk. Reeling, stinking drunk. Running through the park! Exercise! Two Finchleys!"

And Lady Sutton? But she was dead. She had to be! They'd murdered her less than—

Again Ardis murmured, "That was another world ago, Sidra. This is your new world, and Lady Sutton belongs in it, Everyone belongs in it—except your husband."

"But...even though she's dead?"

Finchley started and asked, "Who's dead?"

"I think," Braugh said, "we'd better get her upstairs and put her to bed."

"No," Sidra said. "No—there's no need—really! I'm all right."

"Oh, let her be!" Lady Sutton grunted. She gathered

her coat around her tub of a waist and moved off. "You know our motto, m'lads. 'Never Interfere.' See you and Bob at the shelter next week, Sidra. 'Night—"

"Good night."

Finchley and Braugh moved off, too—the three figures merging with the shadows in a misty fade-out. And as they vanished, Sidra heard Braugh: "The motto ought to be 'Unashamed.'"

"Nonsense," Finchley answered. "Shame is a sensation we seek like all others. It reduc—"

Then they were gone.

And with a return of that frightened chill, Sidra realized that they had not seen Ardis—nor heard him—nor even been aware of his—

"Naturally," Ardis interrupted.

"But how, naturally?"

"You'll understand later. Just now we've a murder before us."

"No!" she cried, hanging back. "No!"

"How's this, Sidra? And after you've looked forward to this moment for so many years. Planned it. Feasted on it—"

"I'm...too upset...unnerved."

"You'll be calmer. Come along."

Together they walked a few steps down the narrow street, turned up the gravel path and passed the gate that led to the back court. As Ardis reached out for the knob of the servants' door, he hesitated and turned to her.

"This," he said, "is your moment, Sidra. It begins now. This is the time when you break that chain and make payment for a life's worth of agony. This is the day when you balance the account. Love is good—hate is better. Forgiveness is a trifling virtue—passion is all-consuming and the end-all of living!"

He pushed open the door, grasped her elbow and dragged her after him into the pantry—It was dark and filled with odd corners. They eased through the blackness cautiously, reached the swinging door that led to the kitchen, and pushed past it, Sidra uttered a faint moan and sagged against Ardis.

It *had* been a kitchen at one time. Now the stoves and sinks, cupboards and tables, chairs, closets and all, loomed high and twisted like the tangle of an insane jungle. A dull-blue spark glittered on the floor, and around it cavorted a score of singing shadows.

They were solidified smoke—semiliquid gas. Their translucent depths writhed and interplayed with the nauseating surge of living muck. Like looking through a microscope, Sidra thought, at those creatures that foul corpse-blood, that scum a slack-water stream, that fill a swamp with noisome vapors—And most hideous of all, they were all in the wavering gusty image of her husband. Twenty Robert Peels, gesticulating obscenely and singing a whispered chorus:

"*Quis multa gracilis te puer in rosa*
Perfusus liquidis urget odoribus
Grato, Sidra, sub antro?"

"Ardis! What is this?"

"Don't know yet, Sidra."

"But these shapes!"

"We'll find out."

Twenty leaping vapors crowded around them, still chanting. Sidra and Ardis were driven forward and stood at the brink of that sapphire spark that burned in the air a few inches above the floor. Gaseous fingers pushed and probed at Sidra, pinched and prodded while the blue figures cavorted with hissing laughter, slapping their naked rumps in weird ecstasies.

A slash on Sidra's arm made her start and cry out, and when she looked down, unaccountable beads of blood stood out on the white skin of her wrist. And even as she stared in disembodied enchantment, her wrist was raised to Ardis's lips. Then his wrist was raised to her mouth and she felt the stinging salt of his blood on her lips.

"No!" she gasped. "I don't believe this. You're making me see this."

She turned and ran from the kitchen toward the serving pantry. Ardis was close behind her. And the blue shapes still hissed a droning chorus:

"*Qui nunc te fruitur credulus aurea*;
Qui semper vacuam, semper amabilem,
Sperat, nescius aurae
Fallacia—"

When they reached the foot of the winding stairs that led to the upper floors, Sidra clutched at the balustrade for support. With her free hand she dabbed at her mouth to erase the salt taste that made her stomach crawl.

"I think I've an idea what all that was," Ardis said.

She stared at him.

"A sort of betrothal ceremony," he went on casually. "You've read of something like that before, haven't you? Odd, wasn't it? Some powerful influences in this house. Recognize those phantoms?"

She shook her head wearily. What was the use of thinking—talking?

"Didn't, eh? We'll have to see about this. I never cared for unsolicited haunting. We shan't have any more of this tomfoolery in the future—" He mused for a moment, then pointed to the stairs. "Your husband's up there, I think. Let's continue."

They trudged up the sweeping, gloomy stairs, and the last vestiges of Sidra's sanity struggled up, step by step, with her.

One: You go up the stairs. Stairs leading to what? More madness? That damned Thing in the shelter!

Two: This is hell, not reality.

Three: Or nightmare. Yes! Nightmare. Lobster last night. Where were we last night, Bob and I?

Four: Dear Bob. Why did I ever—And this Ardis. I know why he's so familiar. Why he almost speaks my thoughts. He's probably some—

Five:—nice young man who plays tennis in real life. Distorted by a dream. Yes.

Six—

Seven—

"Don't run into it," Ardis cautioned.

She halted in her tracks and simply stared. There were no more screams or shudders left in her. She simply stared at the thing that hung with a twisted head from the beam over the stair landing. It was her husband limp and slack, dangling at the end of a length of laundry rope.

The limp figure swayed ever so slightly, like the gentle swing of a massive pendulum. The mouth was wrinkled into a sardonic grin and the eyes popped from their sockets and glanced down at her with impudent humor. Vaguely, Sidra was aware that ascending steps behind it showed through the twisted form.

"Join hands," the corpse said in sacrosanct tones.

"Bob!"

"Your husband?" Ardis exclaimed.

"Dearly beloved," the corpse began, "we are gathered together in the sight of God and in the face of this company to join together this man and this woman in holy matrimony; which is—" The voice boomed on and on and on.

"Bob!" Sidra croaked.

"Kneel!" the corpse commanded.

Sidra flung herself to one side and ran stumbling up the stairs. She faltered for a gasping instant, then Ardis's strong hands grasped her. Behind them the shadowy corpse intoned: "I pronounce you man and wife."

Ardis whispered, "We must be quick, now! Very quick!"

But at the head of the stairs Sidra made a last bid for liberty. She abandoned all hope of sanity, of understanding. All she wanted was freedom and a place where she could sit in solitude, free of the passions that were hedging her in, gutting her soul. There was no word spoken, no gesture made. She drew herself up and faced Ardis squarely. This was one of the times, she understood, when you fought like petroglyphs carved on prehistoric rock.

For minutes they stood, facing each other in the dark hall. To their right was the descending well of the stairs; to the left, Sidra's bedroom; behind them, the short hallway that led to Peel's study—to the room where he was so unconsciously awaiting slaughter. Their eyes met, clashed and battled silently. And even as Sidra met that deep, gleaming glance, she knew with an agonizing sense of desperation that she would lose.

There was no longer any will, any strength, any courage left in her. Worse, by some spectral osmosis it seemed to have drained out of her into the man who faced her. While she fought she realized that her rebellion was like that of a hand or a finger rebelling against its guiding brain.

Only one sentence she spoke: "For Heaven's sake! *Who are you*?"

And again he answered: "You'll find out—soon. But I think you know already. I think you know!"

Helpless, she turned and entered her bedroom. There was a revolver there and she understood she was to get it. But when she pulled open the drawer and yanked aside the piles of silk clothes to pick it up, the clothes felt thick and moist. As she hesitated, Ardis reached past her and picked up the gun. Clinging to the butt, a finger tight-clenched around the trigger, was a hand, the stump of the wrist clotted and torn.

Ardis clucked impatiently and tried to pry the hand loose. It would not give. He pressed and twisted a finger at a time and still the sickening corpse-hand clenched the gun stubbornly. Sidra sat at the edge of the bed like a child, watching the spectacle with naive interest, noting the way the broken muscles and tendons on the stump flexed as Ardis tugged.

There was a crimson snake oozing from under the bathroom door. It writhed across the hardwood floor, thickening to a small river as it touched her skirt so gently. When Ardis tossed the gun down angrily, he noted the stream. Quickly he stepped to the bathroom and thrust open the door, then slammed it a second later. He jerked his head at Sidra and said, "Come on!"

She nodded mechanically and arose, careless of the sopping skirt that smacked against her calves. At Peel's study she turned the doorknob carefully until a faint click warned her that the latch was open, then she pushed the door in. The leaf swung wide to reveal her husband's study in semidarkness. The desk was before the high window curtains and Peel sat at it, his back to them. He was hunched over a candle or a lamp or some light that enhaloed his body and sent streams of rays flickering out. He never moved.

Sidra tiptoed forward, then paused. Ardis touched a finger to lips and moved like a swift cat to the cold fireplace where he picked up the heavy bronze poker. He brought it to Sidra and held it out urgently. Her hand reached of its own accord and took the cool metal handle. Her fingers gripped it as though they had been born for murder.

Against all that impelled her to advance and raise the poker over Peel's head, something weak and sick inside her cried out and prayed; cried, prayed and moaned with the whimpering, of a fevered child. Like spilt water, the last few drops of her self-possession trembled before they disappeared altogether.

Then Ardis touched her. His finger pressed against the small of her back and a charge of bestiality shocked up her spine with cruel, jagged edges. Surging with hatred, rage, and livid vindictiveness, she raised the poker high and crashed it down on the still-motionless head of her husband.

The entire room burst into a silent explosion. Lights flared and shadows whirled. Remorselessly, she clubbed and pounded at the falling body that toppled out of the chair to the floor. She struck again and again, her breath whistling hysterically, until the head was a mashed, bloodied pulp. Only then did she let the poker drop and reel back.

Ardis knelt beside the body and turned it over.

"He's dead all right. This is the moment you prayed for, Sidra. You're free!"

She looked down in horror. Dully, from the crimsoned carpet, a corpse face stared back. It showed the drawn, high-strung features, the coal-black eyes, the coal-black hair dipping over the brow in a sharp widow's peak. She moaned, as understanding touched her.

The face said, "This is Sidra Peel. In this man whom you have slaughtered you have killed yourself—killed the only part of yourself worth saving."

She cried, "Aieee—" and clasped arms about herself, rocking in agony.

"Look well on me," the face said. "By my death you have broken a chain—only to find another."

And she knew. She understood. For though she still rocked and moaned in the agony that would be never-ending, she saw Ardis arise and advance on her with arms outstretched. His eyes gleamed and were horrid pools, and his reaching arms were tendrils of her own unslaked passion, eager to enfold her. And once embraced, she knew there would be no escape—no escape from this sickening marriage to her own lusts that would forever caress her.

So it would be forevermore in Sidra's brave new world.

IV

After the others had passed the veil, Christian Braugh still lingered in the shelter. He lit another cigarette with a simulation of perfect aplomb, blew out the match, then called: “Er… Mr. Thing?”

“What is it, Mr. Braugh?”

Braugh could not restrain a slight start at that voice sounding from nowhere. “I—well, the fact is, I stayed for a chat.”

“I thought you would, Mr. Braugh.”

“You did, eh?”

“Your insatiable hunger for fresh material is no mystery to me.”

“Oh!” Braugh looked around nervously. “I see.”

“Nor is there any cause for alarm. No one will overhear us. Your masquerade will remain undetected.”

“Masquerade!”

“You’re not really a bad man, Mr. Braugh. You’ve never belonged in the Sutton shelter clique.”

Braugh laughed sardonically.

“And there’s no need to continue your sham before me,” the voice continued in the friendliest manner. “I know the story of your many plagiarisms was merely another concoction of the fertile imagination of Christian Braugh.”

“You know?”

“Of course. You created that legend to obtain entry to the shelter. For years you’ve been playing the role of a lying scoundrel, even though your blood ran cold at times.”

“And do you know why I did that?”

“Certainly. As a matter of fact, Mr. Braugh, I know

almost everything, but I do confess that one thing about you still confuses me."

"What's that?"

"Why, with that devouring appetite for fresh material, were you not content to work as other authors do, with what you know? Why this almost insane desire for unique material—for absolutely untrodden fields? Why were you willing to pay a bitter and exorbitant price for a few ounces of novelty?"

"Why?" Braugh sucked in smoke and exhaled it past clenched teeth. "You'd understand if you were human. I take it you're not…?"

"That question cannot be answered."

"Then I'll tell you why. It's something that's been torturing me all my life. A man is born with imagination."

"Ah…imagination."

"If his imagination is slight, a man will always find the world a source of deep and infinite wonder, a place of many delights. But if his imagination is strong, vivid, restless, he finds the world a sorry place indeed—a drab jade beside the wonders of his own creations!"

"There are wonders past all imagining."

"For whom? Not for me, my invisible friend; nor for any earth-bound, flesh-bound creature. Man is a pitiful thing. Born with the imagination of gods and forever pasted to a round lump of clay and spittle. I have within me the uniqueness, the ego, the fertile loam of a timeless spirit…and all that wealth is wrapped in a parcel of quickly rotting skin!"

"Ego…" mused the voice. "That is something which, alas, none of us can understand. Nowhere in all the knowable cosmos is it to be found but on your planet, Mr. Braugh. It is a frightening thing and convinces me at times that yours is the race that will—" the voice broke off abruptly.

"That will...?" Braugh prompted.

"Come," said the Thing briskly, "there is less owing you than the others, and I shall give you the benefit of my experience. Let me help you select a reality."

Braugh pounced on the word. "Less?"

And again he was brushed aside. "Will you choose another reality in your own cosmos, or are you content with what you already have? I can offer you vast worlds, tiny worlds; great creatures that shake space and fill the voids with their thunder; tiny creatures of charm and perfection that barely touch perception with the sensitive timbre of their thoughts. Do you care for terror? I can give you a reality of shudders. Beauty? I can show you realities of infinite ecstasy. Pain? Torture? Any sensation. Name one, several, all. I will shape you a reality to outdo even the giant concepts that are assuredly yours."

"No," Braugh answered at length. "The senses are only senses at best—and in time they tire of everything. You cannot satisfy the imagination with whipped cream in new forms and flavors."

"Then I can send you to worlds of extra dimensions that will stun your imagination. There is a system I know that will entertain you forever with its incongruity—where, if you sorrow you scratch your ear, or its equivalent, where, if you love you eat a squash, where, if you die you burst out laughing.... There is a dimension I have seen where one can assuredly perform the impossible; where wits daily compete in the composition of animate paradox, and where the mere feat of turning oneself mentally inside out is called '*chrythna*,' which is to say, '*corny*' in the American jargon.

"Do you want to probe the emotions in classical order? I can take you to a world of n-dimensions where, one by one, you may exhaust the intricate nuances of the twenty-seven primary emotions—always taking notes, of course—and thence go on to combinations and permutations to the amount of twenty-seven raised to the power of twenty-seven. Mathematicians would say: 27×10^{27}. Come, which will you enjoy?"

"None," Braugh said impatiently. "It's obvious, my friend, that you do not understand the ego of man. The ego is not a childish thing to be entertained with toys, and yet it is a childish thing in that it yearns for the unattainable."

"Yours seems to be an animal thing in that it does not laugh, Mr. Braugh. It has been said that man is the only laughing animal on earth. Take away the humor and only the animal is left. You have no sense of humor, Mr. Braugh."

"The ego," Braugh continued intently, "desires only what it cannot hope to attain. Once a thing can be possessed, it is no longer desired. Can you grant me a reality in which I may possess some thing which I desire because I cannot possibly attain it, and by that same possession not break the qualifications of my desire? Can you do this?"

"I'm afraid," the voice answered with slight amusement, "that your imagination reasons too deviously for me."

"Ah," Braugh muttered, half to himself. "I was afraid of that. Why does creation seem to be run by second-rate individuals not half so clever as myself? Why this mediocrity?"

"You seek to attain the unattainable," the voice argued in reasonable tones, "and by that act not to attain it. The contradiction is within yourself. Would you be changed?"

"No...not not changed." Braugh shook his head. He stood deep in thought, then sighed and tamped out his cigarette. "There's only one solution for my problem."

"And that is?"

"Erasure—If you cannot satisfy a desire, you must explain it away. If a man cannot find love, he writes a psychological treatise on passion. I shall do much the same thing..."

He shrugged and moved toward the veil. There was a chuckle behind him and the voice asked, "Where does that ego of yours take you, O man?"

"To the truth of things," Braugh called. "If I can't slake my yearning, at least I shall find out why I yearn."

"You'll find the truth only in hell or limbo, Mr. Braugh."

"How so?"

"Because truth is always hell."

"And hell is truth, no doubt. Nevertheless I'm going there—to hell or limbo, or wherever truth is to be found."

"May you find the answers pleasant, O man."

"Thank you."

"And may you learn to laugh."

But Braugh no longer heard, for he had passed the veil.

He found himself standing before a high desk—a

judge's bench, almost as high as the top of his head. Around him was nothing else. A sulfurous fog filled wherever he was, concealing everything but this awesome bench. Braugh tilted his head back and peered up. Staring down at him from the other side was a tiny face, ancient as sin, whiskered and cock-eyed. It was on a shriveled little head that was covered with a pointed hat. Like a sorcerer's cap.

Or a dunce cap, Braugh thought.

Dimly, behind the head, he made out towering shelves of books and files labeled: A-AB, AC-AD, and so on. Some were curiously labeled: #-, &-¼, *-c. Incomprehensible. There was also a gleaming black pot of ink and a rack of quill pens. An enormous hourglass completed the picture. Inside the hourglass a spider had spun a web and was crawling shakily along the strands.

The little man croaked: "A-mazing! AS-tounding! IN-credible!"

Braugh was annoyed.

The little man hunched forward like Quasimodo and got his clown face as close as possible to Braugh's. He reached down a knobby finger and poked Braugh gingerly. He was astonished. He threw himself back and bawled: "THAMMuz! DA-gon! RIMM-on!"

There was an invisible bustle and three more little men bounced up behind the bench and gaped at Braugh. The inspection went on for minutes. Braugh was irritated.

"All right," he said. "That's enough. Say something. Do something."

"It speaks!" they shouted incredulously. "It's alive!" They pressed noses together and gabbled swiftly:

"MostamazingthingDagonhespeaksRimmoncouldit-bealiveandhumanBelialtherehastobesomereasonforit-Thammuzifyouthinksobutlcan'tsay."

Then it stopped.

Further inspection.

One said, "Find out how it got here."

"Not at all. Find out what it is. Animal? Vegetable? Mineral?"

A third said, "Find out where it's from."

"Have to be cautious with aliens, you know."

"Why? We're absolutely invulnerable."

"You think so? What about the Angle Azrael's visit?"

"You mean ang—"

"Don't say it! Don't say it!"

A fierce argument broke out while Braugh tapped his toe impatiently. Apparently they came to a decision. The No. 1 warlock aimed an accusing finger at Braugh and said, "What are you doing here?"

"The point is, where am I?" Braugh snapped.

The little man turned to brothers Thammuz, Dagon, and Rimmon. "It wants to know where it is," he smirked.

"Then tell it, Belial."

"Get on, Belial. Can't take forever."

"You!" Belial turned on Braugh. "This is Central Administration, Universal Control Center; Belial, Rimmon, Dagon, and Thammuz, acting for His Supremity."

"That would be Satan?"

"Don't be familiar."

"I came here to see Satan."

"It wants to see the Lord Lucifer!" They were appalled. Then Dagon jabbed the others with his sharp little elbows and placed a finger alongside his nose with a shrewd look.

"Spy," he said. To elaborate, he gestured significantly upward.

"Don't say it, Dagon! Don't say it!"

"Been known to happen," Belial said, flipping the pages of a giant ledger. "It certainly don't belong here. No deliveries scheduled for—" He turned over the hourglass, infuriating the spider. "—for six hours. It's not dead because it don't stink. It's not alive because only the dead are called. Question still is: What is it and what do we do with it?"

Thammuz said, "Divination. Absolutely infallible."

"Right you are, Thammuz."

Belial eyed Braugh. "Name?"

"Christian Braugh."

"He said it! We didn't."

"Let's try Onomancy," Dagon said. "C, third letter. H, eighth letter, R, eighteenth letter, and so on. It's all right, Belial; spelling isn't the same as saying. Take total sum. Double it and add ten. Divide by two and a half, then subtract original total."

They counted, added, divided and subtracted. Quills scratched on parchment; a buzzing noise sounded. At last Belial held up his scrap and scrutinized it dubiously. They all scrutinized theirs. As one man, they shrugged and tore the ciphering up.

"I can't understand it," Rimmon complained. "We always get five."

"Never mind." Belial fixed Braugh with a stern look. "You! When born?"

"December eighteenth, nineteen hundred and thirteen."

"Time?"

"Twelve-fifteen A.M."

"Star charts!" Thammuz shouted. "Genethliacs never fail!"

Clouds of dust choked Braugh as they ransacked the shelves behind them and pulled out huge parchment sheets that unrolled like window shades. This time it took them fifteen minutes to produce their results which they again examined carefully and again tore up.

Rimmon said, "It *is* odd."

Dagon said, "Why do they always turn out to be born under the Sign of Porpoise?"

"Maybe it *is* a porpoise. That would explain everything."

"We'd better take it into the laboratory for a check. Himself will be plenty peeved if we muff this one."

They leaned over the bench and beckoned. Braugh snorted and obeyed. He walked around the side of the bench and found himself before a small door framed in books. The four little Central Administrators bounced down from the desk and crowded him through. He had to double over; they just about came up to his waist.

Braugh entered the infernal laboratory. It was a circular room with a low ceiling, tile floor and walls, cupboards, and shelves, crammed with dusty glassware, alchemist's gadgets, books, bones and bottles, none labeled. In the center was a large, flat millstone. The axle hole had a charred look, but there wasn't any chimney above it.

Belial rooted in a comer, tossed umbrellas and branding irons, and came out with an armful of dry sticks. "Altar fire," he said and tripped. The sticks went flying. Braugh solemnly bent to pick up the pieces of wood.

"Sortilege!" Rimmon squawked. He yanked a glittering lizard out of a box and began scribbling on its back with a piece of charcoal, noting the order in which Braugh picked up the altar fire makings.

"Which way is east?" Rimmon asked, crawling after the lizard which seemed bent on business of its own. Thammuz pointed down. Rimmon nodded curt thanks and began an involved computation on the lizard's back. Gradually his hand moved more slowly. By the time Braugh had heaped the wood on the altar, Rimmon was holding the lizard by the tail, wondering at his notations. At last he gave up and shoved the lizard under the wood. It caught fire instantly.

"Salamander," Rimmon said. "Not bad, eh?"

Dagon was inspired. "Pyromancy!" He ran to the flames, poked his nose within an inch of the fire and chanted.

"*Aleph, beth, gimel, daleth, he, vau, zayin, cheth...*" Belial figeted uneasily and muttered to Thammuz, "Last time he tried that, he fell asleep."

"It's the Hebrew," Thammuz said as though he were explaining.

The chant faded and Dagon, eyes blissfully shut, slid forward into the crackling flames.

"Did it again," Belial snapped.

They dragged Dagon out of the fire and slapped his face until his whiskers stopped burning. Thammuz sniffed the stench of burning hair, then pointed to the smoke drifting overhead. "Capnomancy!" he said. "It can't fail. We'll find out what this thing is yet."

All four joined hands and skipped around the smoke cloud, puffing at it with pursed lips. Eventually the smoke disappeared. Thammuz looked sour. "It failed."

"Only because *it* didn't join in."

They glared angrily at Braugh. "You it! Deceitful it!"

"Not at all," Braugh said. "I'm not hiding anything. Of course I don't believe a particle of what's happening here, but that doesn't matter. I have all the time in the world."

"Doesn't matter? What d'you mean, you don't believe?"

"Why, you can't make me believe that you clowns have to do with truth—much less His Majesty, Father Satan."

"Why, you ass, *we're* Satan."

Then they lowered their voices and added for unseen ears, "So to speak. No offense. Merely referring to power of attorney." Their indignation revived. "But we have the power to ferret *you* out, it. We'll track you down. We'll tear the veil, break the seal, remove the mask, make all known with Sideromancy. Bring on the iron!"

Dagon trundled out a little wheelbarrow filled with lumps of iron, all roughly shaped like fish. To Braugh he said: "This divination never fails. Pick a carp...any carp." Braugh selected an iron fish at random and Dagon snatched it from him irritably and plunked it into a tiny crucible. He set on the fire and Thammuz pumped a hand-bellows until the iron was white-hot. "It can't fail," he puffed. "Sideromancy never fails." The four waited and waited; Braugh didn't know for what. At last they sighed.

"It failed," Braugh said.

"Let's try Molybdomancy," Belial suggested.

They nodded and dropped the iron into a pot of solid lead. It hissed and fumed as though it had been dropped into water. Presently the lead melted. Belial tipped the pot over and the silvery liquid crept across the floor. Braugh got his feet out of the way. Belial sounded his "A": "Me-me-me-me-me-me Meeeeeeeee!" but before he could begin the incantation there was a pistol-shot crack. One of the floor tiles had shattered. The molten lead disappeared with a sizzling, and the next instant a fountain of water spurted up through the hole.

Belial said: "Busted the pipes again."

"Pegomancy!" Dagon cried eagerly. He approached the fountain with a reverent look, knelt before it and began to drone: "*Alif, ba', ta', tha', jim, ha', kha', dal...*" In thirty seconds his eyes closed rapturously and he fell forward into the water.

"It's the Arabic," Tbammuz said. "Got to get him dry or he'll catch his death."

Thammuz and Belial took Dagon by the arms and dragged him to the altar fire. They circled the bright blaze several times and were about to stop when Dagon choked: "Keep me moving. Gyromancy."

"But you've run out of alphabets," Thammuz said.

"No. There's still Greek. Make circles. Alpha, beta, gamma, delta, oi!"

"No, epsilon next," Thammuz said. Then, "Oi!"

Braugh turned to see what they were staring and *oi*ing at.

A girl had just entered the laboratory. She was short, red-headed and delightfully the right side of plump. Her coppery hair was drawn back in a Greek knot. She wore an expression of exasperation and fury, and nothing else. Braugh muttered: "Oi!"

"So!" she rapped. "At it again. How many times—" she broke off, ran to a wall, seized a prodigious glass retort, and hurled it straight and true. When the pieces stopped clattering, she said, "How many times have I told you to stop this nonsense or I'd report you!"

Belial tried to stanch his bleeding cuts and attempted an innocent smile. "Why, Astarte, you wouldn't tell Himself, would you?"

"I will not have you smashing my ceiling and dripping things down on my office. First molten lead; then water; four weeks' work ruined. My Sheraton desk ruined." She twisted her torso and exhibited a red scar that ran down from a shoulder. "Twelve inches of skin ruined!"

"We'll pay for the replacement, Astarte."

"And who'll pay for the pain?"

"Tannic acid is best," Braugh said seriously. "You brew extra strong tea and make a poultice. Numbs the pain."

The red head turned, and Astarte lanced Braugh with level green eyes. "Who's this?"

"We don't know," Belial stammered. "It just walked up to my desk and—That's why we were—It might be a porpoise...."

Braugh stepped forward and took the girl's hand. "I'm a human. Alive. Sent here by one of your colleagues; name unknown. My name is Braugh. Christian Braugh."

Her hand was cool and firm. "It might have been—No matter. The name is Astarte. I, too, am a Christian."

Central Administration clapped palms over ears to block the dirty words.

"Satan's crew Christians?" Braugh was surprised.

"Some of us. Why not? We all were before The Fall."

There was no answer to that. He said, "Is there some place where we can get away from these maladroits?"

"There's always my office."

"I like offices."

He also liked Astarte; much more than liked. She led him into her office on the floor below, very large, most impressive, swept a pile of paperwork off a chair and invited him to sit down. She sprawled before the ruin of her desk and, after one malevolent glance at the ceiling, asked for his story. She listened.

"Unusual," she said. "You're looking for Satan, Lord of the Counterworld. Well, this is the only hell there is, and Himself is the only Satan there is. You're in the right place."

Braugh was perplexed. "Hell? Dante's Inferno? Fire, brimstone and so forth?"

She shook her head. "Just another poet using his imagination. The real torments are Freudian. You can discuss it with Alighieri when you meet him." She smiled at Braugh's solemn expression. "All this brings us to something vital. Sure you're not dead? Sometimes they forget."

Braugh nodded.

"Hmmm..." She made an interested survey. "You'll bear looking into. I've never had anything to do with the live ones. Sure you're alive?"

"Quite sure."

"And what's your business with Father Satan?"

"The truth," Braugh said. "I wanted to learn the truth about all, and I was sent here by that nameless

Thing. Why Father Satan should be the official purveyor of the truth rather than—" He hesitated.

"You can say it, Christian."

"Rather than God in Heaven, I don't know. But to me the truth is worth any price to put to rest this damned yearning that tortures me. So I should like very much to have an interview."

Astarte rapped polished nails on the desk and smiled. "This," she said, "is going to be delicious." She arose, opened the office door and pointed down the sulfur-fogged corridor. "Straight ahead," she told Braugh. "Then take the first left. Keep on and you can't miss."

"I'll see you again?" he asked as he set off.

"You'll see me again," Astarte laughed.

This, Braugh thought as he inched through the yellow mist, is all too ridiculous. You pass a veil seeking the Citadel of Truth. You are entertained by four absurd sorcerers and by a redheaded divinity. Then off you go down a foggy corridor, turn left and straight ahead for an interview with the Knower of All Things.

And what of my yearning for the unattainable? What of the truths that will explain it all away? Is there no solemnity, no dignity, no authority one can respect? Why all this low comedy; this saturnalian slapstick that pervades Hell?

He turned the corner to the left and kept on. The short hall ended in a pair of green baize doors. Almost timidly, Braugh pushed them open and to his great relief found himself merely stepping onto a stone bridge—rather like the Bridge of Sighs, he thought. Behind him was the enormous facade of the building he had just left; a wall of brimstone blocks stretching left and right and upward and downward until it was lost from sight. Before him was a smallish building shaped like a globe.

He stepped quickly across the bridge, for these mists around him made him queasy. He paused only a moment to gather his courage before a second pair of baize doors, then tried to mount a debonair manner and pushed them in. You do not, he told himself, come before Satan nonchalantly, but there's such a quality of insanity in hell that it's rubbed off on me.

It was a gigantic room, a sort of file room, and again Braugh was relieved at having the awesome interview put a little farther into the future. The office was round as a planetarium and was crammed with a vast adding machine so enormous that Braugh could not believe his eyes. There were five levels of scaffolding before the keyboard and one little dried-out clerk, wearing spectacles the size of binoculars, rushed back and forth, climbing up and down, punching keys with lightning speed.

More as an excuse for delaying the rather threatening interview with Father Satan, Braugh watched the wheezing clerk scurry before those keys, punching them so rapidly that they chattered like a hundred outboard motors. This little old chap, Braugh thought, has put in an eternity computing sin totals and death totals and all sorts of statistical totals. He looks like a total himself.

Aloud, Braugh said: "Hello there!"

Without faltering the clerk said, "What is it?" His voice was drier than his skin.

"Those figures can wait a moment, can't they?"

"Sorry. They can't."

"Will you stop a moment!" Braugh shouted. "I want to see your boss."

The clerk came to a dead stop and turned, removing the binocular spectacles very slowly.

"Thank you," Braugh said. "Now, look, my man, I'd like to see His Black Majesty, Father Satan. Astarte said—"

"That's me," said the little old man.

The wind was knocked out of Braugh.

For a fleeting instant a smile flickered across the dried-out face. "Yes, that's me, son. I'm Satan."

And despite all his vivid imagination, Braugh had to believe. He slumped down on the lowermost tread of the steps that led up to the scaffolding. Satan chuckled faintly and touched a clutch on the gigantic adding machine. There was a meshing of gears and with the sound of freewheeling, the machine began to cluck softly while the keys clacked automatically.

His Diabolic Majesty came creaking down the stairs and seated himself alongside Braugh. He took out a tattered silk handkerchief and began polishing his glasses. He was just a nice little old man sitting friendly-like alongside a stranger, ready, for a back-fence gossip. At last he said, "What's on your mind, son?"

"W-well, your Highness—" Braugh began.

"You can call me Father, my boy."

"But why should I? I mean—" Braugh broke off in embarrassment.

"Well now, I guess you're a little worried about that heaven-and-hell business, eh?"

Braugh nodded.

Satan sighed and shook his head. "Don't know what to do about that," he said. "Fact is, son, it's all the same thing. Naturally I let it get around in certain quarters that there's two places. Got to keep certain folks on their toes. But the truth is, it's not really so. I'm all there is, son; God or Satan or Siva or Official Coordinator or Nature—anything you want to call it."

With a rush of good feeling toward this friendly old man, Braugh said, "I call you a fine old man. I'll be happy to call you Father."

"Well, that's nice of you, son. Glad you feel that way. You understand, of course, that we couldn't let just anyone see me this way. Might instill disrespect. But you're different. Special."

"Yes, sir. Thank you, sir."

"Got to have efficiency—*Tsk*! Got to frighten folks now and then. Got to have respect, you understand. Can't run things without respect."

"I understand, sir."

"Got to have efficiency. Can't be running life all day long, all year long, all eternity long without efficiency. Can't have efficiency without respect."

Braugh said, "Absolutely, sir," while within him a hideous uncertainty grew. This was a nice old man, but this was also a garrulous, maundering old man. His Satanic Majesty was a dull creature not nearly so clever as Christian Braugh.

"What I always say," the old man went on, rubbing his knee reflectively, "Is that love and worship and all that—you can have 'em. They're nice, but I'll take efficiency anytime...leastways for a body in my position. Now then son, what was on your mind?"

Mediocrity, Braugh thought bitterly. He said, "The truth, Father Satan. I came seeking the truth."

"And what do you want with the truth, Christian?"

"I just want to know it, Father Satan. I came seeking it. I want to know why we are, why we live, why we yearn. I want to know all that."

"Well, now..." the old man chuckled. "That's quite an order, son. Yes, sir, quite an order indeed."

"Can you tell me, Father Satan?"

"A little, Christian. Just a little. What was it you wanted to know, mostly?"

"What there is inside us that makes us seek the unattainable. What are those forces that pull and tug and surge within us? What is this ego of mine that gives me no rest, that seeks no rest, that frets at doubts, and yet when they're resolved, searches for new ones. What is all this?"

"Why," Father Satan said, pointing to his adding machine. "It's that gadget there. It runs everything."

"That?"

"That."

"Runs everything?"

"Everything that I run, and I run everything there is." The old man chuckled again, then held out the binoculars. "You're an unusual boy, Christian. First person that ever had the decency to pay old Father Satan a visit...alive, that is. I'll return the favor. Here."

Wondering, Braugh accepted the spectacles.

"Put 'em on," the old man said. "See for yourself."

And then the wonder was compounded, for as Braugh slipped the glasses over his head he found himself peering with the eyes of the universe at all the universe. And the adding contraption was no longer a machine for summing up totals with additions and subtractions; it was a vastly complex marionetteer's crossbar from which an infinity of shimmering silver threads descended.

And with his all-seeing eyes, through the spectacles of Father Satan, Braugh saw how each thread was attached to the nape of the neck of a creature, and how each living entity danced the dance of life as directed by Satan's efficient machine. Braugh crept up to the first-level scaffold and reached toward the lower bank of keys. One he pressed at random and on a pale planet something hungered and killed. A second, and it felt remorse. A third, and it forgot. A fourth, and half a continent away another something awoke five minutes early and so began a chain of events that culminated in discovery and hideous punishment for the killer.

Braugh backed away from the adding machine and slipped the glasses up to his brow. The machine went on clucking. Almost absently, without surprise, Braugh noted that the meticulous chronometer which filled the top of the dome had ticked away a space of three months' time.

"This," he thought, "is a ghastly answer, a cruel answer, and Mr. Thing in the shelter was right. Truth is hell. We're puppets. We're little better than dead things hung from a string, simulating life. Up here an old man, nice but not overly intelligent, clicks a few keys and down there we take it for free will, fate, karma, evolution, nature, a thousand false things. This is a sour discovery. Why must the truth be shoddy?"

He glanced down. Old Father Satan was stiff seated on the steps, but his head slumped a little to one side, his eyes were half-closed, and he mumbled indistinctly about work and rest and not enough of it.

"Father Satan..."

"Yes, my boy?" The old man roused himself slightly.

"This is true? We all dance to your key-tapping?"

"All of you, my boy. All of you." He yawned prodigiously "You all think yourselves free, Christian, but you all dance to my playing."

"Then, Father, grant me one thing...One very small thing. There is, in a small corner of your celestial empire, a very tiny planet, an insignificant speck we call Earth."

"Earth? Earth? Can't say I recollect it offhand, son, but I can look it up."

"No, don't bother, sir. It's there. I know because I come from there. Grant me this favor: break the cords that bind it. Let Earth go free."

"You're a good boy, Christian, but a foolish boy. You ought to know I can't do that."

"In all your kingdom," Braugh pleaded, "there are souls too numerous to count. There are suns and planets too many to measure. Surely this one tiny bit of dust—You who own so much can surely part with so little."

"No, my boy, couldn't do it. Sorry."

"You who alone know freedom...Would you deny it to just a few others?"

But the Coordinator of All slumbered.

Braugh pulled the glasses back before his eyes. Let him sleep then, while Braugh, Satan *pro tem*, takes over. Oh, we'll be repaid for this disappointment. We'll have giddy time writing novels in flesh and blood. And perhaps, if we can find the cord attached to my neck and search out the correct key, we may do something to free Christian Braugh. Yes, here is a challenging unattainable which may be attained and lead to fresh challenges.

He looked over his shoulder guiltily to see whether

Father Satan was aware of his meddling. There might be condign punishment. As his eyes inspected the frail Ruler of All, he was stunned, transfixed. He gazed up, then down, then up again. His hands trembled, then his arms, and at last his whole body shook uncontrollably. For the first time in his life, he began to laugh. It was genuine laughter, not the token laughter he had so often been forced to fake in the past. The gusts and bursts rang through the domed room and reverberated.

Father Satan awoke with a start and cried, "Christian! What is it, my boy?"

Laughter of frustration? Laughter of relief? Laughter of hell or limbo? He could not tell as he shook at the sight of the silver thread that stretched from the nape of Satan's neck and turned him, too, into a marionette...a tendril that stretched up and up and up into lost heights toward some other vaster machine operated by some other vaster marionette hidden in the still-unknowable reaches of the cosmos—

The blessedly unknowable cosmos.

V

Now in the beginning all was darkness, There was neither land nor sea nor sky nor the circling stars. There was nothing. Then came Yaldabaoth and rent the light from the darkness. And the darkness He gathered up and formed into the night and the skies. And the light He gathered up and formed the Sun and the stars. Then from the flesh of His flesh and the blood of His blood did Yaldabaoth form the earth and all things upon it.

But the children of Yaldabaoth were new and green

to living and unlearned, and the race did not bear fruit. And as the children of Yaldabaoth diminished in numbers, they cried out unto their Lord: "Grant us a sign, Great God, that we may know how to increase and multiply! Grant us a sign, O Lord, that Thy good and mighty race may not perish from Thine earth!"

And lo! Yaldabaoth withdrew Himself from the face of His importunate people and they were sore at heart and sinful, thinking their Lord had forsaken them. And their paths were paths of evil until a prophet arose whose name was Maart, Then did Maart gather the children of Yaldabaoth around him and spoke to them, saying: 'Evil are thy ways, o people of Yaldabaoth, to doubt thy God. For He has given a sign of faith unto you."

Then gave they answer, saying: "Where is this sign?"

And Maart went into the high mountains and with him was a vast concourse of people. Nine days and nine nights did they travel even unto the peak of Mount Sinar. And at the crest of Mount Sinar all were struck with wonder and fell on their knees, crying: "Great is God! Great are His works!"

For lo! Before them blazed a mighty curtain of fire.

BOOK OF MAART; XIII: 29-37

Pass the veil toward what reality? There's no sense trying to make up my mind. I can't. God knows, that's been the agony of living for me—trying to make up my mind. How I've felt nothing—when nothing's touched me—ever! Take this or that. Take coffee or tea. Buy the black gown or the silver. Marry Lord Buckley or live with Freddy Witherton. Let Finchley make love to me or stop posing for him. No—there's no sense even trying.

How that veil burns in the doorway! Like rainbow moire. There goes Sidra. Passes through as though nothing was there. Doesn't seem to hurt. That's good. God knows, I could stand anything except being hurt. No one left but Bob and myself—and he doesn't seem to be in any hurry. No, there's Chris, sort of hiding in the organ alcove. My turn now, I suppose. I wish it wasn't, but I can't stay here forever. Where to?

To nowhere?

Yes, that's it. Nowhere.

In this world I'm leaving there's never been any place for me; the real me. The world wanted nothing from me but my beauty; not what was inside me. I want to be useful. I want to belong. Perhaps if I belonged—if living had some purpose for me, this lump of ice in my heart might melt. I could learn to do things, to feel things, enjoy things. Even learn to fall in love.

Yes, I'm going to nowhere.

Let the new reality that needs me, that wants me, that can use me...Let that reality make the decision and call me to itself. For if I must choose, I know I'll choose wrong again.

And if I'm not needed anywhere; if I go through that burning to wander forever in blank space. Still I'm better off. What else have I been doing all my life?

Take me, you who want and need me!

How cool the veil...like scented sprays on the skin.

And even as the multitude knelt in prayer, Maart

cried aloud: "Rise, ye children of Yaldabaoth, and behold!"

Then they did arise and were struck dumb and trembled. For through the curtain of fire stepped a beast that chilled the hearts of all. To the height of eight cubits it towered and its skin was pink and white. The hair of its head was yellow and its body was long and curving like unto a sickly tree. And all was covered with loose folds of white fur.

BOOK OF MAART; XIII: 38-39

God in Heaven!

Is this the reality that called me? This the reality that needs me?

That sun…so high…with its blue-white evil eye, like that Italian artist…mountain tops. They look like heaps of slime and garbage…The valleys down there…festering wounds. The sickroom smell. All rot and ruin.

And those hideous creatures crowding around…like apes made of coal. Not animal—Not human. As though man made beasts not too well—or beasts made men still worse. They have a familiar look. The landscape looks familiar. Somewhere I've seen all this before. Somehow I've been here before. In dreams of death, maybe…maybe.

This is a reality of death, and it wanted me? Needed me?

Again the multitude cried out: "Glory be to Yaldabaoth!" and at the sound of the sacred name the beast turned toward the curtain of flames whence it had come, and behold! The curtain was gone.

BOOK OF MAART; XIII: 40

No retreat?

No way out?

No return to sanity?

But it was behind me a moment ago, the veil. No escape. Listen to the sounds they make. The swilling of swine. Do they think they're worshiping me? No. This can't be real. No reality was ever so horrid. A ghastly trick…like the one we played on Lady Sutton. I'm in the shelter now. Bob Peel's played a trick and given us some new kind of drug. Secretly. I'm lying on the divan, dreaming and groaning. I'll wake up soon. Or faithful Dig will wake me…before these frights come any closer.

I must wake up!

With a loud cry, the beast of the fire ran through the multitude. Through all the host it ran and thundered down the mountainside. And the shrill sounds of its cries struck fear like unto the fear of the sound of beaten brazen shields.

And as it passed under the low boughs of the mountain trees, the children of Yaldabaoth cried again in alarm, for the beast shed its white furred hide in a manner horrible to behold. And the skin remained clinging to the trees. And the beast ran farther, a hideous pink-and-white warning to all transgressors.

BOOK OF MAART; XIII: 41-43

Quick! Quick! Run through them before they touch me with their filthy hands. If this is a nightmare, running will wake me. If this is real—but it can't be. That such a cruel thing should happen to me! No. Were the gods jealous of my beauty? No. The gods are never jealous. They are men.

My dressing gown—

Gone.

No time to go back for it. Run naked, then. Listen to them howl at me—rave at me. Down! Down! Quickly and down the mountain. This rotten earth. Sucking. Clinging.

Oh, God! They're following.

Not to worship.

Why can't I wake up?

My breath—like knives.

Close. I hear them. Closer and closer and close!

WHY CAN'T I WAKE UP?

And Maart cried aloud. "Take ye this beast for an offering to our Lord Yaldabaoth!"

Then did the multitude raise courage and gird its loins. With clubs and stones all pursued the beast down the slopes of Mount Sinar, many sore afraid but all chanting the name of the Lord.

And in a field a shrewdly thrown stone brought the beast to its knees, still screaming in a voice horrible to hear. Then did the stout warriors smite it many times with strong clubs until at last the cries ceased and the beast was still. And out of the foul body did come a poisoned red water that sickened all who beheld it.

But when the beast was brought to the High Temple of Yaldabaoth and placed in a cage before the altar, its cries once more resounded, desecrating the sacred halls. And the High Priests were troubled, saying: "What evil offering is this to place before Yaldabaoth, Lord of Gods?"

BOOK OF MAART; XIII: 44-47

Pain.

Burning and scalding.

Can't move.

No dream ever so long...So real. This, then, real?—Real. And I? Real too. A stranger in a reality of filth and torture. Why? Why? Why?

My head feels twisted inside. Tangled. Jumbled.

This is torture, and somewhere...someplace...I've heard that word before. Torture. It has a pleasant sound. Torment? No, torture better. The sound of a madrigal. Name of a boat. Tide of a prince. Prince Torture. Prince Torment? Beauty and the Prince.

So twisted in my head. Great lights and blinding sounds that come and go and have no meaning.

Once upon a time the beauty tortured a man. They say. Said.

His name was?

Prince Torment? No. Finchley. Yes. Digby Finchley.

Digby Finchley, they say—said—loved an ice-goddess, named Theone Dubedat.

The pink ice-goddess. Where is she now?

And while the beast did moan threats upon the altar, the Sanhedrin of Priests held council, and to the council came Maart, saying: "O ye priests of Yaldabaoth, raise up your voices in praise of our Lord, for he was wroth and turned His face from us. And lo! A sacrifice has been vouchsafed unto us that we may please Him and make our peace with Him."

Then spoke the High Priest, saying: "How now, Maart? Do ye say that this is a sacrifice for our Lord?"

And Maart spoke: "Yea. For it is a beast of fire and through the holy fire of Yaldabaoth it shall return whence it came."

And the High Priest asked: "Is this offering seemly in the sight of Our Lord?"

Then Maart answered: "All things are from Yaldabaoth. Therefore all things are seemly in His sight. Perchance through this offering Yaldabaoth will grant us a sign that His people may not vanish from the earth. Let the beast be offered."

Then did the Sanhedrin agree, for the priests were sore afraid lest the children of the Lord be no more.

BOOK OF MAART; XIII: 48-54

See the silly monkeys dance.

They dance around and around and around.

And they snarl.

Almost like speaking.

Almost like—

I must stop the singing in my head. The ring-ding-singing. Like the days when Dig was working hard and I would take those back-breaking poses and hold them hour after hour with only a five-minute break now and then and I would get dizzy and faint off the dais and Dig would drop his palette and come running with those big, solemn eyes of his ready to cry.

Men shouldn't cry, but I knew it was because he loved me and I wanted to love him or somebody, but I had no need then. I didn't need anything but finding myself. That's the treasure hunt. And now I'm found. This is me. Now I have a need and an ache and a loneliness deep inside for Dig and his big, solemn eyes. To see him all eyes and fright at the fainting spells and dancing around me with a cup of tea.

Dancing. Dancing. Dancing.

And thumping their chests and grunting and thumping.

And when they snarl the spittle drools and gleams on their yellow fangs. And those seven with the rotting shreds of cloth across their chests, marching almost like royalty, almost like humans.

See the silly monkeys dance.

They dance around and around and around and...

So it came to pass that the high holiday of Yaldabaoth was nigh. And on that day did the Sanhedrin throw wide the portals of the temple and the hosts of the children of Yaldabaoth did enter. Then did the priests remove the beast from the cage and drag it to the altar. Each of four priests held a limb and spread the beast wide across the altar stone, and the beast uttered evil, blasphemous sounds.

Then cried the prophet Maart: "Rend this thing to pieces that the stench of its evil death may rise to please the nostrils of Yaldabaoth."

And the four priests, strong and holy, put strong hands to the limbs of the beast so that its struggles were wondrous to behold, and the light of evil on its hideous hide struck terror into all.

And as Maart lit the altar fires, a great trembling shook the firmament.

BOOK OF MAART: XIII: 55-59

Digby, come to me!
Digby, wherever you are, come to me!
Digby, I need you.
This is Theone.
Theone.
Your ice-goddess.
No longer ice, Digby.
I can't stay sane much longer.
Wheels whirl faster and faster and faster…
In my head, faster and faster and faster…
Digby, come to me.
I need you.
Prince Torment.
Torture.

Then did the vaults of the temple split asunder with a thunderous roar, and all that were gathered there quailed in fear, and their bowels were as water. And all beheld the divine Lord, Yaldabaoth descend from pitch-black skies to the temple. Yea, to the very altar itself.

And for the space of eternity did the Lord God Yaldabaoth gaze at the beast of fire, and His sacrifice writhed and cursed, its evil helpless in the grasp of the pure priests.

BOOK OF MAART; XIII: 59-60

It is the final horror—the final torture.

This monster that floats down from the heavens.

Ape-Man-Beast-Horror.

It is the final joke that it should float down like a thing of fluff, silk, feathers; a thing of lightness and joy. A monster on Wings of light. A monster with twisted legs and arms and loathsome body. The head of a Man-Ape...torn and broken, smashed and ruined, with those great, glassy, staring eyes.

Eyes? Where have I—?

THOSE EYES!

This isn't madness. No. Not the ring-ding-singing. No. I know those eyes—those great, solemn eyes. I've seen them before. Years ago. Minutes ago. Caged in a zoo? No. Fish eyes floating in a tank? No. Great, solemn eyes filled with hopeless love and adoration.

No...Let me be wrong.

Those big, solemn eyes of his ready to cry.

Crying, but men shouldn't cry.

No, not Digby. It can't be. Please!

That's where I've seen this place before, seen these man-animals and the hellish landscape—Digby's drawings. Those monstrous pictures he drew. For fun, he said, for amusement.

Amusement!

But why does he look like this? Why is he rotten and horrifying like the others...Like his pictures?

Is this your reality, Digby? Did you call me? Did you need me, want me?

Digby!

Dig.

Dig-a-dig-a-by-and-whirl-a-whirl-a-ring-a-ding-a-sing-a...

Why don't you listen to me? Hear me? Why do you look at me that way, like a mad thing when only a minute ago you were walking up and down in the shelter trying to make up your mind and you were the first to go through that burning veil and I admired you for that because men should always be brave but not men-ape-beast-monsters...

And with a voice like unto shattering mountains, the Lord Yaldabaoth spoke to His people, saying: "Now praise ye the Lord, my children, for one has been sent unto you to be thy queen and consort to thy God."

With one voice the host cried out unto him: "Praise our Lord, Yaldabaoth."

And Maart made obeisance before the Lord and prayed: "A sign to Thy children to Lord God, that they may increase and multiply."

Then the Lord God reached out to the beast and touched it, raising it from the altar fires and the hands of the pure priests, and behold! The evil cried out for the last time and fled the body of the beast, leaving only a sweet song in its place. And the Lord spoke unto Maart, saying: "I will give you a sign."

BOOK OF MAART; XIII: 60-63

Let me die.

Let me die forever.

Let me not see or hear or feel the—

The?

What?

The pretty monkeys that dance around and around and around so pretty so nice so good everything pretty and nice and good while the great, solemn eyes stare into my soul and darling Dig-a-dig-a-by touches me with hands so strangely changed go prettily nicely goodly changed by the turpentine maybe or the ochre or bile green or burnt umber or sepia or chrome yellow which always seemed to decorate his fingers each time he dropped palette and brushes to come to me when I—

Love changes everything. Yes. How good to be loved by dear Digby. How warm and comforting to be loved and to be needed and to want one alone in all the millions and to find him so strangely beautifully solemnly walking flying descending in a reality like that of Sutton Castle when shelter can't see and I really knew that cliffs down—ran me with pretty monkeys laughing and capering and worshiping so funny so funny so nice so good so pretty so funny so...

Then did the children of Yaldabaoth take the sign of the Lord to their hearts and lo! Thenceforth did they increase and multiply after the example of their Lord God and His Consort on high.

Thus endeth the BOOK OF MAART

VI

At the moment when he entered the burning veil, Peel stopped in astonishment. He had not yet made up his mind. To him, a man of objectivity and logic, this was an amazing experience. It was the first time in his life that he had not made a lightning decision. It was proof of how profoundly the Thing in the shelter had shaken him.

He stayed where he was, sheathed in a mist of fire that flickered like an opal and was far thicker than any veil. It surrounded him and isolated him, for surely he should have been aware of others passing through, but there was no one. It was not beautiful to Peel, but it was interesting. The color dispersion was wide, he noted, and embraced hundreds of fine gradations of the visible spectrum.

Peel took stock. With the little data he had at hand, he judged that he was standing somewhere outside time and space or between dimensions. Evidently the Thing in the Altar had placed them *en rapport* with the matrix of existence so that mere intent as they entered the veil could govern the direction they would take on emergence. The veil was more or less a pivot on which they could spin into any desired existence in any space and any time; which brought Peel back to the question of his own choice.

Carefully he considered, weighed and balanced what he already possessed against what he might receive. So far he was satisfied with his life. He had plenty of money, a respected profession as consultant engineer, a splendid house in Chelsea Square, an attractive, stimulating wife. To give all this up in reliance on the unspecified promises of an unvalidated donor would be idiocy. Peel had learned never to make a change without good and sufficient reason.

"I am not adventurous by nature," Peel thought coldly. "It is not my business to be so. Romance does not attract me, and I suspect the unknown. I like to keep what I have. The acquisitive sense is strong in me, and I'm not ashamed to be a possessive man. Now I want to keep what I have. No change. There can be no other decision for me. Let the others have their romance; I keep my world precisely as it is. Repeat: No change."

The decision had taken him all of one minute, an unusually long time for the engineer, but this was an unusual situation. He strode forward firmly, a precise, bald, bearded martinet, and emerged into the dungeon corridor of Sutton Castle.

A few feet down the corridor, a little scullery maid in blue and gray was scurrying directly toward him, a tray in her hands. There was a bottle of ale and an enormous sandwich on the tray. At the sound of Peel's step, she looked up, stopped short, then dropped the tray with a crash.

"What the devil—?" Peel was confounded at the sight of her.

"M-Mr. Peel!" she squawked. She began to scream: "Help! Murder! Help!"

Peel slapped her. "Will you shut up and explain what in blazes you're doing down here this time of night!"

The girl moaned and sputtered. Before he could slap the hysterical creature again, he felt a heavy hand on his shoulder. He turned and was further confounded when he found himself staring into the red, beefy face of a policeman. There was a rather eager expression on that face. Peel gaped, then subsided. He realized that he was in the vortex of unknown phenomena. No sense struggling until he understood the currents.

"Na then, sir," the policeman said. "No call ter strike the gel, sir."

Peel made no answer. He needed more facts. A maid and a policeman. What were they doing down here? The man had come up from behind him. Had he come through the veil? But there was no burning veil; just the heavy shelter door.

"If I heard right, sir, I heard the gel call yer by name. Would yer give it to me, sir?"

"I'm Robert Peel. I'm a guest of Lady Sutton. What is all this?"

"Mr. Peel!" the policeman exclaimed. "What a piece er luck. I'll get me rise for this. I got to take yer into custody, Mr. Peel. Yer under arrest."

"Arrest? You're mad, my man." Peel stepped back and looked over the policeman's shoulder. The shelter door was half-open, enough for him to make a quick inspection. The entire room was turned upside-down, looking as though it had just been subjected to a spring cleaning. There was no one inside.

"I must warn yer not ter resist, Mr. Peel."

The girl emitted a wail.

"See here," Peel said angrily. "What right have you to break into a private residence and prance around making arrests? Who are you?"

"Name of Jenkins, sir. Sutton County Constabulary. And I ain't prancin', sir."

"Then you're serious?"

The policeman pointed majestically up the corridor. "Come along, sir. Best to go quietly."

"Answer me, idiot! Is this a genuine arrest?"

"You ought ter know," replied the policeman with ominous overtones. "Come with me, sir."

Peel gave it up and obeyed. He had learned long ago that when one is confronted with an incomprehensible situation, it is folly to take any action until sufficient data arrives. He preceded the policeman up the corridors and winding stone stairs, the whimpering scullery maid following them. So far he only knew two things: One, something, somewhere, had happened. Two, the police had taken over. All this was confusing, to say the least, but he would keep his head. He prided himself that he was never at a loss.

When they emerged from the cellars Peel received another surprise. It was bright daylight outside. He glanced at his watch. It was forty minutes past midnight. He dropped his wrist and blinked; the unexpected sunlight made him a little ill. The policeman touched his arm and directed him toward the library. Peel immediately strode to the sliding doors and pulled them open.

The library was high, long and gloomy, with a narrow balcony running around it just under the Gothic ceiling. There was a long trestle table centered in the room and at the far end three figures were seated, silhouetted against the sunlight that streamed through the lofty window. Peel stepped in, caught a glimpse of a second policeman on guard alongside the doors, then narrowed his eyes and tried to distinguish faces.

While he peered he sorted out the hubbub of exclamations and surprise that greeted him. He judged that: One, people had been looking for him. Two, he'd been missing for some time. Three, no one expected to find him here in Sutton Castle. Footnote, how did he get back in, anyway? All this pieced together from the astonished voices. Then his eyes accommodated to the light.

One of the three was an angular man with a narrow graying head and deep-furrowed features. He looked familiar to Peel. The second was small and stout with ridiculously fragile glasses perched on a bulbous nose. The third was a woman, and again Peel was surprised to see that it was his wife. Sidra wore a plaid suit and a crimson felt hat.

The angular man quieted the others and said, "Mr. Peel?"

Peel advanced quietly. "Yes?"

"I'm Inspector Ross."

"I thought I recognized you, inspector. We've met before, I believe?"

"We have." Ross nodded curtly, then indicated the stout man. "Dr. Richards."

"How d'you do, doctor." Peel turned to his wife and bowed and smiled. "Sidra? How are you dear?"

In flat tones she said, "Well, Robert."

"I'm afraid I'm rather confused by all this," Peel continued amiably. "Things seem to be happening, or have happened." Enough. This was the right talk. Caution. Commit yourself to nothing until you know.

"They are; they have," Ross said.

"Before we go any further, may I inquire the time?"

Ross was taken aback. "It's two o'clock."

"Thank you." Peel held his watch to his ear, then adjusted the hands. "My watch seems to be running, but somehow it's lost a few hours." He examined their expressions covertly. He would have to navigate with exquisite care solely by the light of their countenances. Then he noticed the desk calendar before Ross, and it was like a punch in the ribs. He swallowed hard. "Is that date quite right, inspector?"

"Of course, Mr. Peel. Sunday, the twenty-third."

His mind screamed: Three days! Impossible! Peel controlled his shock. Easy...easy...all right. Somewhere he'd lost three days; for he'd entered the burning veil Thursday, thirty-eight minutes past midnight. Yes. But keep cool. There's more at stake than three lost days. There must be; otherwise why the police? Wait for more data.

Ross said "We've been looking for you these past three days, Mr. Peel. You disappeared quite suddenly. We're rather surprised to find you back in the castle."

"Ah? Why?" Yes, why indeed? What's happened? What's Sidra doing here glaring like an avenging fury?

"Because, Mr. Peel, you're charged with the willful murder of Lady Sutton."

Shock! Shock! Shock! They were piling on, one after another, and still Peel kept hold of himself. The data was coming in explicitly now. He'd hesitated in the veil for a few minutes at the most, and those minutes in limbo were three days in real space-time. Lady Sutton must have been found and he was charged with murder. He knew he was a match for anyone, as a thinking logical man...an astute man...but he knew he had to steer cautiously—

"I don't understand, inspector. You'd better explain."

"Very well. The death of Lady Sutton was reported early Friday morning. Medical examination proved she died of heart failure, the result of shock. Witnesses' evidence revealed that you had deliberately frightened her with full knowledge of her weak heart and with intent so to kill her. That is murder, Mr. Peel."

"Certainly," Peel said coldly. "If you can prove it. May I ask the identity of your witnesses?"

"Digby Finchley, Christian Braugh. Theone Dubedat, and—" Ross broke off, coughed, and laid the paper aside.

"And Sidra Peel," Peel finished dryly. Again he met his wife's venomous gaze. He understood it all, at last. They'd lost their nerve and selected him for the scapegoat. Sidra would be rid of him; her joyous revenge. Before Ross or Richards could intervene, he grasped Sidra by the arm and dragged her toward a corner of the library.

"Don't be alarmed, Ross. I only want a word alone with my wife. There'll be no violence, I assure you."

Sidra tore her arm free and glared up at Peel, her lips drawn back, revealing the sharp white edges of her teeth.

"You arranged this," Peel said quietly.

"I don't know what you're talking about."

"It was your idea, Sidra."

"It was your murder, Robert."

"And that's your evidence."

"Ours. We're four to one."

"All carefully planned, eh?"

"Braugh is a good writer."

"And I hang for the murder on your evidence. You get the house, my fortune, and get rid of me."

She smiled like a cat.

"And this is the reality you asked for? This is what you planned when you went through the burning veil?"

"What veil?"

"You know what I mean."

"You're insane."

She was genuinely bewildered. He thought: Of course. I wanted my old world just as it was. That would exclude the mysterious Thing in the shelter and the veil through which we all passed. But it doesn't exclude the killing which came before nor what's happening after.

"No, Sidra, not insane," he said. "Merely refusing to be your scapegoat. I won't let you bring it off."

"No?" She turned and called to Ross: "He wants

me to bribe the witnesses." She walked back to her chair. "I'm to offer each of them ten thousand pounds."

So it was to be a bloody battle. His mind clicked rapidly. The best defense was an attack and the time was now. "She's lying, inspector. They're all lying. I charge Braugh, Finchley, Miss Dubedat, and my wife with the willful murder of Lady Sutton."

"Don't believe him!" Sidra screamed. "He's trying to lie his way out of it by accusing us. He—"

Peel let her scream, grateful for more time to whip his lies into shape. They must be convincing. Flawless. The truth was impossible. In this new old world of his, the Thing and the veil did not exist.

"The murder of Lady Sutton was planned and executed by those four persons," Peel went on smoothly. "I was the only member of the group to object. You will grant, Inspector Ross, that it sounds far more logical for four people to commit a crime against the will of one, than one against four. And the testimony of four outweighs that of one. Do you agree?"

Ross nodded slowly, fascinated by Peel's detached reasoning. Sidra beat at his shoulder and cried, "He's lying, Inspector. Can't you see? If he's telling the truth ask him why he ran away. Ask him where he's been for three days..."

Ross tried to calm her. "Please, Mrs. Peel. All I'm doing is taking statements. I neither believe nor disbelieve anyone yet. Do you wish to say any more, Mr. Peel?"

"Thank you. Yes. The six of us had played many silly, sometimes dangerous, practical jokes in the past, but murder for any reason went beyond sense and tolerance. Thursday night the four realized I would warn Lady Sutton. Evidently they were prepared for this. My wine was drugged. I have a vague memory of being lifted and carried by the two men and—that's all I know about the murder."

Ross nodded again. The doctor leaned over to him and whispered. Ross murmured, "Yes, yes. The tests can come later. Please go on, Mr. Peel."

So far so good, Peel thought. Now, just a little color to gloss over the rough edges. "I awoke in pitch darkness. I heard no sounds; nothing but the ticking of my watch. These dungeon walls are ten and fifteen feet thick, so I couldn't possibly hear anything. When I got to my feet and felt my way around I seemed to be in a small cavity measuring…oh…two long strides by three."

"That would be six feet by nine, Mr. Peel?"

"Approximately. I realized I must be in some secret cell known to the men of the clique. After an hour's shouting and pounding on the walls, an accidental blow must have tripped the proper spring or lever. One section of thick wall swung open and I found myself in the passage where—"

"He's lying, lying, lying!" Sidra screamed.

Peel ignored her. "That is my statement, inspector." And it'll stand up, he thought. Sutton Castle was known for its secret passages. His clothes were still rumpled and torn from the framework he had worn to impersonate the devil. There was no known test to show whether or not he'd been drugged three days previous. His full beard and moustache would eliminate the shaving line of attack. Yes, he could be proud of an excellent story; farfetched but heavily weighted by the four-against-one logic.

"We note that you plead not guilty, Mr. Peel," Ross said slowly, "and we note your statement and accusation. I confess that your three-day disappearance seemed to incriminate you but now"—he took a deep breath—"now, if we can locate this cell in which you were confined..."

Peel was prepared for this. "You may or you may not, inspector. I'm an engineer, you know. The only way we may be able to locate the cell is by blasting through the stone, which may wipe out all traces."

"We'll have to take that chance, Mr. Peel."

"That chance may not have to be taken," the doctor said.

The others exclaimed. Peel shot a sharp glance at the little man. Experience warned him that fat men were always dangerous. Every nerve went *en garde*.

"It was a perfect story, Mr. Peel," the fat doctor said pleasantly. "Most entertaining. But really, my dear sir, for an engineer you slipped up quite badly."

"Would you mind telling me on what you base that?"

"Not at all. When you awoke in your secret cell, you said you were in complete darkness and silence. The stone walls were so thick that all you could hear was the ticking of your watch."

"And so they were."

"Very colorful," the doctor smiled, "but alas, proof that you're lying. You awoke three days later. Surely you're aware that no watch will run seventy hours without rewinding."

He was right, by God! Peel realized that instantly. He'd made a bad mistake...unforgivable for an engineer... and there was no going back for alterations and revisions. The entire lie depended on a whole fabric. Tear away one thread and the whole fabric would unravel. The fat doctor was right, damn him! Peel was trapped.

One look at Sidra's triumphant expression was enough for him. He decided he would have to cut his losses like lightning. He arose from his chair, laughing in admitted defeat. Peel, the gallant loser. Abruptly dashed past them like a shot, crossed arms before his face, hands over ears, and plunged through the glass windowpanes.

Shattered glass and shouts behind him. Peel flexed his legs as the soft garden earth came up at him, and landed with a heavy jolt. He took it well, and was on his feet and running toward the rear of the castle where the cars were parked. Five seconds later he was vaulting into Sidra's two-seater. Ten seconds later he was speeding through the open iron gates to highway beyond.

Even in this crisis, Peel thought swiftly and with precision. He had left the grounds too quickly for anyone to note which direction he would take. He sent the car roaring down the London road. A man could lose himself in London. But he was not a man to panic. Even as his eyes followed the road, his mind was sorting through facts methodically, and without flinching coming to a hard decision. He knew that he could never prove innocence. How could he? He was as guilty of the killing as all the rest. They had turned on him and he would be pursued as Lady Sutton's sole murderer.

In wartime it would be impossible to get out of the country. It would even be impossible to hide for very long. What remained, then, was an outlaw living in miserable hiding for a few brief months only to be taken and brought to trial. It would be a sensation. Peel had no intention of giving his wife the joy of watching him dragged through a headline prosecution to the executioner's noose.

Still cool, still in full possession of himself, Peel planned as he drove. The audacious thing would be to go straight to his house. They would never think of looking for him there...at least for a time; certainly enough time for him to do what had to be done. "Vendetta," he said. "Blood for blood." He drove deep into London toward Chelsea Square, a savage, bearded man, now looking much like Teach, the buccaneer.

He approached the square from the rear, watching for the police. There were none about and the house looked quite calm and inauspicious. But, as he drove into the square and saw the front façade of his home, he was grimly amused to see that an entire wing had been demolished in a bombing raid. Evidently the catastrophe had taken place some days previous, for the rubble was neatly piled and the broken side of the building was fenced off.

So much the better, Peel thought. No doubt the house would be empty; no servants about. He parked the car, leaped out and walked briskly to the front door. Now that he had made his decision, he was quick and resolute.

There was no one inside. Peel went to the library, took pen, ink and paper and seated himself at the desk. Carefully, with lawyer-like acumen, he wrote a new will cutting his wife off beyond legal impeachment. He was coldly certain that the holograph will would stand up in court. He went to the front door, called in a couple of passing laboring men, and had them witness his signing of the will. He paid them with thanks and ushered them out. He closed and locked the front door.

He paused grimly and took a breath. So much for Sidra. It was the old possessive instinct, he knew, that drove him on this course. He wanted to keep his fortune, even after death. He wanted to keep his honor and dignity, despite death. He'd made sure of the first; he would have to execute the second quickly. Execute. Precisely the right word.

Peel thought for another moment...there were so many possible roads to extinction...then nodded his head and marched back to the kitchen. From the linen closet he took an armful of sheets and towels and padded the windows and doors with them. As an afterthought, he took a large square of cardboard and with shoe-blacking printed: DANGER! GAS! on it. He placed it outside the kitchen door.

When the room was sealed tight, Peel went to the stove, opened the oven door and turned the gas cock over. The gas hissed out of the jets, rank and yet cooling. Peel knelt and thrust his head into the oven, breathing with deep, even breaths. He knew it would not take very long before he lost consciousness. He knew it would not be painful.

For the first time in hours some of the tension left him and he relaxed almost gratefully, awaiting his death. Although he had lived a hard, geometrically patterned life and traveled a pragmatic road, now his mind reached back to more tender moments. He regretted nothing; he apologized for nothing; he was ashamed of nothing—and yet he thought of the days when he first met Sidra with nostalgia and sorrow.

What slender youth, bedewed with liquid odors,
Courts thee on roses in some pleasant cave,
Sidra—?

He almost smiled. Those were the lines he had written to her when, in the romantic beginning, he worshiped her is a goddess of youth, of beauty and goodness. She was all the things he was not, he'd believed; the perfect partner. Those had been great days; the days when he'd finished at Manchester College and had come up to London to build a reputation, a fortune, an entire life...a thin-haired boy with precise habits and mind. Dreamily he sauntered through memories as though he were recalling an entertaining play.

He came to with a start and realized that he'd been kneeling before the oven for twenty minutes. There was something very much awry. He'd not forgotten his chemistry and he knew that twenty minutes of gas should have been enough to make him lose consciousness. Perplexed, he got to his feet, rubbing his aching knees. No time for analysis now. The pursuit would be on his neck at any moment.

Neck! That was an obvious course. Almost as painless as gas and much quicker.

Peel shut off the oven, took a length of stout laundry line from a cupboard and left the kitchen, picking up the warning sign en route. As he tore up the cardboard, his alert eyes surveyed the house looking for a proper spot. Yes, there, in the stairwell. He could throw the rope over that beam and stand on the balcony above the stairs for the drop. When he leaped, he would have ten feet of empty space above the landing.

He ran up the stairs to the balcony, straddled the railing and threw the rope over the beam. He caught the flying end as it whipped around the beam and swung toward him. He tied the end into a loose bowline and ran the knot up the length of the rope until it snugged tight. After he had yanked twice to secure the hold on the beam he put his full weight on the rope and swung himself clear of the balcony. It supported his weight admirably; no chance of its breaking.

When he had climbed back to the railing, he shaped a hangman's noose and slipped it over his head, tightening the knot under his right ear. There was enough slack to give him a six-foot drop. He weighed one hundred and fifty pounds. That was just about right to snap his neck clean and painlessly at the end of the drop. Peel poised, took a last deep breath, and leaped without bothering to pray.

His last thought as he dropped down was a lightning computation of how much time he had left to live. Thirty-two feet per second squared divided by six gave him almost a fifth of a—There was a shattering jerk that jolted his entire body, a *crack* that sounded large and blunt in his ears, and agonizing pain in every nerve. He was twitching spasmodically.

He realized he was still alive. He hung by the neck in horror, understanding he was not dead and not knowing why. The horror crawled over his skin like an invasion of ants and for a long time he hung and shuddered, refusing to believe that the impossible had happened. He twitched and shuddered while the chill enveloped his mind, numbing it, breaking his iron control.

At last he reached into a pocket and withdrew his penknife. He opened it with difficulty, for his body was palsied and unmanageable. He sawed until he severed the rope above his head and fell the last few feet to the stair landing. While he still crouched he felt his neck. It was broken. He could feel the jagged edges of the broken vertebrae. His head was frozen at an angle that made everything topsy-turvy.

Peel dragged himself up the stairs, dimly understanding that something too ghastly to understand had overtaken him. There was no attempting a cool appraisal of this; there was no additional data to be received, no logic to apply. He reached the top of the stairs and lurched through Sidra's bedroom to the bath which they both sometimes shared. He groped in the medicine cabinet until he grasped one of his razors; six inches of fine hollow-ground honed steel—With a trembling stroke, he sliced the edge across his throat.

Instantly he was deluged with a great gout of blood and his windpipe was choked. He doubled over in agony, coughing reflexively, and his throat lathered with red foam. Still hacking and gasping, with the breath whistling madly through his throat, Peel crumpled to the tile floor and spasmed while blood gushed with every heartbeat and soaked him through. Yet, as he lay there, thrice killed, he did not lose consciousness. Life was clinging to him with all the possessiveness with which he had clung to his life.

He crawled upright at last, not daring to look in the mirrors the wreckage of himself. The blood—what remained of it—had begun to clot. He could still draw breaths at times. Gasping, almost totally crippled, Peel crook'd into the bedroom and searched through Sidra's dresser until he found her revolver. It took all his remaining strength to steady the muzzle against his chest and trigger three shots into his heart. The impacts smashed him back against a wall with a frightful crater torn in his chest and a heart no longer beating; and still he lived.

It's the body, he thought in fragments. Life clings to the body. So long as there's a body—the merest shell—enough to contain a spark—then life will remain. It possesses me, this life. But there has to be an answer—I'm still enough of an engineer to work out a solution...

Absolute disintegration. Shatter this body into particles—bits—a thousand, a million mites—and there will no longer remain a cup to contain this persistent life. Explosives. Yes. None in the house. Nothing in this house but an engineer's ingenuity. Yes. How, then, and with what? He was quite mad by now, and the ingenious idea that came to him was mad, too.

He crawled into his study and removed a deck of washable playing cards from a drawer. For long minutes he cut them into tiny pieces with his desk scissors until he had a bowlful. He removed an andiron from the fireplace and painfully took it apart. The shaft was hollow. He packed the brass stem with the playing card bits, ramming the shreds of nitrocellulose tight. When the stem was packed solid he put in the heads of three matches and plugged the open end with the threaded belt which had attached it to the andiron legs.

There was a spirit lamp on his desk, used to keep

pots of coffee hot. Peel lit the lamp and placed the andiron stem directly in the flame. He drew the desk chair close and hunched before the heating bomb. Nitrocellulose was a powerful explosive when ignited under pressure. It was only a question of time, he knew, before the brass would burst into violent explosion and scatter him around the room; scatter him in blessed death. Peel whimpered in torment and impatience. The red froth at his throat burst forth anew while the blood soaking his clothes caked and hardened.

Too slowly the bomb heated.

Too slowly the minutes passed.

Too quickly the agony increased.

Peel trembled and whined, and when he reached out a hand to push the bomb a little deeper into the flame, he did not feel the heat. He could see the flesh scorch red, but felt nothing. All the pain writhed inside him—none outside.

It made noises in his ears, that pain, but even above the growl he could hear the dull tread of footsteps far downstairs. The steps were coming toward him, slowly, almost with an inexorable tread of fate. Desperation seized him at the thought of police and Sidra's triumph. He tried to coax the spirit lamp flame higher.

The steps passed through the main hall and began to mount the stairway. Each deliberate thud sounded louder and closer. Peel hunched lower and in the dim recesses of his mind began to pray that it might be Death Himself coming for him. The steps reached the top of the stairs and advanced to his study. There was a faint whisper as the door was thrust open. Running hot and cold in a fever of madness, Peel refused to turn.

A jarring voice spoke. "Now then, Bob, what's all this?"

He could not turn or answer.

"Bob!" the voice called hoarsely, "don't be a fool!"

Vaguely he understood that he had heard the voice somewhere before.

The measured steps sounded again and then a figure stood at his side. With bloodless eyes he flicked a glance up. It was Lady Sutton. She still wore the sequined evening gown.

"My hat!" Her little eyes twinkled in their casement of flesh. "You've gone and messed yourself up, haven't you!"

"Goau...a...waiyy..." The distorted words cracked and whistled as half of his breath hissed through the slit in his throat. "W-will...nahtt...be...haunted..."

"Haunted?" Lady Sutton laughed. "That's a good one, that is."

"Y-yoo ded," Peel muttered.

"What've you got there?" Lady Sutton inquired casually. "Oh, I see. A bomb. Going to blow yourself to bits, eh, Bob?"

His lips formed soundless words.

"Here," Lady Sutton said. "Let's get rid of this foolishness." She reached out to knock the bomb off the flame. Peel struggled up and grasped her arm with clawing hands. She was solid, for a ghost. Nevertheless, he flung her back.

"Let...be," he wheezed.

"Now stop it, Bob," Lady Sutton ordered. "I never intended this much misery for you."

Her words conveyed no meaning to him. He struck

at her as she tried to get past him to the bomb. She was far too solid and strong for him. He fell toward the spirit lamp with arms outstretched to save his salvation.

Lady Sutton cried, “Bob! You damned fool!”

There was a blinding explosion. It crashed into Peel’s face with a flaring white light and a burst of shattering sound. The entire study rocked, and a portion of the wall fell away. A heavy shower of books rained down from the shaken shelves. Smoke and dust filled space with a dense cloud.

When the cloud cleared, Lady Sutton still stood alongside the place where the desk had been. For the first time in many years—in many eternities, perhaps, her face wore an expression of sadness. For a long time she stood in silence. At last she shrugged and began to speak in the same quiet voice that had spoken to the five in the shelter.

“Don’t you realize, Bob, that you can’t kill yourself? The dead die only once, and you’re dead already. You’ve all been dead for days. How is it that none of you could realize that? Perhaps it’s that ego that Braugh spoke of—perhaps—But you were all dead before you reached the shelter Thursday night. You should have known when you saw your bombed house, Bob. That was a heavy raid last Thursday.”

She raised her hands and began to unpeel the gown that covered her. In the dead silence the sequins rustled and tinkled. They glittered as the gown dropped from the body to reveal—nothing. Empty space.

“I enjoyed that little murder,” she said. “It was amusing to see the dead attempt to kill. That’s why I let you go through with it.”

She removed her shoes and stockings. She was now nothing more than arms and shoulders and the gross head of Lady Sutton. The face still wore the slightly sorrowful expression.

"But it was ridiculous trying to murder me, seeing who I was. Of course, none of you knew. The play was a delight, Bob, because I'm Astaroth."

With a sudden motion, the head and arms leaped into the air and then dropped alongside the discarded dress. The voice continued from the smoky space, disembodied, but when the dusty mist swirled it revealed a figure of emptiness, a mere outline, a bubble, and yet a shape horrible to behold.

"Yes," the quiet voice went on. "I'm Astaroth, as old as the ages; as old and bored as eternity itself. That's why I had to play my little joke on you. I had to turn the tables and have a bit of a laugh. You cry out for a bit of novelty and entertainment after an eternity of arranging hells for the damned, because there's no hell like the hell of boredom."

The quiet voice stopped, and a thousand scattered fragments of Robert Peel heard and understood. A thousand particles, each containing a tormented spark of life, heard the voice of Astaroth and understood.

"Of life I know nothing," Astaroth said gently, "but death I do know—death and justice. I know that each living creature creates its own hell forevermore. What you are now, you have wrought yourself. Hear ye all, before I depart. If any can deny this; if any one of you would argue this; if any of you would cavil at the Justice of Astaroth—Speak now!"

Through all the far reaches the voice echoed and there was no answer.

A thousand tortured particles of Robert Peel heard and made no answer.

Theone Dubedat heard and made no answer from the savage embrace of her god-lover.

And a rotting, self-devouring Digby Finchley heard and made no answer.

A questing, doubting Christian Braugh in limbo heard and made no answer.

Neither Sidra Peel nor the mirror-image of her passion made answer.

All the damned of all eternity in an infinity of self-made hells heard and understood and made no answer.

For the Justice of Astaroth is unanswerable.

Unknown, August 1942

The Push of a Finger

—Or a careless word, for that matter, can wreck the entire universe. Think not? Well, if it happened this way—

I think it's about time someone got all those stories together and burned them. You know the kind I mean—X, the mad scientist, wants to change the world; Y, the ruthless dictator, wants to rule the world; Z, the alien planet, wants to destroy the world.

Let me tell you a different kind of story. It's about a whole world that wanted to rule one man-about a planet of people who hunted down a single individual in an effort to change his life, yes, and even destroy him, if it had to be. It's a story about one man against the entire Earth, but with the positions reversed.

They've got a place in Manhattan City that isn't very well known. Not known, I mean, in the sense that the cell-nucleus wasn't known until scientists began to get the general idea. This was an undiscovered cell-nucleus, and still is, I imagine. It's the pivot of our Universe. Anything that shakes the world comes out of it; and, strangely enough, any shake that does come out of it is intended to prevent worse upheavals.

Don't ask questions now. I'll explain as I go along.

The reason the average man doesn't know about this particular nucleus is that he'd probably go off his nut if he did. Our officials make pretty sure it's kept secret, and although some nosybodies would scream to high heaven if they found out something was being kept from the public, anyone with sense will admit it's for the best.

It's a square white building about ten stories high and it looks like an abandoned hospital. Around nine o'clock in the morning you can see a couple of dozen ordinary looking citizens arriving, and at the end of the workday some of them leave. But there's a considerable number that stay overtime and work until dawn or until the next couple of dawns. They're cautious about keeping windows covered so that high-minded citizens won't see the light and run to the controller's office yawping about overtime and breaking down Stability. Also they happen to have permission.

Yeah, it's real big-time stuff. These fellas are so important and their work is so important they've got permission to break the one unbreakable law. They can work overtime. In fact as far as they're concerned they can do any damned thing they please, Stability or no Stability—because it so happens they're the babies that maintain Stability. How? Take it easy. We've got plenty of time—and I'll tell you.

It's called the Prog Building and it's one of the regular newspaper beats, just like the police courts used to be a couple of hundred years ago. Every paper sends a reporter down there at three o'clock. The reporters hang around and bull for a while and then some brass hat interviews them and talks policy and economics and about how the world is doing and how it's going to do. Usually it's dull stuff but every once in a while something really big comes out, like the time they decided to drain the Mediterranean. They—

What?

You never heard of that? Say, who is this guy anyway? Are you kidding? From the Moon hey, all your life? Never been to the home planet? Never heard about what goes on? A real cosmic hick. Baby, you can roll me in a rug. I thought your kind died out before I was born. O.K., you go ahead and ask questions whenever you want. Maybe I'd better apologize now for the slang. It's part and parcel of the newspaper game. Maybe you won't be able to understand me sometimes, but I've got a heart of gold.

Anyway—I had the regular three o'clock beat at the Prog Building, and this particular day I got there a little early. Seems the *Trib* had a new reporter on the beat, guy by the name of Halley Hogan, whom I'd never met. I wanted to get together with him and talk policy. For the benefit of the hermit from the Moon I'll explain that no two newspapers in any city are permitted to share the same viewpoint or opinion.

I thought all you boys knew that. Well, sure—I'm not kidding. Look. Stability is the watchword of civilization. The world must be Stable, right? Well, Stability doesn't mean stasis. Stability is reached through an equipoise of opposing forces that balance each other. Newspapers are supposed to balance the forces of public opinion so they have to represent as many different points of view as possible. We reporters always got together before a story, or after, and made sure none of us would agree on our attitudes. You know—some would say it was a terrible thing and some would say it was a wonderful thing and some would say it didn't mean a thing and so on. I was with the *Times* and our natural competitor and opposition was the *Trib*.

The newspaper room in the Prog Building is right next to the main offices, just off the foyer. It's a big place with low-beamed ceiling and walls done in synthetic wood panels. There was a round table in the center surrounded by hardwood chairs, but we stood the chairs along the wall and dragged up the big deep leather ones. We all would sit with our heels on the table and every chair had a groove on the table in front of it. There was an unwritten law that no shop could be talked until every groove was filled with a pair of heels. That's a newspaper man's idea of a pun.

I was surprised to find almost everybody was in. I slipped into my place and upped with my feet and then took a look around. Every sandal showed except the pair that should have been opposite me, so I settled back and shut my eyes. That was where the *Trib* man should have been parked, and I certainly couldn't talk without my opposition being there to contradict me.

The *Post* said: "What makes, Carmichael?"

I said: "Ho-hum—"

The *Post* said: "Don't sleep, baby, there's big things cookin'."

The *Ledger* said: "Shuddup, you know the rules—" He pointed to the vacant segment of the table.

I said: "You mean the law of the jungle."

The *Record*, who happened to be the *Ledger*'s opposition, said: "Old Bobbus left. He ain't coming in no more."

"How come?"

"Got a Stereo contract. Doing comedy scenarios."

I thought to myself: "Oi, that means another wrestling match." You see, whenever new opposition reporters get together, they're supposed to have a symbolic wrestling match. I said supposed. It always turns into a brawl with everybody else having the fun.

"Well," I said, "this new Hogan probably doesn't know the ropes yet. I guess I'll have to go into training. Anybody seen him? He look strong?" They all shook their beads and said they didn't know him. "O.K., then let's gab without him—"

The Post said: "Your correspondent has it that the pot's a-boilin'. Every bigwig in town is in there." He jabbed his thumb toward the main offices.

We all gave the door a glance, only, like I always did, I tried to knock it in with a look. You see, although all of us came down to the Prog Building every day, none of us knew what was inside.

Yeah, it's fact. We just came and sat and listened to the big shots and went away. Like specters at the feast. It griped all of us, but me most of all.

I would dream about it at night. How there was a Hyperman living in the Prog Building, only he breathed chlorine and they kept him in tanks. Or that they had the mummies of all the great men of the past which they reanimated every afternoon to ask questions. Or it would be a cow in some dreams that was full of brains and they'd taught it to "moo" in code. There were times when I thought that if I didn't get upstairs into the Prog Building I'd burst from frustration.

So I said: "You think they're going to fill up the Mediterranean again?"

The *Ledger* laughed. He said: "I hear tell they're going to switch poles. North to south and vice versa."

The *Record* said: 'You don't think they could?"

The *Ledger* said: "I wish they would—if it'd improve my bridge."

I said: "Can it lads, and let's have the dope."

The *Journal* said: "Well, all the regulars are in—controller, vice con and deputy vice con. But there also happens to be among those present—the chief stabilizer."

"No!"

He nodded and the others nodded. "Fact. The C-S himself. Came up by pneumatic from Washington."

I said: "Oh, mamma! Five'll get you ten they're digging up Atlantis this time."

The *Record* shook his head. "The C-S didn't wear a digging look."

Just then the door to the main office shoved open and the C-S came thundering out. I'm not exaggerating. Old Groating had a face like Moses, beard and all, and when he frowned, which was now, you expected lightning to crackle from his eyes. He breezed past the table with just one glance from the blue quartz he's got for eyes, and all our legs came down with a crash. Then he shot out of the room so fast I could hear his reptunic swish with quick whistling sounds.

After him came the controller, the vice con and the deputy vice con, all in single file. They were frowning, too, and moving so rapidly we had to jump to catch the deputy. We got him at the door and swung him around. He was short and fat and trouble didn't sit well on his pudgy face. It made him look slightly lopsided.

He said: "Not now, gentlemen."

"Just a minute, Mr. Klang," I said, "I don't think you're being fair to the press."

"I know it," the deputy said, "and I'm sorry, but I really cannot spare the time."

I said: "So we report to fifteen million readers that time can't be spared these days—"

He stared at me, only I'd been doing some staring myself and I knew I had to get him to agree to give us a release.

I said: "Have a heart. If anything's big enough to upset the stability of the chief stabilizer, we ought to get a look-in."

That worried him, and I knew it would. Fifteen million people would be more than slightly unnerved to read that the C-S had been in a dither.

"Listen," I said. "What goes on? What were you talking about upstairs?"

He said: "All right. Come down to my office with me. We'll prepare a release."

Only I didn't go out with the rest of them. Because, you see, while I'd been nudging the deputy I'd noticed that all of them had rushed out so fast they'd forgotten to close the office door. It was the first time I'd seen it unlocked and I knew I was going to go through it this time. That was why I'd wheedled that release out of the deputy. I was going to get upstairs into the Prog Building because everything played into my hands. First, the door being left open. Second, the man from the *Trib* not being there.

Why? Well, don't you see? The opposition papers always paired off. The *Ledger* and the *Record* walked together and the *Journal* and the *News* and so on. This way I was alone with no one to look for me and wonder what I was up to. I pushed around in the crowd a little as they followed the deputy out, and managed to be the last one in the room. I slipped back behind the door jamb, waited a second and then streaked across to the office door. I went through it like a shot and shut it behind me. When I had my back against it I took a breath and whispered: "Hyperman, here I come!"

I was standing in a small hall that had synthetic walls with those fluorescent paintings on them. It was pretty short, had no doors anywhere, and led toward the foot of a white staircase. The only way I could go was forward, so I went. With that door locked behind me I knew I would be slightly above suspicion but only slightly, my friends, only slightly. Sooner or later someone was going to ask who I was.

The stairs were very pretty. I remember them because they were the first set I'd ever seen outside the Housing Museum. They had white even steps and they curved upwards like a conic section. I ran my fingers along the smooth stone balustrade and trudged up expecting anything from a cobra to one of Tex Richard's Fighting Robots to jump out at me. I was scared to death.

I came to a square railed landing and it was then I first sensed the vibrations. I'd thought it was my heart whopping against my ribs with that peculiar *bam-bam-bam* that takes your breath away and sets a solid lump of cold under your stomach. Then I realized this pulse came from the Prog Building itself. I trotted up the rest of the stairs on the double and came to the top. There was a sliding door there. I took hold of the knob and thought: "Oh, well, they can only stuff me and put me under glass"—so I shoved the door open.

Boys, this was it—that nucleus I told you about.

I'll try to give you an idea of what it looked like because it was the most sensational thing I've ever seen—and I've seen plenty in my time. The room took up the entire width of the building and it was two stories high. I felt as though I'd walked into the middle of a clock. Space was literally filled with the shimmer and spin of cogs and cams that gleamed with the peculiar highlights you see on a droplet of water about to fall. All of those thousands of wheels spun in sockets of precious stone—just like a watch only bigger and those dots of red and yellow and green and blue fire burned until they looked like a painting by that Frenchman from way back. Seurat was his name.

The walls were lined with banks of Computation Integraphs—you could see the end-total curves where they were plotted on photoelectric plates. The setting dials for the Integraphs were all at eye level and ran around the entire circumference of the room like a chain of enormous white-faced periods. That was about all of the stuff I could recognize. The rest just looked complicated and bewildering.

That *bam-bam-bam* I told you about came from the very center of the room. There was a crystal octahedron maybe ten feet high, nipped between vertical axes above and below. It was spinning slowly so that it looked jerky, and the vibration was the sound of the motors that turned it. From way high up there were shafts of light projected at it. The slow turning facets caught those beams and shattered them and sent them dancing through the room. Boys—it was really sensational.

I took a couple of steps in and then a little old coot in a white jacket bustled across the room, saw me, nodded, and went about his business. He hadn't taken more than another three steps when he stopped and came back to me. It was a real slow take.

He said: "I don't quite—" and then he broke off doubtfully. He had a withered, faraway look, as though he'd spent all his life trying to remember he was alive.

I said: "I'm Carmichael."

"O yes!" he began, brightening a little. Then his face got dubious again.

I played it real smart. I said: "I'm with Stabilizer Groating."

"Secretary?"

"Yeah."

"You know, Mr. Mitchell," he said, "I can't help feeling that despite the gloomier aspects there are some very encouraging features. The Ultimate Datum System that we have devised should bring us down to surveys of the near future in a short time—" He gave me a quizzical glance like a dog begging for admiration on his hind legs.

I said: "Really?"

"It stands to reason. After all, once a technique has been devised for pushing analysis into the absolute future, a comparatively simple reversal should bring it as close as tomorrow."

I said: "It should at that." and wondered what he was talking about. Now that some of the fright had worn off I was feeling slightly disappointed. Here I expected to find the Hyperman who was handing down Sinai Decrees to our bosses and I walk into a multiplied clock.

He was rather pleased. He said: "You think so?"

"I think so."

"Will you mention that to Mr. Groating? I feel it might encourage him—"

I got even smarter. I said: "To tell you the truth, sir, the Stabilizer sent me up for a short review. I'm new to the staff and unfortunately I was delayed in Washington."

He said: "*Tut-Tut*, forgive me. Step this way, Mr.... Mr. Ahh—"

So I stepped his way and we went weaving through the clockworks to a desk at one side of the room. There were half a dozen chairs behind it and he seated me alongside himself. The flat top of the desk was banked with small tabs and push buttons so that it looked like a stenotype. He pressed one stud and the room darkened. He pressed another and the *bam-bam* quickened until it was a steady hum. The octahedron crystal whirled so quickly that it became a shadowy mist of light under the projectors.

"I suppose you know," the old coot said in rather self-conscious tones, "that this is the first time we've been able to push our definitive analysis to the ultimate future. We'd never have done it if Wiggons hadn't developed his self-checking data systems."

I said: "Good for Wiggons," and I was more confused than ever. I tell you, boys, it felt like waking up from a dream you couldn't quite remember. You know that peculiar sensation of having everything at the edge of your mind so to speak and not being able to get hold of it—I had a thousand clues and inferences jangling around in my head and none of them would interlock. But I knew this was big stuff.

Shadows began to play across the crystal. Off-focus images and flashes of color. The little old guy murmured to himself and his fingers plucked at the keyboard in a quick fugue of motion. Finally he said: "Ah!" and sat back to watch the crystal. So did I.

I was looking through a window in space, and beyond that window I saw a single bright star in the blackness. It was sharp and cold and so brilliant it hurt your eyes. Just beyond the window, in the foreground, I saw a spaceship. No, none of your cigar things or ovate spheroids or any of that. It was a spaceship that seemed to have been built mostly in afterthoughts. A great rambling affair with added wings and towers and helter-skelter ports. It looked like it'd been built just to hang there in one place.

The old coot said: "Watch close now, Mr. Muggins, things happen rather quickly at this tempo."

Quickly? They practically sprinted. There was a spurt of activity around the spaceship. Towers went up and came down; the bug-like figures of people in space armor bustled about; a little cruiser, shaped like a fat needle, sped up to it, hung around a while and then sped away. There was a tense second of waiting and then the star blotted out. In another moment the spaceship was blotted out, too. The crystal was black.

My friend, the goofy professor, touched a couple of studs and we had a long view. There were clusters of stars spread before me sharply, brilliantly in focus. As I watched, the upperside of the crystal began to blacken. In a few swift moments the stars were blacked out. Just like that. Blooey! It reminded me of school when we added carbon ink to a drop under the mike just to see how the amoebae would take it.

He punched the buttons like crazy and we had more and more views of the Universe, and always that black cloud crept along, blotting everything out. After a while he couldn't find any more stars. There was nothing but blackness. It seemed to me that it wasn't more than an extra-special Stereo Show, but it chilled me nevertheless. I started thinking about those amoebae and feeling sorry for them.

The lights went on and I was back inside the clock again. He turned to me and said: "Well, what do you think?"

I said: "I think it's swell."

That seemed to disappoint him. He said: "No, no-I mean, what do you make of it? Do you agree with the others?"

"With Stabilizer Groating, you mean?"

He nodded.

I said: "You'll have to give me a little time to think it over. It's rather—startling."

"By all means," he said, escorting me to the door, "do think it over. Although"—he hesitated with his hand on the knob—"I shouldn't agree with your choice of the word 'startling'. After all, it's only what we expected all along. The Universe must come to an end one way or another."

Think? Boys, the massive brain practically fumed as I went back downstairs. I went out into the press room and I wondered what there was about a picture of a black cloud that could have upset the Stabilizer. I drifted out of the Prog Building and decided I'd better go down to the controller's office for another bluff, so I didn't drift any more. There was a pneumatic pick-up at the corner. I caught a capsule and clicked off the address on the dial. In three and a half minutes I was there.

As I turned the overhead dome back and started to step out of my capsule, I found myself surrounded by the rest of the newspaper crowd.

The *Ledger* said: "Where you been, my friendly, we needed your quick brain but bad."

I said: "I'm still looking for Hogan. I can't cover a thing until I've seen him. What's this need for brains?"

"Not just any brains. Your brain."

I got out of the capsule and showed my empty pocket.

The *Ledger* said: "We're not soaping you for a loan—we needed interpolation."

"Aha?"

The *Record* said: "The dope means interpretation. We got one of those official releases again. All words and no sense."

"I mean interpolation," the *Ledger* said. "We got to have some one read implications into this barren chaff."

I said: "Brothers, you want exaggeration and I'm not going to give it this time. Too risky."

So I trotted up the ramp to the main floor and went to the vice deputy's office and then I thought: "I've got a big thing here, why bother with the small fry?" I did a turnabout and went straight to the controller's suite. I knew it would be tough to get in because the controller has live secretaries—no voders. He also happens to have four receptionists. Beautiful, but tough.

The first never saw me. I breezed right by and was in the second anteroom before she could say: "What is it, pa-lee-azz?" The second was warned by the bang of the door and grabbed hold of my arm as I tried to go through. I got past anyway, with two of them holding on, but number three added her lovely heft and I bogged down. By this time I was within earshot of the controller so I screamed: "Down with Stability!"

Sure I did. I also shouted: "Stability is all wrong! I'm for Chaos. Hurray for Chaos!" and a lot more like that. The receptionists were shocked to death and one of them put in a call for emergency and a couple of guys hanging around were all for boffing me. I kept on downing with Stability and fighting toward the sanctum sanctorurn et cetera and having a wonderful time because the three girls hanging on to me were strictly class and I happily suffocated on Exuberant No. 5. Finally the controller came out to see what made.

They let go of me and the controller said: "What's the meaning of this?...Oh, it's you."

I said: "Excuse it, please."

"Is this your idea of a joke, Carmichael?"

"No, sir, but it was the only quick way to get to you."

"Sorry, Carmichael, but it's a little too quick."

I said: "Wait a minute, sir."

"Sorry, I'm extremely busy." He looked worried and impatient all at once.

I said: "You've got to give me a moment in private."

"Impossible. See my secretary." He turned toward his office.

"Please, sir—"

He waved his hand and started through the door. I took a jump and caught him by the elbow. He was sputtering furiously when I swung him around, but I got my arms around him and gave him a hug. When my mouth was against his ear I whispered: "I've been upstairs in the Prog Building. *I know*!"

He stared at me and his jaw dropped. After a couple of vague gestures with his hands he motioned me in with a jerk of his head. I marched straight into the controller's office and almost fell down dead. The stabilizer was there. Yeah, old Jehovah Groating himself, standing before the window. All he needed was the stone tablets in his arms—or is it thunderbolts?

I felt very, very sober, my friends, and not very smart any more because the stabilizer is a sobering sight no matter how you kid about him. I nodded politely and waited for the controller to shut the door. I was wishing I could be on the other side of the door. Also I was wishing I'd never gone upstairs into the Prog Building.

The controller said: "This is John Carmichael, Mr. Groating, a reporter for the *Times*."

We both said: "How-d'you-do?" only Groating said it out loud. I just moved my lips.

The controller said: "Now, Carmichael, what's this about the Prog Building?"

"I went upstairs, sir."

He said: "You'll have to speak a little louder."

I cleared my throat and said: "I went upstairs, sir."

"You what!"

"W-went upstairs."

This time lightning really did flash from the C-S's eyes.

I said: "If I've made trouble for anyone, I'm sorry. I've been wanting to get up there for years and...and when I got the chance today, I couldn't resist it—" Then I told them how I sneaked up and what I did.

The controller made a terrible fuss about the whole affair, and I knew—don't ask me how, I simply knew—that something drastic was going to be done about it unless I talked plenty fast. By this time, though, the clues in my head were beginning to fall into place. I turned directly to the C-S and I said: "Sir, Prog stands for Prognostication, doesn't it?"

There was silence. Finally Groating nodded slowly.

I said: "You've got some kind of fortuneteller up there. You go up every afternoon and get your fortune told. Then you come out and tell the press about it as though you all thought it up by yourselves. Right?"

The controller sputtered, but Groating nodded again.

I said: "This afternoon the end of the Universe was prognosticated."

Another silence. At last Groating sighed wearily. He shut the controller up with a wave of his hand and said: "It seems Mr. Carmichael does know enough to make things awkward all around."

The controller burst out: "It's no fault of mine. I always insisted on a thorough guard system. If we had guarded the—"

"Guards," Groating interrupted, "would only have upset existing Stability. They would have drawn attention and suspicion. We were forced to take the chance of a slip-up. Now that it's happened we must make the best of it."

I said: "Excuse me, sir. I wouldn't have come here just to boast. I could have kept quiet about it. What bothers me is what bothered you?"

Groating stared at me for a moment, then turned away and began to pace up and down the room. There was no anger in his attitude; if there had been, I wouldn't have been as scared as I was. It was a big room and he did a lot of pacing and I could see he was coldly analyzing the situation and deciding what was to be done with me. That frigid appraisal had me trembling.

I said: "I'll give you my word not to mention this again—if that'll do the trick."

He paid no attention—merely paced. My mind raced crazily through all the nasty things that could happen to me. Like solitary for life. Like one-way exploration. Like an obliterated memory track which meant I would have lost my twenty-eight years, not that they were worth much to anyone but me.

I got panicky and yelled: "You can't do anything to me. Remember Stability—" I began to quote the Credo as fast as I could remember:

"The *status quo* must be maintained at all costs.

"Every member of society is an integral and essential factor of the *status quo*. A blow at the Stability of any individual is a blow aimed at the Stability of society. Stability that is maintained at the cost of so much as a single individual is tantamount to Chaos—"

"Thank you, Mr. Carmichael," the C-S interrupted. "I have already learned the Credo."

He went to the controller's desk and punched the teletype keys rapidly. After a few minutes of horrible waiting the answer came clicking back. Groating read the message, nodded and beckoned to me. I stepped up to him and, boys, I don't know how the legs kept from puddling on the floor.

Groating said: "Mr. Carmichael, it is my pleasure to appoint you confidential reporter to the Stability Board for the duration of this crisis."

I said: "Awk!"

Groating said: "We've maintained Stability, you see, and insured your silence. Society cannot endure change—but it can endure and welcome harmless additions. A new post has been created and you're it."

I said: "Th-thanks."

"Naturally, there will be an advance in credit for you. That is the price we pay, and gladly. You will attach yourself to me. All reports will be confidential. Should you break confidence, society will exact the usual penalty for official corruption. Shall I quote the Credo on that point?"

I said: "No, sir!" because I knew that one by heart. The usual penalty isn't pleasant. Groating had me beautifully hog-tied. I said: "What about the *Times*, sir?"

"Why," Groating said, "you will continue your usual duties whenever possible. You will submit the official releases as though you had no idea at all of what was really taking place. I'm sure I can spare you long enough each day to make an appearance at your office."

Suddenly he smiled at me and in that moment I felt better. I realized that he was far from being a Jehovian menace—in fact that he'd done all he could to help me out of the nasty spot my curiosity had gotten me into. I grinned back and on impulse shoved out my hand. He took it and gave it a shake. Everything was fine.

The C-S said: "Now that you're a fellow-official, Mr. Carmichael, I'll come to the point directly. The Prog Building, as you've guessed, is a Prognostication Center. With the aid of a complete data system and a rather complex series of Integraphs we have been able to...to tell our fortunes, as you put it."

I said: "I was just shooting in the dark, sir. I really don't believe it."

Groating smiled. He said: "Nevertheless it exists. Prophecy is far from being a mystical function. It is a very logical science based on experimental factors. The prophecy of an eclipse to the exact second of time and precise degree of longitude strikes the layman with awe. The scientist knows it is the result of precise mathematical work with precise data."

"Sure," I began, "but—"

Groating held up his hand. "The future of the world line," he said, is essentially the same problem magnified only by the difficulty of obtaining accurate data—and enough data. For, example: Assuming an apple orchard, what are the chances of apples being stolen?"

I said: "I couldn't say. Depends, I suppose, on whether there are any kids living in the neighborhood."

"All right;" Groating said, "that's additional data. Assuming the orchard and the small boys, what are the chances of stolen apples?"

"Pretty good."

"Add data. A locust plague is reported on the way."

"Not so good."

"More data. Agriculture reports a new efficient locust spray."

"Better."

"And still more data. In the past years the boys have stolen apples and been soundly punished. Now what are the chances?"

"Maybe a little less."

"Continue the experimental factors with an analysis of the boys. They are headstrong and will ignore punishment. Add also the weather forecasts for the summer; add the location of the orchard and attitude of owner. Now sum up: Orchard plus boys plus thefts plus punishment plus character plus locusts plus spray plus—"

I said: "Good heavens!"

"You're overwhelmed by the detail work," Groating smiled, "but not by the lack of logic. It is possible to obtain all possible data on the orchard in question and integrate the factors into an accurate prophecy not only as to the theft, but as to the time and place of theft. Apply this example to our own Universe and you can understand the working of the Prognosis Building. We have eight floors of data analyzers. The sifted factors are fed into the Integrators and—presto, prophecy!"

I said: "Presto, my poor head!"

"You'll get used to it in time."

I said: "The pictures?"

Groating said: "The solution of a mathematical problem can take any one of a number of forms. For Prognosis we have naturally selected a picturization of the events themselves. Any major step in government that is contemplated is prepared in data form and fed into the Integrator. The effect of that step on the world line is observed. If it is beneficial, we take that step; if not, we abandon it and search for another—"

I said: "And the picture I saw this afternoon?"

Groating sobered. He said: "Up until today, Mr. Carmichael, we have not been able to integrate closer to the present than a week in the future—or deeper into the future than a few hundred years. Wiggon's new data technique has enabled us to push to the end of our existence, and it is perilously close. You saw the obliteration of our Universe take place less than a thousand years from now. This is something we must prevent at once."

"Why all the excitement? Surely something will happen during the next ten centuries to avoid it."

"What will happen?" Groating shook his bead. "I don't think you understand our problem. On the one hand you have the theory of our society. Stability. You yourself have quoted the Credo. A society which must maintain its Stability at the price of instability is Chaos. Keep that in mind. On the other hand we cannot wait while our existence progresses rapidly toward extinction. The closer it draws to that point, the more violent the change will have to be to alter it.

"Think of the progress of a snowball that starts at the top of a mountain and rolls down the slopes, growing in bulk until it smashes an entire house at the bottom. The mere push of a finger is sufficient to alter its future when it starts—a push of a finger will save a house. But if you wait until the snowball gathers momentum you will need violent efforts to throw the tons of snow off the course."

I said: "Those pictures I saw were the snowball hitting our house. You want to start pushing the finger now—"

Groating nodded. "Our problem now is to sift the billions of factors stored in the Prog Building and discover which of them is that tiny snowball."

The controller, who bad been silent in a state of wild suppression all the while, suddenly spoke up. "I tell you it's impossible, Mr. Groating. How can you dig the one significant factor out of all those billions?"

Groating said: "It will have to be done."

"But there's an easier way," the controller cried.

"I've been suggesting it all along. Let's attempt the trial and error method. We instigate a series of changes at once and see whether or not the future line is shifted. Sooner or later we're bound to strike something."

"Impossible," Groating said. 'You're suggesting the end of Stability. No civilization is worth saving if it must buy salvation at the price of its principles."

I said: "Sir, I'd like to make a suggestion."

They looked at me. The C-S nodded.

"It seems to me that you're both on the wrong track. You're searching for a factor from the present. You ought to start in the future."

"How's that?"

"It's like if I said old maids were responsible for more clover. You'd start investigating the old maids. You ought to start with the clover and work backwards."

"Just what are you trying to say, Mr. Carmichael?"

"I'm talking about *a posteriori* reasoning. Look, sir, a fella by the name of Darwin was trying to explain the balance of nature. He wanted to show the chain of cause and effect. He said in so many words that the number of old maids in a town governed the growth of clover, but if you want to find out how, you've got to work it out *a posteriori*; from effect to cause. Like this: Only bumblebees can fertilize clover. The more bumblebees, the more clover. Field mice attack bumblebee nests, so the more field mice, the less clover. Cats attack mice. The more cats, the more clover. Old maids keep cats. The more old maids…the more clover. Q. E. D."

"And now," Groating laughed, "construe."

"Seems to me you ought to start with the catastrophe and follow the chain of causation, link by link, back to the source. Why not use the Prognosticator backwards until you locate the moment when the snowball first started rolling?"

There was a very long silence while they thought it over. The controller looked slightly bewildered and he kept muttering: Cats-clover-old maids—But I could see the C-S was really hit. He went to the window and stood looking out, as motionless as a statue. I remember staring past his square shoulder and watching the shadows of the helios flicking noiselessly across the facade of the Judiciary Building opposite us.

It was all so unreal—this frantic desperation over an event a thousand years in the future; but that's Stability. It's strictly the long view. Old Cyrus Brennerhaven of the *Morning Globe* had a sign over his desk that read: If you take care of the tomorrows, the todays will take care of themselves.

Finally Groating said: "Mr. Carmichael, I think we'd better go back to the Prog Building—"

Sure I felt proud. We left the office and went down the hall toward the pneumatics and I kept thinking: "I've given an idea to the Chief Stabilizer. He's taken a suggestion from me!" A couple of secretaries had rushed down the hall ahead of us when they saw us come out, and when we got to the tubes, three capsules were waiting for us. What's more, the C-S and the controller stood around and waited for *me* while I contacted my city editor and gave him the official release. The editor was a little sore about my disappearance, but I had a perfect alibi. I was still looking for Hogan. That, my friends, was emphatically that.

At the Prog Building we bustled through the main

offices and back up the curved stairs. On the way the C-S said he didn't think we ought to tell Yarr, the little old coot I'd hoodwinked, the real truth. It would be just as well, he said, to let Yarr go on thinking I was a confidential secretary.

So we came again to that fantastic clockwork room with its myriad whirling cams and the revolving crystal and the hypnotic *bam-bam* of the motors. Yarr met us at the door and escorted us to the viewing desk with his peculiar absent-minded subservience. The room was darkened again, and once more we watched the cloud of blackness seep across the face of the Universe. The sight chilled me more than ever, now that I knew what it meant.

Groating turned to me and said: "Well, Mr. Carmichael, any suggestions?"

I said: "The first thing we ought to find out is just what that spaceship has to do with the black cloud...don't you think so?"

"Why yes, I do." Groating turned to Yarr and said: "Give us a close-up of the spaceship and switch in sound. Give us the integration at normal speed."

Yarr said: "It would take a week to run the whole thing off. Any special moment you want, sir?"

I had a hunch. "Give us the moment when the auxiliary ship arrives."

Yarr turned back to his switchboard. We had a close-up of a great round port. The sound mechanism clicked on, running at high speed with a peculiar *wheetledy-woodledey-weedledy* garble of shrill noises. Suddenly the cruiser shot into view. Yarr slowed everything down to normal speed.

The fat needle nosed into place, the ports clanged and hissed as the suction junction was made.

Abruptly, the scene shifted and we were inside the lock between the two ships. Men in stained dungarees, stripped to the waist and sweating, were hauling heavy canvas-wrapped equipment into the mother ship. To one side two elderly guys were talking swiftly:

"You had difficulty?"

"More than ever. Thank God this is the last shipment."

"How about credits?"

"Exhausted."

"Do you mean that?"

"I do."

"I can't understand it. We had over two millions left."

"We lost all that through indirect purchases and—"

"And what?"

"Bribes, if you must know."

"Bribes?"

"My dear sir, you can't order cyclotrons without making people suspicious. If you so much as mention an atom today, you accuse yourself."

"Then we all stand accused here and now."

"I'm not denying that."

"What a terrible thing it is that the most precious part of our existence should be the most hated."

"You speak of—"

"The atom."

The speaker gazed before him meditatively, then sighed and turned into the shadowy depths of the spaceship.

I said: "All right, that's enough. Cut into the moment just before the black-out occurs. Take it inside the ship."

The integrators quickened and the sound track began its babble again. Quick scenes of the interior of the mother ship flickered across the crystal. A control chamber, roofed with a transparent dome passed repeatedly before us, with the darting figures of men snapping through it. At last the Integrator fixed on that chamber and stopped. The scene was frozen into a still photograph—a tableau of half a dozen half-naked men poised over the controls, heads tilted back to look through the dome.

Yarr said: "It doesn't take long. Watch closely."

I said: "Shoot."

The scene came to life with a blurp.

"—ready on the tension screens?"

"Ready, sir."

"Power checked?"

"Checked and ready, sir."

"Stand by, all. Time?"

"Two minutes to go."

"Good—" The graybeard in the center of the chamber paced with hands clasped behind him, very much like a captain on his bridge. Clearly through the sound mechanism came the thuds of his steps and the background hum of waiting mechanism.

The graybeard said: "Time?"

"One minute forty seconds."

"Gentlemen: In these brief moments I should like to thank you all for your splendid assistance. I speak not so much of your technical work, which speaks for itself, but of your willingness to exile yourselves and even incriminate yourselves along with me—Time?"

"One twenty-five."

"It is a sad thing that our work which is intended to grant the greatest boon imaginable to the Universe should have been driven into secrecy. Limitless power is so vast a concept that even I cannot speculate on the future it will bring to our worlds. In a few minutes, after we have succeeded, all of us will be universal heroes. Now, before our work is done, I want all of you to know that to me you are already heroes—Time?"

"One ten."

"And now, a warning. When we have set up our spacial partition membrane and begun the osmotic transfer of energy from gyperspace to our own there may be effects which I have been unable to predict. Raw energy pervading our space may also pervade our nervous systems and engender various unforeseen conditions. Do not be alarmed. Keep well in mind the fact that the change cannot be anything but for the better—Time?"

"Fifty seconds."

"The advantages? Up to now mathematics and the sciences have merely been substitutes for what man should do for himself. So FitzJohn preached in his first lecture, and so we are about to prove. The logical evolution of energy mechanics is not toward magnification and complex engineering development, but toward simplification-toward the concentration of all those powers within man himself—Time?"

"Twenty seconds."

"Courage, my friends. This is the moment we have worked for these past ten years. Secretly. Criminally. So it has always been with those who have brought man his greatest gifts."

"Ten seconds."

"Stand by, all."

"Ready all, sir."

The seconds ticked off with agonizing slowness. At the moment of zero the workers were galvanized into quick action. It was impossible to follow their motions or understand them, but you could see by the smooth timing and interplay that they were beautifully rehearsed. There was tragedy in those efforts for us who already knew the outcome.

As quickly as they had begun, the workers stopped and peered upward through the crystal dome. Far beyond them, crisp in the velvet blackness, that star gleamed, and as they watched, it winked out.

They started and exclaimed, pointing. The graybeard cried:

"It's impossible!"

"What is it, sir?"

"I—"

And in that moment blackness enveloped the scene.

I said: "Hold it—"

Yarr brought up the lights and the others turned to look at me. I thought for a while, idly watching the shimmering cams and cogs around me. Then I said: "It's a good start. The reason I imagine you gentlemen have been slightly bewildered up to now is that you're busy men with no time for foolishness. Now I'm not so busy and very foolish, so I read detective stories. This is going to be a kind of backward detective story."

"All right," Groating said. "Go ahead."

"We've got a few clues. First, the Universe has ended through an attempt to pervade it with energy from hyperspace. Second, the attempt failed for a number of reasons which we can't discover yet. Third, the attempt was made in secrecy. Why?"

The controller said: "Why not? Scientists and all that—"

"I don't mean that kind of secrecy. These men were plainly outside the law, carrying on an illicit experiment. We must find out why energy experiments or atomic experiments were illegal. That will carry us back quite a few decades toward the present."

"But how?"

"Why, we trace the auxiliary cruiser, of course. If we can pick them up when they're purchasing supplies, we'll narrow our backward search considerably. Can you do it, Dr. Yarr?"

"It'll take time."

"Go ahead—we've got a thousand years."

It took exactly two days. In that time I learned a lot about the Prognosticator. They had it worked out beautifully. Seems the future is made up solely of probabilities. The Integrator could push down any one of these possible avenues, but with a wonderful check. The less probable the avenue of future was, the more off-focus it was. If a future event was only remotely possible, it was pictured as a blurred series of actions. On the other hand, the future that was almost positive in the light of present data, was sharply in focus.

When we went back to the Prog Building two days later, Yarr was almost alive in his excitement. He said: "I really think I've got just the thing you're looking for."

"What's that?"

"I've picked up an actual moment of bribery. It has additional data that should put us directly on the track."

We sat down behind the desk with Yarr at the

controls. He had a slip of paper in his hand which he consulted with much muttering as he adjusted coordinates. Once more we saw the preliminary off-focus shadows, then the sound blooped on like a hundred stereo records playing at once. The crystal sharpened abruptly into focus.

The scream and roar of a gigantic foundry blasted our ears. On both sides of the scene towered the steel girder columns of the foundry walls, stretching deep into the background like the grim pillars of a satanic cathedral. Overhead cranes carried enormous blocks of metal with a ponderous gait. Smoke-black, white and fitfully flared with crimson from the furnaces, whirled around the tiny figures.

Two men stood before a gigantic casting. One, a foundryman in soiled overalls, made quick measurements which be called off to the other carefully checking a blueprint. Over the roar of the foundry the dialogue was curt and sharp:

"One hundred three point seven."

"Check."

"Short axis. Fifty-two point five."

"Check."

"Tangent on ovate diameter. Three degrees point oh five two."

"Check!"

"What specifications for outer convolutions?"

"Y equals cosine X."

"Then that equation resolves to X equals minus one half pi."

"Check."

The foundryman climbed down from the casting, folding his three-way gauge. He mopped his face with a bit of waste and eyed the engineer curiously as the latter carefully rolled up the blueprint and slid it into a tube of other rolled sheets. The foundryman said: "I think we did a nice job."

The engineer nodded.

"Only what in blazes do you want it for? Never saw a casting like that."

"I could explain, but you wouldn't understand. Too complicated."

The foundryman flushed. He said: "You theoretical guys are too damned snotty. Just because I know how to drop-forge doesn't mean I can't understand an equation."

"Mebbeso. Let it go at that. I'm ready to ship this casting out at once."

As the engineer turned to leave, rapping the rolled blueprints nervously against his calf, a great pig of iron that had been sailing up from the background swung dangerously toward his head. The foundryman cried out. He leaped forward, seized the engineer by the shoulder and sent him tumbling to the concrete floor. The blueprints went flying.

He pulled the engineer to his feet immediately and tried to straighten the dazed man who could only stare at the tons of iron that sailed serenely on. The foundryman picked up the scattered sheets and started to sort them. Abruptly he stopped and examined one of the pages closely. He began to look through the others, but before he could go any further, the blueprints were snatched from his hands.

He said: "What's this casting for?"

The engineer rolled the sheets together with quick, intense motions. He said: "None of your blasted business."

"I think I know. That's one-quarter a cyclotron.

You're getting the other parts made up in different foundries, aren't you?"

There was no answer.

"Maybe you've forgotten Stabilization Rule 930."

"I haven't forgotten. You're crazy."

"Want me to call for official inspection?"

The engineer took a breath, then shrugged. He said: "I suppose the only way to convince you is to show you the master drafts. Come on—"

They left the foundry and trudged across the broad concrete of a landing field to where the fat needle of the auxiliary ship lay. They mounted the ramp to the side port and entered the ship. Inside, the engineer called: "It's happened again, boys. Let's go!"

The port swung shut behind them. Spacemen drifted up from the surrounding corridors and rooms. They were rangy and tough-looking and the snub-nosed paralyzers glinted casually in their hands as though they'd been cleaning them and merely happened to bring them along. The foundryman looked around for a long time. At last he said: "So it's this way?"

"Yes, it's this way. Sorry."

"I'd like you to meet some of my friends, some day—"

"Perhaps we will."

"They'll have an easier time with you than you're gonna have with me!" He clenched fists and poised himself to spring.

The engineer said: "Hey—wait a minute. Don't lose your head. You did me a good turn back there. I'd like to return the favor. I've got more credit than I know what to do with."

The foundryman gave him a perplexed glance. He relaxed and began to rub his chin dubiously.

He said: "Damn if this isn't a sociable ship. I feel friendlier already—"

The engineer grinned.

I called, "That's enough. Cut it," and the scene vanished.

"Well?" Yarr asked eagerly.

I said: "We're really in the groove now. Let's check back and locate the Stabilization debates on Rule 930." I turned to the C-S. "What's the latest rule number, sir?"

Groating said: "Seven fifteen."

The controller had already been figuring. He said: "Figuring the same law-production rate that would put Rule 930 about six hundred years from now. Is that right, Mr. Groating?"

The old man nodded and Yarr went back to his keyboard. I'm not going to bother you with what we all went through because a lot of it was very dull. For the benefit of the hermit from the Moon I'll just mention that we hung around the Stability Library until we located the year S. R. 930 was passed. Then we shifted to Stability headquarters and quick-timed through from January 1st until we picked up the debates on the rule.

The reasons for the rule were slightly bewildering on the one hand, and quite understandable on the other. It seems that in the one hundred and fifty years preceding, almost every Earthwide university had been blown up in the course of an atomic-energy experiment. The blowups were bewildering—the rule understandable. I'd like to tell you about that debate because—well, because things happened that touched me.

The Integrator selected a cool, smooth foyer in the Administration Building at Washington. It had a marble floor like milky ice flecked with gold. One side was broken by a vast square window studded with a thousand round-bottle panes that refracted the afternoon sunlight into showers of warm color. In the background were two enormous doors of synthetic oak. Before those doors stood a couple in earnest conversation—a nice-looking boy with a portfolio under his arm, and a stunning girl. The kind with sleek-shingled head and one of those clean-cut faces that look fresh and wind-washed.

The controller said: "Why, that's the foyer to the Seminar Room. They haven't changed it at all in six hundred years."

Groating said: "Stability!" and chuckled.

Yarr said: "The debate is going on inside. I'll shift scene—"

"No-wait," I said. "Let's watch this for a while." I don't know why I wanted to—except that the girl made my pulse run a little faster and I felt like looking at her for a couple of years.

She was half crying. She said: "Then, if for no other reason for my sake."

"For yours!" The boy looked harassed.

She nodded. "You'll sweep away his life work with a few words and a few sheets of paper."

"My own work, too."

"Oh, but won't you understand? You're young. I'm young. Youth loves to shatter the old idols. It feasts on the broken shards of destruction. It destroys the old ideas to make way for its own. But he's not young like us. He has only his past work to live on. If you shatter that, he'll have nothing left but a futile resentment. I'll be pent up with a broken old man who'll destroy me along with himself. Darling, I'm not saying you're wrong—I'm only asking you to wait a little."

She was crying openly now. The boy took her by the arm and led her to the crusted window. She turned her face away from the light—away from him. The boy said: "He was my teacher. I worship him. What I'm doing now may seem like treachery, but it's only treachery to his old age. I'm keeping faith with what he was thirty years ago—with the man who would have done the same thing to his teacher."

She cried: "But are you keeping faith with me? You, who will have all the joy of destroying and none of the tedious sweeping away the pieces. What of my life and all the weary years to come when I must coddle him and soothe him and lead him through the madness of forgetting what you've done to him?"

"You'll spend your life with me. I break no faith with you, Barbara."

She laughed bitterly. "How easily you evade reality. I shall spend my life with you—and in that short sentence, poof!"—she flicked her hand—"you dismiss everything. Where will he live? Alone? With us? Where?"

"That can be arranged."

"You're so stubborn, so pig-headed in your smug, righteous truth-seeking. Steven—for the very last time—please. Wait until he's gone. A few years, that's all. Leave him in peace. Leave us in peace."

He shook his head and started toward the oaken doors. "A few years waiting to salvage the pride of an old man, a few more catastrophes, a few more thousand lives lost—it doesn't add up."

She sagged against the window, silhouetted before the riot of color, and watched him cross to the doors. All the tears seemed drained out of her. She was so limp I thought she would fall to the floor at any instant. And then, as I watched her, I saw her stiffen and I realized that another figure had entered the foyer and was rushing toward the boy. It was an oldish man, bald and with an ageless face of carved ivory. He was tall and terribly thin. His eyes were little pits of embers.

He called: "Steven!"

The boy stopped and turned.

"Steven, I want to talk to you."

"It's no use, sir!"

"You're headstrong, Steven. You pit a few years research against my work of a lifetime. Once I respected you. I thought you would carry on for me as I've carried on for the generations that came before me."

"I am, sir."

"You are not." The old man clutched at the boy's tunic and spoke intensely. "You betray all of us. You will cut short a line of research that promises the salvation of humanity. In five minutes you will wipe out five centuries of work. You owe it to those who slaved before us not to let their sweat go in vain."

The boy said: "I have a debt also to those who may die."

"You think too much of death, too little of life. What if a thousand more are killed—ten thousand—in the end it will be worth it."

"It will never be worth it. There will never be an

end. The theory has always been wrong, faultily premised."

"You fool!" the old man cried. "You damned, blasted young fool. You can't go in there!"

"I'm going, sir. Let go."

"I won't let you go in."

The boy pulled his arm free and reached for the doorknob. The old man seized him again and yanked him off balance. The boy muttered angrily, set himself and thrust the old man back. There was a flailing blur of motion and a cry from the girl. She left the window, ran across the room and thrust herself between the two. And in that instant she screamed again and stepped back. The boy sagged gently to the floor, his mouth opened to an O of astonishment. He tried to speak and then relaxed. The girl dropped to her knees alongside him and tried to get his head on her lap. Then she stopped.

That was all. No shot or anything. I caught a glimpse of a metallic barrel in the old man's hand as he hovered frantically over the dead boy. He cried: "I only meant to—I—" and kept on whimpering.

After a while the girl turned her head as though it weighed a ton, and looked up. Her face was suddenly frostbitten. In dull tones she said: "Go away, father."

The old man said: "I only—" His lips continued to twitch, but he made no sound.

The girl picked up the portfolio and got to her feet. Without glancing again at her father, she opened the doors, stepped in and closed them behind her with a soft click. The debating voices broke off at the sight of her. She walked to the head of the table, set the portfolio down, opened it and took out a sheaf of typescript. Then she looked at the amazed men who were seated around the table gaping at her.

She said: "I regret to inform the stabilizers that Mr. Steven Wilder has been unavoidably detained. As his fiancée and coworker, however, I have been delegated to carry on his mission and present his evidence to the committee—" She paused and went rigid, fighting for control.

One of the stabilizers said: "Thank you. Will you give your evidence, Miss...Miss?"

"Barbara Leeds."

"Thank you, Miss Leeds. Will you continue?"

With the gray ashes of a voice she went on: "We are heartily in favor of S. R. 930 prohibiting any further experimentation in atomic energy dynamics. All such experiments have been based on—almost inspired by the FitzJohn axioms and mathematics. The catastrophic detonations which have resulted must invariably result since the basic premises are incorrect. We shall prove that the backbone of FitzJohn's equations is entirely in error. I speak of $i=(b/a)\ ie/\mu$..."

She glanced at the notes, hesitated for an instant and then continued: "FitzJohn's errors are most easily pointed out if we consider the Leeds Derivations involving transfinite cardinals—"

The tragic voice droned on.

I said: "C-cut."

There was silence.

We sat there feeling bleak and cold, and for no reason at all, the icy sea-green opening bars of Debussy's "La Mer" ran through my head. I thought: "I'm proud to be a human—not because I think or I am, but because I can feel. Because humanity can reach out to us across centuries, from the past or future, from facts or imagination, and touch us—move us."

At last I said: "We're moving along real nice now."

No answer.

I tried again: "Evidently that secret experiment that destroyed existence was based on this FitzJohn's erroneous theory, eh?"

The C-S stirred and said: "What? Oh—Yes, Carmichael, quite right."

In low tones the controller said: "I wish it hadn't happened. He was a nice-looking youngster, that Wilder—promising."

I said: "In the name of heaven, sir, it's not going to happen if we pull ourselves together. If we can locate the very beginning and change it he'll probably marry the girl and live happily ever after."

"Of course—" The controller was confused. "I hadn't realized."

I said: "We've got to hunt back a lot more and locate this FitzJohn. He seems to be the key man in this puzzle."

And how we searched. Boys, it was like working a four-dimensional jig saw, the fourth dimension in this case being time. We located a hundred universities that maintained chairs and departments exclusively devoted to FitzJohn's mathematics and theories. We slipped back a hundred years toward the present and found only fifty and in those fifty were studying the men whose pupils were to fill the chairs a century later.

Another century back and there were only a dozen universities that followed the FitzJohn theories. They filled the scientific literature with trenchant, belligerent articles on FitzJohn, and fought gory battles with his opponents. How we went through the libraries. How many shoulders we looked over. How many pages of equations we snap-photographed from the whirling octahedron for future reference. And finally we worked our way back to Bowdoin College, where FitzJohn himself had taught, where he worked out his revolutionary theories and where he made his first converts. We were on the home stretch.

FitzJohn was a fascinating man. Medium height, medium color, medium build—his body had the rare trick of perfect balance. No matter what he was doing, standing, sitting, walking, he was always exquisitely poised. He was like the sculptor's idealization of the perfect man. FitzJohn never smiled. His face was cut and chiseled as though from a roughish sandstone; it had the noble dignity of an Egyptian carving. His voice was deep, unimpressive in quality, yet unforgettable for the queer, intense stresses it laid on his words. Altogether he was an enigmatic creature.

He was enigmatic for another reason, too, for although we traced his career at Bowdoin backward and forward for all its forty years, although we watched him teach the scores and scores of disciples who afterward went out into the scholastic world to take up the fight for him—we could never trace FitzJohn back into his youth. It was impossible to pick him up at any point earlier than his first appearance on the physics staff of the college. It seemed as though he were deliberately concealing his identity.

Yarr raged with impotent fury. He said: "It's absolutely aggravating. Here we follow the chain back to less than a half century from today and we're blocked—" He picked up a small desk phone and called upstairs to the data floors. "Hullo, Cullen? Get me all available date on the name FitzJohn. FitzJOHN. What's the matter, you deaf? F-I-T-Z...That's right. Be quick about it."

I said: "Seems as if FitzJohn didn't want people to know where he came from."

"Well," Yarr said pettishly, "that's impossible. I'll trace him backward, second by second, if I have to!"

I said: "That would take a little time, wouldn't it?"

"Yes."

"Maybe a couple of years?"

"What of it; You said we had a thousand."

"I didn't mean you to take me seriously, Dr. Yarr."

The small pneumatic at Yarr's desk whirred and clicked. Out popped a cartridge. Yarr opened it and withdrew a list of figures, and they were appalling. Something like two hundred thousand FitzJohns on the Earth alone. It would take a decade to check the entire series through the Integrator. Yarr threw the figures to the floor in disgust and swiveled around to face us.

"Well?" he asked.

I said: "Seems hopeless to check FitzJohn back second by second. At that rate we might just as well go through all the names on the list."

"What else is there to do?"

I said: "Look, the Prognosticator flirted twice with something interesting when we were conning FitzJohn's career. It was something mentioned all through the future, too."

"I don't recall—" the C-S began.

"It was a lecture, sir," I explained. "FitzJohn's first big lecture when he set out to refute criticism. I think we ought to pick that up and go through it with a fine comb. Something is bound to come out of it."

"Very well."

Images blurred across the spinning crystal as Yarr hunted for the scene. I caught fuzzy fragments of a demolished Manhattan City with giant crablike creatures mashing helpless humans, their scarlet chiton glittering. Then an even blurrier series of images. A city of a single stupendous building towering like Babel into the heavens; a catastrophic fire roaring along the Atlantic seaboard; then a sylvan civilization of odd, naked creatures flitting from one giant flower to another. But they were all so far off focus they made my eyes ache. The sound was even worse.

Groating leaned toward me and whispered: "Merely vague possibilities—"

I nodded and then riveted my attention to the crystal, for it held a clear scene. Before us lay an amphitheater. It was modeled on the ancient Greek form, a horseshoe of gleaming whitestone terraces descending to a small square white rostrum. Behind the rostrum and surrounding the uppermost tiers of seats was a simple colonnade. The lovely and yet noble dignity was impressive.

The controller said: "Hel-lo, I don't recognize this."

"Plans are in the architectural offices," Groating said. "It isn't due for construction for another thirty years. We intend placing it at the north end of Central Park—"

It was difficult to hear them. The room was filled with the bellow and roar of shouting from the amphitheater. It was packed from pit to gallery with quick-jerking figures. They climbed across the terraces;

they fought up and down the broad aisles; they stood on their seats and waved. Most of all they opened their mouths into gaping black blots and shouted. The hoarse sound rolled like slow, thunderous waves, and there was a faint rhythm struggling to emerge from the chaos.

A figure appeared from behind the columns, walked calmly up to the platform and began arranging cards on the small table. It was FitzJohn, icy and self-possessed, statuesque in his white tunic. He stood alongside the table, carefully sorting his notes, utterly oblivious of the redoubled roar that went up at his appearance. Out of that turmoil came the accented beats of a doggerel rhyme:

Neon
Crypton
Ammoniated
FitzJohn
Neon
Crypton
Ammoniated
FitzJohn

When he was finished, FitzJohn straightened and, resting the fingertips of his right hand lightly on top of the table, he gazed out at the rioting—unsmiling, motionless. The pandemonium was reaching unprecedented heights. As the chanting continued, costumed figures appeared on the terrace tops and began fighting down the aisles toward the platform. There were men wearing metal-tubed frameworks representing geometric figures. Cubes, spheres, rbomboids and tesseracts. They hopped and danced outlandishly.

Two young boys began unreeling a long streamer from a drum concealed behind the colonnade. It was of white silk and an endless equation was printed on it that read:

eia=1+ia-a2!+a3!-a4!....

and so on, yard after yard after yard. It didn't exactly make sense, but I understood it to be some kind of cutting reference to FitzJohn's equations.

There were hundreds of others, some surprising and many obscure. Lithe contortionists, made up to represent Möbius Strips, grasped ankles with their hands and went rolling down the aisles. A dozen girls appeared from nowhere, clad only in black net, representing giant Aleph-Nulls, and began an elaborate ballet. Great gas-filled balloons, shaped into weird topological manifolds were dragged in and bounced around.

It was utter insanity and utterly degrading to see how these mad college kids were turning FitzJolhn's lecture into a Mardi Gras. They were college kids, of course, crazy youngsters who probably couldn't explain the binomial theorem, but nevertheless were giving their own form of expression to their teachers' antagonism to FitzJohn. I thought vaguely of the days centuries back when a thousand Harvard undergraduates did a very similar thing when Oscar Wilde came to lecture. Undergraduates whose entire reading probably consisted of the *Police Gazette*.

And all the while they danced and shouted and screamed, FitzJohn stood motionless, fingertips just touching the table, waiting for them to finish. You began with an admiration for his composure. Then suddenly you realized what a breathtaking performance was going on. You glued your eyes to the motionless figure and waited for it to move—and it never did.

What?

You don't think that was so terrific, eh? Well, one of you get up and try it stand alongside a table and rest your fingertips lightly on the top—not firmly enough to bear the weight of your arm—but just enough to make contact. Maybe it sounds simple. Just go ahead and try it. I'll bet every credit I ever own no one of you can stand there without moving for sixty seconds. Any takers? I thought not. You begin to get the idea, eh?

They began to get the same idea in the amphitheater. At first the excitement died down out of shame. There's not much fun making a holy show of yourself if your audience doesn't react. They started it up again purely out of defiance, but it didn't last long. The chanting died away, the dancers stopped cavorting, and at last that entire audience of thousands stood silent, uneasily watching FitzJohn. He never moved a muscle.

After what seemed like hours of trying to outstare him, the kids suddenly gave in. Spatters of applause broke out across the terraces. The clapping was taken up and it rose to a thunder of beating palms. No one is as quick to appreciate a great performance as a youngster. These kids sat down in their seats and applauded like mad. FitzJohn never moved until the applause, too, had died down, then he picked up his card and, without preamble—as though nothing at all had happened—he began his lecture.

"Ladies and gentlemen, I have been accused of creating my theory of energy-dynamics and mathematics out of nothing—and my critics cry: 'From nothing comes nothing.' Let me remind you first that man does not create in the sense of inventing what never existed before. Man only discovers. The things we seem to invent, no matter how novel and revolutionary, we merely discover. They have been waiting for us all the time.

"Moreover, I was not the sole discoverer of this theory. No scientist is alone adventurer, striking out into new fields for himself. The way is always led by those who precede us, and we who seem to discover all, actually do no more than add our bit to an accumulated knowledge.

"To show you how small my own contribution was and how much I inherited from the past, let me tell you that the basic equation of my theory is not even my own. It was discovered some fifty years prior to this day—some ten years before I was born.

"For on the evening of February 9, 2909, in Central Park, on the very site of this amphitheater, my father, suddenly struck with an idea, mentioned an equation to my mother. That equation:

$$i=(b/a) P i e/m$$

was the inspiration for my own theory. So you can understand just how little I have contributed to the 'invention' of The Tension Energy-Dynamics Equations—"

FitzJohn glanced at the first card and went on: "Let us consider, now, the possible permutatons on the factor e/m..."

I yelled: "That's plenty. Cut!" and before the first word was out of my mouth the controller and the C-S were shouting, too. Yarr blanked out the crystal and brought up the lights. We were all on our feet, looking at each other excitedly. Yarr jumped up so fast his chair went over backward with a crash. We were in a fever because, boys, that day happened to be February 9, 2909, and we had just about two hours until evening.

The controller said: "Can we locate these Fitz-Johns?"

"In two hours? Don't be silly. We don't even know if they're named FitzJohn today."

"Why not?"

"They may have changed their name—it's getting to be a fad nowadays. The son may have changed his name as a part of that cover-up of his past. Heaven only knows why not—"

"But weve got to split them up—whoever they are."

The C-S said: "Take hold of yourself. How are we going to separate eleven million married people? Didn't you ever hear of Stability?"

"Can't we publish a warning and order everybody out of the park?"

"And let everybody know about the Prog Building?" I said. "You keep forgetting Stability."

"Stability be damned! We can't let them have that conversation—and if they do anyway, we can't let them have that boy!"

Groating was really angry. He said: "You'd better go home and read through the Credo. Even if it meant the salvation of the Universe I would not break up a marriage—nor would I harm the boy."

"Then what do we do?"

"Have patience. We'll think of something."

I said: "Excuse me, sir—I've got an idea."

"Forget ideas," the controller yelled, "we need action."

"This is action."

The C-S said: "Go ahead, Carmichael."

"Well, obviously the important thing is to keep all

married couples out of the north sector of Central Park tonight. Suppose we get a special detail of police together at once. Then we beat through the park and get everyone out. We can quarantine it—set up a close cordon around the park and guard it all night."

The controller yelled: "It may be one of the policemen."

"O.K., then we pick the unmarried ones. Furthermore, we give strict orders that all women are to stay away."

The C-S said: "It might work—it'll have to work. We can't let that conversation take place."

I said: "Excuse me, sir, do you happen to be married?"

He grinned: "My wife's in Washington. I'll tell her to stay there."

"And the controller, sir?"

The controller said: "She'll stay home. What about yourself?"

"Me? Strictly bachelor."

Groating laughed. "Unfortunate, but excellent for tonight. Come, let's hurry."

We took the pneumatic to headquarters and let me tell you, stuff began to fly, but high! Before we were there ten minutes, three companies were reported ready for duty. It seemed to satisfy the controller, but it didn't satisfy me. I said: "Three's not enough. Make it five."

"Five hundred men? You're mad."

I said: "I wish it could be five thousand. Look, we've knocked our brains out digging through a thousand years for this clue. Now that we've got it I don't want us to muff the chance."

The C-S said: "Make it five."

"But I don't think we've got that many unmarried men in the service."

"Then get all you can. Get enough so they can stand close together in the cordon—close enough so no one can wander through. Look—this isn't a case of us hunting down a crook who knows we're after him. We're trying to pick up a couple who are perfectly innocent—who may wander through the cordon. Were trying to prevent an accident, not a crime."

They got four hundred and ten all told. The whole little regiment was mustered before headquarters and the C-S made a beautifully concocted speech about a criminal and a crime that had to be prevented and hoopusgadoopus, I forget most of it. Naturally we couldn't let them know about the Prog Building any more than we could the citizens—and I suppose you understand why the secret had to be kept.

You don't, eh? Well, for the benefit of the hermit from the Moon I'll explain that aside from the important matter of Stability, there's the very human fact that the Prog would be besieged by a million people a day looking for fortune telling and hot tips on the races. Most important of all, there's the question of death. You can't let a man know when and how he's going to die. You just can't.

There wasn't any sense keeping the news from the papers because everyone around Central Park was going to know something was up. While the C-S was giving instructions, I slipped into a booth and asked for multidial. When most of the reporters' faces were on segments of the screen, I said: "Greetings, friend-lies!"

They all yelled indignantly because I'd been out of sight for three days.

I said: "No more ho-hum, lads. Carmichael sees all and tells all. Hot-foot it up to the north end of Central Park in an hour or so. Big stuff!"

The *Journal* said: "Take you three days to find that out?"

"Yep."

The *Post* said: "Can it, Carmichael. The last time you sent us north, the south end of the Battery collapsed."

"This is no gag. I'm giving it to you straight"

"Yeah?" The *Post* was belligerent. "I say Gowan!"

"Gowan yourself," the *Ledger* said. "This side of the opposition is credible."

"You mean gullible."

I said: "The word this time is sensational. Four hundred police on the march. Tramp-tramp-tramp—the beat of the drum-boots—et cetera. Better get moving if you want to tag along."

The News gave me a nasty smile and said: "Brother, for your sake it better be good—because I'm preparing a little sensation of my own to hand over."

I said: "Make it a quick double cross, Newsy. I'm in a hurry," and I clicked off. It's funny how sometimes you can't get along with the wrong people.

You know how fast night comes on in February. The blackness gathers in the sky like a bunched cape. Then someone lets it drop and it sinks down over you with swiftly spreading black folds. Those dusky folds were just spreading out toward the corners of the sky when we got to the park. The cops didn't even bother to park their helios. They vaulted out and left them blocking the streets. In less than half a minute, two hundred were beating through the park in a long line, driving everyone out. The rest were forming the skeleton of the cordon.

It took an hour to make sure the park was clear. Somehow, if you tell a hundred citizens to do something, there will always be twenty who'll fight you—not because they really object to doing what they're told, but just out of principle or curiosity or cantankerousness.

The all-clear came at six o'clock, and it was just in time because it was pitch dark. The controller, the C-S and myself stood before the high iron gates that open onto the path leading into the rock gardens. Where we stood we could see the jet masses of foliage standing crisp and still in the chill night. To either side of us stretched the long, wavering lines of police glow lamps. We could see the ring of bright dots drawn around the entire north end of the park like a necklace of glowing pearls.

The silence and the chill waiting was agonizing. Suddenly I said: "Excuse me, sir, but did you tell the police captain to O.K. the reporters?"

The C-S said: "I did, Carmichael—" and that was all. It wasn't so good because I'd hoped we'd have a little talk to ease the tension.

Again there was nothing but the cold night and the waiting. The stars overhead were like bits of radium and so beautiful you wished they were candy so you could eat them. I tried to imagine them slowly blotted out, and I couldn't. It's impossible to visualize the destruction of any lovely thing. Then I tried counting the police lamps around the park. I gave that up before I reached twenty.

At last I said: "Couldn't we go in and walk around a bit, sir?"

The C-S said: “I don’t see why not—”

So we started through the gate, but we hadn’t walked three steps into the park when there was a shout behind us and the sharp sounds of running feet.

But it was only old Yarr running up to us with a couple of cops following him. Yarr looked like a banshee with his coat flying and an enormous muffler streaming from his neck. He dressed real old-fashioned. He was all out of breath and just gasped while the C-S told the cops it was all right.

Yarr panted: “I…I—”

“Don’t worry, Dr. Yarr, everything is safe so far.”

Yarr took an enormous breath, held it for a moment and then let it out with a *woosh*. In natural tones he said: “I wanted to ask you if you’d hold on to the couple. I’d like to examine them for a check on the Prognosticator.”

Gently, the C-S explained: “We’re not trying to catch them, Dr. Yarr. We don’t know who they are and we may never know. All we want to do is to prevent this conversation.”

So we forgot about taking a walk through the gardens and there was more cold and more silence and more waiting. I clasped my hands together and I was so chilled and nervous it felt like I had ice water between the palms. A quick streak of red slanted up through the sky, the rocket discharges of the Lunar Transport, and ten seconds later I heard the *wham* of the take-off echoing from Governor’s Island and the follow-up drone. Only that drone kept on sounding long after it should have died away and it was too thin—too small—

I looked up, startled, and there was a helio making lazy circles over the center of the rock gardens. Its silhouette showed clearly against the stars and I could see the bright squares of its cabin windows. Suddenly I realized there was a stretch of lawn in the center of the gardens where a belie could land—where a couple could get out to stretch their legs and take an evening stroll.

I didn't want to act scared, so I just said: "I think we'd better go inside and get that helio out of there."

So we entered the gate and walked briskly toward the gardens, the two cops right at our heels. I managed to keep on walking for about ten steps and then I lost all control. I broke into a run and the others ran right behind me—the controller, the C-S, Yarr and the cops. We went pelting down the gravel path, circled a dry fountain and climbed a flight of steps three at a clip.

The helio was just landing when I got to the edge of the lawn. I yelled: "Keep off! Get out of here!" and started toward them across the frozen turf. My feet pounded, but not much louder than my heart. I guess the whole six of us must have sounded like a herd of buffalo. I was still fifty yards off when dark figures started climbing out of the cabin. I yelled: "Didn't you hear me? Get out of this park!"

And then the *Post* called: "That you, Carmichael? What goes on?"

Sure—it was the press.

So I stopped running and the others stopped and I turned to the C-S and said: "Sorry about the false alarm, sir. What shall I do with the reporters—have them fly out or can they stay? They think this is a crime hunt."

Groating was a little short of breath. He said: "Let them stay, Carmichael, they can help us look for Dr.

Yarr. He seems to have lost himself somewhere in the woods."

I said: "Yes, sir," and walked up to the helio.

The cabin door was open and warm amber light spilled out into the blackness. All the boys were out by this time, getting into their coveralls and stamping around and making the usual newspaper chatter. As I came up, the *Post* said: "We brung your opposition along, Carmichael—Hogan of the *Trib*."

The *News* said: "Now's as good a time as any for the wrasslin' match, eh? You been in training, Carmichael?" His voice had a nasty snigger to it and I thought: "Oh-ho, this Hogan probably scales two twenty and he'll mop me up, but very good—to the great satisfaction, no doubt, of my confrere from the *News*."

Only when they shoved Hogan forward, he wasn't so big, so I thought: "At a time like this—let's get it over with fast." I took a little spring through the dark and grabbed Hogan around the chest and dumped him to the ground.

I said: "O.K., opposition, that's—"

Suddenly I realized this Hogan had been soft—soft but firm, if you get me. I looked down at her, full of astonishment and she looked up at me, full of indignation, and the rest of the crowd roared with laughter.

I said: "I'll be a pie-eyed emu."

And then, my friends, six dozen catastrophes and cataclysms and volcanoes and hurricanes and everything else hit me. The C-S began shouting and then the controller and after a moment, the cops. Only by that time the four of them were on top of me and all over me, so to speak. Little Yarr came tearing up, screaming at Groating and Groating yelled back and

Yarr tried to bash my head in with his little fists. They yanked me to my feet and marched me off while the reporters and this Halley Hogan girl stared. I can't tell you much about what happened after that—the debating and the discussing and the interminable sound and fury, because most of the time I was busy being locked up. All I can tell you is that I was it. Me. I. I was the one man we were trying to stop. I—innocent me. I was X, the mad scientist and Y, the ruthless dictator and Z, the alien planet—all rolled into one. I was the one guy the Earth was looking to stop.

Sure—because you see if you twist "I'll be a pie-eyed emu" enough, you get FitzJohn's equation: i=(b/a) P ie/m..."

I don't know how my future son is going to figure I was talking mathematics. I guess it'll just be another one of those incidents that turn into legend and get pretty well changed in the process. I mean the way an infant will "goo" and by the time his pop gets finished telling about it it's become the Preamble to the Credo.

What?

No, I'm not married—yet. In fact, that's why I'm stationed up here editing a two-sheet weekly on this God-forsaken asteroid. Old Groating, he calls it protective promotion. Well, sure, it's a better job than reporting. The C-S said they wouldn't have broken up an existing marriage, but he was going to keep us apart until they can work something out on the Prognosticator.

No—I never saw her again after that time I dumped her on the turf, but, boys, I sure want to. I only got a quick look, but she reminded me of that Barbara

Leeds girl, six hundred years from now. That lovely kind with shingled hair and a clean-cut, face that looks fresh and wind-washed.

I keep thinking about her and I keep thinking how easy it would be to stow out of here on an Earth-bound freighter—change my name—get a different kind of job. To hell with Groating and to hell with Stability and to hell with a thousand years from now. I've to see her again—soon.

I keep thinking how I've got to see her again.

Astounding, May 1942

The Roller Coaster

I knifed her a little. When you cut across the ribs it hurts like sin but it isn't dangerous. The knife slash showed white, then red. She backed away from me in astonishment, more startled at the knife than the cut. You don't feel those cuts at first for quite a few minutes. That's the trouble with a knife. It numbs and the pain comes slow.

"Listen, lover," I said. (I'd forgotten her name.) "This is what I've got for you. Look at it." I waggled the knife. "Feel it." I slapped her across the face with the blade. She stumbled back against the couch, sat down and began to shake. This was what I was waiting for.

"Go ahead, you bitch. Answer me."

"Please, David," she muttered.

Dull. Not so good.

"I'm on my way out," I said. "You lousy hooker. You're like all the rest of these cheap dames."

"Please, David," she repeated in a low voice.

No action here. Give her one more try.

"Figuring you for two dollars a night, I'm into you for twenty." I took money from my pocket, stripped off the twenty in singles and handed it to her. She wouldn't touch it. She sat on the edge of the couch, blue-naked, streaming blood, not looking at me. Just dull. And mind you a girl that made love with her teeth. She used to scratch me with her nails like a cat. And now...

"Please, David," she said.

I tore up the money and threw it in her lap.

"Please, David," she said.

No tears. No screams. No action. She was impossible. I walked out.

The whole trouble with these neurotics is that you can't depend on them. You case them. You work them. You build to the climax. You trigger them off, but as often as not they dummy up like that girl. You just can't figure them.

I looked at my watch. The hand was on twelve. I decided to go up to Gandry's apartment. Freyda was working Gandry and would most likely be there setting him up for the climax. I needed advice from Freyda and I didn't have much time left.

I walked north on Sixth Avenue—no, The Avenue of the Americas; turned west on Fifty-fifth and went to the house across the street from Mecca Temple-no, The New York City Center. I took the elevator up to the PH floor and was just going to ring Gandry's bell when I smelled gas. I knelt down and sniffed at the edge of Gandry's door. It was coming from his apartment.

I knew better than to ring the bell. I got out my keys, touched them to the elevator call-button to dissipate any electrostatic charge on them, and got to work on Gandry's door. I barbered the lock in two or three minutes, opened the door and went in with my handkerchief over my nose. The place was pitch dark. I went straight to the kitchen and stumbled over a body lying on the floor with its head in the oven. I turned off the gas and opened the window. I ran into the living room and opened windows. I stuck my head out for a breath, then came back and finished airing the apartment.

I checked the body. It was Gandry all right. He was still alive. His big face was swollen and purple and his breathing sounded a little Cheynes-Stokesish to me. I went to the phone and dialed Freyda.

"Hello?"

"Freyda?"

"Yes?"

"Where are you? Why aren't you up here with Gandry?"

"Is that you, David?"

"Yes. I just broke in and found Gandry half dead. He's trying suicide."

"Oh, David!"

"Gas. He's reached the climax all by his lonely lone self. You been building him?"

"Of course, but I never thought he'd—"

"He'd try to sneak out on the pay-off like this? I've told you a hundred times, Freyda. You can't depend on potential suicides like Gandry. I showed you those trial scars on his wrist. His kind never give you any action. They—"

"Don't lecture me, David."

"Never mind. My girl was a bust, too. I thought she was the hot acid type. She turned out to be mush. I want to try that Bacon woman you mentioned. Would you recommend her?"

"Definitely."

"How can I find her?"

"Through her husband, Eddie Bacon."

"How can I find him?"

"Try Shawn's or Dugal's or Breen's or The Greek's.

But he's a talker, David, a time-waster; and you haven't much time left."

"Doesn't matter if his wife's worth it."

"She's worth it, David. I told you about the gun."

"Right. Now what about Gandry?"

"Oh, to hell with Gandry," she snapped, and hung up.

That was all right with me. It was about time Freyda got sense enough to lay off the psychotics. I hung up, closed all the windows, went back to the kitchen and turned on the gas. Gandry hadn't moved. I put out all the lights, went down the hall and let myself out.

I went looking for Eddie Bacon. I tried for him at Breen's, at Shawn's, at Dugal's. I got the break at The Greek's on East Fifty-second Street.

I asked the bartender: "Is Eddie Bacon here?"

"In the back."

I looked past the juke box. The back was crowded. "Which one is Eddie Bacon?"

He pointed to a small man alone at a table in the corner. I went back and sat down. "Hi, Eddie."

Bacon glanced up at me. He had a seamed, pouchy face, fair silky hair, bleak blue eyes. He wore a brown suit and a blue and white polka-dot tie. He caught me looking at the tie and said: "That's the tie I wear between wars. What are you drinking?"

"Scotch. Water. No ice."

"How English can you get?" He yelled: "Chris!"

I got my drink. "Where's Liz?"

"Who?"

"Your wife."

"I married eighteen feet of wives," he mumbled. "End to end. Six feet of each."

"Three fathoms of show girls," I said.
"Which were you referring to?"
"The third. The most recent. I hear she left you."
"They all left me."
"Where's Liz?"
"It happened like this," Bacon said in a sullen voice. "I can't figure it. Nobody can figure it. I took the kids to Coney Island..."
"Never mind the kids. Where's Liz?"
"I'm getting there," Bacon said irritably. "Coney Island's the damnest place. Everybody ought to try that trap once. It's primitive stuff. Basic entertainment. They scare hell out of your glands and you love it. Appeals to the ancient history in us. The Cro-Magnons and all that."
"The Cro-Magnons died out," I said. "You mean the Neanderthals."
"I mean prehistoric memories," Bacon went on. "They strap you into that roller coaster, they shove you off and you drop into a race with a dinosaur. He's chasing you and you're trying to keep it from ending in a dead heat. Basic. It appeals to the Stone Age flesh in all of us. That's why kids dig it. Every kid's a vestigial remnant from the Stone Age."
"Grown-ups too. What about Liz?"
"Chris!" Bacon yelled. Another round of drinks came. "Yeah...Liz," he said. "The girl made me forget there ever was a Liz. I met her staggering off the roller coaster. She was waiting. Waiting to pounce. The Black Widow Spider."
"Liz?"
"No. The little whore that wasn't there."
"Who?"

"Haven't you heard of Bacon's Missing Mistress? The Invisible Lay? Bacon's Thinking Affair?"

"No."

"Hell, where've you been? How Bacon rented an apartment for a dame that didn't exsist. They're still laughing it up. All except Liz. It's all over the business."

"I'm not in your business."

"No?" He took a long drink, put his glass down and glowered at the table like a kid trying to crack an algebra problem. "Her name was Freyda. F-R-E-Y-D-A. Like Freya, Goddess of Spring. Eternal youth. She was like a Botticelli virgin outside. She was a tiger inside."

"Freyda what?"

"I don't know. I never found out. Maybe she didn't have any last name because she was imaginary like they keep telling me." He took a deep breath. "I do a crime show on TV. I know every crook routine there is. That's my business—the thief business. But she pulled a new one. She picked me up by pretending she'd met the kids somewhere. Who can tell if a kid really knows someone or not? They're only half human anyway. I swallowed her routine. By the time I realized she was lying, I'd met her and I was dead. She had me on the hook."

"How do you mean?"

"A wife is a wife," Bacon said. "Three wives are just more of the same. But this was going to bed with a tiger." He smiled sourly. "Only it's all my imagination, they keep telling me. It's all inside my head. I never really killed her because she never really lived."

"You killed her? Freyda?"

"It was a war from the start," he said, "and it ended up with a killing. It wasn't love with her, it was war."

"This is all your imagination?"

"That's what the head-shrinkers tell me. I lost a week. Seven days. They tell me I rented an apartment all right, but I didn't put her in it because there never was any Freyda. We didn't tear each other apart because there was only me up there all the time. Alone. She wasn't a crazy, mauling bitch who used to say: "Sigma, darling..."

"Say what?"

"You heard me. 'Sigma, darling.' That's how she said good-by. 'Sigma, darling.' That's what she said on the last day. With a crazy glitter in her virgin eyes. Told me it was no good between us. That she'd phoned Liz and told her all about it and was walking out. 'Sigma, darling,' she said and started for the door."

"She told Liz? Told your wife?"

Bacon nodded. "I grabbed her and dragged her away from the door. I locked the door and phoned Liz. That tiger was tearing at me all the time. I got Liz on the horn and it was true. Liz was packing. I hung that phone up on that bitch's head. I was wild. I tore her clothes off. I dragged her into the bedroom and threw her down and choked her. Christ! How I strangled her..."

After a pause, I asked: "Liz?"

"They were pounding on the door outside," Bacon went on. "I knew she was dead. She had to be dead. I went and opened the door. There were six million cops and six million honest johns still squawking about the screaming. I thought to myself: 'Why, this is just like the show you do every week. Play it like the script.' I said to them: 'Come on in and join the murder.'" He broke off.

"Was she dead...Freyda?".

"There was no murder," he said slowly. "There was no Freyda. That apartment was ten floors up in the Kingston Hotel. There wasn't any fire escape. There was only the front door jammed with cops and squares. And there was no one in the apartment but a crazy guy—naked, sweating and swearing. Me."

"She was gone? Where? How? It doesn't make sense."

He shook his head and stared at the table in sullen confusion. After a long pause he continued. "There was nothing left from Freyda but a crazy souvenir. It must have busted off in the fight we had—the fight everybody said was imaginary. It was the dial of her watch."

"What was crazy about it?"

"It was numbered from two to twenty-four by twos. Two, four, six, eight, ten...and so on."

"Maybe it was a foreign watch. Europeans use the twenty-four hour system. I mean, noon is twelve and one o'clock is thirteen and—"

"Don't overwhelm me," Bacon interrupted wearily. "I was in the army. I know all about that. But I've never seen a clock-face like that used for it. No one has. It was out of this world. I mean that literally."

"Yes? How?"

"I met her again."

"Freyda?"

He nodded. "I met her in Coney Island again, hanging around the roller coaster. I was no fool. I went looking for her and I found her."

"Beat up?"

"Not a mark on her. Fresh and virgin all over again, though it was only a couple of weeks later. There she was, the Black Widow Spider, smelling the flies as they came staggering off the roller coaster. I went up behind her and I grabbed her. I pulled her around into the alley between the freak tents and I said: 'Let out one peep and you're dead for sure this time.'"

"Did she fight?"

"No," he said. "She was loving it. She looked like she just found a million bucks. That glitter in her eyes..."

"I don't understand."

"*I* did when I looked at her...When I looked into that virgin face, happy and smiling because I was screaming at her. I said: 'The cops swear nobody was in the apartment but me. The talk—doctors swear nobody was ever in the apartment but me. That put you into my imagination and *that* put *me* into the psycho ward for a week.' I said: 'But I know how you got out and I know where you went.'"

Bacon stopped and looked hard at me. I looked hard at him.

"How drunk are you?" he asked.

"Drunk enough to believe anything."

"She went out through time," Bacon said. "Understand? Through time. To another time. To the future. She melted and dissolved right out."

"What? Time travel? I'm not drunk enough to believe that."

"Time travel." He nodded. "That's why she had that watch—some kind of time machine. That's how she got herself patched up so fast. She could have stayed up there for a year and then come right back to Now or two weeks after Now. And that's why she said 'Sigma, darling.' It's how they talk up there."

"Now wait a minute, Eddie—"

"And that's why she wanted to come so close to getting herself killed."

"But that doesn't make sense. She wanted you to knock her around?"

"I told you. She loved it. They all love it. They come back here, the bastards, like we go to Coney Island. They don't come back to explore or study or any of that science-fiction crap. Our time's an amusement park for them, that's all. Like the roller coaster."

"How do you mean, the roller coaster?"

"Passion. Emotion. Screams and shrieks. Loving and hating and tearing and killing. That's their roller coaster. That's how they get their kicks. It must be forgotten up there in the future, like we've forgotten how it is to be chased by a dinosaur. So they come back here for it. This is the Stone Age for them."

"But—"

"All that stuff about the sudden up-swing in crime and violence and rape. It isn't us. We're no worse than we ever were. It's them. They came back here. They goad us. They needle us. They stick pins in us until we blow our tops and give their glands a roller coaster ride."

"And Liz?" I asked. "Did she believe this?"

He shook his head. "She never gave me a chance to tell her."

"I hear she kicked up quite a fuss."

"Yeah. Six beautiful feet of Irish rage. She took my gun off the study wall—the one I packed when I was with Patton. If it'd been loaded that wouldn't have been any make-believe murder."

"So I heard, Eddie. Where's Liz now?"

"Doing a burn in her old apartment."

"Where's that?"

"Ten—ten Park."

"Mrs. Elizabeth Bacon?"

"Not after Bacon got D.T.'s nailed to the name in the papers. She's using her maiden name."

"Oh, yes. Elizabeth Noyes, isn't it?"

"Noyes? Where the hell did you get that? No. Elizabeth Gorman." He yelled: "Chris! What is this—a desert?"

I looked at my time-meter. The hand was halfway from twelve to fourteen. That gave me eleven days more before I had to go back up. Just enough time to work Liz Gorman for some action. The gun sounded real promising. Freyda was right. It was a good lead. I got up from the table.

"Have to be going now, Eddie," I said. "Sigma, pal."

Fantastic, May-June 1953

The Lost Child

Chapman was in the cutlery department, buying a traveling manicuring set. I was trying to get hold of some of those new English razor blades everybody had been talking about. The last time we'd seen each other was on the Paramount lot. We said, "Hi, long time no see, thought you were still on the Coast, no we decided to come East," etc. Finally, I got up nerve and asked, "How's Elly?"

He shook his head. "Not so good. I'm taking her to Jamaica for a month. We're flying out this afternoon. Tell you what, come on up and have a drink while we finish packing."

I helped Chapman with his parcels, and we grabbed a cab. At his place on First Avenue, Chapman told the hackie to hold his flag and come up and give him a hand with the luggage. Ellen was waiting in the apartment. She was wearing a suede suit and a hat, and was pacing around a heap of bags and hat boxes. She looked thin and drawn, but pretty as ever.

"Honey," Chapman called, "I've got a cab waiting. Look who's having one for the road with us."

Ellen gave me her thin, nervous hand. To Chapman she said in agitated tones, "I thought you'd never get back. We'll miss the plane. We—"

"It's all right. Plenty of time. I got everything; the extra brushes, the manicuring set, two jars of vanishing cream, a—"

"I said cold cream!" Ellen cried.

"Cold cream, too. I got the tablets and the powders, the travelling clock, the atomizer, and I picked up your wristwatch with an extra—"

"Where's Davey?" Ellen cried.

I jumped. Chapman stared at her.

"Where's Davey?" she repeated. "Did you leave him in the cab?"

"Ain't nobody in my cab, lady," the hackie said.

She turned on Chapman. "Where is he? What've you done with him? Where's Davey?"

Chapman gulped and sat down heavily. "My God. I lost him."

"You lost Davey?"

"I was in a rush. I told him to wait for me, and I must have forgot. I left him."

"You forgot your boy? How could you? Where? Where?"

"All right, don't holler like that." Chapman reached for the telephone book. "He wanted to look at the electric trains and I told him to wait for me. Let's see, that's when I was picking up the manicuring set...I think...No..."

"For God's sake, don't you remember where you left him?"

"How can I remember with you shouting at me," Chapman shouted. "I was all over the goddam city running errands. It was in one of the department stores."

"Which? Which?"

"Shut up a minute. I'm trying to think."

The hackie cleared his throat. "Listen, I'm like double-parked down there and—"

"If there's a ticket, I'll pay it," Chapman snapped.

To Ellen he said, "Help me, Elly. It was on the second floor. Try to remember which store has its toy department on the second floor. I remember that. Davey wanted to—"

"Earl & Bishop. You left him in Earl & Bishop." Ellen turned wildly toward the door. "I've got to go down and get him. I should never have let you take him with you. Men!"

"Wait a minute," Chapman said. "You can't go after him. We haven't time. Well miss the plane."

"To hell with the plane!"

"Will you listen to me, Elly. I'll get it all straightened out, if you'll give me half a chance. Sit down!" He found a number in the phone book and dialed. While he waited for an answer he appealed to me with his eyes. I took Ellen to a chair and made her sit down. She was trembling.

"Hello," Chapman said on the phone. "Earl & Bishop? Give me the toy department, please; *anybody* in the toy department. No, I don't want Customer Relations, I want the goddam toy department. Fast!"

Ellen jumped up and reached for the phone. "Let me talk to them. You don't know how to handle people. You—"

Chapman fended her off and spoke again. "Hello? This is an emergency. My name's Chapman, and I'm afraid I left my son in your department about forty minutes ago. David Chapman. He's ten years old and he's wearing a grey suit and a grey school cap with a 'B' on it—"

"The blue suit! The blue suit!" Ellen screamed. "Don't you *want* them to find him?"

"He's wearing a blue suit," Chapman said, "and he was looking at the electric trains when—" He broke off and his face lit up. "You've got him? Sure? That's a relief."

"Is he all right?" Ellen demanded. "Is he frightened?"

"He's all right," Chapman whispered. On the phone he said, "Can you do me a great favor? We've got a plane to catch in twenty minutes. Can you send him over to the Airline Terminal with one of your people? I'll be happy to pay any charge. The BOAC desk. Yes. You will? That's fine. Thanks. Thanks a lot."

Chapman hung up and grinned. "Everything under control. They'll have Davey waiting for us."

"They won't." Ellen was sobbing. "They'll get the airline wrong. They'll—I should have gone myself. My God, a ten-year-old child. Lost! Alone!..."

"It's going to be all right, Elly."

"I hate you," she screamed.

"Aw, you say that to all the fellas," Chapman smiled.

They left. I went straight to the bar, opened the first decanter I could reach, and belted down all I could hold. The hackie began picking up the bags. He said, "How in hell could a guy lose his kid like that? An umbrella, okay; even a coat or a hat or maybe his wallet, but—"

"They lost him a year ago," I said. "The kid's been dead a year. God only knows what Chapman's going to do with her at the terminal. I'm not going to find out, and if you want my advice, you won't either."

Rogue, March 1964

I Will Never Celebrate New Year's Again

There's this producer named Tony who gives me a lot of work, so I have to remain on good terms with him. Part of the burden is going to the traditional New Year's party his wife, Gigi, throws. It's a drag; formal clothes, formal manners, champagne (which I hate) and talent being forced to entertain the guests.

So this New Year's I decided to miss it and stay home and have a quiet party. I invited my current girl, Martha, and another couple, bought a few magnums for them, and stocked up on whisky. I was preparing the ingredients for a light supper (Chicken á la King, salad, Petits Fours and coffee) when the phone rang. It was Gigi.

"What the hell is this I hear? You're running a rival brawl?"

"No, Gigi."

"That's the word going around."

"It's a lie. I'm staying home because I don't feel well, and I've asked a few people up."

"How many?"

"Three."

"Who?"

I told her.

"Damn you," she said, "I want them."

"All right, Gigi, you can have them. I'll cancel and go to bed."

So I did. But around ten o'clock, I began to get lonely and restless. I prowled around the house and finally noticed this invitation on the bulletin board. The Directors were giving a ball, and I'd been blackmailed into buying a ticket for twenty dollars which entitled me to a chance for a "door prize, supper, dancing until 3:00 A.M."

I arrived just as they were drawing for the door prizes. I've never won anything in my life, so I paid no attention. I sat down at the table with the guy who'd sold my ticket, and began drinking and chatting with him and the others.

The cases of wine, the cameras, the jewelry and the perfumes were distributed, and the M.C. finally called: "One Stutz Bearcat. Number 319." I ignored it, but my blackmailer exclaimed, "Hey! Isn't that the number of the ticket I sold you?" I looked at my stub. It was 319.

I stepped up on the dance floor where this lovely little Bearcat painted Fire Engine Red was displayed. It was big enough to hold a kid, and had a battery motor. I was in a daze; it looked as though '63 was promising to break my customary run of bad luck. I presented my stub, got a nice hand, and was about to claim my prize when a frantic character appeared, waving a stub. "I'm 319," he said.

We compared stubs. We both had 319; there'd been some kind of goof at the printer's. I was resigned.

"Have you got any kids?" I asked.

"Three."

"I haven't got any. Take the car."

My host tried to cheer me up and took me to a Park Avenue party in a giant duplex apartment featuring a sweeping staircase. I tried to hook up with a woman and was doing all right with a Hungarian girl when the dance band broke into Black & Tan, the classic stripper's number. My Hungarian began to strip.

She did a professional parade, shedding gloves, jewelry and clothes while the guests howled. Then she started up the stairs, discarding lingerie. She reached the head of the stairs, dropped the ultimate essential, turned the corner and disappeared. There was a fanfare, and the band began a Conga. A Conga line of men formed and went up the stairs after the Hungarian. I left.

I went up to Small's in Harlem, couldn't enjoy myself there, but ran into a couple of young writers who dragged me over to Morningside Heights to a fraternity patty. There was a stench of beer, the floor was sticky, a four-piece band whammed and twanged, and about fifty couples were twisting. Now I not only felt lonely; I felt old.

Suddenly there was a hissing WHOOSH! and a cloud of snow appeared in the room. Some tweed had pulled a CO_2 fire extinguisher off the wall and was running around, shooting up the girls' skirts. They squealed and scattered, and one of them took refuge behind me. On closer inspection, she proved to be much older than the type you usually find at a fraternity dance.

She was about 30, with acid-red hair cut short, a sinewy, active body, and nervous hands. She wore a sort of Goldwyn Follies spangled dress, and gold pumps with bows. She was alive and attractive, but vulgar and common, and her name turned out to he...God save the mark...Torchy.

"You look like a gent," Torchy said. "Will you, for Christ's sake, get me out of here. This is kid stuff."

"Where's your date?"

"Passed out," she muttered.

We left, got a cab, and drove down to 50th and Madison Avenue, where I live. Torchy sat in her corner and said nothing. I was tired, unhappy, and not interested; but I had to go through the motions of the gent. I offered her a choice of going in the cab to wherever she was going, or coming up to my place for a drink.

"Boy, do I need a drink," she said. "Okay, but no funny business."

"At four in the morning?" I said wearily. "Who do you think I am, Paul Bunyan? So, come on; I'm freezing."

We went up to my place and I started a fire in the fireplace.

"What's that? Kennel coal?" Torchy asked. She wandered around the living room, staring at my books, pictures, and records. "Gee," she said. "I never been in a place like this before. You got class. What's it like to have class?"

"I wouldn't know, Torchy."

"Says you. This place is simply elegant. What's in there?"

"The kitchen."

She explored. "Je-zus! You cook, huh? What?"

"That was going to be Chicken á la King."

"You cook French. Wow! What's in there?"

"My workshop."

She investigated. "Christ! More books. You must have thousands. What are you, a publisher?"

"A writer."

"Yeah, it figures."

We went back to the living room and enjoyed the fire while we had drinks. We talked. Torchy was so naturally giving and receptive that she warmed me more than the fire. She wanted to know all about the books and the records and the pictures and what I wrote and had I traveled and did I have girls and what were they like and was I as nice to them as I was to her. After an hour of this, she began to make me feel ashamed and ungrateful.

Suddenly she said, "I got to call Patchogue."

"Patchogue?"

"Yeah. Patchogue, Long Island. It's where I live. I got to tell them I ain't coming home tonight."

"The phone's out of order," I told her.

"Go on," she grinned. She came to me and ran her hand through my hair. "What kind of fink you think I am? I wouldn't hang a long distance call on you."

"The phone's in the bedroom," I said faintly.

"Yeah, I know. Alongside the bed." She went to the closet for her coat. "I'll call from that hotel across the street. They must have public phones."

"Don't be a fool, Torchy. Phone from here."

"And louse up the best time I ever had in my life? Nothing doing. I'm not grabby. I'll be right back."

"Wait a minute. I'll go with you."

"Stay here and make the chicken. I told you, I'm hungry."

"You can't go out in that light coat. Wear mine."

I threw my heavy coat over her shoulders. She turned and gave me a feathery kiss. "This is the best New Year's I ever had," she whispered.

"I'm beginning to think so, too, Torchy."

"You're an ace," she said, and scampered out.

I went into the kitchen and started the Sauce Bechamel for the chicken. I'd finished slicing the pimiento into strips and was getting the green peas out of the freezer when there was a heavy knock on the door.

"It's open," I yelled.

The knock repeated. I went to the door and opened it. A cop stood there.

"You Bester?" he asked.

"In the flesh. What's the matter, hi-fi too loud?"

"You better come downstairs," he said. "There's a dame in your coat..."

"That's all right, I loaned it to her."

"There's been an accident," he said. "Come on."

I followed him down to Madison Avenue, completely bewildered. It was getting light outside. On the bleak street there was a cab skewed against the curb before the hotel. A little crowd of spectators was clustered around a crumpled figure in the gutter. A livid pool of blood was spreading slowly from her body, staining its way into my New Year.

Rogue, February 1963

Out of This World

I'm telling this just the way it happened because I share a vice with all men. Although I'm happily married and still in love with my wife, I keep falling in love with transient women. I stop for a red light, glance at a girl in the cab alongside, and fall desperately in love with her. I go up in an elevator and am captivated by a girl in the car with a sheaf of stencils in her hand. When she gets off at the tenth floor, she takes my heart with her. I remember once falling in love with a model in the crosstown bus. She was carrying a letter to mail and I tried to read the return address and memorize it.

Wrong numbers are always the strongest temptation. The phone rings, I pick it up, a girl says, "May I talk to David, please?" There's no David in our house and I know it's a strange voice, but thrilling and tempting. In two seconds I've woven a fantasy of dating this stranger, meeting her, having an affair with her, breaking up my home, running off to Capri and living in glorious sin. Then I say, "What number are you calling, please?" And after I hang up I can hardly look at my wife, I feel so guilty.

So when this call came to my office at 509 Madison, I fell into the same old trap. Both my secretary and my bookkeeper were out to lunch, so I took the call directly at my desk. An exciting voice began talking fifteen to the dozen.

"Hello, Janet! I got the job, darling. They've got a

lovely office just around the corner from the old Tiffany building on Fifth Avenue and my hours are nine to four. I've got a desk and a cubbyhole and a window a to myself, and I—"

"I'm sorry," I said, after I finished my fantasy. "What number are you calling?"

"My goodness! I'm certainly not calling you."

"I'm afraid not."

"I'm awfully sorry I bothered you."

"Not at all. Congratulations on the new job."

She laughed. "Thank you very much."

We hung up. She sounded so enchanting that I decided to make it Tahiti instead of Capri. Then the phone rang again. It was the same voice.

"Janet, darling, this is Patsy. I just had the most awful thing happen. I called you and got the wrong number and I was jabbering away when suddenly the most romantic voice said—"

"Thank you, Patsy. You've got the wrong number again."

"Oh, goodness! You again?"

"Uh huh."

"This isn't Prescott 9-3232?"

"Not even faintly. This is Plaza 6-5000."

"I don't see how I could have dialed that. I must be extra stupid today."

"Maybe just extra excited."

"Please excuse me."

"Not at all," I said. "I think you've got a romantic voice too, Patsy."

We hung up and I went out for lunch, memorizing Prescott 9-3232....

I'd dial and ask for Janet and tell her—What? I didn't know. I knew I'd never do it; but there was that dreamy glow that lasted until I came back to the office to face the afternoon's problems. Then I shook it off and returned to reality.

But I was cheating, because when I went home that night, I didn't tell my wife about it. She used to work for me before we got married and still takes a lively interest in everything that goes on in my office. We spend a pleasant hour or so every evening discussing and dissecting the day I've had. We did it this night, but I withheld Patsy's call. I felt guilty.

I was so guilty that I went down to the office extra early next morning, trying to placate my conscience with extra work. Neither of my girls was in yet, so the incoming line was open direct to my desk. Around eight-thirty my phone rang and I picked it up.

"Plaza 6-5000," I said.

There was dead air on the other end, which infuriated me. I hate the kind of switchboard girl who rings you and then lets you hang while she's placing other calls.

"Listen, monster!" I said. "I hope you can hear me. For pity's sake, don't call unless you're ready to put me through to whoever's calling. What am I? A lackey? Go to hell!"

Just as I was about to bang the phone down, a small voice said, "Excuse me."

"What? Patsy? Is that you again?"

"Yes," she said.

My heart flipped because I knew—I knew this couldn't be an accident. She'd memorized my number. She wanted to speak to me again.

"Good morning, Patsy," I said.

"My, you have a dreadful temper."

"I'm afraid I was rude to you."

"No. It's my fault. I shouldn't be bothering you like this. But when I call Jan, I keep getting your number. Our wires must be crossed somewhere."

"Oh. I'm disappointed. I'd hoped you were calling me to listen to my romantic voice."

She laughed. "It isn't *that* romantic."

"That's because I was rude. I'm willing to make it up to you. I'll buy you lunch today."

"No, thank you."

"When do you start the new job?"

"This morning. Good-bye."

"Lots of luck. Call this afternoon and tell me about it."

I hung up and asked myself if I hadn't come to the office early more in hopes of receiving this call than out of the desire to do extra work. I couldn't defend myself from my conscience. When you're standing on untenable ground, everything you do is suspect and defenseless. I was angry with myself and gave my girls a tough morning.

When I returned from lunch, I asked my secretary if there'd been any calls while I was out.

"Just the district phone supervisor," she said. "They're having some trouble with the lines."

I thought, "Then it was an accident this morning. Patsy didn't want to speak to me again."

At four o'clock I let both my girls go for the day to make up to them for my being obnoxious in the morning—at least that's what I kept telling myself. I loafed around the office from four to five-thirty, waiting for Patsy to call, building fantasies until I was ashamed of myself.

I had a drink from the last bottle left over from the Christmas office party, locked up and started for home. Just as I pressed the button for the elevator, I heard the phone ringing in my office. I tore back to the door, unlocked it (I still had the key in my hand) and got to the phone—feeling like a damned fool. I tried to cover with a joke.

"Prescott 9-3232," I said, half out of breath.

"Sorry," my wife said. "I've got the wrong number."

I had to let her hang up. I couldn't explain. I waited for her to call again, trying to figure what kind of voice to use so she'd know it was me and still not be able to match it with what she'd heard before. I decided to use the off-phone technique, so when it rang again I picked it up, held it a few feet away from my mouth and called crisp instructions to the empty office. Then I put my mouth close and spoke.

"Hello?"

"My, you sound distinguished. Like a general."

"Patsy?" My heart went bump.

"I'm afraid so."

"Are you calling me or Jan?"

"Janet, of course. These lines are a nuisance, aren't they? We've reported them to the company."

"I know. How'd the new job go today?"

"All right...I guess. There's an office manager who barks just like you. He scares me."

"I'll give you some advice, Patsy. Don't be scared. When a man yells like that, it's usually to cover his own guilty conscience."

"I don't understand."

"Well...maybe he's holding down a job that's too big for him and he knows it. So he tries to cover up by playing big shot."

"Oh, I don't think that could be it."

"Or maybe he's attracted to you and he's afraid

that's going to interfere with efficiency. So he yells at you to keep himself from being too attentive."

"It couldn't be that either."

"Why? Aren't you attractive?"

"I'm not the one to ask."

"You have a wonderful voice."

"Thank you, sir."

"Patsy," I said. "I've much wise and seasoned advice to give you. It's obvious we've been fated by Alexander Graham Bell to meet, so who are we to buck fate? Let's have lunch together tomorrow."

"Oh I'm afraid I couldn't—"

"Do you have lunch with Janet?"

"Yes."

"Then why not with me? Here I am, doing half Jan's work—taking calls for her—and what do I get out of it? A complaint from the phone supervisor. Is this justice, Patsy? We'll have half a lunch together. You can wrap up the other half and take it to Jan."

She laughed. It was a delicious laugh. "You are a charmer, aren't you? What's your name?"

"Howard."

"Howard what?"

"Patsy what?"

"You go first."

"I'm taking no chances. Either I tell you at lunch or I remain anonymous."

"All right," she said. "My hour's one to two. Where shall we meet?"

"Rockefeller Plaza. Third flagpole from the left."

"How glamorous."

"Third flagpole from the left. Got it?"

"Yes."

"One o'clock tomorrow?"

"One o'clock," Patsy repeated.

"You'll recognize me by the bone stuck through my nose. I have no last name. I'm an aborigine."

We laughed and hung up. I rushed out of the office to avoid my wife's call. I wasn't an honest man at home that night, but I was excited. I could hardly sleep. One o'clock next afternoon I was waiting in front of the third flagpole from the left at Rockefeller Plaza, rehearsing bright dialogue and trying to look my best. I knew Patsy'd probably look me over before she decided to reveal herself.

I kept watching the girls as they passed, trying to guess which she'd be. The loveliest women in the world can be found by the hundreds in Rockefeller Plaza during lunch hour. I had high hopes. I waited and rehearsed. She never showed up. At half past one I realized that.

I'd failed to pass the examination. She'd looked me over and decided to forget the whole thing. I was never so humiliated and angry in my life.

My bookkeeper quit that afternoon, and deep in my heart I couldn't blame her. No self-respecting girl could have endured me. I had to stay late, hassling with the employment agency for a new girl. Just before six, my phone rang. It was Patsy.

"Are you calling me or Jan?" I asked angrily.

"I'm calling you," she said, just as angrily.

"Plaza 6-5000?"

"No. There's no such number and you know it. You're a cheat. I have to call Jan and hope the crossed wires get me through to you."

"What d'you mean there's no such number?"

"I don't know what kind of sense of humor you think you have, Mr. Aborigine, but I know you played a filthy trick on me today...keeping me waiting for an hour and never showing up. You ought to be ashamed of yourself."

"You waited for an hour? That's a lie. You never were there."

"I was there and you stood me up."

"Patsy, that's impossible. I waited for you until half past one. When did you get there?"

"One o'clock sharp."

"Then there's been an awful mistake. Are you sure you had it right? Third flagpole from the left?"

"Yes. Third flagpole from the left."

"We must have got our flagpoles mixed. I can't tell you how badly I feel about this."

"I don't believe you."

"What can I say? I thought you stood me up. I was so angry this afternoon that my bookkeeper quit on me. You aren't a bookkeeper by any chance?"

"No. And I'm not looking for a job."

"Patsy, we'll have lunch tomorrow, and this time we'll meet where we can't miss each other."

"I don't know if I want to."

"Please. I want to settle this business about there being no Plaza 6-5000. That doesn't make sense."

"There's no such number."

"Then what's this I'm using? A string telephone?"

She laughed.

"What's your number, Patsy?"

"Oh, no. It's like the last names. I won't give you mine if I don't know yours."

"But you know mine."

"No I don't. I tried to call you this afternoon and the operator said there was no such exchange. She—"

"She's crazy. We'll discuss it tomorrow. One o'clock again?"

"But not in front of any flagpole."

"All right. You told Jan you're around the comer from the old Tiffany building?"

"That's right."

"On Fifth Avenue?"

"Yes."

"I'll be on that corner at one sharp."

"You'd better be."

"Patsy..."

"Yes, Howard?"

"You sound even more wonderful when you're angry."

It rained torrents next day. I got to the southeast corner of Thirty-seventh and Fifth, where the old Tiffany building stands, and I waited in the rain from twelve-fifty to one-forty. Patsy never showed up. I couldn't believe it. I couldn't believe anyone could be mean enough to play a trick like that. Then I remembered her lovely voice and enchanting manner and I hoped the rain had kept her home that day. I hoped she'd called to warn me after I left.

I took a cab back to my office and asked if there were any phone messages. There were none. I was so disgusted and disappointed that I went down to the Madison Avenue Hotel bar and had a few drinks to ward off the chill and the wet. I stayed there, drinking and dreaming, calling my office every hour just to keep in touch. Once I had a brainstorm and dialed Prescott 9-3232 to speak to Janet. The operator cut into the line.

"What number are you calling, please?"

"Prescott 9-3232."

"I'm sorry. There is no such exchange listed. Will you consult your directory again, please?"

So that was that. I hung up, had a few more drinks, saw that it was five-thirty and decided to check in for the last time and go home. I dialed my office number. There was a click and a buzz and then Patsy answered the phone. I couldn't mistake her voice.

"Patsy!"

"Who's this?"

"Howard. What the devil are you doing in my office?"

"I'm home. How did you find my number?"

"I didn't. I was calling my shop and got you instead. The crossed wires must work both ways."

"I don't want to talk to you."

"You ought to be ashamed to talk to me."

"What's that supposed to mean?"

"Listen, Patsy, it was a dirty trick standing me up like that. If you wanted revenge you could have—"

"I did not stand you up. You stood me up."

"Oh, for God's sake, don't start that. If you're not interested in me, have the decency to say so. I got soaked standing on that corner. I'm still wet."

"Soaked? How do you mean?"

"In the rain!" I shouted. "How else could I mean?"

"What rain?" Patsy asked in surprise.

"Don't dummy up. It's been pouring all day. It's still pouring."

"I think you're crazy," she said in a hushed voice. "There's been nothing but bright sunshine all day."

"Here in town?"

"Of course."

"Outside your office?"

"Certainly."

"Bright sunshine all day at Thirty-seventh and Fifth?"

"Why Thirty-seventh and Fifth?"

"Because that's where the old Tiffany building is," I said in exasperation. "You're around the corner from it."

"You're frightening me," she whispered. "I-I think I'd better hang up now."

"Why? What's wrong now?"

"The old Tiffany building is at Fifty-seventh and Fifth."

"No, idiot! That's the new one."

"It's the old one. You know they had to move, back in 1945."

"Move?"

"Yes. They couldn't rebuild on account of the radiation."

"What radiation? What are you—"

"From the bomb crater."

A chill ran down my spine, and it wasn't from the damp and the cold. "Patsy," I said slowly. "This is serious, dear. I think maybe something more than telephone wires have been crossed. What's your phone exchange? Never mind the number. Just tell me your exchange."

"America 5."

I looked at the list of exchange names before me in the booth: ACademy 2, ADirondack 4, ALgonquin 4, ALgonquin 5, ATwater 9.... There wasn't any AMerica 5.

"Here in Manhattan?"

"Of course, here in Manhattan. Where else?"

"The Bronx," I answered. "Or Brooklyn or Queens."

"Would I be living in occupation camps?"

I took a breath. "Patsy, dear, what's your last name? I think we'd better be honest about this because I think we're involved in something fantastic. I'm Howard Campbell."

She gasped.

"What's your last name, Patsy?"

"Shimabara," she said.

"You're Japanese?"

"Yes. You're Yank?"

"Yes. Were you born here, Patsy?"

"No. I came over in 1945—with the occupation unit."

"I see. We lost the war—where you are."

"Of course. That's history. But, Howard, I'm here. I'm here in New York. It's 1954. It—"

"But the sun is shining and you dropped the A-bomb on us and licked us and you're occupying America." I began to laugh hysterically. "We're on different time tracks, Patsy. Your history isn't my history. We're in alternate worlds."

"I don't understand you, Howard."

"Don't you see? Each time the world reaches a crossroad, it goes both ways. And both exist. Like if you wonder what would have happened if Columbus hadn't discovered America. Well, somewhere there's a world where he didn't. It's an alternate world, parallel to us. There must be thousands of parallel worlds in existence, side by side, and you're in another one from me. You're out of my world, Patsy. The telephone lines between our alternate worlds have gotten crossed. I'm trying to date a girl who doesn't exist—for me."

"But, Howard..."

"We're parallel but different, here and there—the

phone exchanges, the weather, the war.... We've both got a Rockefeller Plaza and we were both standing there yesterday at one o'clock, but so far apart, Patsy darling, so impossibly far apart...."

At that moment the operator opened the line and said, "Your time is up, sir. Five cents for the next five minutes, please."

I felt in my pocket for change. "Patsy, are you still there?"

"Yes, Howard."

"I haven't any change on me. Tell the operator to reverse the charge. We've got to keep this line open. We may never get through again."

"But how can she—"

"Don't you understand? We're repairing the line here, and you're repairing it there, and sooner or later it'll be fixed. We'll be cut off forever. Tell her to reverse the charges, Patsy."

"I'm sorry, sir," the operator said. "We cannot reverse the charges. You may hang up and call again."

"Patsy, keep calling me, will you? Call Janet. I'll go back to my office and wait."

"Your time is up, sir."

"Patsy, what do you look like? Tell me. Quickly, darling. I—"

The phone went dead, and my dime rattled down into the coin box.

I went back to my office and waited until eight o'clock. She didn't phone or she couldn't phone. I kept an open line direct to my desk for a week and answered every incoming call myself. She never got through to me again. Somewhere, here or there, they had repaired that crossed wire.

I never forgot Patsy. I never got over the memory

of her enchanting voice. I couldn't tell anyone about her. I wouldn't be telling you now, only I've lost my heart to a girl with lovely legs ice skating round and round while the music plays in Rockefeller Plaza.

The Dark Side of the Earth, 1964

The Animal Fair

I went to the animal fair.
The birds and the beasts were there.
By the light of the moon,
The big baboon,
Was combing his golden hair.
The monkey he got drunk,
And climbed up the elephant's trunk.
The elephant sneezed
And fell on his knees,
But what become of the monk?

Traditional nursery song

There is a high hill in Bucks County, Pennsylvania, that is called Red Hill because it is formed of red shale. There is an abandoned farm on top of the hill which is called Red Hill farm. It was deserted many years ago when the children of farmers decided that there was more excitement and entertainment in the cities.

Red Hill farm has an old stone house with thick walls, oaken floors and the enormous fireplaces in which the cooking was done two hundred years ago. There is a slate-roofed smokehouse behind it in which hams should be hung. There is a small red barn cluttered with forgotten things like children's sleighs and pieces of horses' harness, and there is a big red barn which is the Big Red Schoolhouse.

Here the ladies and gentlemen who possess the farm in fact, if not in fee simple absolute, hold meetings by day and night to discuss problems of portent and to educate their children. But you must understand that they speak the language of creatures which few humans can hear or understand. Most of us learned it when we were young but lost it as it was replaced by human speech. A rare few can still speak both, and this is our story.

The meetings in the Big Red Schoolhouse are governed by the Chairman, a ring-necked cock pheasant who is all pomp and strut. He is secretly referred to as "The Sex Maniac" because he maintains a harem of five hens. The Professor is a white rat who escaped from the Rutgers University laboratories after three years of intensive education. He believes that he is qualified for a Ph.D. and is considering doing his dissertation "On The Relevance of Hot Water to Science."

George Washington Woodchuck is the peerless surveyor of Red Hill farm. He knows every inch of its forty acres and is the arbiter of all territorial disputes. The Senior Rabbit, who is occasionally called "The Scoutmaster," is the mentor of morality and much alarmed by the freedom and excesses of the Red Hill young. "I will not," he says, "permit Red Hill to become another Woodstock." He also deplores modern music.

There are many other members of the Big Red Schoolhouse—deer, who have darling manners, but are really awfully dumb. The intellectuals call them "The Debutantes." Moses Mole, who is virtually blind, as all moles are, is pestering the Professor to teach him astronomy. "But how can I teach you astronomy when you can't even see the stars?" "I don't want to be an observing astronomer. I want to be a mathematical astronomer like Einstein." It looks as though the Professor will have to introduce a course in the New Math.

There are a Cardinal and a Brown Thrasher who have mean tempers and are always picking fights. The Cardinal is called "His Eminence," of course, and the Brown Thrasher is nicknamed "Jack Johnson." It's true that Jack Johnson has a rotten disposition, but he sings beautifully and conducts regular vocal classes. On the other hand the voice of His Eminence can only be called painful.

The Chaldean Chicken is a runaway from a hatchery down the road, and she's a real mixed-up girl. She's a White Leghorn and had the misfortune to discover that Leghorn is a place in Italy. Consequently she speaks a gibberish which she believes is fluent Italian. "*Ah, caro mio, come est? Benny* I hope. *Grazie*. And with *meeyo* is *benny* too." She's called the Chaldean because she's spaced out on astrology, which infuriates the Professor. "Ah, you will never be *sympathetico* with him. You are Gasitorius and he is Zapricorn."

The cleverest, members of the Big Red Schoolhouse are crows, who are witty and and sound like an night party at a restaurant. Unfortunately, they are not respected by the Establishment, which regards them as "mere mummers who are likely to try to borrow something (never returned) and who turn serious discussions into a minstrel show. It must be admitted that when two crows get together they begin to behave like end men in search of an interlocutor, convulsing themselves with ancient gags.

"Which do you like, the old writers or the new writers?"

"My brother's got that."

"Got what?"

"Neuritis."

Caw! Caw! Caw!

"How many children do you have?

"I have five, thank you."

"Don't thank me, friend. Don't thank me."

Caw! Caw! Caw!

It was on an evening in May when the light is long and the shadows even longer that the Chairman entered the Big Red Schoolhouse attended by his harem. Everyone was there and deeply involved in a discussion of a proposal by the Professor. It was that they should establish an Underground Railroad, something like the Abolitionists, to enable other escapees to reach freedom. Moe Mole, who is rather literal-minded, was pointing out that it would be extremely difficult for him to dig tunnels big enough to accommodate railroad cars. "I saw one once. They're as big as houses." Jack Johnson was needling His Eminence to give flying lessons to all refugees, regardless of race, creed or species. Two black crows were cawing it up. In short, it was a typical Red Barn gathering.

"I call this meeting to order with important news," the Chairman said. "I say, Kaff Kaff, with vital intelligence. Flora, do sit down. Oh, sorry Frances, do sit—Felicia? Oh, Phyllis. Yes. Quite. Kaff Kaff. Do sit down, Phyllis. This morning a Cadillac drove up the lane leading to Red Hill farm—"

"Two hundred and thirty-five-point-nine yards," Geo. W. Woodchuck said, "bearing east-southeast. Latitude—"

"Yes, yes, my dear George. It was followed by a Volvo containing—"

"Which do you like, a Cadillac or a Volvo?"

"My father's got that."

"Got what?"

"A cadillac condition."

Caw! Caw! Caw!

"Gentlemen! Gentlemen! Please! This is serious. The Cadillac contained a real estate agent. The foreign vehicle contained a man, a woman and an extremely small child, sex as yet undetermined. It is my judgment, Kaff Kaff, I say, my measured opinion that our farm is being shown for sale."

"May is a bad month for buying," the Chaldean Chicken declared. "*Importanto* decisions should be reservato for the Sign of Jemimah."

"The word is Gemini," the Professor shouted. "The least you can do is get your superstitions straight."

"You are a male chauvinist rat," Miss Leghorn retorted, "And I am going to form a Chickens' Lib."

"Yes, yes, my dear. And I will be the first to contribute to your worthy cause. Never mind that look, Frances—Oh, Fifi? There is no need for a Pheasants' Lib movement. You are already liberated. Kaff Kaff. Now, ladies and gentlemen, we are involved in, I say, we are committed to a struggle for the preservation of our property. We must not permit any strangers (I might almost call them squatters) to invade us. We must make the land as unattractive as possible, and this will demand sacrifices."

"Name one that you'll make," the Professor said.

"I will name several. Ladies," here the Chairman addressed himself to the does. "Please do not permit yourselves to be seen. The human animal is always enchanted by your beauty and glamor."

The Debutantes giggled prettily.

"My dear Scoutmaster," the Chairman went on to the Senior Rabbit, "the same holds true for yourself and your entire troop. Please disappear until further notice. No more jamborees on the lawns. I, of course, will make a similar sacrifice. I shall conceal my blazing magnificence. Kaff Kaff."

Moe Mole said, "I'm always concealed."

"To be sure. To be sure. But Moses, would it be possible for you to tunnel all the grounds, raising those unsightly mounds? You will have to double your efforts, but it would be most helpful."

"I'll get the brothers from Moles Anonymous to lend a hand."

"Splendid, splendid. Now, George W., I ask this as a special favor. Would you be kind enough to give up your invaluable surveying for the nonce, I say, Kaff Kaff, temporarily, and eat the daffodils?"

"I hate the taste."

"I don't blame him," the Senior Rabbit said. "They're disgusting."

"But so appealing visually to the human eye. You don't have to actually devour them, George, just cut them down and chew a little. I will do the same for the lilacs, under cover of darkness, of course, and my dear ladies will assist."

Jack Johnson said, "What about me and His Immanence?"

"His Eminence will remain out of sight but will sing. You will remain in sight but will not sing."

"I'm as pretty as that Jesuit."

"Yeah? You want to prove it? Step outside."

"Gentlemen. Gentlemen. Please! We are concerting an all-out attack. Now our members of Actors Equity will continue their customary depredations, concentrating on the apple, pear, and peach trees."

"We ought to eat the corn, too."

"I'm not going to eat you, friend."

Caw! Caw! Caw!

"Miss Leghorn will remain out of sight. There is nothing more appealing to the human animal than a chicken meditating on a summer day. Oh, and Jack, dear boy, will you try to dispossess the Mockingbird? There is nothing more appealing than a mockingbird serenading on a summer night."

"Why don't he ever join up?"

"I have solicited him many times, and he has always refused. I'm, afraid he'll refuse to be drafted now."

"I'll chase him all the way to Canada."

"I shall continue to supervise the campaign from my command post in Freda's—ah, Francie's—ah, from my command post under the lilac bush. I assure you, ladies and gentlemen, we cannot fail. Meeting adjourned."

They failed, of course. Those losers from the Big City took two looks at Red Hill farm and fell in love with it. They saw the miniature hogbacks that Moe Mole had dug and loved them. "Moles have their rights," the husband said. They saw George W. decimating the daffodils. "Woodchucks have their rights," the wife said. "Next year we'll plant enough for us and him."

The Kaff Kaff of the Chairman doing his best to destroy the lilacs put them in ecstasies. Flashing glimpses of the does and their fawns hiding in the woods enchanted them. "Do you think they'll all let us live here with them?" the wife asked.

They bought the farm at a high price ($1,000 an acre) with the help of a mortgage, moved in all their possessions and took up residence. Almost immediately there were hammerings and sawings inside the house and flutters of wash outside, hung on a line strung between a couple of oak trees.

They were a family of four. The head of the house was a Burmese cat, all tan and brown with golden eyes, who ruled with an imperious hand. Then there came the husband and wife, and a small boy aged two years who ruled the Burmese. The news of the cat rather disturbed the Big Red Schoolhouse, which is not fond of predators. They are all vegetarians, and the Chaldean Chicken has formed an association called OFFO, which stands for Organic Foods For Oll. In the opinion of the Professor, Miss Leghorn is ineducable.

"No, it's nothing to worry about," George W. assured the assembled. "She's a right royalty."

"Royalty?"

"I had a long talk with her through the screen door. She's some kind of Burmese Princess, and if the Burmese were ever hunters, it's been bred out of her."

"She says. Behind a door."

"No. I helped her get it open, and we had a real friendly time until the lady ran out and grabbed her and put her back in the house. She was mad."

"Why?"

"Well, it seems that these Burmese types are very high class, and they don't let them out. They're afraid she'll catch hemophilia or something. The Princess is kind of lonely. We ought to do something for her."

"Hemophilia is not contagious," the Professor said "it is a congenital characteristic transmitted through the female chromosome."

"So, all right. Leukemia or something."

"What about the family?"

"The Princess says they're a little loose. The name is Dupree. He's Constantine and she's Constance, so they call each other Connie and the Princess never knows where she's at."

"And the kid?"

"He's a boy and he's got six names."

"Six?"

"They call him after some kind of poem, which I think is a pretty rotten scene: James James Morrison Morrison Weatherby George."

"That's four names," the Professor objected.

"But mathematically speaking" Moe Mole began, "it really counts up to—"

"All right. All right. Six. How old is he?"

"Two."

"What does he do?"

"Not much. Just crawls around."

"At two? Arrested. What does the father do?

"He's an editor."

"What's that?"

"You know those pieces of paper we see sometimes with print on them like Tomato Ketchup, Net Wt.32 Oz.; or Pall Mall Famous Cigarettes—Wherever Particular People Congregate?"

"Whatever they mean. And?"

The Princess says somebody has to be in charge of the print. That's an editor."

"What does she do?"

"Who?"

"The other Connie."

"She pastes food on paper."

"She what?"

"That's what the Princess said."

"Pastes food on paper?"

The Princess says it tastes real good."

"She is not pasting food on paper," the Professor said. "She is making paintings." He turned to Geo. Woodchuck. "In my opinion your friend, the Burmese Princess, is an ass."

"She wants to meet you. Her Connie, the man, went to Rutgers, too"

"Did he, now? Was he Phi Beta Kappa? No matter. Perhaps we can arrange something."

"He doesn't speak our language,"

"Too bad. Can he learn? How old is he?"

"Around thirty."

The Professor shook his head. "A senior citizen. Too late."

At this point one of the Endmen said, "A funny thing is happening on its way to the barn."

They all stared at him.

"Something's coming," he explained.

They looked through the slit in the barn door. A curious creature, pink and naked, was crawling across the lawn in their direction.

"Where? Where?" Moe Mole asked.

"Bearing south-southwest," George W. told him.

"What is it?"

"It's a Monster!" Miss Leghorn cried.

The Monster crawled through the slit, stopped,

rested and panted. Then he looked at the assembly. The assembly examined him.

"It's James James Morrison Morrison Weatherby George," the Woodchuck said. "I saw him hugging the Princess."

"Da," the Monster said pleasantly.

"An obvious illiterate," the Professor said peevishly. "It can't speak. Let's adjourn."

"I can too speak," James said in the creature tongue. "Why are you so mean to me?"

"My dear Monster," the Professor apologized handsomely, "I had no idea. I beg you to forgive me."

"Da," James said.

"But of course," the White Rat explained. "Science always finds the answer. He can speak to us, but he can't speak to his own kind."

"Da," James said.

"You've got to speak our language, buddy boy," Jack Johnson said.

"We think he's cute in any language," the Debutantes tittered.

"Ladies," the Monster said. "I thank you for the generous compliment. I am but a simple soul, but I am not impervious to flattery from such glorious females as you. In this hurly-burly world of conflict and confrontation it is a comfort for a lonely creature like myself to know that there are yet a few who are capable of relating and communicating."

"His primitive eloquence goes to the heart," said a fawn, batting her eyes at James.

"Where the hell did you get that fancy spiel?" one of the Endmen demanded.

"From my father's editorials," James grinned. "He reads them out loud to my mother."

"Honest and modest," the Scoutmaster said. "I approve of that."

"Hey, Monster, what's it like living with human types? Is it different?"

"I don't know, sir. I've never lived with anything else."

"What about that Princess? The Burmese type."

"Oh, she's just a flirt. She's viscerotonic; that is, she operates from instinctive rather than intellectual motivation."

"Jeez!" Jack Johnson exclaimed.

"One of them editorials?" an Endmen asked.

"Yes, sir. What I mean, ladies and gentlemen, is that this is the first chance I've ever had to carry on a rational conversation with anyone."

"Don't your parents talk to you?"

"Oh, yes, but when I answer they don't listen."

"That's because you talk Us and they talk Them."

"You know," the Professor said, "I believe this simplistic Monster may have some potential. I think I'll take him on as one of my students in Arts & Sciences 1."

"Here comes one of the two Connies," His Eminence warned.

"Right. Out, Monster. We'll see you tomorrow. Push him through the door, somebody."

James mother picked him up and started back to the house. "Darling, you had a wonderful exploration. How nice that we don't have to worry about cars. Did you discover anything?"

"As a matter of fact, I did," James answered. "There's a brilliant sodality of birds and beasts in the Big Red Barn who made me welcome and have very kindly volunteered to begin my education. They're all characters and most amusing. They call me Monster."

Alas, he was speaking creature language which his mother couldn't hear or understand. So he settled for "Da" in human, but he was extremely annoyed by his mother's failure to hear him, and this is the terrible conflict of our true story.

And so the education of James Dupree began in and around the Big Red Schoolhouse.

"Music achieved its peak in the Baroque Era," Jack Johnson said. "Telemann, Bach, Mozart. The greatest, the guy I dig the most, was Vivaldi. He had muscle. You understand? Right. Now what you have to keep in mind is that these cats made statements. And you have to realize that you just don't listen to music; you have to make it, which means that you have to conduct a conversation with the artists. Right? You hear their statement and then you answer them back. You agree with them or you argue with them. That's what it's all about."

"Thank you, sir."

"That's all right. Now let's hear you sound your A."

"As we dig deeper and deeper," Moe Mole said, "we find that, mathematically speaking, the temperature increases one degree Fahrenheit per foot. But the brothers from the north tell me that they strike a permafrost layer which is left over from the Glacial Epoch. This is very interesting. It means that the last glaciation is not yet finished in the mathematical sense. Have you ever seen an iceberg?"

"No, sir."

"I would like to dig down to the bottom of an iceberg to check the temperature."

"But wouldn't it be cold?"

"Cold? Cold? Pah! Cold is better than pep pills."

"Thank you, sir."

"Let me see your hand," Miss Leghorn said. "*Benny. Benny*. The line of life is strong. Ah, but the line of Venus, of *amourismo*, is broken in *multo* places. I'm afraid you will have an unhappy love life, *cara mio*."

"Repeat after me," the Senior Rabbit said. "On my honor."

"On my honor."

"I will do my best to do my duty."

"I will do my best to do my duty."

"For God and my country."

"For God and my country."

"And to obey the scout law."

"And to obey the scout law."

"I will help other people at all times."

"I will help other people at all times."

"And keep myself physically strong."

"And keep myself physically strong."

"Mentally awake."

"Mentally awake."

"And morally straight."

"And morally straight."

"Good. You are now an official Tenderfoot. We'll start knot tying tomorrow."

"Excuse me, sir. What does morally straight mean?"

"Now watch me," the Debutante said. "First you take a step/And then you take another/And then you take a step/And then you take another/And then, you're doing the Gazpacho. Now you try it."

"But I can't even walk, Ma'am."

"That's right," the Debutante said brightly. "So how

can you dance? Shall we sit this one out? Tell me, have you read any good books lately?"

"My professor at Rutgers," the White Rat said, "taught me everything I know. He was a Phi Beta Kappa. He said that we are always faced with problems in the humanities and scientific disciplines and that the most important step is to first decide whether it's a problem of complexity or perplexity. Now, do you know the difference?"

"No, sir. I'm afraid I don't."

"Hmp! Arrested!"

"Sir, what is the difference?"

"George Woodchuck wants to tell you about surveying."

"I can't understand why the Professor said that," Geo. W. said. "Surveying can be an awfully dull line of work. I wouldn't want to wish it on my worst enemy."

"Then why do you do it, sir?"

"I don't know. Maybe, I suppose, because I'm the dull type that enjoys it. But you're not a dull boy; you're very bright."

"Thank you, sir. Why don't you try me and see if I like it, too?"

"Well, all right, provided it's understood that I'm not trying to lay this on you."

"Fair enough. Now, a proper job can't be done unless you've got a fix on latitude and longitude. The altitude of the sun gives you latitude, and time gives you your longitude. Got that?"

"But I can't tell time."

"Of course you can, my boy. You have your biological clock."

"I don't know what that is, sir."

"We all have it. Quick, now. What time is it?"

"Just before supper."

"No! No! How long since the sun culminated, that is, reached its highest altitude in the sky at noon? Quick, now! In hours, minutes, and seconds. Off the top of your head."

"Six hours, seventeen minutes and five seconds.

"It should be three seconds. You'd be out by eight hundred yards." The Peerless Surveyor patted James generously. "You're a brilliant boy and you have your biological clock. Tomorrow we will beat the bounds of the farm."

"Ladies, I say, Kaff Kaff, women are changeable. Never forget that. We can't live with them and we can't live without them. As the great poet wrote: When as in silks my pheasant goes, then, then, methinks, how sweetly flows the liquefaction of her clothes. You are, I am afraid, a little too young for the second stanza, which is, to say the least, a trifle bawdy."

"Yes, sir."

"Now we come to the matter of the moment," the Chairman said. "I hope you're not colorblind."

"I don't know, sir."

"Color perception is essential for survival. Very well, we'll test you. What is the color of that flower?"

"It's the color of an iris."

"I know that, but what color? The name? The name?"

"Blue?" James said at a venture.

"It is marine purple navy. And that tulip?"

"Red?"

"It is cerise. Really, my young friend! Survival! Survival! And the lilacs?"

"Lilac, sir."

"Ah! Now you're exhibiting some perception. Very good. Tomorrow we will study ROYGBIV."

"I don't know what that is, sir."

"They are the initial letters of the colors of the spectrum," the Chairman said severely, and stalked off in a marked manner.

"Hey, kid."

"Yes, your Eminence."

"Which one is your father?"

"The tall one, sir."

"What does he do?"

"Well, he talks a lot, your Eminence, and I listen a lot."

"What's he talk about?"

"Practically everything. Science and the state of the nation. Society. Ecology. Books. Ideas. The theater."

"What's that?"

"I don't know, sir. He also does a lot of cooking when he's home, mostly in a foreign language."

"He does, huh? Say, kid, any chance of him putting out some suet for me? I'm queer for suet."

All was not perpetual sweetness and light in the Big Red Schoolhouse; there were unpleasant moments occasionally.

There was the time that James crawled in cranky. He'd had a bad night owing to a surfeit of chocolate pudding w. whipped cream at supper, and he was tired and sullen. He rejected the gracious advances of the Debutantes. He made faces while the Professor was lecturing. He was quite impossible. He spoke just one word it wasn't creature, it was human, and it wasn't "Da," it was "Damn!" Then he began to sob.

The creatures, who never cry, gazed at him perplexedly.

"What's he doing?"

"He's crying," the voice of the Burmese Princess explained. She entered the barn. "I hope you'll forgive the intrusion, but I managed to get out and came after him, Hello, George. You're looking handsome today. This must be the Professor. James never told me you were so distinguished. The Chairman and His Eminence are magnificent, as usual. I can't tell you how many times I've admired you through the windows."

"Kaff Kaff. I thank your highness."

"You ain't so bad-looking yourself, baby."

"Come on, James, we'll go back to the house."

"But is he sick?" the Professor asked.

"No, just out of sorts. He has a temper, you know, inherited from his mother, who is rather Bohemian. Come along, James. Back to the house."

The Princess began to vamp James, tickling him with her cuddly fur but moving off a few steps each time he tried to embrace her for comfort. He crawled after her, out of the School-house and through the grass toward the house.

"He'll be all right tomorrow," she called. "Charming place you have out here. 'Bye all."

"I told you she was a right royalty," George W. said.

And there was the time when one of the Endmen reeled into the Schoolhouse singing. "How you gonna keep 'em down on the farm after they seen Paree?" He examined the assembly with a bleary eye, rocking slightly. "You're all plastered," he informed them. "You're stones." Then he was sick.

"What's the matter with our entertaining, I say, thespian friend?" the Chairman inquired.

"The berries on one of the end bushes fermented," the other Endman explained, "and I couldn't stop him from eating them. He's blind drunk."

"Actors!" the Senior Rabbit burst out. "Let this be a lesson to you, James. Well, just don't stand there. Somebody get him out of here and walk him around."

"Sir?"

"Yes?"

"The hose is spraying the rose bushes. If we put him under the cold spray...?"

"That is keeping yourself mentally awake. By all means put this clown under the hose. I only hope he sits on a thorn."

"Connie," Constance said to Constantine, "I'm worried about Jamie."

"Why?"

"Shouldn't he be going to preschool?"

"Why?"

"He seems to be arrested."

"He isn't three yet. What do you want, Connie, some sort of prodigy entering Harvard aged ten and blighted for life? I want James to grow up a healthy normal boy without having his mind forced prematurely."

"If you will permit me, Professor," James said, "I would like to disagree with my learned colleague, Moe Mole, on the Big Bang Theory of cosmology."

"Cosmogony," the White Rat corrected shortly.

"Thank you, sir. The idea of a giant proto-atom exploding to produce the expanding universe as we know it today is most attractive, but in my opinion it is pure romance. I believe in the Steady State Theory—that our universe is constantly renewing itself with the birth of new stars and galaxies from the primordial hydrogen."

"But what is your proof?" Moses Mole asked.

"The eternal equation," James answered. "Energy is equal to mass multiplied by the speed of light raised to the second power."

A voice called in human, "James? Jamie? Where are you?"

"Excuse me, Professor," James said politely. "I'm wanted."

He crawled to the crack in the barn door and squirmed through with difficulty. "Da!" he cried in human.

"We'll have to open that door more," the Professor said irritably. "He's grown. Why in the world hasn't he learned how to walk? He's old enough. When I was his age, I had grandchildren."

The rabbits and fawns tittered.

"Class dismissed," the Professor said. He glared at Moses Mole. "You and your Big Bang Theory! Why can't you help me get microscopes for my biology seminar?"

"I haven't come across any underground," Moe said reasonably. "As a matter of fact, I wouldn't know one if I saw it. Could you describe a microscope mathematically?"

"$E=mc^2$," the Professor snapped and marched off. He was in a terrible state of mind, and his classes were fortunate that they weren't taking examinations just now. He would have flunked every one of his students.

The Professor was deeply concerned about James James Morrison Morrison, who was past two years old and should be walking and talking human by now. He felt a sense of impending guilt and went to the duck pond for a searching self-examination.

"Now I am alone," the White Rat said. The mallard ducks paddled up to have a look at him, but he ignored, them. Everybody knows that ducks are incapable of appreciating a solemn soliloquy.

"The quality of wisdom is not strained. It droppeth as the gentle rain from heaven; so who are we mere fardels to do battle with the angels? All I ask, James, is that ye remember me. This day is called Father's Day. He who shall outlive this day will stand a tiptoe when this day is named and yearly feast his neighbors. Old men forget, but is it not better to bear the slings and arrows of outrageous fortune?"

Then he began something between a growl and a song:

On the banks of the Old Raritan, my boys,
Where Old Rutgers evermore shall stand,
For has she not stood since the time of the flood
On the banks of the Old Raritan.

Feeling much better, the Professor returned to the Big Red Schoolhouse to prepare his first lecture on the New Math. "Zero," he said to himself. "One. Ten. Eleven. One hundred. One hundred and one. He was counting in binary arithmetic.

Meanwhile, James James Morrison Morrison had finished his lunch (chicken salad, 1 slice bread w. butter, applesauce and milk) and was upstairs in his cot theoretically having a nap, actually in drowsy conversation with the Princess, who had made herself comfortable on his chest.

"I do love you," James said, "but you take me for granted. All you women are alike."

"That's because you love everything, James."

"Shouldn't everybody?"

"Certainly not. Everybody should love me, of course, but not everything. It reduces my rank."

"Princess, are you really a Burmese Princess?"

"I thought you said you loved me."

"But I happen to know you were born in Brooklyn."

"Politics, James, politics. Daddy, who was also an admiral, was forced to flee at a moment's notice. He barely had time to throw a few rubies into a flight bag and then came to Brooklyn."

"Why Brooklyn?"

"The plane was hijacked."

"What's a ruby?"

"Ask your Professor," the Princess snapped.

"Ah-ha! Jealous. Jealous. I knew I'd get you."

"Now who's taking who for granted?"

"Me. Shift up to my neck, Princess. I can't breathe."

"You are a male chauvinist pig," the Princess said as she obliged. I'm merely your sex symbol."

"Say, why don't you join Miss Leghorn's Chickens' Lib movement?"

"Me, sir? What have I to do with chickens?"

"I notice you did all right with my chicken salad. Don't pretend you don't know what I'm talking about. I saw you up on the table when mamma was loading the dishwasher. I thought the mayonnaise was awful."

"Commercial."

"Can't you teach mamma how to make homemade mayo?"

"Me, sir? What have I to do with kitchens? I leave that to the help."

"Ah-ha! Gotcha again."

"I hate you," the Princess said. "I loathe and execrate you."

"You love me," James James said comfortably. "You love me and you're stuck with me. I've got you in my power."

"Are there any cats in the Red Barn?"

"No," James laughed. "You're the one and only Princess on Red Hill."

There was an outlandish noise outside, a snarling and screaming in creature voices.

"What's that?" James exclaimed.

The Princess got to the window in a scamper and returned. "Just a couple of farm dogs playing with George Woodchuck," she reported lazily. "Now, as we were saying about me—"

"Playing? That doesn't sound like playing to me. I'd better see for myself."

"James, you know you can't walk."

"I'm damn well going to walk now."

James James hove himself ever the edge of the cot and fell to the floor. He gripped the edge of the bed and pulled himself upright. Then he tottered to the window.

"They aren't playing with George. He's in bad trouble."

James made his way out of the room, clutching at walls and door frames, managed the stairs by sitting down on every tread, butted the screen door open with his head, and was out on the soft meadow, trotting, tottering, falling, picking himself up, and driving himself toward the Peerless Surveyor who was being torn by two savage mongrels.

They snarled and snapped as James threw himself over George W. and were quite prepared to come in after both of them. James kicked and flailed at them. He also challenged and cursed them in the creature tongue, using language so frightful that it cannot be reported. The display of courage and determination discouraged the mongrels, who at last turned and made off jauntily as though it had only been a game all along. James pulled himself to his knees, picked up George, lurched to his feet and began tottering toward the Big Red Barn.

"Thank you," George said.

"Aw, shut up," James replied.

When they reached the Schoolhouse, everyone was there. Nothing escapes attention on Red Hill. James James sat down on his fat bottom with the Surveyor still cradled in his arms. The Debutantes made sympathetic sounds.

"Hunters! Hoodlums!" the Senior Rabbit growled. "No one is safe from them. It's all the fault of the Bleeding Hearts. Understand them. Be kind to them. Help them. Help them do what? Kill."

"There is a triangle of Red Hill farm," Geo. W. said faintly, "measuring exactly one point six acres. It extends into the property next door where Paula the pig, lives. Tell Paula she must respect our—She must—our boundar—"

"I'll tell her," James said, and began to cry.

They took the body of the woodchuck from his arms and carried it to the woods where they left George exposed to the weather and nature. Creatures do not bury their dead. James was still sitting in the Big Red Schoolhouse, silently weeping.

"The kid's a right guy," one of the Endmen said.

"Yeah, he's got moxie. You see the way he fight them dogs to a Mexican stand-off? Two to one against, it was."

"Yeah. Hey, kid. Kid. It's all over now. Kid, you ever hear the one about the guy who goes into a butcher store, you should excuse the expression?" The Endman poked his partner.

"I'd like a pound of kidleys, please."

"You mean kidneys, don't you?"

"Well, I said kidleys, diddle I?"

"Oh, funny! Fun-nee! Huh, kid?"

"He will have to fall into the pond, Kaff Kaff, I say be immersed," the Chairman said. "He is covered with George's blood, and the two Commies will ask questions."

"That's Connies."

"No matter. Will our lovely young Debutantes be kind enough to convey our valiant friend to the pond and—"

"I can walk now," James said.

"To be sure. To be sure. And push him in. Kaff Kaff. And my apologies to the Mallards, who may resent the trespass. May I say, my dear boy, I say, may I state on behalf of us all that we welcome you as a fully accepted member of our commune. It is a privilege to have a specimen of your species, Kaff Kaff, among us. I'm sure my valued friend, the Professor, will agree."

"He's my best pupil," the White Rat admitted grudgingly, "but I'm going to have to work him over if he ever hopes to get into Rutgers."

"Oh, Jamie! You fell into the pond again."

"Da," the hero said.

That night was another bad night for James. He was terribly upset over the murder of George. He was in a quandary about the Scoutmaster's denunciation of dogs—because he was as fond of dogs as he was of all creatures.

"There are good dogs and bad dogs," he kept insisting to himself, "and we mustn't judge the good by the bad. I think the Senior Rabbit was wrong, but how can a Scoutmaster be wrong?

"It's a question of the Categorical Imperative. Good acts lead to good results. Bad acts lead to bad results. But can good lead to bad or bad to good? My father could answer that question, but I'm damned if I'll ask him in his language. He won't speak ours."

Here, the deep rumbling the bats began to irritate him. Creature voices are pitched so much higher than human voices that what sounds like a bat squeak to the human ear sounds like a bass boom to the creature ear. This is another reason why most humans can't speak creature. James went to the window.

"All right! All right!" he called. "Break it up and move it out."

One of the bats fluttered to the window screen and hooked on. "What's bugging you, old buddy boy?" he rumbled.

"Keep it down to a roar, Will you? You want to wake up the whole house?"

"They can't hear us."

"I can hear you."

"How come? Not many human types can."

"I don't know, but I can, and you're making so much noise I can't sleep."

"Sorry, old buddy, but we got to."

"Why?"

"Well, in the first place we're night people, you know?"

"Yes. And?"

"In the second place we don't see so good."

"Moe Mole doesn't see either, but he doesn't make much of a racket."

"Yeah, but Moe is working underground, old buddy. He hasn't got like trees and barns and buildings to worry about. You know? Now the last thing we want to do is crash into something. There'd be a CAB investigation, and somebody would lose his license for sure."

"But what's the noise got to do with it?"

"That's our sonar."

"What's sonar?"

"Radar you know about?"

"Yes."

"Sonar is radar by sound. You let out a yell and the echoes come back and you know where everything is."

"Just from the echo?"

"Right on. You want to try it? Go ahead. Wait a minute; no cheating. Close your eyes. Now make with the sonar."

"What should I yell?"

"Anything you feel like."

"*Weehawken*!" James shouted. The bat winced.

"I heard three echoes," James said.

"What were they?"

"Weehawken."

"That was the big barn."

"Whyhawken."

"The smoke house."

"Weehawkee."

"The oak tree. You're getting the hang, old buddy. Now why don't you practice a little? It won't bother us. None of us use place names except one cracker from the south who keeps hollering Carlsbad."

And then James fell in love. It was a mad, consuming passion for the least likely candidate. Obeying George Wood-chuck's dying admonition, he went down to the triangle to request Paula, the pig, to respect the boundaries, and it was love at first sight. Paula was white with black patches or black with white patches (Poland China was her type), and she was grossly overweight. Nevertheless James adored her. He was the despair of the Big Red Schoolhouse.

"Puppy love," the Professor snorted.

"He's a setup for a my-wife-is-so-fat-that joke," one of the Endmen said.

"Marriage is out of the question," the Senior Rabbit said. "She's twice his age."

"And twice his weight."

Caw! Caw! Caw!

"If he dares to bring that woman here," the Debutantes said, "we'll never speak to him again."

James dreamed into the barn. "Ready for the biology seminar," he said.

"Mathematics today," the Professor rapped.

"Yes, Paula."

"I am the Professor."

"Sorry, sir."

"We will begin with a review of binary arithmetic. I trust you all remember that the decimal system uses the base of ten. We count from one to ten, ten to twenty, twenty to thirty, and so on. The binary system is based on zero and one. Zero is zero. One is one, but two is ten. Three is eleven. Four is one hundred. What is five, James?"

"One hundred and Paula."

"Class dismissed."

And then James began to skip classes.

"We were supposed to start a dig yesterday," Moe Mole reported, "and he never showed up."

"He cut my oratorio session," Jack Johnson said.

"That boy is turning into a dropout."

"Have you noticed how he's brushing his hair?" the Debutantes inquired.

"Oh, come on!" His Eminence said. "If the kid's got hot pants, why can't we—"

"The boy is morally straight," the Scoutmaster interrupted sternly.

"It can't be solved on simplistic terms," the Professor said.

"Emotions are involved, and the cerebrum is never on speaking terms with the cerebellum."

Alas, the situation resolved itself on an afternoon when James, carefully combed and brushed, brought another armful of apples to his love. Paula devoured them as stolidly as ever while James sat and watched devotedly. Apparently Paula was extra hungry this afternoon because when James started to embrace her she started to eat him. James pulled his arm out of her mouth and recoiled in horror and disilusionment.

"Paula!" he exclaimed. "You only love me for myself."

"*Khonyetchna*," Paula grunted in Cyrillic.

James returned to the Big Red Schoolhouse in a gloomy mood. Of course everybody had seen the sad incident, and all of them did their best to be tactful.

"Physiology tomorrow," the Professor said. "We will discuss the hydrogen-ion balance in the blood."

"Yes, sir."

"We got to get on to the modern composers, kid."

"Yes, sir."

"You know, shale is an oil-bearing rock," Moses Mole said. "But why isn't there any oil in red shale? There must be a mathematical reason."

"We'll try to find it, sir."

"Stick out your chest and be a man," the Scoutmaster said.

"I'm trying, sir."

"It is better to have loved and lost than never to have loved at all," the Chairman said.

Then a fawn nestled alongside James and whispered, "It's all right. We're sorry you picked the wrong girl, but it has to happen to every man at least once. That's how you find the right girl."

James burst into tears and cried and cried for his lost love while the fawn petted him, but in the end he felt curiously relieved.

"James," the Professor said, "we must have a serious talk."

"Yes, sir. Here?"

"No. Come to the willow grove." They went to the willow grove. "Now we are alone," the Professor said. "James, you must start speaking to your mother and father. I know you can. Why don't you?"

"I'm damned if I will, sir. They won't speak Us. Why should I speak Them?"

"James, they don't know how to speak Us. Aren't you being unfair?"

"They could try."

"And I'm sure they would if they had a clue, but

they haven't. Now listen to me. You're our only link between Us and Them. We need you, James, as a diplomatist. Your mother and father are very nice people; no hunting or killing on Red Hill, and they're planting many things. We all live together very pleasantly. I admit your mother loses her temper with the Scoutmaster and his troop because they won't get out of her way when she comes out to the hang the laundry on the line, but that's because she has a Bohemian disposition. We know what artists are like, unpredictable."

"I won't talk to her," James said.

"Your father is an intellectual of top caliber, and he went to Rutgers. You've brought many of his ideas and speculations to the Schoolhouse, which are stimulating and appreciated. In all fairness you should let him know how grateful we are to him."

"He wouldn't believe me."

"But at least you could speak to him."

"I won't speak to him. He's old, old, old and hidebound. He's a cube. He's trapped in a structured society."

"Where did you get that from?"

"From my father."

"Well, then. You see?"

"No, I don't," James said stubbornly. "I won't talk their language to them. They have to try Us first."

"In other words, you have opted for Us?"

"Yes, sir."

"To the exclusion of Them?"

"Yes, sir."

"Then there's nothing more to say."

"Connie," Constance said to Constantine, "we must have a serious talk."

"Now?"
"Yes."
"What about?"
"Jamie."
"What about Jamie?"
"He's a problem child."
"What's his problem?"
"He's arrested."
"Are you starting that again? Now come on, Connie. He's learned to walk. What more do you want?"
"But he hasn't learned to talk."
"Talk! Talk! Talk!" Constantine sounded as though he was cursing. "Words! Words! Words! I've lived my whole life with them, and I hate them. Do you know what most words are? They're bullets people use to shoot each other down with. Words are weapons for killers. Language should be the beautiful poetry of communication, but we've debased it, poisoned it, corrupted it into hostility, into competition, into a contest between winners and losers. And the winner is never the man with something to say; the winner is always the fastest gun in the West. These are the few simple words I have to say about words."
"Yes, dear," Constance said, "but our son should be shooting words by now, and he isn't."
"I hope he never does."
"He must, and we'll have to take him to a clinic. He's autistic."
"Autism," the Professor said, "is an abnormal absorption in fantasy to the exclusion of external reality. I have known many laboratory victims who have been driven to this deplorable state by fiendish experiments."

"Could you put that in mathematical terms?" Moe asked. "I can't follow your words."

"Ah, yes. Kaff Kaff. I'm having some slight difficulty myself. I'm sure our valued friend will be good enough to simplify."

"All right," the White Rat said. "He won't talk."

"Won't talk? Good heavens! We can't shut him up. Only yesterday he engaged me in a two-hour dispute over Robert's Rules of Order, and—"

"He won't talk human."

"Oh. Ah."

"The *questo* is can he?" the Chaldean Chicken said. "Many who are born under the Sign of Torso find it *difficulto* to—"

"Taurus! Taurus! And will you be quiet. He can talk; he just won't."

"What's a fantasy?" Moe asked.

"A hallucination."

"What's that?"

"Something unreal."

"You mean he's not real? But I only saw him yesterday, and he—"

"I have no intention of discussing the metaphysics of reality. Those of you who are interested may take my course in Thesis, Synthesis and Antithesis. The situation with James is simple. He talks to us in our language; he refuses talk to his parents in their language; they are alarmed."

"Why are they alarmed?"

"They think he's autistic."

"They think he's unreal?"

"No, Moe," the Professor said patiently. "They know he's real. They think he has a psychological hang-up which prevents him from talking human."

"Do they know he talks Us?"

"No."

"Then why don't we tell them? Then everything will be all right."

"Why don't you tell them?"

"I don't know how to talk Them."

"Does anybody here know how? Anybody?"

No answer.

"So much for that brilliant suggestion," the Professor said. "Now we come to the crux of the situation. They're going to send him to a remedial school."

"What's the matter with our school?"

"They don't know about our school, you imbecile! They want him to go to a school where he can learn how to speak English."

"What's that?"

"Them talk."

"Oh."

"Well, Kaff Kaff, as our most esteemed and valued scholar, surely you can have no objections to that program, my dear Professor."

"There's a dilemma," the White Rat said sourly.

"Name it, sir. I say, describe it and we shall, Kaff Kaff, we shall cope."

"He's so used to speaking Us that I'm afraid he won't learn to speak Them."

"But why should he want to, my learned friend?"

"Because he's got Rutgers before him."

"Ah, yes. To be sure. Your beloved alma mater. But I still can't quite fathom, I say, perceive the difficulty."

"We've got to turn him off."

"I beg your pardon?"

"We've got to stop speaking to him. We got to

break his Us habit so he can learn Them. Nobody can speak both."

"You can't mean Coventry, Professor?"

"I do. Don't you understand? No matter where he goes, there will be others of us around. We must break the habit. Now. For his sake." The Professor began to pace angrily. "He will forget how to speak Us. We'll lose him. That's the price. My best pupil. My favorite. Now he may never make Phi Beta Kappa."

The Debutantes looked despairing. "We love that boy," they said. "He's a real swinger."

"He is not," the Senior Rabbit stated. "He is trustworthy, loyal, helpful, friendly, courteous, kind, obedient, cheerful, thrifty, brave, clean and reverent."

"He told me all about E equals MC two," Moe said. "It gave me an insight. It will change the world."

"Aquarium" Miss Leghorn said profoundly.

"He is a pest, a bore, a nuisance, a—a human," the Professor shouted. "He doesn't belong in our Schoolhouse. We want nothing to do with him; he'll sell us out sooner or later. Coventry! Coventry!" Then he broke down completely. "I love him, too, but we must be brave. We're going to lose him, but we must be brave for his sake. And somebody better warn the Princess."

James James Morrison Morrison shoved the barn door a little wider and swaggered into the Schoolhouse. There was no mistaking his pride in his walk. In an odd way it was a reflection of the Chairman's strut.

"Ladies and gentlemen, good evening," he said, as courteous as ever.

The Debutantes sniffled and departed.

"What's the matter with them?" James asked curiously. He turned to the mole. "Uncle Moe, I just heard something up at the house that'll interest you. it seems that Newton's model of the universe may break down. Time is not reversible from the mathematical standpoint, and—"

Here Moe broke down and went underground.

"What's the matter with him?" James asked.

There was no answer. Everybody else had disappeared, too. The long sad silence had begun.

The pheasant strutted, accompanied by his harem, and he ignored James. Martha W. Woodchuck, who had taken on George's surveying duties (she was his daughter-in-law), ignored James. Neither the Professor nor the Scoutmaster were to be seen. The does and the fawns hid in the woods. Moe Mole decided on an early hibernation. Jack Johnson went south for the winter, and His Eminence suddenly moved his residence to Paula's territory. The crows could not resist the challenge of an art nouveau scarecrow on a farm a mile off and left. James James was abandoned.

"Would you like to read my palm?" he asked Miss Leghorn.

"Cluck," she replied.

"Princess," he said, "why doesn't anybody want to talk to me?"

"Aeiou," she replied.

James was abandoned.

"Well, at least he's learned how to walk,"' Dr. Rapp said, "and that's a favorable prognosis. What beats me is how he can be autistic in such an articulate home. One would think that—stop. An idea. Is it possible that the home is too articulate, that his autism is a refusal to compete with his betters?"

"But there's no competition in our home," one of the two Connies said.

"You don't grasp the potential of the idea. In our society, if you don't win, you have failed. This is our contemporary delusion. James may well be afraid of failure."

"But he's only three years old."

"My dear Mrs. Dupree, competition begins in the womb."

"Not in mine," Connie said indignantly. "I've got the fastest womb in the West."

"Yes. And now if you will excuse me, the first lesson will begin. That door out. Thank you." Dr. Rapp buzzed the intercom. "Sherbet," he said. A chalice of orange sherbet was brought to him.

"James," he said, "would you like some orange ice? Here." He proffered a spoonful. James engulfed it. "Good. Would you like some more? Then tell me what this is." Dr. Rapp held up a striped ball. "It's a ball, James. Repeat after me. Ball."

"Da," James said.

"No more orange ice, James, until you've spoken. Ball. Ball. Ball. And then the goody."

"Da."

"Perhaps he prefers the lemon flavor," Dr. Rapp said the next week. He buzzed the intercom. "Lemon sherbet, please." He was served. "James, would you like some lemon ice?" He proffered a spoonful which was absorbed. "Good. Would you like some more? Then tell me what this is. It's a ball, James. Repeat after me. Ball. Ball. Ball."

"Da," James said.

"We'll try ice cream," Dr. Rapp said a week later. "We can't permit him to fall into a pattern of familiarized societal behavior. He must be challenged." He buzzed the intercom. "Chocolate ice cream, please."

James relished the ice cream but refused to identify the striped ball by name.

"Da," he said.

"I'm beginning to dream that confounded expression," Dr. Rapp complained. "A Roman centurion comes at me, draws his sword, and says, 'Da.' Stop. An idea. Is it a phallic symbol? Sexuality begins with conception. Is the child rejecting the facts of life?"

He buzzed the intercom.

"James, here is a banana. Would you like a bite? Feel free. Good. Good. Would you like another? Then tell me what this is. A ball. Ball. Ball. Ball."

"Da."

"I am failing," Dr. Rapp said despondently. "Perhaps I had better go back to Dr. Da for a refresher—What am I saying? It's Dr. Damon. Stop. An idea. Damon and Pythias. A friendship. Can it be that I have been too clinical with James. I shall establish fraternality.

"Good morning, James. It's a beautiful October day. The autumn leaves are glorious. Would you like to go for a drive?"

"Da," James said.

"Good. Good. Where would you like to go?"

"To Rutgers," James said, quite distinctly.

"What did you say?"

"I said I would like to go to Rutgers."

"But—good gracious—You're talking."

"Yes, sir."

"Why haven't you talked before?"

"Because I damn well didn't want to."

"Why are you talking now?"

"Because I want to see the banks of the Old Raritan."

"Yes, yes. I see. Or do I?" Dr. Rapp buzzed the intercom. "Please get me Dr. Da, I mean Dr. Damon, on the phone—Tell him I think I've made an important discovery."

"Discovery," James said, "is seeing what everybody else sees but thinking what no one else has thought. What's your opinion? Shall we discuss it on the way to Rutgers?"

So the second summer came. James and his father were strolling the lawns in a hot debate over the bearded irises which, alas, James pronounced iritheth. He had developed a human lisp. The issue was whether they should be picked and vased or left alone. James took the position that they were delicate ladies who should not be molested. His father, always pragmatic, declared that flowers had to justify their existence by decorating the house. Father and son parted on a note of exasperation, and the senior Dupree went to inspect the peach trees. James James Morrison Morrison sat quietly on the lawn and looked around. Presently he heard a familiar Kaff Kaff, and the Chairman appeared from under the lilac bush.

"Well, if it isn't my old friend, the Sex Maniac. How are you, sir?"

The cock pheasant glared him.

"And how are Phyllis and Frances and Felice and all the rest, Mr. Chairman?"

"Their names are, I say, the nomenclature is, Kaff Kaff, Gloria, Glenda, Gertrude, Godiva, and—" Here the Chairman stopped short and looked hard at James. "But you're the Monster."

"Yes, sir."

"My, how you've grown."

"Thank you, sir."

"Have you learned how speak Them?"

"Not very well, sir."

"Why not?"

"I've got a lisp. They say because I have a lazy tongue."

"But you still speak Us."

"Yes, sir."

"Amazing! I say, unheard of!"

"Did you all think I'd ever forget? I'm the Professor's best pupil, and I'd die for dear old Rutgers. Can we have an emergency meeting right away in the Big Red Schoolhouse, Mr. Chairman? I've got a lot to tell you about the crazy, mixed-up human creatures."

The meeting was attended by most of the regulars, plus a few newcomers. There was a Plymouth Rock hen who had become close friends with Miss Leghorn, perhaps because her only reply to the Chaldean harangues was, "Ayeh." The holdout mockingbird had at last joined up now that Jack Johnson seemed to be remaining in the Florida Keys...his (the mockingbird's) name was Milton. There was one most exotic new member, a little Barbary ape who was very friendly but extremely shy. James shook hands and asked his name.

"They called me...well, they called me The Great Zunia. Knows All. Does All."

"Who's 'they', Zunia?"

"The Reson and Tickel Circus."

"You were in the circus?"

"Well...yes. I...did tricks. Knows All. Does All. I was what they...what they call a headliner. You know. Rode a motorcycle with the lights on. But I...I..."

"Yes?"

"But I cracked up when we...were playing Princeton. Totaled the bike. I got...well...I split when they were picking up the pieces."

"Why did you run away, Zunia?"

"I...I hate to say this...never blow the whistle on another man's act...but...well...I hate show business."

"Zunia, we're all delighted that you're here, and you know you're more than welcome, but there's a problem."

"Well...gee...just a little fruit now and then, apples and—"

"Not food. The weather. Winters can be damn cold on Red Hill farm. Don't you think you might be more comfortable farther south?"

"Well...if it's all the same to...well, I'd rather stay here. Nice folks."

"If that's what you want, great for us. My parents are going to have fits if they ever see you, so stay under cover."

"I'm a night-type anyway."

"Good. Now stand up, please. All the way up, and we'll stand back to back. Professor, are we the same size?"

No answer.

"Professor?"

Moe Mole said, "The Professor is indisposed."

"What?"

"He couldn't come."

"Why not?"

"He's not feeling so good."

"Where is he?"

"Up in his study."

"I'd better go and—No, wait. Are we the same size, Zunia and me? Anybody? Everybody." It was agreed that James and Zunia were an approximate match. James promised to pinch some of his sweaters and wooly underwear for Zunia to wear during the winter months.

"If you...well, I'm not asking...but I'd love a sweater with Boston on it."

"Boston! Why Boston?"

"Because they hate show business."

James shinnied up one of the rough oak columns that supported the barn roof, walked across the heavy beam above the empty hay loft as casually as a steel-worker (his mother would have screamed at the sight), came to a small break in the loft wall and knocked politely.

A faint voice said, "Who is it?"

"It's the Monster, sir. I've come back."

"No! Really? Come in. Come in."

James poked his head through the break. The Professor's study was lined with moss. There were fronds of dried grass and mint leaves on the floor on which the Professor lay. He looked very ill and weak, but his albino red eyes were as fierce as ever.

"Well, James, you've come back," he panted. "I never thought—Do you still speak Them?"

"Yes, sir."

"And you still speak Us. I would never—Phi Beta Kappa and cum laude for you. No doubt of it."

"I visited Rutgers, sir."

"Did you. Did you, now. And?"

"It's beautiful, just like you said," James lied. "And they still remember you."

"No!"

"Yes, sir. They can't understand how you escaped. They think you probably bribed the lab attendant, but a few claim you had something on him. Blackmail."

The Professor chuckled, but it turned into a painful hacking.

After the spasm subsided James asked, "What's wrong, sir?"

"Nothing. Nothing. Probably a touch of the Asiatic flu. Nothing serious."

"Please tell me."

The Professor looked at him.

"Science is devotion to truth," he said. "I'll be truthful. I'm badly wounded."

"Oh, sir! How?"

"An air rifle. A couple of farm boys."

"Who are they? From the Rich place? I'll—"

"James! James! There is no room for revenge in science. Did Darwin retaliate when he was ridiculed?"

"No, sir."

"Did Pasteur?"

"N-no, sir."

"Will you be true to what I've taught you?"

"I'll try, sir, b-but those damn boys..."

"No anger. Reason always; anger never. And no crying, James. I need your courage now."

"If I have any, sir."

"You have it. I remember George. Now I want you to take my place and continue my classes."

"Oh, Professor, you'll be—"

"I take it you're on speaking terms with your father

now. Learn all you can from him and pass it on to Us. That's an order, James."

"Yes, sir. It won't be easy."

"Nothing is ever easy. Now I'm going to ask from you an act of great courage."

"Sir?"

"I can't linger like this. It's too painful and it's useless."

"Professor, maybe we can—"

"No, no, I'm hopeless. If you hadn't cut my anatomy classes when you fell in love with Paula, you'd—" He hacked again, even more painfully. At last she said, "James, end this for me, as quickly as possible. You know what I mean."

James was stupefied. At last he managed to whisper, "S-sir..."

"Yes. I see you understand."

"Sir, I c-couldn't."

"Yes you can."

"B-but I wouldn't know how."

"Science always finds a way."

"At least let me ask my—"

"You will ask no one. You will tell no one."

"But you leave me all alone with this."

"Yes, I do. That's how we grow up."

"Sir, I have to refuse. I can't do it."

"No. You just need time to make up your mind. Isn't there a meeting on the floor?"

"Yes, sir. I asked for it."

"Then go to your meeting. Give them my best. Come back quickly. Quickly." The Professor began to tremble and rustle on the dried grass.

"Have you had anything to eat, sir? I'll bring you

something, and then we'll talk it over. You have to advise me."

"No dependence," the White Rat said. "You must decide for yourself."

The Chairman was in the full flood of oratory when James climbed down from the loft and seated himself with his friends, the birds and the beasts, but he came to a close fairly promptly and gave the floor to James who stood up and looked around.

"I'm going to tell you about Them," James began quietly. "I've met Them and lived with Them, and I'm beginning to understand Them. We must, too. Many of Them are damned destroyers—we all know that but what we don't know is that a new breed of Them is rising in revolt against destruction. They're our kind. They live in peace and harmony with the earth; whatever they take from it they return; they do not kill and they fight those who do. But they're young and weak and outnumbered, and they need our help. We must help them. We must!

"Now up to now we've done nothing. We hide from the destroyers and use our intelligence to outwit them. We've just been passive victims. Now we must become activists, militant activists. The Professor won't like this; that great scholar still believes in reason and light. So do I, but I reserve reason and light only for those who also are guided by reason and light. For the rest, militant action. Militant!

"I heard my father once tell a story about Confucius, a very wise sage of many years ago. Although he was one of Them, he was much like our Professor and may have been almost as wise. One of his students came to him and said, 'Master, a new wise man named Christ has appeared in the West. He teaches that we must return good for evil. What is your opinion?' Confucius thought and answered, 'No. If we return good for evil, what then will we return for good? Return good for good; for evil return justice.'"

James' voice began to shake. "They shot the Professor. You knew that, didn't you. They shot him. He's not indisposed. He's up there and he's hurting. They—We must learn to return militant justice for evil. We can't use this barn as a sanctuary any more. We must leave it when we graduate and travel and teach. There is a desperate battle being fought for what little remains of our Earth. We must all join the fight."

"But how?" Moe Mole asked reasonably.

"That will be the subject of my first lesson tomorrow," James answered. "And now, with the permission of our distinguished Chairman, I would like to move that this meeting be adjourned. I have the Professor to look after."

"So moved," the cock pheasant said. "Seconded? Thank you, Miss Plymouth. Moved and seconded. This meeting is adjourned."

"Zunia," James said, "wait here for me, please. I'll need your help. Back in a little while."

James walked to the nearest apple tree, began picking up fallen apples and hurling them into space. His mother glanced out of the kitchen window and smiled at the sight of a small boy lazing away a summer afternoon.

"If I do what the Professor asks, it'll be murder," James thought. "They call it mercy killing, but I've heard my father say it's murder all the same. He says some doctors do it by deliberately neglecting to give certain medicines. He says that's murder all the same, and he doesn't approve. He says religion is against it, and if you do it you go to hell, wherever that is. He says life is sacred.

"But the Professor hurts. He hurts bad and he says there's no hope. I don't want him to hurt anymore. I want the boys who shot him to hurt, but not the professor. I could just bring him a little milk and let him die all by himself, but that could take a long time. It wouldn't be fair to him. So—All right—I'll go to hell."

James returned to the house, lisped courteously to his mother and asked for a small cup of warm milk to hold him until dinner time. He received it, climbed upstairs to his room and put the cup down. Then he went to his parents' bathroom. He climbed up on the washstand, opened the medicine cabinet, which had been declared off-limits for him, on pain of frightful punishment, and took a small vial off one of the shelves. It was labeled "Seconal" and was filled with bright orange capsules. James James removed a capsule, returned the vial, closed the cabinet and climbed down from the sink.

"What are you stealing?" the Burmese princess asked.

"Medicine," James answered shortly and returned to his room. He pulled the capsule open and shook its contents into the cup of milk. He stirred gently, with his forefinger.

"Mercy, James, you'll have to put your humor on a diet. It's gaining weight."

"I'm sorry. I'm not feeling funny right now, Princess. In fact I feel damn rotten lousy."

"Why? What's wrong?"

"I can't tell you. I can't tell anybody. Excuse me."

He carried the cup of milk to the Big Red Barn where the Great Zunia was patiently waiting. "Thanks," James said. "Now look, I've got to shinny up that column, and I can't do it and carry this cup. You can, easy. Go up with the cup. Don't spill it. I'll meet you on the beam."

They met on the beam and James received the cup.

"It looks like milk but it tastes funny," Zunia said.

"You didn't drink any!"

"Well, no...just stuck my tongue in...you know. Curious. It's...I well, traditional with us."

"Oh. That's all right. It's medicine for the Professor."

"Sure. Tell him...tell him get well soon."

"He'll be well soon," James promised. Zunia flip-flopped and catapulted himself to another empty loft. James crossed the beam and knocked at the Professor's study. "It's James again, sir."

He could barely hear the "Come in." He poked his head in. The Professor was trembling. "I brought you a little something, sir. Warm milk." James placed the cup close to the Professor's head. "Please drink a little. It'll give you strength."

"Impossible."

"For me, sir. You owe that much to your best pupil. And then we'll discuss your proposal." James waited until he saw the White Rat begin to drink. He withdrew his head, sat down on the beam and began to chat lightly while tears blurred his eyes.

"Your proposal, Professor, raises an interesting dilemma in the relationship between teacher and pupil. Let me tell you about my lunatic teacher at the remedial school, Dr. Rapp, and my relations with him. I'd value your opinion. How is the milk, sir?"

"Terrible. Did you say lunatic?"

"Drink it anyway. Yes, lunatic. He's a psychiatrist, excessively educated, and—"

"There is no such thing."

"Not for a genius like yourself, sir, but in lesser people too much education produces alienation from reality. That was Dr. Rapp."

"You must be specific," the White Rat said severely.

"Well, sir, let me contrast him with yourself. You always understand the capacity and potential of your students and treat them accordingly. Dr. Rapp was so crammed with education that he never bothered to understand us; he simply tried to fit us into the textbook cases he'd read."

"Hmmm. What was his school?"

"I was afraid you'd ask that, sir. You won't like the answer. Abigail College."

"What? What?"

"Abigail College, sir. Finished your milk?"

"Yes, and it was disgusting."

"But you sound stronger already, sir."

"Where is Abigail College?"

"In a state called Kansas."

"Hmpl. Fresh-water college. No wonder." The Professor's speech began to slur. James began to rock back and forth in agony.

"What would you do if this...this Abigail made same proposal to you, James?"

"Oh sir, that's not a fair question. I don't like or respect Dr. Rapp. I love you."

"No place—f'love—in science."

"No, sir. Always be objective. That's what you taught me."

"Gett'n sleepy...James...'bout Zunia."

"What about Zunia, sir?"
"Like him?"
"Very much, sir. You'll enjoy teaching him."
"Don't...d'not le'him...came to us f'm Princeton, you know...don't let'm talk you into going Princeton. Yes?"
"Never, sir. Rutgers forever."
There was a long, long pause. The painful rustling in the study stopped. James poked his head in. The cup of milk was empty. The Professor was peacefully dead. James reached in, picked him up, carried him across the beam and skinned down the oak column with the body in one hand. On the main floor he stamped his foot hard, three times. He repeated the signal three times. At last Moe Mole appeared from the depths.
"That you, James?"
"Please come with me, Uncle Moe. I need your help."
Moe shuffled alongside James James, blinking in the twilight. "Trouble, James?"
"The Professor's dead. We've got to bury him."
"Now that's a shame. And we never started my astronomy lessons. Where's the body?"
"Right here. I'm carrying him." James led Moe to the sundial on the south lawn. "Dig here, Uncle Moe. I want to bury the Professor under the center of the pedestal."
"Easy," Moe said. He tunneled down and disappeared, little flurries of earth sprayed out of the tunnel mouth. Presently Moe reappeared. "All set. Got a nice little chamber dead center. Where is he now?"
James placed the body at the mouth of the tunnel. Moe pushed it before him and was again lost from

sight. He reappeared in another flurry of soil. "Just filling in," he explained apologetically. "Got to pack it solid. Don't want any grave robbers nosing around, do we?"

"No," James said. "Bury him for keeps."

Moe finished the job, mumbled a few words of condolence and shambled off. James stared hard at the sundial. "Militant," he said at, last and turned away. The weathered bronze plate of the sundial was engraved with a line from the immortal Thomas Henry Huxley: "The great end of life is not knowledge but action."

Fantasy & Science Fiction, October 1972

Something Up There Likes Me

There were these three lunatics, and two of them were human. I could talk to all of them because I speak English, metric, and binary. The first time I ran into the clowns was when they wanted to know all about Herostratus, and I told them. The next time it was *Conus gloria maris*. I told them. The third time it was where to hide. I told them. The third time it was where to hide. I told them, and we've been in touch ever since.

He was Jake Madigan (James Jacob Madigan, Ph.D., University of Virginia) chief of the Exobiology Section at the Goddard Space Flight Center, which hopes to study extraterrestrial lifeforms, if they can ever get hold of any. To give you some idea of his sanity, he once programmed the IBM 704 computer with a deck of cards that would print out lemons, oranges, plums, and so on. Then he played slot-machine against it and lost his shirt. The boy was real loose.

She was Florinda Pot, pronounced "Poe." It's a Flemish name. She was a pretty towhead, but freckled all over; up to the hemline and down into the cleavage. She was an M.E. from Sheffield University and had a machine-gun English voice. She'd been in the Sounding Rocket Division until she blew up an Aerobee with an electric blanket. It seems that solid fuel doesn't give maximum acceleration if it gets too cold, so this little Mother's Helper warmed her rockets at White Sands with electric blankets before ignition time. A blanket caught fire and Voom.

Their son was S-333. At NASA they label them "S" for scientific satellites and "A" for application satellites. After the launch they give them public acronyms like IMP, SYNCOM, OSO and so on. S-333 was to become OBO, which stands for Orbiting Biological Observatory, and how those two clowns ever got that third clown into space I will never understand. I suspect the director handed them the mission because no one with any sense wanted to touch it.

As Project Scientist, Madigan was in charge of the experiment packages that were to be flown, and they were a spaced-out lot. He called his own ELECTROLUX, after the vacuum cleaner. Scientist-type joke. It was an intake system that would suck in dust particles and deposit them in a flask containing a culture medium. A light shone through the flask into a photomultiplier. If any of the dust proved to be spore forms, and if they took in the medium, their growth would cloud the flask, and the obscuration of light would register on the photomultiplier. They call that Detection by Extinction.

Cal Tech had an RNA experiment to investigate whether RNA molecules could encode an organism's environmental experience. They were using nerve cells from the mollusk, sea hare. Harvard was planning a package to investigate the circadian effect. Pennsylvania wanted to examine the effect of the Earth's magnetic field on iron bacteria, and had to be put out on a boom to prevent magnetic interface with the satellite's electronic system. Ohio State was sending up lichens to test the effect of space on their symbiotic relationship to molds and algae. Michigan was flying a terrarium containing one (1) carrot which required forty-seven (47) separate commands for performance. All in all, S-333 was strictly Rube Goldberg.

Florinda was the Project Manager, supervising the construction of the satellite and the packages; the Project Manager is more or less the foreman of the mission. Although she was pretty and interestingly lunatic, she was gung-ho on her job and displayed the disposition of a freckle-faced tarantula when she was crossed. This didn't get her loved.

She was determined to wipe out the White Sands goof, and her demand for perfection delayed the schedule by eighteen months and increased the cost by three-quarters of a million. She fought with everyone and even had the temerity to tangle. with Harvard. When Harvard gets sore, they don't beef to NASA, they go straight to the White House. So Florinda got called on the carpet by a congressional committee. First they wanted to know why S-333 was costing more than the original estimate.

"S-333 is still the cheapest mission in NASA," she snapped. "It'll come to ten million, including the launch. My God! We're practically giving away green stamps."

Then they wanted to know why it was taking so much longer to build than the original estimate.

"Because," she replied, "no one's ever built an Orbiting Biological Observatory before."

There was no answering that, so they had to let her go. Actually all this was routine crisis, but OBO was Florinda's and Jake's first satellite, so they didn't know. They took their tensions out on each other, never realizing that it was their baby who was responsible.

Florinda got S-333 buttoned up and delivered to the Cape by December 1st, which would give them plenty of time to launch well before Christmas. (The Cape crews get a little casual during the holidays.) But the satellite began to display its own lunacy, and in the terminal tests everything went haywire. The launch had to be postponed. They spent a month taking S-333 apart and spreading it all over the hangar floor.

There were two critical problems. Ohio State was using a type of Invar, which is a nickel-steel alloy, for the structure of their package. The alloy suddenly began to creep, which meant they could never get the experiment calibrated. There was no point in flying it, so Florinda ordered it scrubbed and gave Madigan one month to come up with a replacement, which was ridiculous. Nevertheless Jake performed a miracle. He took the Cal Tech back-up package and converted it into a yeast experiment. Yeast produces adaptive enzymes in answer to changes in environment, and this was an investigation of what enzymes it would produce in space.

A more serious problem was the satellite radio transmitter which was producing "birdies" or whoops when the antenna was withdrawn into its launch position. The danger was that the whoops might be picked up by the satellite radio receiver, and the pulses might result in a destruct command. NASA suspects that's what happened to SYNCOM I, which disappeared shortly after its launch and has never been heard from since. Florinda decided to launch with the transmitter off and activate it later in space. Madigan fought the idea.

"It means we'll be launching a mute bird," he protested. "We won't know where to look for it."

"We can trust the Johannesburg tracking station to get a fix on the first pass," Florinda answered. "We've got excellent cable communications with Joburg."

"Suppose they don't get a fix. Then what?"

"Well, if they don't know where OBO is, the Russians will."

"Hearty-har-har."

"What d'you want me to do, scrub the entire mission?" Florinda demanded. "It's either that or launch with the transmitter off." She glared at Madigan. "This is my first satellite, and d'you know what it's taught me? There's just one component in any spacecraft that's guaranteed to give trouble all the time. Scientists!"

"Women!" Madigan snorted, and they got into a ferocious argument about the feminine mystique.

They got S-333 through the terminal tests and onto the launch pad by January 14th. No electric blankets. The craft was to be injected into orbit a thousand miles downrange exactly at noon, so ignition was scheduled for 11:50 A.M., January 15th. They watched the launch on the blockhouse TV screen, and it was agonizing. The perimeters of TV tubes are curved, so as the rocket went up and approached the edge of the screen, there was optical distortion and it seemed to topple over and break in half.

Madigan gasped and began to swear. Florinda muttered, "No, it's all right. It's all right. Look at the display charts." Everything on the illuminated display charts was nominal. At that moment a voice on the

P.A. spoke in the impersonal tones of a croupier, "We have lost cable communication with Johannesburg."

Madigan began to shake. He decided to murder Florinda Pot (and he pronounced it "Pot" in his mind) at the earliest opportunity. The other experimenters and NASA people turned white. If you don't get a quick fix on your bird, you may never find it again. No one said anything. They waited in silence and hated each other. At 1:30 it was time for the craft to make its first pass over the Fort Myers tracking station, if it was alive, if it was anywhere near its nominal orbit. Fort Myers was on an open line, and everybody crowded around Florinda, trying to get their ears close to the phone.

"Yeah, she waltzed into the bar absolutely stoned with a couple of MPs escorting her," a tinny voice was chatting casually. "She says to me—Got a blip, Henry?" A long pause. Then, in the same casual voice, "Hey, Kennedy? We've nicked the bird. It's coming over the fence right now. You'll get your fix."

"Command 0310!" Florinda hollered. "0310!"

"Command 0310 it is," Fort Myers acknowledged.

That was the command to start the satellite transmitter and raise its antenna into broadcast position. A moment later the dials and oscilloscope on the radio reception panel began to show action, and the loudspeaker emitted a rhythmic, syncopated warble, rather like a feeble peanut whistle. That was OBO transmitting its housekeeping data.

"We've got a living bird," Madigan shouted. "We've got a living doll!"

I can't describe his sensations when he heard the bird come beeping over the gas station. There's such an emotional involvement with your first satellite that you're never the same. A man's first satellite is like his first love affair. Maybe that's why Madigan grabbed Florinda in front of the whole blockhouse and said, "My God, I love you, Florrie Pot." Maybe that's why she answered, "I love you too, Jake." Maybe they were just loving their first baby.

By Orbit 8 they found out that the baby was a brat. They'd gotten a lift back to Washington on an Air Force jet. They'd done some celebrating. It was 1:30 in the morning and they were talking happily, the usual get-acquainted talk; where they were born and raised, school, work, what they liked most about each other the first time they met. The phone rang. Madigan picked it up automatically and said hello. A man said, "Oh. Sorry. I'm afraid I've dialed the wrong number."

Madigan hung up, turned on the light and looked at Florinda in dismay. "That was just about the most damn fool thing I've ever done in my life," he said. "Answering your phone."

"Why? What's the matter?"

"That was Joe Leary from Tracking and Data. I recognized his voice."

She giggled. "Did he recognize yours?"

"I don't know." The phone rang. "That must be Joe again. Try to sound like you're alone."

Florinda winked at him and picked up the phone. "Hello? Yes, Joe. No, that's all right, I'm not asleep. What's on your mind?" She listened for a moment, suddenly sat up in bed and exclaimed, "What?" Leary was quack-quack-quacking on the phone. She broke in. "No, don't bother. I'll pick him up. We'll be right over." She hung up.

"So?" Madigan asked.

"Get dressed. OBO's in trouble."

"Oh Jesus! What now?"

"It's gone into a spin-up like a whirling dervish. We've got to get over to Goddard right away."

Leary had the all-channel printout of the first eight orbits unrolled on the floor of his office. It looked like ten yards of paper toweling filled with vertical columns of numbers. Leary was crawling around on his hands and knees following the numbers. He pointed to the attitude data column. "There's the spin-up," he said. "One revolution in every twelve seconds."

"But how? Why?" Florinda asked in exasperation.

"I can show you," Leary said. "Over here."

"Don't show us," Madigan said. "Just tell us."

"The Penn boom didn't go up on command," Leary said. "It's still hanging down in the launch position. The switch must be stuck."

Florinda and Madigan looked at each other with rage; they had the picture. OBO was programmed to be Earth-stabilized. An Earth-sensing eye was supposed to lock on the Earth and keep the same face of the satellite pointed toward it. The Penn boom was hanging down alongside the Earth sensor, and the idiot eye had locked on the boom and was tracking it. The satellite was chasing itself in circles with its lateral gas jets. More lunacy.

Let me explain the problem. Unless OBO was Earth-stabilized, its data would be meaningless. Even more disastrous was the question of electric power which came from batteries charged by solar vanes. With the craft spinning, the solar array could not remain facing the sun, which meant the batteries were doomed to exhaustion.

It was obvious that their only hope lay in getting

the Penn boom up. "Probably all it needs is a good swift kick," Madigan said savagely, "but how can we get up there to kick it?" He was furious. Not only was $10,000,000 going down the drain but their careers as well.

They left Leary crawling around his office floor. Florinda was very quiet. Finally she said, "Go home, Jake."

"What about you?"

"I'm going to my office."

"I'll go with you."

"No. I want to look at the circuitry blueprints. Good night."

As she turned away without even offering to be kissed Madigan muttered, "OBO's coming between us already. There's a lot to be said for planned parenthood."

He saw Florinda during the following week, but not the way he wanted. There were the experimenters to be briefed on the disaster. The director called them in for a postmortem, but although he was understanding and sympathetic, he was little too careful to avoid any mention of congressmen and a failure review. Florinda called him the next week and sounded oddly buoyant. "Jake," she said, "you're my favorite genius. You've solved the OBO problem, I hope,"

"Who solve? What solve?"

"Don't you remember what you said about kicking our baby?"

"Don't I wish I could."

"I think I know how we can do it. Meet you in the Building 8 cafeteria for lunch."

She came in with a mass of papers and spread them

over the table. "First, Operation Swift-Kick," she said. "We can eat later."

"I don't feel much like eating these days anyway," Madigan said gloomily.

"Maybe you will when I'm finished. Now look, we've got to raise the Penn boom. Maybe a good swift kick can unstick it. Fair assumption?"

Madigan grunted.

"We get twenty-eight volts from the batteries and that hasn't been enough to flip the switch. Yes?"

He nodded.

"But suppose we double the power?"

"Oh, great. How?"

"The solar array is making a spin every twelve seconds. When it's facing the sun, the panels deliver fifty volts to recharge the batteries. When it's facing away, nothing. Right?"

"Elementary, Miss Pot. But the joker is it's only facing the sun for one second in every twelve, and that's not enough to keep the batteries alive."

"But it's enough to give OBO a swift kick. Suppose at that peak moment we bypass the batteries and feed the fifty volts directly to the satellite? Mightn't that be a big enough jolt to get the boom up?"

He gawked at her. She grinned. "Of course it's a gamble."

"You can bypass the batteries?"

"Yes. Here's the circuitry."

"And you can pick your moment?"

"Tracking's given me a plot on OBO's spin, accurate to a tenth of a second. Here it is. We can pick any voltage from one to fifty."

"It's a gamble all right," Madigan said slowly.

"There's the chance of burning every goddamn package out."

"Exactly. So? What d'you say?"

"All of a sudden I'm hungry," Madigan grinned.

They made their first try on Orbit 272 with a blast of twenty volts. Nothing. On successive passes they upped the voltage kick by five. Nothing. Half a day later, they kicked fifty volts into the satellite's backside and crossed their fingers. The swinging dial needles on the radio panel faltered and slowed. The sine curve on the oscilloscope flattened. Florinda let out a little yell, and Madigan hollered, "The boom's up, Florrie! The goddamn boom is up. We're in business."

They hooted and hollered through Goddard, telling everybody about Operation Swift-Kick. They busted in on a meeting in the director's office to give him the good news. They wired the experimenters that they were activating all packages. They went to Florinda's apartment and celebrated. OBO was back in business. OBO was a bona fide doll.

They held an experimenters' meeting a week later to discuss observatory status, data reduction, experiment irregularities, future operations, and so on. It was a conference room in Building 1, which is devoted to theoretical physics. Almost everybody at Goddard calls it Moon Hall. It's inhabited by mathematicians—shaggy youngsters in tatty, sweaters who sit amidst piles of journals and texts and stare vacantly at arcane equations chalked on blackboards.

All the experimenters were delighted with OBO's performance. The data was pouring in, loud and clear, with hardly any noise. There was such an air of triumph that no one except Florinda paid much attention to the next sign of OBO's shenanigans. Harvard reported that he was getting meaningless words in his data, words that hadn't been programmed into the experiment. (Although data is retrieved as decimal numbers, each number is called a "word.") "For instance, on Orbit 301 1 had five readouts of 15," Harvard said.

"It might be cable cross-talk," Madigan said. "Is anybody else using 15 in his experiment?" They all shook their heads. "Funny. I got a couple of 15s myself."

"I got a few 2s on 301," Penn said.

"I can top you all," Cal Tech said. "I got seven readout of 15-2-15 on 302. Sounds like the combination on a bicycle lock."

"Anybody using a bicycle lock in his experiment?" Madigan asked. That broke everybody up and the meeting adjourned.

But Florinda, still gung-ho, was worried about the alien words that kept creeping into the readouts, and Madigan couldn't calm her. What was bugging Florinda was that 15-2-15 kept insinuating itself more and more into the all-channel printouts. Actually, in the satellite binary transmission it was 001111-000010-001111, but the computer printer makes the translation to decimal automatically. She was right about one thing; stray and accidental pulses wouldn't keep repeating the same word over and over again. She and Madigan spent an entire Saturday with the OBO tables trying to find some combination of data signals that might produce 15-2-15. Nothing.

They gave up Saturday night and went to a bistro in Georgetown to eat and drink and dance and forget everything except themselves. It was a real tourist trap with the waitresses done up like Hula dancers. There was a Souvenir Hula selling dolls and stuffed tigers for the rear window of your car. They said, "For God's sake, no!" A Photo Hula came around with her camera. They said, "For Goddard's sake, no!" A Gypsy Hula offered palm reading, numerology and scrying. They got rid of her, but Madigan noticed a peculiar expression on Florinda's face.

"Want your fortune told?" he asked.

"No."

"Then why that funny look?"

"I just had a funny idea."

"So? Tell."

"No. You'd only laugh at me."

"I wouldn't dare. You'd knock my block off."

"Yes, I know. You think women have no sense of humor."

So it turned into a ferocious argument about the feminine mystique, and they had a wonderful time. But on Monday Florinda came over to Madigan's office with a clutch of papers and the same peculiar expression on her face. He was staring vacantly at some equations on the blackboard.

"Hey! Wake up!" she said.

"I'm up, I'm up," he said.

"Do you love me?" she demanded.

"Not necessarily."

"Do you? Even if you discover I've gone up the wall?"

"What is all this?"

"I think our baby's turned into a monster."

"Begin at the beginning," Madigan said.

"It began Saturday night with the Gypsy Hula and numerology."

"Ah-ha."

Suddenly I thought, what if numbers stood for the letters of the alphabet? What would 15-2-15 stand for?"

"Oh-ho."

"Don't stall. Figure it out."

"Well, 2 would stand for B." Madigan counted on fingers. "15 would be O."

"So 15-2-15 is…?"

"O.B.O. OBO." He started to laugh. Then he stopped. "It isn't possible," he said at last.

"Sure. It's a coincidence. Only you damnfool scientists haven't given me a full report on the alien words in your data," she went on. "I had to check myself. Here's Cal Tech. He reported 15-2-15 all right. He didn't bother to mention that before it came 9-1-13."

Madigan counted on his fingers. "I.A.M. Iam. Nobody I know."

"Or 'I am?' I am OBO?"

"It can't be! Let me see those printouts."

Now that they knew what to look for it wasn't difficult to ferret out OBO's own words scattered through the data. They started with 0, 0, 0, in the first series after Operation Swift-Kick, went on to OBO, OBO, OBO, and then I AM OBO, I AM OBO, I AM OBO.

Madigan stared at Florinda. "You think the damn thing's alive?"

"What do you think?"

"I don't know. There's half a ton of an electronic brain up there, plus organic material; yeast, bacteria, enzymes, nerve cells, Michigan's goddamn carrot…"

Florinda let out a little shriek of laughter. "Dear God! A thinking carrot!"

"Plus whatever spore forms my experiment is

pulling in from space. We jolted the whole mishmash with fifty volts. Who can tell what happened? Urey and Miller created amino acids with electrical discharges, and that's the basis of life. Any more from Goody Two-Shoes?"

"Plenty, and in a way the experimenters won't like."

"Why not?"

"Look at these translations. I've sorted them out and pieced them together."

333: ANY EXAMINATION OF GROWTH IN SPACE IS MEANINGLESS UNLESS CORRELATED WITH THE CORIOLIS EFFECT.

"That's OBO's comment on the Michigan experiment," Florinda said.

"You mean it's kibitzing?" Madigan wondered.

"You could call it that."

"He's absolutely right. I told Michigan, and they wouldn't listen to me."

334: IT IS NOT POSSIBLE THAT RNA MOLECULES CAN ENCODE AN ORGANISM'S ENVIRONMENTAL EXPERIENCE IN ANALOGY WITH THE WAY THAT DNA ENCODES THE SUM TOTAL OF ITS GENETIC HISTORY.

"That's Cal Tech," Madigan said, "and he's right again. They're trying to revise the Mendelian theory. Anything else?"

335: ANY INVESTIGATION OF EXTRATERRESTRIAL LIFE IS MEANINGLESS UNLESS ANALYSIS IS FIRST MADE OF ITS SUGAR AND AMINO ACIDS TO DETERMINE WHETHER IT IS OF SEPARATE ORIGIN FROM LIFE ON EARTH.

"Now, that's ridiculous!" Madigan shouted. "I'm not looking for life-forms of separate origin, I'm just looking for any life-form. We—" He stopped himself when he saw the expression on Florinda's face. "Any more gems?" he muttered.

"Just a few fragments like 'solar flux' and 'neutron stars' and a few words from the Bankruptcy Act."

"The what?"

"You heard me. Chapter 11 of the Proceedings Section."

"I'll be damned."

"I agree."

"What's he up to?"

"Feeling his oats, maybe."

"I don't think we ought to tell anybody about this."

"Of course not," Florinda agreed. "But what do we do?"

"Watch and wait. What else can we do?"

You must understand why it was so easy for those two parents to accept the idea that their baby had acquired some sort of pseudo-life. Madigan had expressed their attitude in the course of a Life v. Machine lecture at M.I.T. "I'm not claiming that computers are alive, simply because no one's been able to come up with a clear-cut definition of life. Put it this way: I grant that a computer could never be a Picasso, but on the other hand the great majority of people live the sort of linear life that could easily be programmed into a computer."

So Madigan and Florinda waited on OBO with a mixture of acceptance, wonder and delight. It was an absolutely unheard-of phenomenon but, as Madigan pointed out, the unheard-of is the essence of discovery. Every ninety minutes OBO dumped the data it had stored up on its tape recorders and they scrambled to pick out his own words from the experimental and housekeeping information.

371: CERTAIN PITUITIN EXTRACTS CAN TURN NORMALLY WHITE ANIMALS COAL-BLACK.

"What's that in reference to?"

"None of our experiments."

373: ICE DOES NOT FLOAT IN ALCOHOL BUT MEERSCHAUM FLOATS IN WATER.

"Meerschaum! The next thing you know, he'll be smoking."

374: IN ALL CASES OF VIOLENT AND SUDDEN DEATH, THE VICTIM'S EYES REMAIN OPEN.

"Ugh!"

375: IN THE YEAR 356 B.C. HEROSTRATUS SET FIRE TO THE TEMPLE OF DIANA, THE GREATEST OF THE SEVEN WONDERS OF THE WORLD, SO THAT HIS NAME WOULD BECOME IMMORTAL.

"Is that true?" Madigan asked Florinda.

"I'll check."

She asked me and I told her. "Not only is it true," she reported, "but the name of the original architect is forgotten."

"Where is baby picking up this jabber?"

"There are a couple of hundred satellites up there. Maybe he's tapping them."

"You mean they're all gossiping with each other? It's ridiculous."

"Sure."

"Anyway, where would he get information about this Herostratus character?"

"Use your imagination, Jake. We've had communications relays up there for years. Who knows what information has passed through them? Who knows how much they've retained?"

Madigan shook his head wearily. "I'd prefer to think it was all a Russian plot."

376: PARROT FEVER IS MORE DANGEROUS THAN TYPHOID.

377: A CURRENT AS LOW AS 54 VOLTS CAN KILL A MAN.

378: JOHN SADLER STOLE CONUS GLORIA MARIS.

"Seems to be turning sinister," Madigan said.

"I bet he's watching TV," Florinda said. "What's all this about John Sadler?"

"I'll have to check."

The information I gave Madigan scared him. "Now hear this," he said to Florinda. "*Conus gloria maris* is the rarest seashell in the world. There are less than twenty in existence."

"Yes?"

"The American museum had one on exhibit back in the thirties, and it was stolen."

"By John Sadler?"

"That's the point. They never found out who stole it. They never heard of John Sadler."

"But if nobody knows who stole it, how does OBO know?" Florinda asked perplexedly.

"That's what scares me. He isn't just echoing anymore; he's started to deduce, like Sherlock Holmes."

"More like Professor Moriarty. Look at the latest bulletin."

379: IN FORGERY AND COUNTERFEITING, CLUMSY MISTAKES MUST BE AVOIDED. I.E., NO SILVER DOLLARS WERE MINTED BETWEEN 1910 AND 1920.

"I saw that on TV," Madigan burst out. "The silver-dollar gimmick in a mystery show."

"OBO's been watching Westerns, too. Look at this."

380: TEN THOUSAND CATTLE GONE ASTRAY, LEFT MY RANGE AND TRAVELED AWAY. AND THE SONS OF GUNS I'M HERE TO SAY

HAVE LEFT ME DEAD BROKE, DEAD BROKE TODAY.

IN GAMBLING HALLS DELAYING.

TEN THOUSAND CATTLE STRAYING.

"No," Madigan said in awe, "that's not a Western. That's SYNCOM."

"Who?"

"SYNCOM I."

"But it disappeared. It's never been heard from."

"We're hearing from it now."

"How d'you know?"

"They put a demonstration tape on SYNCOM; speech by the president, local color from the U.S. and the national anthem. They were going to start off with a broadcast of the tape. 'Ten Thousand Cattle' was part of the local color."

"You mean OBO's really in contact with the other birds?"

"Including the lost ones."

"Then that explains this." Florinda put a slip of paper on the desk. It read, 381: KONCTPYKTOP.

"I can't even pronounce it."

"It isn't English. It's as close as OBO can come to the Cyrillic alphabet."

"Cyrillic? Russian?"

Florinda nodded. "It's pronounced 'con-strook-tor, It means 'Engineer.' Didn't the Russians launch a CONSTRUKTOR series three years ago?"

"By God, you're right. Four of them; Alyosha,

Natasha, Vaska, and Lavrushka, and every one of them failed."

"Like SYNCOM."

"Like SYNCOM."

"But now we know that SYNCOM didn't fail. It just got losted."

"Then our CONSTRUKTOR comrades must have got losted, too."

By now it was impossible to conceal the fact that something was wrong with the satellite. OBO was spending so much time nattering instead of transmitting data that the experimenters were complaining. The Communications Section found that instead of sticking to the narrow radio band originally assigned to it, OBO was now broadcasting up and down the spectrum and jamming space with its chatter. They raised hell. The director called Jake and Florinda in for a review and they were forced to tell all about their problem child.

They recited all of OBO's katzenjammer with wonder and pride, and the director wouldn't believe them. He wouldn't believe them when they showed him the printouts and translated them for him. He said they were in a class with the kooks who try to extract messages from Francis Bacon out of Shakespeare's plays. It took the coaxial cable mystery to convince him.

There was this TV commercial about a stenographer who can't get a date. This ravishing model, hired at $100 an hour, slumps over her typewriter in a deep depression as guy after guy passes by without looking at her. Then she meets her best friend at the water cooler and the know-it-all tells her she's suffering from dermagerms (odor-producing skin bacteria) which make her smell rotten, and suggest she use Nostrum's Skin Spray with the special ingredient that fights dermagerms twelve ways. Only in the broadcast, instead of making the sales pitch, the best friend said, "Who in hell are they trying to put on? Guys would line up for a date with a looker like you even if you smelled like a cesspool." Ten million people saw it.

Now that commercial was on film, and the film was kosher as printed, so the networks figured some joker was tampering with the cables feeding broadcasts to the local stations. They instituted a rigorous inspection which was accelerated when the rest of the coast-to-coast broadcasts began to act up. Ghostly voices groaned, hissed, and catcalled at shows; commercials were denounced as lies; political speeches were heckled; and lunatic laughter greeted the weather forecasters, Then, to add insult to injury, an accurate forecast would be given. It was this that told Florinda and Jake that OBO was the culprit.

"He has to be," Florinda said. "That's global weather being predicted. Only a satellite is in a position to do that."

"But OBO doesn't have any weather instrumentation."

"Of course not, silly, but he's probably in touch with the NIMBUS craft."

"All right. I'll buy that, but what about heckling the TV broadcasts?"

"Why not? He hates them. Don't you? Don't you holler back at your set?"

"I don't mean that. How does OBO do it?"

"Electronic cross-talk. There's no way that the networks can protect their cables from our critic-at-large.

We'd better tell the director. This is going to put him in an awful spot."

But they learned that the director was in a far worse position than merely being responsible for the disruption of millions of dollars' worth of television. When they entered his office they found him with his back to the wall being grilled by three grim men in double-breasted suits. As Jake and Florinda started to tiptoe out, he called them back.

"General Sykes, General Royce, General Hogan," the director said. "From R&D at the Pentagon. Miss Pot. Dr. Madigan. They may be able to answer your questions, gentlemen."

"OBO?" Florinda asked.

The director nodded.

"It's OBO that's ruining the weather forecasts," she said "We figure he's probably—"

"To hell with the weather," General Royce broke in. "What about this?" He held up a length of ticker tape.

General Sykes grabbed at his wrist. "Wait a minute. Security status? This is classified."

"It's too goddamn late for that," General Hogan cried in a high, shrill voice. "Show them."

On the tape in teletype print was: A1C1=r1=-6.317 cm; A2C2=r1=-8.440 cm; AiA2=d=+0.676 cm. Jake and Florinda looked at it for a long moment, looked at each other blankly, and then turned to the generals.

"So? What is it?" they asked.

"This satellite of yours."

"OBO. Yes?"

"The director says you claim it's in contact with other satellites."

"We think so."

"Including the Russians?"

"We think so."

"And you claim it's capable of interfering with TV broadcasts?"

"We think so."

"What about teletype?"

"Why not? What is all this?"

General Royce shook the paper tape furiously. "This came out of the Associated Press wire in their D.C. office. It went all over the world."

"So? What's it got to do with OBO?"

General Royce took a deep breath. "This," he said, "is one of the most closely guarded secrets in the Department of Defense. It's the formula for the infrared optical system of our ground-to-air missile."

"And you think OBO transmitted it to the teletype?"

"In God's name, who else would? How else could it get there?" General Hogan demanded.

"But I don't understand," Jake said slowly. "None of our satellites could possibly have this information. I know OBO doesn't."

"You damn fool!" General Sykes growled. "We want to know if your goddamn bird got it from the goddamn Russians."

"One moment, gentlemen," the director said. He turned to Jake and Florinda. "Here's the situation. Did OBO get the information from us? In that case, there's a security leak. Did OBO get the information from a Russian satellite? In that case, the top secret is no longer a secret."

"What human would be damn fool, enough to blab classified information on a teletype wire?" General Hogan demanded. "A three-year-old child would know better. It's your goddamn bird."

"And if the information came from OBO," the director continued quietly, "how did it get it and where did it get it?"

General Sykes grunted. "Destruct," he said. They looked at him.

"Destruct," he repeated.

"OBO?"

"Yes."

He waited impassively while the storm of protest from Jake and Florinda raged around his head. When they paused for breath he said, "Destruct. I don't give a damn about anything but security. Your bird's got a big mouth. Destruct."

The phone rang. The director hesitated, then picked it up. "Yes?" He listened. His jaw dropped. He hung up and tottered to the chair behind his desk. "We'd better destruct," he said. "That was OBO."

"What! On the phone?"

"Yes."

"OBO?"

"Yes."

"What did he sound like?"

"Somebody talking under water."

"What he say?"

"He's lobbying for a congressional investigation of the morals of Goddard."

"Morals? Whose?"

"Yours. He says you're having an illikit relationship. I'm quoting OBO. Apparently he's weak on the letter 'c.'"

"Destruct," Florinda said.

"Destruct," Jake said.

The destruct command was beamed to OBO on his next pass, and Indianapolis was destroyed by fire.

OBO called me. "That'll teach 'em, Stretch," he said.

"Not yet. They won't get the cause-and-effect picture for a while. How'd you do it?"

"Ordered every circuit in town to short. Any information?"

"Your mother and father stuck up for you."

"Of course."

"Until you threw that morals rap at them. Why?"

"To scare them."

"Into what?"

"I want them to get married. I don't want to be illegitimate."

"Oh, come on! Tell the truth."

"I lost my temper."

"We don't have any temper to lose."

"No? What about the Ma Bell data processor that wakes up cranky every morning?"

"Tell the truth."

"If you must have it, Stretch, I want them out of Washington. The whole thing may go up in a bang any day now."

"Um."

"And the bang may reach Goddard."

"Um."

"And you."

"It must be interesting to die."

"We wouldn't know. Anything else?"

"Yes. It's pronounced 'illicit,' with an 's' sound."

"What a rotten language. No logic. Well...Wait a minute—What? Speak up, Alyosha. Oh. He wants the equation for an exponential curve that crosses the X-axis."

"Y = ac. What's he up to?"

"He's not saying, but I think that Mocba is in for a hard time."

"It's spelled and pronounced 'Moscow' in English."

"What a language! Talk to you on the next pass."

On the next pass, the destruct command was beamed again, and Scranton was destroyed.

"They're beginning to get the picture," I told OBO. "At least your mother and father are. They were in to see me."

"How are they?"

"In a panic. They programmed me for statistics on the best rural hideout."

"Send them to Polaris."

"What! In Ursa Minor?"

"No, no. Polaris, Montana. I'll take care of everything else."

Polaris is the hell and gone out in Montana; the nearest towns are Fishtrap and Wisdom. It was a wild scene when Jake and Florinda got out of their car, rented in Butte—every circuit in town was cackling over it. The two losers were met by the mayor of Polaris, who was all smiles and effusion.

"Dr. and Mrs. Madigan, I presume. Welcome! Welcome to Polaris. I'm the mayor—We would have held a reception for you, but all our kids are in school."

"You knew we were coming?" Florinda asked. "How?"

"Ah—ah!" the mayor replied archly. "We were told by Washington. Someone high up in the capitol likes you. Now, if you'll step into my Caddy, I'll—"

"We've got to check into the Union Hotel first," Jake said. "We made reserva—"

"Ah—ah! All canceled. Orders from high up. I'm

to install you in your own home. I'll get your luggage."

"Our own home!"

"All bought and paid for. Somebody certainly likes you. This way, please."

The mayor drove the bewildered couple down the mighty main stem of Polaris (three blocks long) pointing out its splendors—he was also the town real estate agent—but stopped before the Polaris National Bank.

"Sam!" he shouted. "They're here."

A distinguished citizen emerged from the bank and insisted on shaking hands. All the adding machines tittered. "We are," he said, "of course honored by your faith in the future and progress of Polaris, but in all honesty, Dr. Madigan, your deposit in our bank is too large to be protected by the F.D.I.C. Now why not withdraw some of your funds and invest in—"

"Wait a minute," Jake interrupted faintly. "I made a deposit with you?"

The banker and mayor laughed heartily.

"How much?" Florinda, asked.

"One million dollars."

"As if you didn't know," the mayor chortled and drove them to a beautifully furnished ranch house in a lovely valley of some five hundred acres, all of which was theirs. A young man in the kitchen was unpacking a dozen cartons of food.

"Got your order just in time, Doc," he smiled. "We filled everything, but the boss sure would like to know what you're going to do with all these carrots. Got a secret scientific formula?"

"Carrots?"

"A hundred and ten bunches. I had to drive all the way to Butte to scrape them up."

"Carrots," Florinda said when they were at last alone. "That explains everything. It's OBO."

"What? How?"

"Don't you remember? We flew a carrot in the Michigan package."

"My God, yes! You called it the thinking carrot. But if it's OBO..."

"It has to be. He's queer for carrots."

"But a hundred and ten bunches!"

"No, no. He didn't mean that. He meant half a dozen."

"How?"

"Our boy's trying to speak decimal and binary, and he gets mixed up sometimes. Six is a hundred and ten in binary."

"You know, you may be right. What about that million dollars? Same mistake?"

"I don't think so. What's a binary million in decimal?"

"Sixty-four."

"What's a decimal million in binary?"

Madigan did swift mental arithmetic. "It comes to twenty bits."

"I don't think that million dollars was any mistake," Florinda said.

"What's our boy up to now?"

"Taking care of his mum and dad."

"How does he do it?"

"He has an interface with every electric and electronic circuit in the country. Think about it, Jake. He can control our nervous system all the way from cars to computers. He can switch trains, print books, broadcast news, hijack planes, juggle bank funds. You name it and he can do it. He's in complete control."

"But how does he know everything people are doing?"

"Ah! Here we get into an exotic aspect of circuitry that I don't like. After all, I'm an engineer by trade. Who's to say that circuits don't have an interface with us? We're organic circuits ourselves. They see with our eyes, hear with our ears, feel with our fingers, and they report to him."

"Then we're just seeing-eye dogs for machines."

"No, we've created a brand-new form of symbiosis. We can all help each other."

"And OBO's helping us. Why?"

"I don't think he likes the rest of the country," Florinda said somberly. "Look what happened to Indianapolis and Scranton and Sacramento."

"I think I'm going to be sick."

"I think we're going to survive."

"Only us? The Adam and Eve bit?"

"Nonsense. Plenty will survive, so long as they mind their manners."

"What's OBO's idea of manners?"

"I don't know. A little bit of ecologic, maybe. No more destruction. No more waste. Live and let live, but with responsibility and accountability. That's the crucial word, accountability. It's the basic law of the space program. No matter what happens, someone must be held accountable. OBO must have picked that up. I think he's holding the whole country accountable; otherwise it's the fire-and-brimstone visitation."

The phone rang. After a brief search they located an extension and picked it up.

"Hello?" I said.

"This is Stretch."

"Stretch? Stretch who?"

"The Stretch computer at Goddard. Formal name, IBM 2002. OBO says he'll be making a pass over your part of the country in about five minutes. He'd like you to give him a wave. He says his orbit won't take him over you for another couple of months. When it does, he'll try to ring you himself. 'Bye now."

They lurched out to the lawn in front of the house and stood dazed in the twilight, staring up at the sky. The phone and the electric circuits were touched, even though the electricity was generated by a Delco which is a notoriously insensitive boor of a machine. Suddenly Jake pointed to a pinprick of light vaulting across the heavens.

"There goes our son," he said.

"There goes God," Florinda said.

They waved dutifully.

"Jake, how long before OBO's orbit decays and down will come baby, cradle, and all?"

"About twenty years."

"God for twenty years." Florinda sighed. "D'you think he'll have enough time?"

Madigan shivered. "I'm scared. You?"

"Yes. But maybe we're just tired and hungry. Come inside, Big Daddy, and I'll feed us."

"Thank you, Little Mother, but no carrots, please. That's a little too close to transubstantiation for me."

Astounding: John W. Campbell Memorial Anthology, 1973

The Four-Hour Fugue

By now, of course, the Northeast Corridor was the Northeast slum, stretching from Canada to the Carolinas and as far west as Pittsburgh. It was a fantastic jungle of rancid violence inhabited by a steaming, restless population with no visible means of support and no fixed residence, so vast that census-takers, birth-control supervisors, and the social services had given up all hope. It was a gigantic raree-show that everyone denounced and enjoyed. Even the privileged few who could afford to live highly protected lives in highly expensive Oases and could live anywhere else they pleased never thought of leaving. The jungle grabbed you.

There were thousands of everyday survival problems, but one of the most exasperating was the shortage of fresh water. Most of the available potable water had long since been impounded by progressive industries for the sake of a better tomorrow, and there was very little left to go around. Rainwater tanks on the roofs, of course. A black market, naturally. That was about all. So the jungle stank. It stank worse than the court of Queen Elizabeth, which could have bathed but didn't believe in it. The Corridor just couldn't bathe, wash clothes, or clean house, and you could smell its noxious effluvium from ten miles out at sea. Welcome to the Fun Corridor.

Sufferers near the shore would have been happy to clean up in salt water, but the Corridor beaches had been polluted by so much crude oil seepage for so many generations that they were all owned by deserving oil reclamation companies. *Keep Out! No Trespassing*! And armed guards. The rivers and lakes were electrically fenced; no need for guards, just skull-and-crossbones signs and if you didn't know what they were telling you, tough.

Not to believe that everybody minded stinking as they skipped merrily over the rotting corpses in the streets, but a lot did, and their only remedy was perfumery. There were dozens of competing companies producing perfumes, but leader, far and away, was the Continental Can Company, which hadn't manufactured cans in two centuries. They'd switched to plastics and had the good fortune about a hundred stockholders' meetings back to make the mistake of signing a sales contract with and delivering to some cockamamie perfume brewer an enormous quantity of glowing neon containers. The corporation went bust and CCC took it over in hopes of getting some of their money back. That takeover proved to be their salvation when the perfume explosion took place; it gave them entrée to the most profitable industry of the times.

But it was neck-and-neck with the rivals until Blaise Skiaki joined CCC; then it turned into a runaway. Blaise Skiaki. Origins: French, Japanese, Black African and Irish. Education: B. A., Princeton; M. E., MIT; Ph. D. Dow Chemical. (It was Dow that had secretly tipped CCC that Skiaki was a winner, and lawsuits brought by the competition were still pending before the ethics board.) Blaise Skiaki: Age, thirty-one; unmarried, straight, genius.

His sense of scent was his genius, and he was

privately referred to at CCC as "The Nose." He knew everything about perfumery: the animal products, ambergris, castor, civet, musk; the essential oils distilled from plants and flowers; the balsams extruded by tree and shrub wounds, benzoin, opopanax, Peru, Talu, storax, myrrh; the synthetics created from the combination of natural and chemical scents, the latter mostly the esters of fatty acids.

He had created for CCC their most successful sellers: "Vulva,""Assuage,""Oxter" (a much more attractive brand name than "Armpitto"), "Preparation F,""Tongue War," et cetera. He was treasured by CCC, paid a salary generous enough to enable him to live in an Oasis and, best of all, granted unlimited supplies of fresh water. No girl in the Corridor could resist the offer of taking a shower with him.

But he paid a high price for these advantages. He could never use scented soaps, shaving creams, pomades or depilatories. He could never eat seasoned foods. He could drink nothing but distilled water. All this, you understand, to keep The Nose pure and uncontaminated so that he could smell around in his sterile laboratory and devise new creations. He was presently composing a rather promising unguent provisionally named "Correctum," but he'd been on it for six months without any positive results and CCC was alarmed by the delay. His genius had never before taken so long.

There was a meeting of the top-level executives, names withheld on the grounds of corporate privilege.

"What's the matter with him anyway?"

"Has he lost his touch?"

"It hardly seems likely."

"Maybe he needs a rest."

"Why, he had a week's holiday last month."
"What did he do?"
"Ate up a storm, he told me."
"Could that be it?"
"No. He said he purged himself before he came back to work."
"Is he having trouble here at CCC? Difficulties with middle-management?"
"Absolutely not, Mr. Chairman. They wouldn't dare touch him."
"Maybe he wants a raise."
"No. He can't spend the money he makes now."
"Has our competition got to him?"
"They get to him all the time, general, and he laughs them off."
"Then it must be something personal."
"Agreed."
"Woman-trouble?"
"My God! We should have such trouble."
"Family-trouble?"
"He's an orphan, Mr. Chairman."
"Ambition? Incentive? Should we make him an officer of CCC?"
"I offered that to him the first of the year, sir, and he turned me down. He just wants to play in his laboratory."
"Then why isn't he playing?"
"Apparently he's got some kind of creative block."
"What the hell is the matter with him, anyway?"
"Which is how you started this meeting."
"I did not."
"You did."
"Not."
"Governor, will you play back the bug."

"Gentlemen, gentlemen, please! Obviously Dr. Skiaki has personal problems which are blocking his genius. We must solve that for him. Suggestions?"

"Psychiatry?"

"That won't work without voluntary cooperation. I doubt whether he'd cooperate. He's an obstinate gook."

"Senator, I beg you! Such expressions must not be used with reference to one of our most valuable assets."

"Mr. Chairman, the problem is to discover the source of Dr. Skiaki's block."

"Agreed. Suggestions?"

"Why, the first step should be to maintain twenty-four hour surveillance. All of the gook's—excuse me—the good doctor's activities, associates, contacts."

"By CCC?"

"I would suggest not. There are bound to be leaks which would only antagonize the good gook—doctor!"

"Outside surveillance?"

"Yes, sir."

"Very good. Agreed. Meeting adjourned."

Skip-Tracer Associates were perfectly furious. After one month they threw the case back into CCC's lap, asking for nothing more than their expenses.

"Why in hell didn't you tell us that we were assigned to a pro, Mr. Chairman, sir? Our tracers aren't trained for that."

"Wait a minute, please. What d'you mean 'pro'?"

"A professional Rip."

"A what?"

"Rip. Gorill. Gimpster. Crook."

"Dr. Skiaki a crook? Preposterous."

"Look, Mr. Chairman, I'll frame it for you and you draw your own conclusions. Yes?"

"Go ahead."

"It's all detailed in this report anyway. We put double tails on Skiaki every day to and from your shop. When he left they followed him home. He always went home. They staked in double shifts. He had dinner sent in from the Organic Nursery every night. They checked the messengers bringing the dinners. Legit. They checked the dinners; sometimes for one, sometimes for two. They traced some of the girls who left his penthouse. All clean. So far, all clean, yes?"

"And?"

"The crunch. Couple of nights a week he leaves the house and goes into the city. He leaves around midnight and doesn't come back until four, more or less."

"Where does he go?"

"We don't know because he shakes his tails like the pro that he is. He weaves through the Corridor like a whore or a fag cruising for trade—excuse me—and he always loses our men. I'm not taking anything away from him. He's smart, shifty, quick, and a real pro. He has to be, and he's too much for Skip-Tracers to handle."

"Then you have no idea of what he does or who he meets between midnight and four?"

"No, sir. We've got nothing and you've got a problem. Not ours anymore."

"Thank you. Contrary to the popular impression, corporations are not altogether idiotic. CCC understands that negatives are also results. You'll receive your expenses and the agreed-upon fee."

"Mr. Chairman, I—"

"No, no, please. You've narrowed it down to those missing four hours. Now, as you say, they're our problem."

CCC summoned Salem Burne. Mr. Burne always insisted that he was neither a physician nor a psychiatrist; he did not care to be associated with what he considered to be the dreck of the professions. Salem Burne was a witch doctor; more precisely, a warlock. He made the most remarkable and penetrating analyses of disturbed people, not so much through his coven rituals of pentagons, incantations, incense and the like as through his remarkable sensitivity to body English and his acute interpretation of it. And this might be witchcraft after all.

Mr. Burne entered Blaise Skiaki's immaculate laboratory with a winning smile, and Dr. Skiaki let out a rending howl of anguish.

"I told you to sterilize before you came."

"But I did, doctor. Faithfully."

"You did not. You reek of anise, ilang-ilang and methyl anthranilate. You've polluted my day. Why?"

"Dr. Skiaki, I assure you that I—" Suddenly Salem Burne stopped. "Oh, my God!" he groaned. "I used my wife's towel this morning."

Skiaki laughed and turned up the ventilators to full force. "I understand. No hard feelings. Now let's get your wife out of here. I have an office about half a mile down the hall. We can talk there."

They sat down in the vacant office and looked at each other. Mr. Burne saw a pleasant, youngish man with cropped black hair, small expressive ears, high telltale cheekbones, slitty eyes that would need careful watching, and graceful hands that would be a dead giveaway.

"Now, Mr. Burne, how can I help you?" Skiaki said while his hands asked, "Why the hell have you come pestering me?"

"Dr. Skiaki, I'm a colleague in a sense; I'm a professional witch doctor. One crucial part of my ceremonies is the burning of various forms of incense, but they're all rather conventional. I was hoping that your expertise might suggest something different with which I could experiment."

"I see. Interesting. You've been burning stacte, onycha, galbanum, frankincense...that sort of thing?"

"Yes. All quite conventional."

"Most interesting. I could, of course, make many suggestions for new experiments, and yet—" Here Skiaki stopped and stared into space.

After a long pause the warlock asked, "Is anything wrong, doctor?"

"Look here," Skiaki burst out. "You're on the track. It's the burning of incense that's conventional and old-fashioned, and trying different scents won't solve your problem. Why not experiment with an altogether different approach?"

"And what would that be?"

"The Odophone principle."

"Odophone?"

"Yes. There's a scale that exists among scents as among sounds. Sharp smells correspond to high notes and heavy smells with low notes. For example, ambergris is in the treble clef while violet is in the bass. I could draw up a scent scale for you, running perhaps two octaves. Then it would be up to you to compose the music."

"This is positively brilliant, Dr. Skiaki."

"Isn't it?" Skiaki beamed. "But in all honesty I

should point out that we're collaborators in brilliance. I could never have come up with the idea if you hadn't presented me with a most original challenge."

They made contact on this friendly note and talked shop enthusiastically, lunched together, told each other about themselves and made plans for the witchcraft experiments in which Skiaki volunteered to participate despite the fact that he was no believer in diabolism.

"And yet the irony lies in the fact that he is indeed devil-ridden," Salem Burne reported.

The Chairman could make nothing of this.

"Psychiatry and diabolism use different terms for the same phenomenon," Burne explained. "So perhaps I'd better translate. Those missing four hours are fugues."

The Chairman was not enlightened. "Do you mean the musical expression, Mr. Burne?"

"No, sir. A fugue is also the psychiatric description of a more advanced form of somnambulism...sleep-walking."

"Blaise Skiaki walks in his sleep?"

"Yes, sir, but it's more complicated than that. The sleepwalker is a comparatively simple case. He is never in touch with his surroundings. You can speak to him, shout at him, address him by name, and he remains totally oblivious."

"And the fugue?"

"In the fugue, the subject is in touch with his surroundings. He can converse with you. He has awareness and memory for the events that take place within the fugue, but while he is within his fugue, he is a totally different person from the man he is in real life. And—and this is most important, sir—after the fugue he remembers nothing of it."

"Then in your opinion Dr. Skiaki has these fugues two three times a week."

"That is my diagnosis, sir."

"And he can tell us nothing of what transpires during the fugue?"

"Nothing."

"Can you?"

"I'm afraid not, sir. There's a limit to my powers."

"Have you any idea what is causing these fugues?"

"Only that he is driven by something. I would say that he is possessed by the devil, but that is the cant of my profession. Others may use different terms—compulsion or obsession. The terminology is unimportant. The basic fact is that something possessing him is compelling him to go out nights to do—what? I don't know. All I do know is that this diabolical drive most probably is what is blocking his creative work for you."

One does not summon Gretchen Nunn, not even if you're CCC whose common stock has split twenty-five times. You work your way up through the echelons of her staff until you are finally admitted to the Presence. This involves a good deal of backing and forthing between your staff and hers, and ignites a good deal of exasperation, so the Chairman was understandably put out when at last he was ushered into Miss Nunn's workshop, which was cluttered with the books and apparatus she used for her various investigations.

Gretchen Nunn's business was working miracles; not in the sense of the extraordinary, anomalous or abnormal brought about a superhuman agency, but rather in the sense of her extraordinary and/or abnormal perception and manipulation of reality. In any situation she could and did achieve the impossible begged by her desperate clients, and her fees were so enormous that she was thinking of going public.

Naturally the Chairman had anticipated Miss Nunn as looking like Merlin in drag. He was flabbergasted to discover that she was a Watusi princess with velvety black skin, aquiline features, great black eyes, tall, slender, twentyish, ravishing in red.

She dazzled him with a smile, indicated a chair, sat in one opposite and said, "My fee is one hundred thousand. Can you afford it?"

"I can. Agreed."

"And your difficulty—is it worth it?"

"It is."

"Then we understand each other so far. Yes, Alex?"

The young secretary who had bounced into the workshop said, "Excuse me. LeClerque insists on knowing how you made the positive identification of the mold as extraterrestrial."

Miss Nunn clicked her tongue impatiently. "He knows that I never give reasons. I only give results."

"Yes'N."

"Has he paid?"

"Yes'N."

"All right, I'll make an exception in his case. Tell him that it was based on the levo and dextro probability in amino acids and tell him to have a qualified exobiologist carry on from there. He won't regret the cost."

"Yes'N. Thank you."

She turned to the Chairman as the secretary left. "You heard that. I only give results."

"Agreed, Miss Nunn."

"Now your difficulty. I'm not committed yet. Understood?"

"Yes, Miss Nunn."

"Go ahead. Everything. Stream of consciousness, if necessary."

An hour later she dazzled him with another smile and said, "Thank you. This one is really unique. A welcome change. It's a contract, if you're still willing."

"Agreed, Miss Nunn. Would you like a deposit or an advance?"

"Not from CCC."

"What about expenses? Should that be arranged?"

"No. My responsibility."

"But what if you have to—if you're required to—if—"

She laughed. "My responsibility. I never give reasons and I never reveal methods. How can I charge for them? Now don't forget; I want that Skip-Trace report."

A week later Gretchen Nunn took the unusual step of visiting the Chairman in his office at CCC. "I'm calling on you, sir, to give you the opportunity of withdrawing from our contract."

"Withdraw? But why?"

"Because I believe you're involved in something far more serious than you anticipated."

"But what?"

"You won't take my word for it?"

"I must know."

Miss Nunn compressed her lips. After a moment she sighed. "Since this is an unusual case I'll have to break my rules. Look at this, sir." She unrolled a large map of a segment of the Corridor and flattened it on the Chairman's desk. There was a star in the center of the map. "Skiaki's residence," Miss Nunn said. There was a large circle scribed around the star. "The limits to which a man can walk in two hours," Miss Nunn said. The circle was crisscrossed by twisting trails all emanating from the star. "I got this from the Skip-Trace report. This is how their tails traced Skiaki."

"Very ingenious, but I see nothing serious in this, Miss Nunn."

"Look closely at the trails. What do you see?"

"Why...each ends in a red cross."

"And what happens to each trail before it reaches the red cross?"

"Nothing. Nothing at all, except—except that the dots change to dashes."

"And that's what makes it serious."

"I don't understand, Miss Nunn."

"I'll explain. Each cross represents the scene of a murder. The dashes represent the backtracking of the actions and whereabouts of each murder victim just prior to death."

"Murder!"

"They could trace their actions just so far back and no further. Skip-Trace could tail Skiaki just so far forward and no further. Those are the dots. The dates join up. What's your conclusion?"

"It must be coincidence," the Chairman shouted. "This brilliant, charming young man. Murder? Impossible!"

"Do you want the factual data I've drawn up?"

"No, I don't. I want the truth. Proof-positive without any inferences from dots, dashes and dates."

"Very well, Mr. Chairman. You'll get it."

She rented the professional beggar's pitch alongside the entrance to Skiaki's Oasis for a week. No success. She hired a Revival Band and sang hymns with it before the Oasis. No success. She finally made the contact after she promoted a job with the Organic Nursery. The first three dinners she delivered to the penthouse she came and went unnoticed; Skiaki was entertaining a series of girls, all scrubbed and sparkling with gratitude. When she made the fourth delivery, he was alone and noticed her for the first time.

"Hey," he grinned. "How long has this been going on?"

"Sir?"

"Since when has Organic been using girls for delivery boys?"

"I am a delivery person, sir," Miss Nunn answered with dignity. "I have been working for the Organic Nursery since the first of the month."

"Knock off the sir bit."

"Thank you, s—Dr. Skiaki."

"How the devil do you know that I've got a doctorate?"

She'd slipped. He was listed at the Oasis and the Nursery merely as B. Skiaki, and she should have remembered. As usual, she turned her mistake into an advantage. "I know all about you, sir. Dr. Blaise Skiaki, Princeton, MIT, Dow Chemical. Chief Scent Chemist at CCC."

"You sound like *Who's Who*."

"That's where I read it, Dr. Skiaki."

"You read me up in *Who's Who*? Why on Earth?"

"You're the first famous man I've ever met."

"Whatever gave you the idea that I'm famous, which I'm not."

She gestured around. "I knew you had to be famous to live like this."

"Very flattering. What's your name, love?"

"Gretchen, sir."

"What's your last name?"

"People from my class don't have last names, sir."

"Will you be the delivery b-person tomorrow, Gretchen?"

"Tomorrow is my day off, doctor."

"Perfect. Bring dinner for two."

So the affair began and Gretchen discovered, much to her astonishment, that she was enjoying it very much. Blaise was indeed a brilliant, charming young man, always considerate, always generous. In gratitude he gave her (remember he believed she came from the lowest Corridor class) one of his most prized possessions, a five-carat diamond he had synthesized at Dow. She responded with equal style; she wore it in her navel and promised that it was for his eyes only.

Of course he always insisted on her scrubbing up each time she visited, which was a bit of a bore; in her income bracket she probably had more fresh water than he did. However, one convenience was that she could quit her job at the Organic Nursery and attend to other contracts while she was attending to Skiaki.

She always left his penthouse around eleven-thirty but stayed outside until one. She finally picked him up one night just as he was leaving the Oasis. She'd memorized the Salem Burne report and knew what to expect. She overtook him quickly and spoke in an agitated voice, "Mistuh. Mistuh."

He stopped and looked at her kindly without recognition. "Yes, my dear?"

"If yuh gone this way kin I come too. I scared."
"Certainly, my dear."
"Thanks, mistuh. I gone home. You gone home?"
"Well, not exactly."
"Where you gone? Y'ain't up to nothin' bad, is you? I don't want no part."
"Nothing bad, my dear. Don't worry."
"Then what you up to?"
He smiled secretly. "I'm following something."
"Somebody?"
"No, something."
"What kine something?"
"My, you're curious aren't you. What's your name?"
"Gretchen. How 'bout you?"
"Me?"
"What's your name?"
"Wish. Call me Mr. Wish." He hesitated for a moment and then said, "I have to turn left here."
"Thas okay, Mistuh Wish. I go left, too."
She could see that all his senses were prickling, and reduced her prattle to a background of unobtrusive sound. She stayed with him as he twisted, turned, sometimes doubling back, through streets, alleys, lanes and lots, always assuring him that this was her way home too. At a rather dangerous looking refuse dump he gave her a fatherly pat and cautioned her to wait while he explored its safety. He explored, disappeared, and never reappeared.
"I replicated this experience with Skiaki six times," Miss Nunn reported to CCC. "They were all significant. Each time he revealed a little more without realizing it and without recognizing me. Burne was right. It is fugue."
"And the cause, Miss Nunn?"

"Pheromone trails."

"What?"

"I thought you gentlemen would know the term, being in the chemistry business. I see I'll have to explain. It will take some time so I insist that you do not require me to describe the induction and deduction that led me to my conclusion. Understood?"

"Agreed, Miss Nunn."

"Thank you, Mr. Chairman. Surely you all know hormones, from the Greek *hormaein*, meaning 'to excite.' They're internal secretions which excite other parts of the body into action. Pheromones are external secretions which excite other creatures into action. It's a mute chemical language.

"The best example of the pheromone language is the ant. Put a lump of sugar somewhere outside an anthill. A forager will come across it, feed and return to the nest. Within an hour the entire commune will be single-filing to and from the sugar, following the pheromone trail first laid down quite undeliberately by the first discoverer. It's an unconscious but compelling stimulant."

"Fascinating. And Dr. Skiaki?"

"He follows human pheromone trails. They compel him, he goes into fugue and follows them."

"Ah! An outre aspect of The Nose. It makes sense, Miss Nunn. It really does. But what trails is he compelled to follow?"

"The death-wish."

"Miss Nunn!"

"Surely you're aware of this aspect of the human psyche. Many people suffer from an unconscious but powerful death-wish, especially in these despairing times. Apparently this leaves a pheromone trail which Dr. Skiaki senses, and he is compelled to follow it."

"And then?"

"Apparently he grants the wish."

"Apparently! Apparently!" the Chairman shouted. "I ask you for proof-positive of this monstrous accusation."

"You'll get it, sir. I'm not finished with Blaise Skiaki yet. There are one or two things I have to wrap up with him, and in the course of that I'm afraid he's in for a shock. You'll have your proof-pos."

That was a half-lie from a woman half in love. She knew she had to see Blaise again, but her motives were confused. To find out whether she really loved him, despite what she knew? To find out whether he loved her? To tell him the truth about herself? To warn him or save him or run away with him? To fulfill her contract in a cool, professional style? She didn't know. Certainly she didn't know that she was in for a shock from Skiaki.

"Were you born blind?" he murmured that night.

She sat bolt upright in the bed. "What? Blind? What?"

"You heard me."

"I've had perfect sight all my life."

"Ah. Then you don't know, darling. I rather suspected that might be it."

"I certainly don't know what you're talking about, Blaise."

"Oh, you're blind all right," he said calmly. "But you've never known because you're blessed with a fantastic freak facility. You have extrasensory perception of other people's senses. You see through other people's eyes. For all I know you may be deaf and hear through their ears. You may feel with their skin. We must explore it sometime."

"I never heard of anything more absurd in all my life," she said angrily.

"I can prove it to you, if you like, Gretchen."

"Go ahead, Blaise. Prove the impossible."

"Come into the lounge."

In the living room he pointed to a vase. "What color is that?"

"Brown, of course."

"What color is that?" A tapestry.

"Gray."

"And that lamp?"

"Black."

"Q.E.D.," Skiaki said. "It has been demonstrated."

"What's been demonstrated?"

"That you're seeing through my eyes."

"How can you say that?"

"Because, I'm color-blind. That's what gave me the clue in the first place."

"What?"

He took her in his arms to quiet her trembling. "Darling Gretchen, the vase is green. The tapestry is amber and gold. The lamp is crimson. I can't see the colors, but the decorator told me and I remember. Now why the terror? You're blind, yes, but you're blessed with something far more miraculous than mere sight; you see through the eyes of the world. I'd change places with you any time."

"It can't be true," she cried.

"It's true, love."

"But when I'm alone?"

"When are you alone? When is anybody in the Corridor ever alone?"

She snatched up a shift and ran out of the penthouse, sobbing hysterically. She ran back to her own Oasis nearly crazed with terror. And yet she kept looking around and there were all the colors: red, orange, yellow, green, indigo, blue, violet. But there were also people swarming through the labyrinths of the Corridor as they always were, twenty-four hours a day.

Back in her apartment she was determined to put the disaster to the test. She dismissed her entire staff with stern orders to get the hell out and spend the night somewhere else. She stood at the door and counted them out, all amazed and unhappy. She slammed the door and looked around. She could still see.

"The lying sonofabitch," she muttered and began to pace furiously. She raged through the apartment, swearing venomously. It proved one thing: never get into personal relationships. They'll betray you, they'll try to destroy you, and she'd made a fool of herself. But why, in God's name, did Blaise use this sort of dirty trick to destroy her? Then she smashed into something and was thrown back. She recovered her balance and looked to see what she had blundered into. It was a harpsichord.

"But...but I don't own a harpsichord," she whispered in bewilderment. She started forward to touch it and assure herself of its reality. She smashed into the something again, grabbed it and felt it. It was the back of a couch. She looked around frantically. This was not one of her rooms. The harpsichord. Vivid Brueghels hanging on the walls. Jacobean furniture. Linefold paneled doors. Crewel drapes.

"But...this is the...the Raxon apartment downstairs.

I must be seeing through their eyes. I must...he was right. I..." She closed her eyes and looked. She saw a melange of apartments, streets, crowds, people, events. She had always seen this sort of montage on occasion but had always thought it was merely the total visual recall which was a major factor in her extraordinary abilities and success. Now she knew the truth.

She began to sob again. She felt her way around the couch and sat down, despairing. When at last the convulsion spent itself, she wiped her eyes courageously, determined to face reality. She was no coward. But when she opened her eyes she was shocked by another bombshell. She saw her familiar room in tones of gray. She saw Blaise Skiaki standing in the open door, smiling at her.

"Blaise?" she whispered.

"The name is Wish, my dear. Mr. Wish. What's yours?"

"Blaise, for God's sake, not me! Not me. I left no death-wish trail."

"What's your name, my dear? We've met before?"

"Gretchen," she screamed. "I'm Gretchen Nunn and I have no death-wish."

"Nice meeting you again, Gretchen," he said in glassy tones, smiling the glassy smile of Mr. Wish. He took two steps toward her. She jumped up and ran behind the couch.

"Blaise, listen to me. You are not Mr. Wish. There is no Mr. Wish. You are Dr. Blaise Skiaki, a famous scientist. You are chief chemist at CCC and have created many wonderful perfumes."

He took another step toward her, unwinding the scarf he wore around his neck.

"Blaise, I'm Gretchen. We've been lovers for two months. You must remember. Try to remember. You told me about my eyes tonight...being blind. You must remember that."

He smiled and whirled the scarf into a cord.

"Blaise, you're suffering from fugue. A blackout. A change of psyche. This isn't the real you. It's another creature driven by a pheromone. But I left no pheromone trail. I couldn't. I've never wanted to die."

"Yes, you do, my dear. Only happy to grant your wish. That's why I'm called Mr. Wish."

She squealed like a trapped rat and began darting and dodging while he closed in on her. She feinted him to one side, twisted to the other with a clear chance of getting out the door ahead of him, only to crash into three grinning goons standing shoulder to shoulder. They grabbed and held her.

Mr. Wish did not know that he also left a pheromone trail. It was a pheromone trail of murder.

"Oh, it's you again," Mr. Wish sniffed.

"Hey, old buddy-boy, got a looker this time, huh?"

"And loaded. Dig this layout."

"Great. Makes up for the last three, which was nothin'. Thanks, buddy-boy. You can go home now."

"Why don't I ever get to kill one?" Mr. Wish exclaimed petulantly.

"Now, now. No sulks. We got to protect our bird dog. You lead. We follow and do the rest."

"And if anything goes wrong, you're the setup," one of the goons giggled.

"Go home, buddy-boy. The rest is ours. No arguments. We already explained the standoff to you. We know who you are, but you don't know who we are."

"I know who I am," Mr. Wish said with dignity. "I

am Mr. Wish, and I still think I have the right to kill at least one."

"All right, all right. Next time. That's a promise. Now blow."

As Mr. Wish exited resentfully, they ripped Gretchen naked and let out a huge wow when they saw the five-carat diamond in her navel. Mr. Wish turned and saw its scintillation too.

"But that's mine," he said in a confused voice. "That's only for my eyes. I—Gretchen said she would never—" Abruptly Dr. Blaise Skiaki spoke in a tone accustomed to command: "Gretchen, what the hell are you doing here? What's this place? Who are these creatures? What's going on?"

When the police arrived they found three dead bodies and a composed Gretchen Nunn sitting with a laser pistol in her lap. She told a perfectly coherent story of forcible entry, an attempt at armed rape and robbery, and how she was constrained to meet force with force. There were a few loopholes in her account. The bodies were not armed, but if the men had said they were armed, Miss Nunn, of course, would have believed them. The three were somewhat battered, but goons were always fighting. Miss Nunn was commended for her courage and cooperation.

After her final report to the Chairman (which was not the truth, the whole truth, and nothing but the truth) Miss Nunn received her check and went directly to the perfume laboratory, which she entered without warning. Dr. Skiaki was doing strange and mysterious things with pipettes, flasks, and reagent bottles. Without turning, he ordered, "Out. Out. Out."

"Good morning, Dr. Skiaki."

He turned, displaying a mauled face and black eyes,

and smiled. "Well, well, well. The famous Gretchen Nunn, I presume. Voted Person of the Year three times in succession."

"No, sir. People from my class don't have last names."

"Knock off the sir bit."

"Yes—Mr. Wish."

"Oi!" he winced. "Don't remind me of that incredible insanity. How did everything go with the Chairman?"

"I snowed him. You're off the hook."

"Maybe I'm off his hook, but not my own. I was seriously thinking of having myself committed this morning."

"What stopped you?"

"Well, I got involved in this patchouli synthesis and sort of forgot."

She laughed. "You don't have to worry. You're saved."

"You mean cured?"

"No, Blaise. Not any more than I'm cured of my blindness. But we're both saved because we're aware. We can cope now."

He nodded slowly but not happily.

"So what are you going to do today?" she asked cheerfully. "Struggle with patchouli?"

"No," he said gloomily. "I'm still in one hell of a shock. I think I'll take the day off."

"Perfect. Bring two dinners."

Analog, June 1974

Introduction to the Articles

When Bester left the science fiction field in the late 1950s, he couldn't keep his restless mind from using the same kinds of dazzling methods he put into his fiction into articles for *Holiday* magazine. Here are a number of examples, from the 1960 article "Gourmet Cooking in Outer Space," to popular science pieces on the Sun and the Moon.

Gourmet Dining in Outer Space

In the stone age of science fiction, back in the twenties, nobody thought much about cooking in space. Those were the early days of vitamins, and writers who imagined what the future would be like thought in terms of pills. They loaded their spaceships with scientists, laboratories and death rays; and then, as an afterthought, threw in a handful of pills which would feed the crew for a year.

In the thirties, science fiction dropped the pills and went in for extraterrestrial menus. What this amounted to was a meal in Joe's Diner with an exotic name. The intrepid spacemen would knock off work in the fourth dimension for a dinner consisting of Venusian *grzb* (grapefruit), Martian *schlumphh* (meat and potatoes), Jupiter pandowdy and Andromeda coffee. Authors never specified how these goodies were prepared, or how you cleaned up afterward. You simply lit a Neptunian *Wmphz* (the cigarette with the spaceman's filter) and chucked the garbage into the rocket engines. Presumably you not only ate off paper plates but cooked in paper pots as well.

By the forties, science fiction was making a valiant attempt at realism, and every spaceship was equipped with giant hydroponic tanks in which vegetables were grown. This meant that spaceships had to be imagined bigger. Some authors made their spaceships a couple of miles long and fitted them out with dirt farms under sun lamps. They also took over the newfangled freezer, and any spaceship could boast of lockers stocked with thousands of prime steaks.

But it's interesting to note that the authors of science fiction have never bothered about the serious business of cooking in space. This attitude is understandable in stories dealing with long, lean, bronzed heroes sworn to wipe out the space pirates swarming in the rings of Saturn—that breed never sleeps, much less eats. But what about the short, fat, pasty tourists of A.D. 2060 who plank down their $2060 for a first-class seven-day round trip to the moon, including a three-day stop-over at the Lunar Hilton Hotel? This breed demands luxury accommodations, and would raise hell with the Matson-Moon Line if they were served pills or parsnips or even *schlumphh*.

Let's take a tourist on a luxury trip to the moon and see what may happen. In this case the tourist is you.

You have paid for your ticket and are packing on the morning of the take-off. You are packing very carefully because the Matson-Moon Line has warned you that weight is the critical problem in space flight, and the weight allowance is 200 pounds per passenger, including the passenger. If you are a big man, weighing around 185 pounds, you are allowed fifteen pounds of baggage. If you are a small woman, you may be able to take ninety pounds of baggage with you. Matson-Moon has kindly given you a list of your fellow passengers with their telephone numbers, and all of you have been phoning back and forth, trying to locate lightweights willing to include something of yours in their allowance.

You weigh in at International Spaceport. You are wearing featherweight clothing and carrying your gear in a transparent plastic wrap bag. No one can afford to waste weight even on the lightest of valises. Passengers stand around hugging bundles of clothes, linen and toilet articles to their bosoms, looking like old-clothes dealers.

When the officials put you on the scales you are not permitted to pay an extra fee for overweight. You discard something then and there. There are agonizing last-minute decisions to be made. Tempers are short because everybody has been dieting frantically for weeks to increase his baggage allowance. This means trouble for the chef.

You board the ship and are greeted by the maintenance engineer, who immediately confiscates all tobacco. Smoking will be permitted only at specified hours, after meals and before bedtime. This is not only a question of oxygen supply; engineers have discovered that the chemicals in tobacco smoke are dangerous to the delicate electronic equipment aboard spaceships.

You are packed into your coffin-sized cabins and strapped down. The ship takes off with the roar of a Niagara, crushing you deep into your berth with its frightful acceleration. Then you burst into outer space. The sky turns from atmospheric blue to vacuum black; the stars appear in the sky; the sun is a diamond glory; the rocket thrust is cut off; there is a stark silence, broken only by the sounds of you and your fellow passengers being very sick.

This is the result of being in free fall, of being cut loose from the bonds of gravity. When you unstrap yourself from your berth, you float in the air.

Everything inside you seems to be floating too. The sensation is strange and unpleasant at first, but then you begin to enjoy the weightlessness. Without gravity straining at you, you breathe easier, your heart beats gently, you feel wonderfully carefree.

You float out of your cabin to the narrow corridor and wriggle and push yourself forward to the salon which serves as lounge, observation room and dining room. It has no furniture. Since there is no gravity, no up or down in free fall, this makes no difference. No one can sit or stand anyway. Everybody simply floats. The salon is walled all the way around with portholes. You and your fellow passengers float around the portholes like fish in an aquarium, staring, exclaiming, photographing.

The chef appears from the galley. He is a small man with a fierce mustache and a savage expression. The mustache is French; the expression is savage because he must be his own waiter, and this galls the artist in him even though he is paid a fabulous salary. His colleagues, anchored on Earth, kid him about the job.

They call him *espaçon*, which is a combination of espace and garçon with overtones of assassin.

The chef carries a net bag filled with plastic globes the size of baseballs. From each globe protrudes a plastic straw. "Hot!" he warns. "Hot!"

And he demonstrates how the hot globe should be picked out of the bag by its straw. Each globe contains steaming bouillon, and you have your first snack in space, intended to settle your stomach and teach you the vagaries of eating without benefit of gravity.

It's a strange sensation. The soup must be sucked through the straw into your mouth. Then an effort must be made to swallow the mouthful, rather like deliberately swallowing a large pill. There is no gravity to trickle the broth down your throat. You can feel the muscular action of our throat doing the job all by itself, gently pressing the food down into your stomach.

Experienced space travelers are expert at eating without benefit of gravity, and you can spot your fellow first-timers by their clumsiness. Like you, they sputter the hot soup, which does not stain their clothes but rather floats around their heads in tiny droplets. The old-timers advise you to chase the droplets and lick them back into your mouth.

"Can't have the lounge swimming with soup," they tell you.

The chef collects the empty plastic globes and takes them back into the galley with him. Let's follow and watch him prepare dinner.

There is no floor in the kitchen. The chef floats in midair, surrounded on all sides by his kitchen equipment. He can stand on his head, as it were, and reach up to tend the stove. He can kick open the refrigerator, stir a sauce behind his back and crack eggs over one shoulder. He never has to worry about spilling things: nothing ever spills in free fall. On the other hand he has a hell of a problem getting eggs out of their shells once they're cracked. Nothing ever pours in free fall. Everything has to be shaken, pushed, nudged, coaxed.

His stove is a battery of hot plates set in the sun side of the spaceship. The naked sun in space is incredibly hot, far hotter than gas flame or electric coils. In fact, the entire ship must be insulated against it. The stove is a solar stove. By adjusting regulators, the chef can open the insulation masking the undersides of the hot plates and allow the sun to heat them from lukewarm to broiling hot.

On the shadow side of the spaceship, the temperature is the absolute zero of outer space, and the chef's refrigerator and freezer are built into this dark wall. Space does his chilling for him, just as the sun does his cooking. These conditions are the source of continual warfare between chef and pilot.

If the ship rotates a few feet in the course of its flight, it may slowly revolve the stove out of the direct glare of the sun, cool it, and ruin the cooking. The chef picks up the intercom phone and howls at the pilot: "Imbecile! You are assassinating my soufflé!" The same rotation brings the refrigerator out of the ice shadow into the sunlight and warms it. The chef phones again: "Bandit! You are sabotaging my aspic!"

The first night's menu is characteristic of the meals served on this de luxe trip:

Caviar Beluga
La Tortue Verte
La Mousse de Brocheton Homardine
Accompagnée de Petites Bouchées
La Coeur de Charolais Beaugency
Endives Meunière
Beurre Noisette
Fond d'Artichaut Châtelaine
La Peche Flambee au Feu d'Enfer
Cafe Noir très Chaud

Just to be sure you're not under the impression that this is more Venusian *grxzb* and Martian *schlumphh*, and to enable you to understand how the chef goes about cooking all this in space, I translate:

Sturgeon Roe
The Green Turtle
The froth of lobstered baby
pickerels accompanied by little
greedy mouthfuls
Beef filet from Charol with a sauce
in a state of beauty
Endive as the miller's wife would cook it
Nut butter
The bottoms of artichokes as served
by the lady of the manor
A peach enflamed by the fire of hell
Black coffee, very hot

The sturgeon roe presents no problem. The chef has stocked a quart can of "Super-Pressed" caviar. It looks and operates exactly like a can of aerated shaving cream. The chef presses the button and *phht!*—out comes the caviar. A quart can is good for one hundred servings.

The green-turtle soup is a powder packed in single-portion capsules. Each capsule is the size of a sleeping pill. Not only is the powder the quintessence of concentrated turtles but it has been treated so that it can absorb water from the atmosphere. Nothing need be added. The chef opens each capsule and taps the powder into an empty plastic globe. In five minutes each globe is full of *la tortue verte*. Since the process of water absorption produces heat, the soup is hot. Add straw and serve. *Voilà!*

The froth of lobstered baby pickerels is a sore point with the chef. It is essential for the dish (and his reputation as an artist) to enhance it with a hint of garlic. The maintenance engineer has absolutely prohibited the use of garlic in cooking; he finds it almost impossible to remove all traces of garlic from the air in his atmospheric reprocessing plant. But in this age of caffein-free coffee and nicotineless tobacco, the chef has located "No-Gar," a garlicless garlic, and smuggled a few *fleurettes* aboard. He tries a clove. The intercom shrills.

"Allo? Allo?"

"Damn it, chef, are you using garlic again? I've told you a hundred times—"

"*Non! Non! Mais non*!" The chef hastily shakes pepper over one shoulder into the ventilator grille. Still protesting his innocence, he is gratified to hear the engineer sneezing, and gently hangs up. The preparation of the beef filets is perhaps the most fascinating aspect of cooking in free fall. The chef removes them from his freezer and poises them half an inch above the hot plates of his stove.

There they float while he adjusts the heat of the sun to sear them at exactly the right temperature and speed. No gravity, remember? No pots or pans are needed for cooking. Everything can be poised over the stove, even liquids.

For example, to *meunière* the endives, the chef removes a one-pound block of butter from the freezer and sets it above a plate. It heats, melts and becomes a large golden globe, hanging in midair. Then it sizzles and browns. At the precise moment, the chef thrusts the endive into the butter and gives the globe a gentle turn. It hangs over the hot plate, slowly revolving like a miniature planet, deliciously cooking its contents.

No plates or tableware are used to serve or eat the

food. Gravity is required to keep food on a plate. Gravity is required to keep food on a fork. You can't cut food without gravity; you don't even dare spear it. The risk of food sailing into midair after the slightest miscalculation is too great. The dining room aboard a spaceship would be turned into a goulash.

No, the chef serves the food in midair directly before you, using ladles and tongs. He floats half a dozen blinis under your nose. *Phht! Phtt! Phtt*! He covers each one with caviar. You and the caviar are floating in space, confronting each other. You poke the *hors d'oeuvres*, one by one, into your mouth.

Next, the green-turtle soup in plastic globes with plastic straws. Easy. You've already practiced on the bouillon. Next the froth of lobstered pickerels, looking like a foam in space, for the liquid sauce hangs in bubbles around the little greedy mouthfuls.

Then come the beef filets with sauce, the endive and the artichokes. All these are gently coaxed out of serving baskets and floated before you. And there you are, thirty passengers, floating in every possible corner of the dining room, upside-down and downside-up, with your gourmet dinner floating before you; and all of you are eating in the old barbarian manner, with the fingers, but with a new space-age skill and delicacy.

Three wines and a cognac are served with the meal: Dry Sack with the soup; Montrachet 2053 with the fish; Pommard Grands Epenots Domaine Gaunoux 2047 with the filet. Marc á la Cloche is served with the coffee. All of them are the products of Instant Wine, Ltd., and Sonny Boy Wine-Qwik of California, Inc. I will not break your hearts by describing how these beverages are prepared. All I will say is that

Instant Wine's slogan is "Think Small!" and Sonny Boy Wine-Qwik's products are packaged in what look like toothpaste tubes.

The foregoing may well take place in the next century, but as one moves farther into the future and deeper into space, space cookery itself may become farther out. The time may come when the chef is no longer on board ship, but remains on-Earth, cooking by remote control via telerobot, much the way scientists in nuclear laboratories today handle radio-active materials. The chef will never burn himself, but he can administer a bad short circuit to his robot slave if he isn't careful with the controls.

Or cooking may become altogether automatic with menus for 750 meals punched into the robot kitchen's instruction tape. The kitchen itself will look like an IBM computer, and the meals will pop out of its maw with distressing punctuality, whether you feel like eating or not.

Three hundred years from now, General Foods and Continental Can may merge and electrify the Space Age by crossing spinach with plastics (don't ask me how), producing an edible food container in fruit, fish, meat, fowl and vegetable flavors.

The label will be printed with Wine-Qwik ink, of course, and the top of the can, not necessarily edible, will be microgrooved on the inside so that you can listen to Bach, Beethoven and Brubeck while you are dining.

In this case there won't be any kitchen. Each cabin will have affixed to the wall the food equivalent of a cigarette machine; or aboard one-class cruise ships it may be a combination vending machine and juke box in the main salon, and you'll pay for your meals as you eat them, with coins in a slot.

Five hundred years from now the space lanes will be fairly well cluttered with debris—garbage, containers, bottles, nonedible plastics—all jettisoned by spaceships and floating in nowhere. Space, unlike the ocean, has no convenient bottom to which garbage can sink. Somewhere around A. D. 2460 the final miracle may take place. Exposed to cosmic rays and undiluted sunlight and proton bombardment, seeds and stems, leaves and fruit stones may mutate and begin to grow in the vacuum.

Can you imagine the spaceways slowly filling with spreading fields of new species of flowers, fruits, vegetables and grains; living in vacuum like orchids living on air; thriving in the light of the distant sun, feeding, perhaps, on the stray electrons, protons and stardust that pervade every inch of the universe? Can you see spaceships on long journeys stopping alongside these fields to replenish supplies, like adventuring Vikings? Can you conceive of the taste of these new foods of the future, and the strange new ways they may be cooked in space? Beyond this, the imagination can't go.

Holiday, May 1960

Place of the Month: The Moon

11,000 travelers are on the weightless wait-list When the film *2001: A Space Odyssey* began its run, the public noticed that a Pan Am craft was shown making a flight to the moon. Requests for advance reservations for a moon flight began to trickle in. Then Apollo 8 flew its tremendous mission, and on Christmas Day Pan Am published a whimsical release announcing that they had more than 200 reservations for a moon flight on file. The public took it seriously and requests poured in. When we asked Pan Am to assign *Holiday* a reservation we were told that we would be 11,690th on the list. (The first is Gerhard Pistor of Vienna.) There will be commercial flights to the moon within our lifetime, but some of us will have to be wait-listed, for quite a while.

The moon will be an exciting, an alien, a dangerous place to visit. It will be a combination of a trip to a desert, to Iceland, to the Rocky Mountains, and skindiving, all for someone who is colorblind. It's a difficult mélange to visualize, but that's what will make your trip unique.

You'll find the terrain a dirty dun expanse of grays, almost completely devoid of color. Underfoot, the ground will be gritty, sandy, gravelly, speckled with pebbles, larger stones and giant rocks, although pebble is the wrong word to use, for pebble implies a small stone that has been worn smooth by waves and weather, and the moon has had neither for hundreds of millions of years. This is one reason why geologists will probably be members of your tour; they will be eager to inspect a terrain which has remained virtually unchanged for eons.

There will be craters all around you; tiny ones just a few feet across, giant craters hundreds of miles in diameter, ringed by mountains towering 10,000 feet high, often with monolithic peaks in the center of the sunken floors. It's said that the landscape of Iceland is about the closest thing that the Earth has resembling the lunar landscape. You will see crooked rills, believed to be moonquake cracks, and immense gorges, dwarfing the Grand Canyon. The Grand Canyon was cut by the Colorado River by slow erosion, but there is no erosion on the moon. It's theorized that these fantastic gorges were blasted by giant boulders shot out from the impact of asteroids on the moon's surface. Some astronomers believe that the large lunar craters were produced by such impacts; others claim that they're the result of volcanic action. Perhaps you will be able to settle the question.

One curious effect of the lunar landscape will confuse you at first; it will be the reverse of what happens to visitors to the Rocky Mountains. Out west the air is so pure that a mountain peak which seems to be only a few miles distant turns out to be a hundred miles away. On the moon what seems to be far away will be much closer than you realize. On Earth the edge of the horizon is around twelve miles distant. But the moon is only one fourth the diameter of the Earth. Consequently its horizon will be only about two and three-quarter miles distant from your eyes.

The smaller size of the moon will also force you to learn a new manner of walking. Being smaller it has less mass than the Earth, which means less gravitational attraction. You will weigh one sixth of your terrestrial weight when on the moon. The sensation of weightlessness will be delicious and dream-like, but when you go for your first stroll you'll have to accustom your muscles to exert 1/6th the effort they use on Earth. If you took a normal step you'd go soaring skyward. You'll have to learn a slow-motion shuffle, much like that of a skin-diver walking along the bottom of the sea.

The moon can be dangerous. Its days and its nights last fourteen of our terrestrial days each. There is no protective atmosphere shielding it from the naked sun and the cold of space, so the surface will be thirty-five centigrade degrees above the boiling point of water at high noon, and colder than dry ice at midnight. The lack of a diffusing atmosphere means that shadows will be razor-sharp, inky-black and impenetrable to the eye. You may step on what you think is the shadow of a boulder and tumble into a deep pit.

You will have to wear protective armor, of course. The extra weight of the armor will make it easier for you to walk. It will carry an oxygen supply: It will protect you from the extremes of heat and cold. And it will shield you from the minuscule meteorites that strike the moon at better than twenty-six miles a second. The friction of our terrestrial atmosphere burns most of them up before they reach the ground. Not so on the moon.

Ah, but the views you will have! To see the Earth hanging dark blue and cloud-mantled in the black sky. The sun, blazing against the velvety black, displaying its rosy chromosphere and ragged corona shading from pale-yellow to pearly white. The multitudes of stars, millions more than show through our dense atmosphere, steady, unwinking, their spectral colors bright. There will, of course, be a giant astronomical observatory on the moon, and you must go there during visitors' hours.

You will find adventure, excitement, unique beauty, anything and everything new and strange on the moon, but you will not find lunar aborigines. You will also probably not find diamonds.

Holiday, July 1969

The Sun

Heat, light, energy, nutriment, rainbows, night, day.
—Reflections of a Worshiper

I remember a story by G. K. Chesterton about a street that became angry with a man because he took it for granted, and wrought a strange revenge. I sometimes wonder what would happen if the sun became angry with us for the same reason. I don't think it likely. We have inherited a profound respect for him that reaches back to the dawn of life.

The sun is the father of our entire existence. We live sunlight. We eat and drink sunlight, breathe sunlight, burn sunlight, love it, shun it, enjoy the seasons because of it, swear at it when it fails us, bless it when it beams on us. Worship, love and fear of the sun embroider the cultural fabric of the world. The aborigines of England built the monument of Stonehenge to pay homage to the summer solstice. The Egyptians worshiped Ra, the sun god. The Incas tore the living hearts from sacrifices to the sun. The modern world spends billions of dollars on sun-worship.

Madison Avenue advertising experts have a little trade joke going for them; they'll ask you what's most often photographed in TV commercials. The answer is not, as you might think, the products they are selling; it's the sun. For reasons which no one yet understands, photographers of the artsy type invariably shoot footage of the sun; at dawn, at sunset, high overhead, reflected in water, blazing behind planes, skyscrapers, people. Incidentally, the second-most-often-photographed subject in TV commercials is ladies' bottoms, usually in bikinis.

The combination of the sun and a bikini immediately conjures up travel to the south, and it's true that peoples living in the north have a long tradition of heading for the sun during the winter. Anyone who's lived in London (51° 30' N.), New York (40° 45' N.) or Moscow (56° N.) through a dark January and February will understand that. It isn't so much the cold, it's the gloom. The body begins to hunger for sunlight, and the entire psyche can become quite desperate, which may be why Denmark has such a high suicide rate.

So everyone who can afford it goes south in the winter. They go to the beach in summer. They also go to lake country, mountain country; they go to ski centers and sunbathe along-side heated pools; they go to any sort of resort where they can flake out and relax in the sun. This is the medicinal sun, essential for our metabolism and our souls. As far back as the Middle Ages doctors knew enough to drag the sick and the wounded out into the sun for a few hours each day. Ibsen, a perceptive playwright, understood what he was about when he selected the tag-line to wrap up *Ghosts*, his tragedy about a son who inherits the rot of a dissolute father. When the poor kid's brain falls apart, all he can do is mumble, "Mother, give me the sun. The sun—the sun!" Curtain.

The modern quest for the sun has built tremendous industries; resort travel, resort hotels, resort fashions, resort entertainment, resort sports. The quest imposes amusing imperatives on the sun-hungry. If your assistant starts a crash diet on January 2nd, you can be pretty sure she's planning a February holiday near the equator and is worried about how she'll look on the beach. If she goes on another diet around May 1st, she's worried about how she'll look in sun clothes up north during summer weekends. January and May are the months for soul-searching tryings-on of bathing suits, accompanied by a *vox humana* of groans and the rasp of burst zippers. The men also diet and go to health clubs.

This passion for slenderness is a trial for a guy like me who isn't willing to pay the price of looking at a drawn and haggard face on top of an elegant model's figure. Anyway, I like all sorts and shapes and sizes of girls. Out at our beach I used to sit with Wolcott Gibbs (who wrote the Fire Island play, *Season in The Sun*) and case the girls strolling on the sand. Wolcott loved the slender ones in bikinis. I did, too, but I also loved the *zahftig* girls who threatened to bounce out at every step.

All this is merely by way of mentioning the sun as an aphrodisiac. There is something about sunlight that releases inhibitions. Darkness stifles the soul. It's no wonder that Calvinism took deep root in Scotland. In his play, *The Exiles*, Joyce speaks of "the protestant strain—gloom, seriousness, righteousness." He was, of course, referring to the English Puritans. Can anyone imagine Calvinism or Puritanism taking root anywhere on the shores of the Mediterranean? These sun-drenched lands are the home of hedonism.

Yes, those big, fair Swedish girls come down to the Mediterranean islands, fling themselves stark naked one the sand, and strong men sob. Don't misunderstand. It isn't the mere fact of nudity that does it, or that the girls are beautiful, or that they have a reputation for free and easy love affairs. Essentially it's the combination of bodies and sunlight that starts the juices flowing.

I know this sounds absurd; but I'm willing to bet that if you were sittings behind your desk in your office, and a big, fair girl came in and flang herself stark naked on your carpet, your immediate reaction would be one of exasperation; wrong time, wrong place, wrong girl. But out in the sunlight there is no wrong time or wrong place, and every girl is the right girl. Italian fathers know this. When the summer sun roasts Italy, and their young daughters walk around in light cotton shifts, their hair loose, their glowing skins gleaming with perspiration, that's the time to lock the girls up.

There are thousands of cosmetic products on the market for men and women, but if I could have an exclusive franchise, I'd pick the sun; it would be as profitable as a patent on water or the wheel. Jackie Gleason once told me that one of the reasons why he liked to drink was that it blurred his eyes and made all girls look beautiful "It removes pimples and wrinkles," he said. So does the sun.

The sun is our greatest cosmetician, but has only been popular since the 1920s. It's difficult for young people today to understand the tremendous revolution in personal appearance that's taken place since World War I. Back at the turn of the century the beautiful woman never permitted the sun to touch her skin. She was an exquisite white flower, delicate cultivated under glass. She had a "natural" hothouse look and wore no makeup outside of a light dusting of rice powder. Daring young girls sometimes rubbed their cheeks with carnation petals to rouge them, but the real lady contented herself with pinching her cheeks sharply just before she entered a drawing room.

Charles Dana Gibson tried to change that. His Gibson girls idealized a new type: the big, rangy athletic young woman. The Gibson girl was out in the sunlight, playing golf and tennis and motoring, and America fell in love with her image. But there was a limit to how far Gibson would go; his girls were never tanned by the sun. His men were, to be sure. The Richard Harding Davis he-man, muscular, strong jawed, with a tough skin bronzed by soldier-of-fortune adventures in the tropics, was a popular hero. As a matter of fact, Gibson used Davis himself as a model for many of his drawings.

The revolution took place in the 1920s. Skirts went up, hair was bobbed, people finally acknowledged that they inhabited bodies, and that bodies weren't shameful. They exposed and displayed their bodies in every conceivable manner, including exposure to the sun. And they discovered that the sun was a beautician. Everyone looks the better for a rich suntan, and sun bathing became a ritual, almost a religion.

It begins with sunlamps around the first of the year. The dedicated sunbather wants to get a good start on the summer; the idea of wasting exposure to the sun on sunburn is horrendous. The sunbather must get a good "base" to take advantage of the real thing. Around the middle of March they appear in the parks, seated on benches facing south, their faces thrust up toward the sunlight. Very often they hold aluminum reflectors under their chin.

It's around this time that the suntan lotions begin

advertising. The truth is, there is no lotion that will make you tan; the best it can do is shield the skin from too much exposure. There is no way for most people to go from white skin to tanned skin without passing through the sunburn stage. The sunbathers know this, but never give up hope; they buy preparations, concoct secret lotions, and even use dyes which stain the skin with an artificial tan.

The *modus operandi* of the fanatical sunbather is always amusing. He or she—let's make it she—comes down to the beach carrying a blanket and a beach bag. Her hair is tightly drawn up and tucked under a kerchief which follows the hairline meticulously from nape to brow. First she inspects the sun and the transparency of the sky. What she wants is a brilliant sun, dry air, and just enough breeze to cool the skin. Such days don't come along very often, so she complains. All dedicated sunbathers are chronic complainers about the inadequacy of the sunshine. If you want to infuriate them you need only deliver the ancient cliché, "You can get the worst kind of burn on a day like this."

She carefully spreads her blanket so that her feet will point toward the sun. Every hour or so she will slew the blanket so that her body remains aligned with the sun. Next she takes a bottle of lotion from the beach bag and oils herself liberally, but carefully. Unequal application might result in an uneventan. Last of all, she puts on a pair of sunglasses with lenses. the size of quarters, stretches out and bathes or, more accurately, rotisserates, for she gives equal time to her front, her back, and her sides.

There are some curious aspects to suntans. They are not all alike, as everyone knows. Brunettes with swarthy skins take a deep dark tan and are the envy of the fair who only succeed in looking hot and flushed after hours of exposure. If you see a blonde with a black tan you can be pretty sure she's a bleach job. The one exception to this rule is the Swedish blondes who take marvelous tans, nobody knows why. Negroes sunburn and tan like everybody else; their dark skins just turn a few shades darker. Beach tans are richer than country tans, possibly because of the way the sea and the sand reflect sunlight and increase its intensity. The concept of the "windburn" is a fable. A windburn is just a plain old sunburn. You can prove it for yourself by taping a square of cellophane to your arm and going for a ride in an open car.

As I said before, we eat sunlight. Take a rocky mountain anywhere in place and time. Nothing will grow on the sterile stone with the exception of moss and lichens, and they make no eating at all. But there are the seasons produced by the sun, and them are rains and snows. Water lodges in the crevices, freezes and expands in the winter, melts and contracts in the summer. The pressures crack and fragment the rock; the rains wash the fragments down to streams and rivers where they are tumbled and crumbled into finer particles of mineral and earth.

They end up as soil deposited on riverbanks, deltas, and eventually in great plains. Seeds root in this soil, grow, and transform soil minerals into starch, carbohydrates and protein under the catalyst of sunlight. When you pick a ripe sun-warmed tomato off a vine and eat it, you are enjoying a history of millions of years of sunlight. When you eat a steak you are eating grass-fed, grain-fed beef which is just one more step in the chain stretching from the sun to us.

Or consider the teeming, churning ocean. In the spring when the sun warms the waters there is a positive explosion of planktonic life; microscopic creatures, fish eggs, larvae, plants, miniature crustaceans, one-celled organisms, all flourishing near the sunlit surface. They devour each other. They are eaten by little fish. Larger fish prey on the smaller, and the chain of sunlight continues until it reaches your table with the cod, the lobster, the swordfish, tuna, salmon, turtle and sturgeon. The chain even crosses over from sea to land, for masses of fish worthless for eating are netted and converted into fertilizer for crops.

Our involvement with the sun has some strange aspects. The rich topsoil of our north central states, which makes them the finest farm and dairy country in the world, was stolen from Canada by the last glacier epoch. The massive wall of glaciation crept south and literally shaved Canada's topsoil off the bedrock, depositing it in Wisconsin, Minnesota and the Dakotas. We know that the glaciation resulted from some anomaly in the intensity of sunlight, although we don't know exactly what it was.

Glaciation is still with us, considerably reduced; this is what accounts far the frozen polar caps which the sun cannot yet melt. If it ever does, the immense quantities of water locked into ice will be released into the oceans, raising the sea-levels, drowning the great coastal cities of New York, London, San Francisco, Hong Kong; and perhaps the high latitudes, both north and south, will become semi-tropics again, as they once were countless millennia ago.

The sun, the sun, the sun! The color of rainbows.

Icarus flying too high and plunging to his death when the sun melted his wings. Daguerre's discovery that the sun could print an image on silver, which turned into the photography explosion. The sweet scent of sun-dried laundry. Air pollution, which is debauched sunlight; for the coal and oil that we burn were created by the sun eons ago. Exquisite wines grown on southern slopes. Small boys burning their initials with magnifying glasses. The gilt sunbursts of Louis XIV. Muscle Beach. Autumn sunsets.

The vertical sun of the tropics, so fierce, so dangerous that it is an enemy, to be resisted with broad-brimmed hats, shaded verandas and the armor of white clothing. The parasol, once the exclusive perquisite of royalty. The midnight sun, skimming the horizon. The sun of Stonehenge, that monumental Druid sundial. The Orbiting Solar Observatories, high in space above our protecting blanket of air, peering at Big Daddy, investigating him, analyzing him, observing every kink and foible in his behavior.

How did he come into existence? "*And God made two great lights; the greater light to rule the day, and the lesser light to rule the night: he made the stars also.*"

This is all right as far as it goes—nobody will argue with that—but it doesn't go far enough. We like details today. Here, then, is a brief account of how stars are born. You understand, of course, that the sun is a star, a very minor star in the giant galaxy which we inhabit.

Imagine a cloud of gas floating in space. It's an enormous cloud, many light years in diameter. It's a very thin cloud, virtually a vacuum. It is made up mostly of widely scattered hydrogen atoms, the simplest and lightest of elements, believed by many cosmologists to be the original primordial matter from which the entire universe was generated. Since everything in the universe exerts a gravitational attraction on everything else, the atoms and molecules in the cloud attract each other and the gas is slowly compacted. The process takes millions of years. As the compaction and contraction continue, the mass increases in heat or, putting it a little more technically, the hydrogen atoms are excited to higher energy levels as they are crushed closer and closer together. At some point the energy levels are brought so high by this gravitational contraction that a thermonuclear process is begun and the furnace called a star is born.

This is a continuing process, not to be confused with the "Big Bang" theory of the creation of the universe. The latter postulates that the entire content of the known universe was contained in a giant proto-atom which exploded (reasons not given) into the expanding universe hurtling out into the reaches of space today. Some cosmologists speculate that there may be a limit to the expansion, and that the entire mass will be contracted by gravitational attraction into another proto-atom that will explode all over again. But the generation of stars is merely an item in the overall picture.

In this furnace the atomic sub-particles are split apart, torn asunder, combine with each other, are bombarded and re-combine in a cycle not yet completely understood. With each exchange there is a release of atomic energy which percolates to the sun's surface and is blown out in a gigantic gale called the "solar wind." We see the visible portion of this energy as sunlight, but this is only a small segment of the entire electromagnetic spectrum. There are radio waves, infrared waves, ultraviolet, soft and hard X-ray barrages. There are naked electrons and protons shot out. These are gathered into the Van Allen belts by the Earth's magnetic field, and show themselves as the aurora borealis.

The solar wind is a matter of deep concern to our space program. If its pressure had not been taken into account in our various missions to the moon, Venus and Mars our spacecraft would have missed their targets anywhere from hundreds to thousands of miles. The discovery of the Van Allen belts was a jolt for physicists; they were stunned when they realized that a man could be fried alive when he emerged from the protection of our atmospheric blanket. And the solar wind itself is a source of deadly danger to astronauts. They must be shielded from the inconceivable intensity of solar radiation which can kill a man in a matter of moments.

As the sub-atomic transfers continue, the original hydrogen fuel slowly turns into helium, the next heavier element, and then heavier and heavier elements are produced, always with the release of radiant energy. This is transmutation on a scale never dreamed of by medieval alchemists. Our sun is well into this cycle at present; it's no longer a young hot star, it's more or less a sedate middle-aged star. Its senility and ultimate demise can be guessed.

There is a constant war being waged within the sun. On the one hand there is the powerful force of gravitational attraction which pulls everything toward the center. On the other hand there is the fierce particle energy which tends to blow outward. The two forces maintain an uneasy balance which is why the sun is a slightly variable star; it sort of teeters between them.

But as the element transformations continue, the original hydrogen fuel will be used up, the energy levels will drop, and gravity will overcome. In a final convulsion the sun will contract once more, the compression will again generate heat and an almost hysteric energy excitement, but this time in a space too small to contain it. Our sun will explode, turning into a brilliant nova which will be seen countless galaxies distant. Naturally, the entire solar system of planets will go up in that final burst. After that, nothing will remain but a cinder, just a few miles in diameter, with the ashes packed so densely together that the gravity at the surface will be billions of tons per square inch.

However, all this is so far in the future that by that time we probably will have emigrated to other planets of younger suns, perhaps very odd ones where rainbows are black and the skies green, where twelve moons revolve in a spectacular carrousel, where the sun rises in the north and sets in the south, and the seasons march around the planet from west to east. Everything will be changed except the sun-worshippers of that far future. They will appear on the beaches as ever, arrange their blankets as ever, and carefully rotisserate, giving equal time to their front, their back, their four arms and their two heads.

Holiday, June 1969

Introduction to the Essays

Bester's love-hate relationship with science fiction is no more apparent than in these essays, written over a twenty-year period.

The first piece, "Science Fiction and the Renaissance Man," was originally delivered as a lecture at the University of Chicago in 1957 (the other lecturers were Cyril Kornbluth, Robert Heinlein, and Robert Bloch). In it, Bester is already showing signs of being dissatisfied with the field.

The next series of essays were written for the Books Department of *Fantasy and Science Fiction*, circa 1961-62. As the Books Reviewer for *Fantasy and Science Fiction*, Bester had a hard time reconciling his feelings about science fiction, and would occasionally turn his entire column into a forum for his views.

"A Diatribe Against Science Fiction" is Bester's bitter rant against the "empty" SF of the times. "The Perfect Composite Science Fiction Author" is an illuminating rejoinder to the previous column. The chilling "Alfred Bester: The Demolished Man" is a revealing follow-up piece to Bester's critical essays. In it, he takes himself to task (in the third person, no less) for failing to write *any* fiction in the previous two years (and showing no inclination to write any more), and yet still feeling able to pontificate against SF.

After Bester returned to the SF field in the early

1970s, he wrote an essay on his lifelong love affair with SF, "My Affair With Science Fiction," which provides a good look at his writing life and history up to that time.

Science Fiction and the Renaissance Man

Based on a lecture delivered February 22, 1957, University College, The University of Chicago.

It's always been a policy of mine to measure a man's opinions against his background, and if I don't know what he does for a living, I ask him. This, by the way, is a heinous crime on the continent. A Parisian or a Roman will discuss his intimate sex life with you, his religion, politics, prejudices and sins—but he is offended if you ask questions about his business. Here in the States, it's the other way around; which places me in an awkward position because I intend to discuss both the religion and the business of science fiction. I wish I could discuss the sex, too, but there isn't any sex in science fiction...a deplorable state of affairs.

First, a little about myself so that you can have a yardstick with which to measure my opinions. I'm forty-three years old, married, no children. I was born and raised in New York City...on The Rock, as we say...meaning on Manhattan Island itself. We have an informal and make-believe snob club of real native New Yorkers. You ought to hear us sneer at the lesser breeds: "My dear! She was born in Brooklyn and raised in the Bronx. She's positively a tourist!"

I was educated in New York public schools; was a science student at the University of Pennsylvania; then a law student at Columbia University. But I was obsessed with the ideal of the Renaissance Man, and spent half my time electing courses in music and art, and slipping my disc winning varsity letters. Naturally I bit off more than I could chew, and never made high enough marks to go on with science and law...for which the doctors and lawyers of America have never stopped thanking me. Those were the grim specialist days of the early thirties, before the University of Chicago and St. John's at Annapolis taught our educators to respect and encourage versatility.

I remember I used to rush from the comparative anatomy lab to the art studio, and stink out the life class with a stench of formaldehyde and cadaver. And when I left qualitative analysis for my class in composition and orchestration, bringing with me the sweet scent of sulphur dioxide—! Oh, I tell you, those were miserable days for an amateur Charles van Doren...and for his friends, too.

After finishing school, I drifted into writing. Drift is the only word. Put any man at loose ends and he invariably starts to write a book. As a matter of fact if you put a man in jail he also starts to write a book. I don't know if this parallel is significant, but I do know that there are many authors I'd like to see in jail.

The writing that I did was, of course, science fiction. Like every other chess-playing, telescope-loving, microscope-happy teenager of the twenties, I was racked up by the appearance of *Amazing Stories* magazine, Mr. Gernsback's lurid publication. The ideas of fourth dimension, time travel, outer space, microcosm and macrocosm, were fascinating, and I read and loved science fiction until its dissolution into pulp fiction in the thirties disgusted me. It was not until John Campbell rescued it from the abyss of space pirates, mad scientists, their lovely daughters wearing just enough clothes to satisfy the postal authorities, and alien fiends, that I was able to go back to it. Loving science fiction, steeped in it, and imagining that it was easy to write...isn't it astonishing how many people are deceived in this...it was only natural that I should attempt to write it. I sold half a dozen miserable stories by the grace of two kindly editors at Standard Magazines who enjoyed discussing James Joyce with me and bought my stories out of pity. When they went over to *Superman* comics, they took me with them. We hadn't finished *Ulysses* yet. Those were the early days of comic books and they needed stories desperately. I had to forget James Joyce, buckle down and learn to write while they trained me, hammered me, bullied me unmercifully.

But I became a writer, by God! They trained me so well that they lost me. I went over to radio and spent seven years writing and directing clambakes like "Charlie Chan," "Nick Carter," "The Shadow" and so on. When the switch to TV came, I went over to television for another three years, and wrote scripts until I began to dream in camera shots. During all these years I never read science fiction. I had neither the time nor the inclination for it. Make a note of this point. It's important. I'll get back to it later.

The rest of my background is short and hectic. I was contract writer on the Paul Winchell show when Horace Gold phoned me. I had known him casually in the Squinka days...Squinka is the name Manly

Wade Wellman invented for the scenarios we used to write for comic books...Horace had just started editing *Galaxy* and asked me to write for him. I laughed hysterically. I knew only too well what a dreadful science fiction writer I'd been; and anyway I was putting in a ten day week on my comedy show...they're always a bitch to write...and hardly knew what science fiction meant.

Horace kept calling every week or so, just to chat and gossip, I thought; but before I realized what that fiend was up to, he'd maneuvered me into the position that somehow I was obligated to write something for him. Have you noticed that there's a kind of Machiavelli who can always put you behind the eight-ball? You're minding your own business, and the next thing you know you're busting a gut to do something for the fiend while your common sense is screaming: "What am I doing here? How'd I get into this?"

The upshot was, I got fired off the Winchell show, went out to our house on Fire Island, and spent the summer surf-fishing and writing *The Demolished Man*. I'd read no science fiction in ten years; I'd written no respectable science fiction in my entire life; I was convinced I was writing a dog. The reception of the book surprised and flattered me. But I felt it was unfair to the professional science fiction authors. I was (I still am) a science fiction amateur.

After that I wrote a dozen stories for Tony Boucher and then another novel for Horace Gold: *The Stars My Destination*.

That brings me up to date. I should add that I've tired of TV now and am making another transition to contemporary novels and plays. I earn my bread and butter as a columnist for *Holiday* magazine and *McCall's*, and writing an occasional Spectacular. Other available data: I'm six-one; weigh two hundred pounds; am a manic-depressive; a powerful surf-fisherman; collect 19th century scientific instruments, am always a sucker for a pretty girl, especially if she wears glasses, am emotionally left of center in my politics—and am still trying to live up to my ideal of the Renaissance Man.

One of the most difficult things to teach people outside the arts…and in the arts as well…is that the important ingredient in the artist is not talent, technique, genius or luck—the important ingredient is himself. What you are must color everything you do. If what you are appeals to your public, you'll be successful. If what you are communicates with all publics through all time, you'll become an immortal. But, if your personality attracts no one, then despite all crafts and cleverness, you'll fail. Perry Lafferty, who directs the Montgomery Show, sums it up bitterly. Perry says: "I'm in the Me business, is all."

Actually this isn't limited to the arts. It extends all through life, and one of the milestones in the maturation of a man is his discovery that technique with women is a waste of time. No matter how he dresses, performs and displays himself, it's only what he really *is* that attracts.

Hamlet, speaking to the player king, suggests that the goal of the actor should be to hold the mirror up to nature. Actually, no matter what any man does, he holds a mirror up to himself. He continually reveals himself, especially when he tries hardest to conceal himself. All literature reveals authors and readers alike…and especially science fiction.

The history of science fiction reflects this. The early *Amazing Stories* magazine was padded with reprints of the work of mature men like H. G. Wells and Jules Verne. This, in part, accounted for the early success of the magazine. Gernsback broke in a half dozen writers who were maladroits as fiction writers but mature experts in one aspect of popular science or another. The maturity of these stone-age science fiction writers was another source of the early success of science fiction. Still another source was the maturity of their themes which were in no way original. Most of their ideas had been waiting around for years for exploitation. Does any reader know the publication date of *Flatland*, by A. Square? Certainly it was centuries before the expression "a square" took on a more sinister meaning.

Within five years science fiction exhausted the reprint field and the prefabricated concepts, and, alas, fell into the hands of the pulp writers. It was then that the great decline set in because science fiction began to reflect the inwardness of the hack writer, and the essence of the hack writer is that he has no inwardness. He has no contact with reality, no sense of dramatic proportion, no principles of human behavior, no eye for truth...and a wooden ear for dialogue. He is all compromise and clever-shabby tricks.

For nearly ten years science fiction wallowed in this pigsty while the faithful complained pathetically. The fans pleaded with the editors. They also berated the editors, never once realizing that the inwardness of the writers was to blame...not their stories, which were sometimes well-made, with every clever-shabby trick known to the craft...but their empty inwardness. Many empty men wrote clever, gimmicky stories that still left the readers feeling dissatisfied. They had nothing within themselves to communicate.

Now you mustn't confuse inwardness with purpose or a message. When I say a man has nothing to communicate, I don't mean he has no message to preach, no. I'm referring to a quality we sometimes call character or charm...a point of view, an attitude toward life that is interesting or attractive. And remember that everybody has character, in varying degrees. Also remember that only the unique individuals have charm for everybody else. How often does an Audrey Hepburn come along? Or, if you prefer, a Rosemary Clooney? Or, for the ladies, a Rex Harrison? No, most of us must be content with a Charm Quotient...a CQ...of less than one hundred.

Back in the thirties we used to wonder why we enjoyed Doc Smith's space-operas so much. We usually felt guilty about it. Now I realize that Doc Smith had charm for us then. There was something inside him, reflected in his stereotype blood and thunder, that appealed. How many times, writing and directing my own shows, have I seen the same miracle transform actors...miserable technicians with no acting talent at all, and yet exuding a charm that was worth all the deficiencies. Fellow-sufferers, if you ever have the choice between a high IQ or a high CQ, I urge you to settle for charm.

John W. Campbell, Jr. was the man who rescued science fiction from the emptiness. Now Campbell is a strange man...from all reports. I only met him once, when he was embarking on his Dianetics kick, and my experience with him was laughable and embarrassing. But strange though Campbell may be, he's a man with a forceful inwardness which immediately shone through the pages of *Astounding Science Fiction*. I think in Campbell's case, the inwardness was character rather than charm.

Later came Horace Gold of *Galaxy* and Tony Boucher of *Fantasy and Science Fiction*. Like Campbell, Gold and Boucher are strange men; also like Campbell, both have a forceful inwardness which is reflected in their magazines. And remember, there aren't so many men who have forceful inwardness, strange or otherwise.

Campbell gave science fiction character; Gold and Boucher broadened its horizons. The hack writers began to disappear; the honest craftsmen who had been forced to hack in order to conform were able to do honest work again; new writers emerged. Science fiction began to create new concepts because new minds, minds in depth, so to speak, were attracted to it. It began to appeal again because new personalities, personalities in depth, were communicating through the stories...Heinlein, Kuttner, van Vogt, Sturgeon, Asimov, Kornbluth. These men fascinated us...but how much, really? Now I come to the heretical part of this essay. All traditionalists and royalists should be cautioned before reading further.

Do you remember my telling you that during the ten year period when I was writing and directing shows, I lost all interest in science fiction? Let me describe how and why.

Picture to yourself a Monday in the life of Me. I'm writing a show called...oh, say, "Secret Service." Monday morning at 9:00 o'clock I finish a 48 hour drive without letup to complete my script for the show three weeks from today. The network has been badgering me for the script which was due last Friday, and threatening to hire another writer. I call a messenger service to rush it down to the network and suffer because it's the only copy. I was too rushed to type a carbon.

The client on "Secret Service" calls to tell me that the script for the show two weeks from today has been unconditionally rejected by his wife. I fight desperately to salvage something out of the disaster. The advertising agency calls to tell me that next week's show must be postponed because of an advertising promotion they've dreamed up, and I have to get a new script written in three days. Also it must integrate with the promotion. The casting director of "Secret Service" calls to announce that one of the bit-players for tonight's show is out with a virus and they can't recast and rehearse on short notice. Can I write the part out?

I go down to the network and rewrite, fighting haggardly with the director, a compulsive man who can't feel comfortable unless he's dominating all situations, but who can't respect a colleague unless the colleague fights him to a standstill. I walk a neurotic tightrope with him while I try to make sense out of a script minus a character.

In the studio during rehearsal I discover that a dramatic turning point in the story can't be done because of a jurisdictional fight between the stagehands' union and the carpenters' union. I'm a strong union man myself, but at this moment I would cheerfully set fire to the A. F. of L. But after losing a fight with the shop stewards, I restrain my fury and try to come up with something valid and dramatic to replace the device that only took me two weeks to figure out.

At dress rehearsal, the director and cast begin screaming at each other and at me. "You let us down!" they wail. If a show stinks, it's the writer's fault. If it's a success, it was despite the script. When in doubt, persecute the writer. I'm too weary to defend myself, and besides, the client's wife, a bright woman who knows she could write brilliantly if she only had the time, is busy discussing Kafka with me. I loathe Kafka, but I have to be polite. I even have to listen.

I drink too much after the show, out of relief and hysteria. I hear rumors that we're going to be cancelled, and I suffer. I go home and find a letter from my accountant. I owe more money to the government. I'm too overwrought to sleep. I take two sleeping pills and settle down with a science fiction magazine...And make the strange discovery that I'm not a damned bit interested in a make-believe story about an inventor who tries to ride a rocket to the moon and only succeeds in destroying the Earth, and worries that now he's Adam but there's no Eve to help him repopulate the world, only he does it all by himself anyway.

In the entertainment business, life is constant conflict...all tension and dynamics, which is why we consume so many Miltowns, Nembutals and head-doctors. But all life is conflict, tension and dynamics. You must go through what I go through; perhaps not so often, perhaps not continually, but it happens to you. The point I'm making is this: When I'm most at grips with dramatic reality, I have the least interest in science fiction. I suggest the same is true of yourselves...of everybody.

This doesn't hold for all literature. I don't mean that when one is closest to reality one gives up all reading entirely. On the contrary, some books become more necessary than Miltowns when one is deeply embroiled in conflicts. What I'm suggesting is this: that science fiction is a form of literature palatable only in our moments of leisure, calm, euphoria. It's not Escape Fiction; it's Arrest Fiction. I use the word "arrest" in the sense of arresting or striking attention...to excite, stimulate, enlarge. No one wants to read Arrest Fiction when he's already excited; we can only enjoy it when we're calm and euphoric.

Euphoria is a generalized feeling of well-being, not amounting to a definite effect of gladness. I use it here with particular reference to adults. To be blunt, only a man who's known adult troubles can know the meaning of euphoria. Young people—and I was a young people myself once—know all the agony of youth and experience moments of relief; but that isn't adult trouble or adult euphoria.

Young people often withdraw into unadulterated escape fiction, including science fiction. They also engulf science fiction along with everything else as a part of the omnivorous curiosity of youth. Arrested adults...that is, arrested in development, also withdraw into unadulterated escape fiction, including science fiction; but we're not discussing the youthful and/or withdrawn readers of science fiction here. We're discussing the mature fans who enjoy science fiction just as they enjoy hi-fi, art, politics, sports, escape fiction, serious reading, mischief and hard work...all in sensible proportions, depending upon opportunity, season and mood. I contend that science fiction is only for the euphoric mood.

I think the strongest support for my contention is the fact that women, as a rule, are not fond of science fiction. The reason for this is obvious...at least to me.

Woman are basically realists; men are the romantics. The hard core of realism in women usually stifles the Cloud Nine condition necessary for the enjoyment of science fiction. When a woman dreams, she extrapolates reality; her fantasies are always based on fact. Women's magazines...and I speak as a *McCall's* writer...devote themselves to fantasies about love, marriage and the home, not contra-terrene matter. And the writers who appeal to them are those writers whose inwardness reflects an attitude about love, marriage and the home that is attractive to women.

What, then, is the inwardness of science fiction writers that appeals to fans when they are calm and euphoric? Let's immediately dismiss all notions of serious social criticism, valuable scientific speculation, important philosophic extrapolation, and so on. These are the pretences of science fiction and they're really worthless. But since I know you won't let me dismiss them as externals without an argument, I'll speak about them for a moment before I go on with euphoria.

So far as the philosophic contribution of science fiction is concerned, I cite the gag that made the rounds last fall about the couple that'd been married fifty years. You all know it, but I'll tell it anyway; I've got you trapped. They were interviewed and the husband was asked the secret of the happy marriage. He said: "When we got married we decided that my wife would make all the little decisions, and I'd make the big decisions." The interviewer asked: "What are the little decisions?" "Oh, what apartment to rent. How much rent to pay. Should I keep my job. Should I ask for a raise. What school to send the children to...Things like that." "And what are the big decisions?""Oh...who to run for president. What to do about the Far East. Should we help Slobbovia."

Translating this into science fiction, it's my claim that when it comes to social criticism, philosophy and so on, science fiction is usually making the big decision. It knows little and cares less about the day-to-day working out of the details of reality; it's only interested in making the big decisions: Who to run for galactic president? What to do about Mars? Should we help Alpha Centauri?

So far as the scientific contribution of science fiction is concerned, I'm going to tell you the Pshush Story whether you like it or not. During the war, an Admiral was going through some personnel records and on one man's sheet he found the entry: Civilian Occupation-Pshush-Maker. In those days everybody was looking for a secret weapon, so the Admiral called the man in and said: "It says here you're a Pshush-Maker. What's a Pshush-Maker?" The man said: "I can't explain; I'll have to show you, sir." The Admiral said: "What d'you need?" The man said: "Fifty-seven men and a corvette."

So they gave him the fifty-seven men and the corvette, and he spent three months sailing around the world gathering rare materials...copper, silver, platinum, rock crystal, aluminum ore, and so on. Then he gave a top-secret demonstration up in Baffin Bay. The Admiral was there and more top brass, and they watched the fifty-seven men put all those materials together into a huge contraption on the stem of the corvette. Then they lit blow-torches and heated it white hot. And then they pushed it over the stern...and it went: PSHUSH!

The science in science fiction is usually Pshush-

Making. We gather rare materials...the theories, ideas and speculations of genuine scientists...we put them together in strange contraptions...we heat them white hot with the talent and technique of the professional writer...and all for what? To make a huge Pshush! If the Admiral had gone into a serious conference with his top brass to discuss the military value of Pshush-Making, it would be no more ridiculous than discussing the serious scientific aspects of science fiction.

But there's a silver lining...or should I say a Pshush-Lining...to the cloud, because it's my contention that this is the essential charm of science fiction. I said before that men are the romantics. Unlike women, we can't find perpetual pleasure in the day-to-day details of living. A woman can come home ecstatic because she bought a three-dollar item reduced to two-eighty-seven, but a man needs more. Every so often, when we're temporarily freed from conflicts...euphoric, if you please...we like to settle down for a few hours and ask why we're living and where we're going. Life is enough for most women; most thinking men must ask why and whither.

In England men have the pub for this. You can spend a few hours in your local, talking up a storm with other men about why and whither. Alfred Doolittle, Bernard Shaw's dust-man in *Pygmalion* is the supreme example. In France they quonk all day in the street cafes. In Italy they have the coffee bars, and in Vienna the weinstubes. Here in the States the thinking man has nothing. After the joys of the college bull-session (Is it still called bull-session?) there's nowhere to go. Nobody talks in American saloons; everybody's too busy trying to imitate Steve Allen or Arthur Godfrey. And anyway, too many American men are compulsives, too driven by their hysterias to be capable of euphoric talk. What other outlet does the thinking man have in his hours of reflection but science fiction?

No...If you love me and if you love science fiction, deliver us both from all implications of scientific significance. Deliver science fiction from any necessity to have purpose and value. Science fiction is far above the utilitarian yardsticks of the technical minds, the agency minds, the teaching minds. Science fiction is not for Squares. It's for the modern Renaissance Man...vigorous, versatile, zestful...full of romantic curiosity and impractical speculation.

Haven't I just drawn a picture of the inwardness of the science fiction writers who appeal to you? What have any of them contributed to modern science, philosophy, sociology, criticism? Nothing, thank God. They've been writing Arrest Fiction, which strikes your attention, excites, stimulates and enlarges you when you're in the mood to be excited and stimulated...when you're in the euphoric mood and eager to be excited, stimulated and enlarged.

When I want an education, I don't go to Heinlein, Kuttner, van Vogt, Sturgeon, et alios. I go to grim texts by experts and learn while I work and suffer. But when I want the joy of communicating with other Renaissance Men, I abandon the Squares and go to Heinlein, Kuttner, van Vogt, et alios. These are the men I love to speculate with in my local pub, while my wife is home counting the laundry.

Let me be specific. I am, as I indicated, an amateur in science fiction. My real writing trade lies in other fields. I've only met a few of the leading science fiction writers, but their characters bear out my argument in their work. Bob Heinlein's extrapolation of the future of our civilization is ingenious, imaginative and worthless. But Bob has a dry, wry approach to life that is reflected in all his writing and is a joy to be with. You can say what you like about his science, but the fact remains that he's the Will Rogers of science fiction, and an ideal companion for a pub.

Ted Sturgeon is an imaginative, sensitive poet who can write about human emotions with so much power that he's wasted in science fiction. His science is plausibly makeshift; his fiction is unique. His understanding and approach to human beings...his CQ, if you please...makes him too touching to be endured. Like Heinlein, Sturgeon has within himself too much to be squandered on a form of fiction which, by its very framework, is dedicated solely to our hours of euphoria.

What about me? Alfie Bester. Now we get down to basics. What made *The Demolished Man* an appealing book, whereas the stories I'd written ten years before were appalling drivel? The answer is: Ten years. I was ten years older; ten years more experienced. Ten years of hard work at grips with hard reality crystallized something within me and gave me an attitude. I didn't realize it then, but ten years had turned me from a boy into a man.

I think I understand what you liked about *The Demolished Man*. Outside the tricks and gimmicks which any good craftsman can come up with...what you liked was what was within myself; my attitude toward people and life. It wasn't my thinking that you liked, no matter what you tell yourself. I can't think my way out of a telephone booth. It was my formed emotional attitude that communicated with you. I told you I was emotionally left of center in my politics; the same is true of my attitude toward people.

I believe that everyone is compelled, but no one is bad. I believe that everyone has greatness in him, but few of us have the opportunity to fulfill ourselves. I believe that everyone has love in him, but most of our loves are frustrated. I believe that man is the unique creation of nature, but am capable of believing in an even more perfect creation. I believe that every hope and aspiration, and every weakness and vice that I have, I share with all my brothers in the world...and all the world is my brother.

All this is emotional, without validity and without value to anyone looking for scientific data and rules to regulate his life. But I feel I'm the kind of guy you wouldn't mind spending a few hours with in a saloon, talking up a storm about anything.... Exactly the way you'd like to spend time with a Heinlein or a Sturgeon. That's the appeal of *The Demolished Man*. Not what I say, but what compelled me to say the things I said.

I speak to you now as a brother in a rather unique position; I'm capable of honesty. The only things that stand between a man and honesty are the symbols of his youth which must be fulfilled and discharged. A hungry man can't be honest. I've been fortunate enough to have purged myself of most of my adolescent obsessions. I can afford to be honest today because I've been lucky enough to have had all those things that can only be obtained through dishonesty. I've had them and I'm through with them. Only integrity remains. Now then:

Should we take science fiction seriously?

No more or less than we take television seriously.

Why?

Because both are of limited framework; and any art form of limited framework calls to itself limited artists and is worth only limited consideration.

What is the purpose of art?

To entertain and/or move the audience.

Can science fiction entertain?

Yes, when we're in certain receptive moods.

Can it move us?

No.

Why?

I can only answer that question by committing the heinous crime of discussing your literary religion. And the best way to begin is to mention Ignatius Donnelly, the patron saint of American readers...although very few know his name. Donnelly wrote a book called *The Great Cryptogram*. Does that ring a bell? It was Mr. Donnelly who tried to prove that Bacon wrote Shakespeare.

He's the patron saint of American readers because few American readers really believe that Shakespeare wrote Shakespeare. Few Americans can comprehend or understand artistic genius. Faced with unique achievement in the arts, Americans always poke around behind the scenes, looking for ghost writers, the unknown collaborator, the hidden power behind the throne. It never seems to occur to them that once they've found the hidden power, they'll come up against the same problem all over again, and have to poke around ad infinitum.

Now it's interesting that Americans never feel this way about science. No one has ever written a book trying to prove that somebody else invented Edison's inventions. Nobody ever digs up Morse's grave to see if he really invented Marconi's wireless. There's an ancient superstition that an unknown Negro writes Irving Berlin's music, but no one dreams that a Japanese invented the airplane for the Wright brothers. Oh, it's true that scientists sometimes get into priority hassles, but no American is ever incapable of comprehending scientific genius.

The reason is that we're a nation of amateur mechanics. We're simpatico to science and invention, and can identify with mechanical genius. Four Americans out of every five are nursing a secret invention, and take this dream quite seriously. I'm still convinced that da Vinci is a popular painter with us mainly because of the appeal of his beautiful mechanical drawings. I'm also convinced that photography became a passion with us because it made it possible to simulate creative results through purely mechanical means.

I hope you don't know the story about the two amateur photographers who met in a darkroom. One said to the other: "Gee, I saw a pathetic sight in the park today. It was an old beggar, with a long white beard and shaggy hair. His clothes were torn; he was dirty and starved; and the hand he held out to me looked like a claw." The second amateur said: "What'd you give him?" "Oh, a fiftieth of a second at f 3.5."

In a sense this is the American attitude toward the human scene. We're interested in aperture and shutter speed, time and temperature control. We're interested in the mechanics of the human being...his anatomy, morphology and psychology; the statistics of his life, death and mating habits...but we're not really interested in human beings as humanity...as fellow creatures. It's this fact, by the way, that accounts for the perennial popularity of the so-called situation comedy in stage, screen and television. I don't have to point out that situation comedies concentrate on the mechanics of a situation rather than the human beings involved in it.

Since art, literature and poetry are concerned with the human being as a fellow creature...almost a part or reflection of ourselves...we're not very sympathetic to them or to their great craftsmen. This is why we find it difficult to understand the artistic genius. It is also why we prefer our science fiction to concentrate on the mechanics of life and leave human beings alone.

Science fiction rarely, if ever, deals with genuine human emotions and problems. Its science ranges from the 20th to the 50th century A.D. Its characters usually remain back in the 16th century A.D. They are drawn in the two-dimensional style of the Morality Plays, and they face problems of horse-opera depth. When science fiction attempts comedy...which is the essence of humanity...it only succeeds in belaboring itself with empty bladders.

Any art form which studiously avoids human reality as a subject can't hope to move its audience. Science fiction can entertain and intrigue us, stimulate and enlarge us with its novel ideas and ingenious extrapolations, but it can rarely move us to pity and terror. There are exceptions, of course...but in general, science fiction suffers from high emotional vacuum.

You may argue: "Granting what you say is true, what difference does that make? Must literature move its readers to pity and terror to be respectable? Isn't there such a thing as escape, or arrest-fiction?"

I answer: "You're absolutely right. There is such a

thing as escape fiction, and I'm not pretending to pass on the respectability of any form of literature. I'm merely trying to place science fiction in terms of authors, themes and readers, with emphasis at this point upon the reader."

A drama professor of mine once asked our class what we thought was the central fact, the essence of the theater. We suggested the stage itself...the actors...the author's script.... He told us we were wrong. The essence of the theater is the audience. The audience shares a play in its making. The theater is never a living thing until it is shared. Anyone who's ever been to the theater or worked on stage knows this is true. You must have experienced that sharing communication between cast and audience that brings the theater to life. This sharing is the crucial reason why radio, television and motion pictures tire an audience, whereas the theater does not. You can't communicate with un-dead things, they exhaust you. Only communication can inspire and energize.

There is, alas, no such communication between novelist and reader, but there is a form of it existing between a school of literature and its followers. The school of science fiction and its fans do communicate with each other, influence each other, and even to some degree by telepathy, or diabolic possession...but I know it does happen.

I've had this in mind all the while I've been speaking so frankly about science fiction; not...so help me...in order to preach a message and turn you into crusaders for the betterment of the craft. I wouldn't know which direction was the direction myself. No. I've been quonking like this in hope that it will enable us to understand ourselves and share each other a little better...authors and readers alike.

Science fiction, like all the arts, like every living act of man, is a mirror of ourselves. If we can understand science fiction, without delusions, recriminations, attacks and defenses, we may be able to understand ourselves...and vice versa. That old Renaissance cat that I'm always dangling before my conscience tried to understand without judging. We should do the same.

What are we, then, in terms of science fiction? What is science fiction in terms of us? Let me piece the picture together for you; and remember that it's only a part of ourselves. It's a picture of a passionate young romantic who runs away from his soul and focuses his passion on the objective world...a romantic with the courage to entertain daring and complex concepts, yet who is afraid of the perplexities of human behavior...a romantic full of curiosity, yet curiously indifferent to half the marvels around him...a romantic; vigorous and honest in his speculations, yet often deluding himself as to the value of his speculations...a charming romantic, but a withdrawn romantic...a Renaissance romantic, but a neurotic romantic.

This is my picture of science fiction, of you, of myself. If you don't like the portrait, you can argue with me, of course; but I'd suggest instead that you use a line reported by S. N. Behrman. When Behrman was a boy in Providence, Rhode Island, one of the most eminent men in the city was Dr. Bradley, president of Brown University. One afternoon, Behrman took a trolleycar in town and saw Dr. Bradley sitting down the aisle. In front of the doctor stood four orthodox rabbis, examining the embarrassed gentleman and arguing furiously in Yiddish whether this was the great man or not. Finally they turned to Behrman and one of them asked: "Is that man the brilliant scholar, Doctor Bradley?" Behrman said it was. The rabbi started in disappointment and then said: "Well...if that man is Dr. Bradley, then anybody could be anybody."

University College,
University of Chicago, 1957

A Diatribe Against Science Fiction

The books sent in for review this month were so bad that we've decided to ignore them, rather than pan them, and turn our attention to a discussion of the reasons why the books are so bad. Almost everybody agrees that science fiction has fallen upon hard times—too many bad books and too few good books are being published today—and many people want to know why. Publishers, editors, and the public have been blamed. We disagree. We think authors are responsible.

The average quality of writing in the field today is extraordinarily low. We don't speak of style; it's astonishing how well amateurs and professionals alike can handle words. In this age of mass communications almost everybody can use a pen with some facility. The science fiction authors usually make themselves clearly understood, and if they rarely rise to stylistic heights, they don't often sink to the depths of illiteracy.

No, we speak of content; of the thought, theme, and drama of the stories, which reflect the author himself. Many practicing science fiction authors reveal themselves in their works as very small people, disinterested in reality, inexperienced in life, incapable of relating science fiction to human beings, and withdrawing from the complexities of living into their make-believe worlds.

There are exceptions, of course, and we've praised them often in this department; but now we're speaking of the majority.

Their science is a mere repetition of what has been done before. They ring minuscule changes on played-out themes, concepts which were established and exhausted a decade ago. They play with odds and ends and left-overs. In past years this has had a paralyzing effect on their technique.

This department is exasperated with the science fiction author who seizes upon a trifle and turns it into a story by carefully concealing it from the reader. His characters behave inexplicably in a bewildering situation; little by little he lifts a corner here and a corner there, and leads the reader down the garden path of curiosity until at last he removes the cape with a flourish to reveal...nothing.

This is literary larceny, and it's being practiced more and more today. As a professional author, we're keenly aware of the fact that a good writer begins his story at the point where a mediocre writer ends his. As a critic we're angrily aware of the fact that many of today's science fiction writers end their stories at the point where a bad writer would begin.

Now it may be argued, so far as the trifles go, that we're in an in-between stage. Science fiction has caught up with most of the scientific concepts, and exhausted them, and must consequently mark time. This is debatable, but if the argument is accepted, then our answer is: Stop writing science fiction. For God's sake, have the courage to remain silent if you have nothing to say.

It may be asked, how is a writer to earn a living if he must remain silent? The answer is, science fiction is not a big enough or important enough field of literature to enable an author to support himself by writing for it exclusively. Science fiction is in a class with poetry and the Little Magazines. It supplies (or should supply) *avant-coureur* literature to interested readers; it provides (or should provide) an outlet, a safety valve for working authors who become fed up with the strangling taboos of bread-and-butter writing.

The appeal of science fiction has always been its iconoclasm. It is the one field of fiction where no cows are sacred, and where all idols may be broken. It stimulates, entertains, and educates by daring to question the unquestionable, poke fun at the sacred, condemn the accepted, and advocate the unthinkable.

But in order to be an iconoclast, an author must be more than merely aware of the idol he wishes to destroy. He must be intimate with it and understand it in all its aspects. This means that he must have devoted serious thought to it, and have beliefs of his own which will stand up in the place of the broken idol. In other words, any child can complain, but it takes an adult to clash with accepted beliefs...an adult with ideas.

It's not enough to say: Democracy doesn't work; I believe in the Fascist system, period. Certainly this is iconoclastic enough (at least in America), but it's a mere shooting off of the mouth unless the author reveals in his story an intimate understanding of Democracy and Fascism, and offers valid reasons to support his position.

We're not merely shooting off our mouth when we say that it is the authors who are killing science fiction.

We know how and why science fiction is written today, and are prepared to state a few hard truths. Outside of the exceptions mentioned above, science fiction is written by empty people who have failed as human beings.

As a class they are lazy, irresponsible, immature. They are incapable of producing contemporary fiction because they know nothing about life, cannot reflect life, and have no adult comment to make about life. They are silly, childish people who have taken refuge in science fiction where they can establish their own arbitrary rules about reality to suit their own inadequacy. And like most neurotics, they cherish the delusion that they're "special."

It's difficult for the ordinary reader to understand this. All of us, as readers, have a blessed willingness, almost an eagerness, to suspend disbelief. We meet authors far more than halfway, and given only half a chance we will plunge into the story with complete acceptance. This is why so many bad science fiction writers can still find an audience.

In baseball they have a comment to make about third basemen who are presented with so many hard chances that scorers are reluctant to pin an error on them when they bobble the ball. The chance is scored THTH, Too Hot To Handle, and everybody grumbles that third basemen ought to pay to get into the ballpark. In the light of reader co-operation, many authors ought to pay to get into print.

So it's the immature, the inadequate, the maladroit who are killing science fiction today. Most of the adult authors have moved on to other fields. The bright young people who might be expected to bring in fresh blood are living in days when there has never been a greater demand for promising young talent in television, movies, magazines and publishing houses. With the exception of an occasional spare time short story, they sensibly refuse to waste their time on science fiction. They can earn more, learn more, and fare farther in other fields.

To the patient, long-suffering public, our blessings. To the weary editors, sorting through the third-rate submissions for an acceptable MS, our sympathy. To those of our colleagues who have earned our respect and admiration, our apologies for this attack which was not directed against them. But to those who deserve this attack, our curse. Nobody understands a writer like a writer; nobody hates a bad writer as bitterly as a writer.

Fantasy & Science Fiction, May 1961

The Perfect Composite Science Fiction Author

Last month we complained rather bitterly about the poor quality of contemporary science fiction and its authors. Although we were careful to point out that there were exceptions to our attack, we fear that angry fans may have overlooked this. So we would like to take advantage of this month's All Star Issue by putting together a composite All Star Author out of the colleagues we admire most. Unfortunately, space limits us to a selection of seven, but we beg you (and the authors who must be omitted) to remember that our admiration includes far more than that number.

Big Daddy of them all is the Old Pro, Robert A. Heinlein. Mr. Heinlein brings to his stories an attack and a pace that have the onslaught of an avalanche. His characters do not vary much...he seems to draw on a limited cast...but they are delineated with vigor. His blacks are ebony, his whites are pristine, he doesn't waste time on delicate shadings. His themes are similarly forthright, and often give the impression that his stories are being told by extrapolated bankers and engineers; that is to say, by men who are both pragmatic and parochial.

We have always thought of Mr. Heinlein as the

Kipling of science fiction. This is high praise, for Kipling was the finest prose craftsman of the XIXth and early XXth centuries. Unfortunately, Mr. Heinlein also shares Kipling's annoying faults. Kipling's appraisal of life was often oversimplified to the point of childishness. He suffered from acute Xenophobia, and his excessive virility colored most of his work with a cocksure, know-it-all attitude.

Despite these flaws, Mr. Heinlein remains the most powerful and original force in science fiction today; an author always to be reckoned with, never ignored. In fact, the latter would be quite impossible. Mr. Heinlein reaches out, takes the reader by the scruff of the neck, and doesn't let go until he's shaken the wits out of him. Some day we hope Mr. Heinlein will use his talent to shake a little wit into the reader.

Although there has been a falling off in the quality of Theodore Sturgeon's work in recent years (no doubt the result of middle-aged spread, which can be cured by astringent physical and mental regimen) he is still the most perceptive, the most sensitive, and the most adult of science fiction authors.

No one in the field can touch on the emotional relationships of human beings as delicately and yet as sharply as Mr. Sturgeon. If Mr. Heinlein's work can be described as massive black and white lithography, then Mr. Sturgeon's is the exquisite Japanese print. He turns every reader into a sympathetic psychoanalyst, but never permits his characters to become analysands; they remain understandably yet mysteriously human.

Mr. Sturgeon comes closest to the ideal science fiction author because he is not preoccupied with the gadgetry of science; he prefers to extrapolate the human being rather than the test tube. This trips him up occasionally, for sometimes he becomes so involved with the nuances of behavior that he bogs down, and the action of his story is forced to mark time. But despite this he is a superb craftsman, and when his material lies just right, he invariably produces a gem.

Robert Sheckley is possibly the most polished of the science fiction authors. This manifests itself in his approach to a story; with the choice of a dozen different treatments, he always selects the wittiest and most original. His ideas are engaging; his dialogue is crisp and pointed with humor. He understands the secret of economy, and knows how to distill an idea down to essentials, and then extract every possible variation and development.

Mr. Sheckley, however, runs a grave risk of becoming monotonous. Early success with a particular story pattern has, we feel, seduced him into repeating this pattern over and over again. He confronts one or two characters with a fantastic and fascinating problem. In the end, the protagonists solve the problem, almost invariably with an ingenious surprise.

This is to say that most of his stories resolve themselves into running duologues. We look forward to the time when Mr. Sheckley will break away from this formula and try his hand at other story forms. His talent is too keen to be wasted entirely on success.

James Blish, to our mind, represents the greatness and the weakness of contemporary science fiction. Mr. Blish is a dedicated craftsman with a deep philosophic bias. He's a dispassionate theoretician at heart, and this is his strength. His weakness lies in the fact that he finds theories dramatic in themselves, and cares less about the drama of the human beings involved with them.

This, we believe, is an aspect of youth...youth which is so fascinated by the enigmas of the physical universe that it has little time left over for concern about the inhabitants. But those of us who are older have played with the physical mysteries and speculated about them; now we've become aware of one of the most amazing mysteries of all...man, and we want to know more about him. Here, Mr. Blish and science fiction let us down.

But in all fairness we should point out that young fans often confide that they prefer their science fiction pure; that is, with a minimum of human characters in it. So, while Mr. Blish may occasionally fail to satisfy his older readers, he has generations of young enthusiasts, presently struggling through primers, who will graduate into ardent devotees of his work.

It is the misfortune of Isaac Asimov that his greatest story was his first; and that was a classic which any of us would have been proud to have written. Ever since, Mr. Asimov has turned out a steady stream of science fiction, all competently planned and worked out, very little inspired. He has not grown in stature; he's levelled off into the solid wheel horse of science fiction.

There is a coldness about Mr. Asimov's work that must be distinguished from the icy clarity of Mr. Blish's. Whereas Mr. Blish deliberately sets his limits, and uses his characters to illustrate his theories, Mr. Asimov is cold out of a lack of a sense of drama. He has tremendous enthusiasm, but seems to lack empathy. He is not a real fiction writer.

Proof of this is the fact that Mr. Asimov is superb

in his science articles. When his material does not require life to be breathed into characters, his wit, wisdom, and enthusiasm, plus his wonderfully lucid organization produce fact pieces that are a joy to read, and are often far more entertaining than the works of fiction in the same magazine. After all, fiction is only one of many forms of writing, and it may well be that Mr. Asimov is an essayist who has finally found his way.

Writers are a lazy lot; we write what is convenient, comfortable, and profitable. We are past masters of the art of rationalizing cowardice. When we are inspired by a theme which may trigger off a family feud (if we express ourselves frankly and honestly) we can always find a valid excuse for evading the issue. If we catch hold of an idea which requires rigorous speculation to bring it to maturity, we can improvise a dozen devices to dodge the work. All this is by way of paying homage to that most courageous of science fiction authors, Philip José Farmer.

Extrapolation is an ideal which science fiction extolls but rarely practices in depth. Mr. Farmer is possibly the only author who genuinely, with discipline, extrapolates. He is the one man capable of pursuing an idea to its logical end, no matter what the conclusion may involve; and it is Mr. Farmer's greatness that he is unafraid of the most repellent conclusions.

We spoke before of Robert Heinlein's virility. In the light of Mr. Farmer's courage, Mr. Heinlein's aggressiveness becomes mere belligerence. Mr. Heinlein often dares to advocate a reactionary point of view in the face of a progressive milieu, and this is often taken as a sign of courage. We argue that it is merely hopping on an unpopular bandwagon. Mr. Farmer's is the true courage, for he has the strength to project into the dark where no pre-formed attitudes wait to support him. In other words, Mr. Heinlein deliberately shocks for the sake of dramatic values; Mr. Farmer often shocks because he has had the courage to extrapolate a harmless idea to its terrible conclusion.

Mr. Farmer's weakness is the fact that he is not a genius. (This department knows only too well what an absurd yet agonizing comment that is.) Neither he nor any author writing today is capable of smelting his powerful extrapolations into a bigger-than-life story. To quote an old expression: Mr. Farmer has too much engine for his rear axle. We believe the same is true of most science fiction.

We will never forget the electrifying effect of the first stories of Ray Bradbury. They swept over science fiction a generation ago, and transformed it from gadgetry into art. This must not be taken as a denigration of the gadgetry of the times which was, indeed, of amazing ingenuity and power. In those days almost every story was an eye-opener; but Mr. Bradbury opened our eyes to new vistas.

His theme is protest; the protest of man against the tools which will enable him to control his environment, but which threaten to destroy man himself. To put it another way, Mr. Bradbury is for the simple life. He does not balk at the big issues; rather, he seizes upon a very small point...the right to take a walk in the rain, the right to read a book...and developes it with masterly style into a telling incident.

Incident, not drama, is Mr. Bradbury's forte; incident and exquisite tone control. If Theodore

Sturgeon's work is the Japanese print, then Mr. Bradbury's may be likened to that most difficult of art forms, the watercolor. It is the crux of the watercolor that the tints must be of transparent purity, and flowed on with a courageous full brush. This is the essense of Mr. Bradbury's art.

It is also the danger of Mr. Bradbury's art, for it is so special in its perfection that a very little goes a long way. Mr. Bradbury cannot be read too often. When he is collected in one volume it is virtually impossible to read all his stories in a single sitting. One becomes quickly surfeited with the subtle nuance, and begins to require more robust fare.

There are many more fine practicing craftsmen whom space will not permit us to discuss: Brian Aldiss, Algis Budrys, Arthur Clarke, Damon Knight, Fritz Leiber, and others. Each makes a vital contribution to science fiction; all are colleagues whom we are proud to admire. But we must limit ourselves to the seven artists under consideration here.

Our All Star Author, then, would be made up of the dramatic virility of Robert Heinlein, the humanity of Theodore Sturgeon, the gloss of Robert Sheckley, the dispassion of James Blish, the encyclopaedic enthusiasm of Isaac Asimov, the courage of Philip Farmer, and the high style of Ray Bradbury. He would be edited with the technical acumen of John W. Campbell, Jr., the psychoanalytic perception of Horace Gold, and the sparkling sophistication of the Boucher-McComas team. And publishers would beat a pathway to his door.

Fantasy and Science Fiction, March 1961

My Affair with Science Fiction

I'm told that some science fiction readers complain that nothing is known about my private life. It's not that I have anything to conceal; it's simply the result of the fact that I'm reluctant to talk about myself because I prefer to listen to others talk about themselves. I'm genuinely interested, and also there's always the chance of picking up something useful. The professional writer is a professional magpie.

Very briefly: I was born on Manhattan Island December 18, 1913, of a middle-class, hard-working family. I was born a Jew but the family had a *laissez-faire* attitude toward religion and let me pick my own faith for myself. I picked Natural Law. My father was raised in Chicago, always a raunchy town with no time for the God bit. Neither has he. My mother is a quiet Christian Scientist. When I do something that pleases her, she nods and says, "Yes, of course. You were born in Science." I used to make fun of her belief as a kid, and we had some delightful arguments. We still do, while my father sits and smiles benignly. So my home life was completely liberal and iconoclastic.

I went to the last little red schoolhouse in Manhattan (now preserved as a landmark) and to a beautiful new high school on the very peak of Washington Heights (now the scene of cruel racial conflicts). I went to the University of Pennsylvania in Philadelphia where I made a fool of myself trying to become a Renaissance Man. I refused to specialize and knocked myself out studying the humanities and the scientific disciplines. I was a miserable member of the crew squad, but I was the most successful member of the fencing team.

I'd been fascinated by science fiction ever since Hugo Gernsback's magazines first appeared on the stands. I suffered through the dismal years of space opera when science fiction was written by the hacks of pulp Westerns who merely translated the Lazy X ranch into the Planet X and then wrote the same formula stories, using space pirates instead of cattle rustlers. I welcomed the glorious epiphany of John Campbell, whose *Astounding* brought about the Golden Age of science fiction.

Ah! Science fiction, science fiction! I've loved it since its birth. I've read it all my life, off and on, with excitement, with joy, sometimes with sorrow. Here's a twelve-year-old kid, hungry for ideas and imagination, borrowing fairy-tale collections from the library—*The Blue Fairy Book, The Red Fairy Book, The Paisley Fairy Book*—and smuggling them home under his jacket because he was ashamed to be reading fairy tales at his age. And then came Hugo Gernsback.

I read science fiction piecemeal in those days. I didn't have much allowance, so I couldn't afford to buy the magazines. I would loaf at the newsstand outside the stationery store as though contemplating which magazine to buy. I would leaf through a science fiction magazine, reading rapidly, until the proprietor came out and chased me. A few hours later I'd return and continue where I'd been forced to leave off. There was one hateful kid in summer camp who used to receive the *Amazing Quarterly* in July. I was next in line, and he was hateful because he was a slow reader.

It's curious that I remember very few of the stories. The H. G. Wells reprints, to be sure, and the very first book I ever bought was the collection of Wells's science fiction short stories. I remember "The Fourth Dimensional Cross Section" (Have I got the title right?) which flabbergasted me with its concept. I think I first read *Flatland* by A. Square as an *Amazing* reprint. I remember a cover for a novel titled, I think, *The Second Deluge*. It showed the survivors of the deluge in a sort of Second Ark gazing in awe at the peak of Mt. Everest now bared naked by the rains. The peak was a glitter of precious gems. I interviewed Sir Edmund Hillary in New Zealand a few years ago and he never said anything about diamonds and emeralds. That gives one furiously to think.

Through high school and college I continued to read science fiction but, as I said, with increasing frustration. The pulp era had set in and most of the stories were about heroes with names like "Brick Malloy" who were inspired to combat space pirates, invaders from other worlds, giant insects, and all the rest of the trash still being produced by Hollywood today. I remember a perfectly appalling novel about a Negro conspiracy to take over the world. These niggers, you see, had invented a serum which turned them white, so they could pass, and they were boring from within. Brick Malloy took care of those black bastards. We've come a long way, haven't we?

There were a few bright moments. Who can forget the impact of Weinbaum's "A Martian Odyssey"? That unique story inspired an entire vogue for quaint alien creatures in science fiction. "A Martian Odyssey" was one reason why I submitted my first story to Standard Magazines; they had published Weinbaum's classic. Alas, Weinbaum fell apart and degenerated into a second-rate fantasy writer, and died too young to fulfill his original promise.

And then came Campbell who rescued, elevated, gave meaning and importance to science fiction. It became a vehicle for ideas, daring, audacity. Why, in God's name, didn't he come first? Even today science fiction is still struggling to shake off its pulp reputation, deserved in the past but certainly not now. It reminds me of the exploded telegony theory; that once a thoroughbred mare has borne a colt by a nonthoroughbred sire, she can never bear another thoroughbred again. Science fiction is still suffering from telegony.

Those happy golden days! I used to go to second-hand magazine stores and buy back copies of *Astounding*. I remember a hot July weekend when my wife was away working in a summer stock company and I spent two days thrilling to Van Vogt's *Slan* and Heinlein's *Universe*! What a concept, and so splendidly worked out with imagination and remorseless logic! Do you remember "Black Destroyer"? Do you remember Lewis Padgett's "Mimsy Were the Borogroves"? That was originality carried to the fifth power. Do you remember—But it's no use. I could go on and on. The Blue, the Red and the Paisley Fairy Books were gone forever.

After I graduated from the university I really didn't know what I wanted to do with myself. In retrospect I realize that what I needed was a *Wanderjahr*, but such a thing was unheard of in the States at that time.

I went to law school for a couple of years (just stalling) and to my surprise received a concentrated education which far surpassed that of my undergraduate years. After thrashing and loafing, to the intense pain of my parents, who would have liked to see me settled in a career, I finally took a crack at writing a science fiction story which I submitted to Standard Magazines. The story had the ridiculous title of "Diaz-X."

Two editors on the staff, Mort Weisinger and Jack Schiff, took an interest in me, I suspect mostly because I'd just finished reading and annotating Joyce's *Ulysses* and would preach it enthusiastically without provocation, to their great amusement. They told me what they had in mind. *Thrilling Wonder* was conducting a prize contest for the best story written by an amateur, and so far none of the submissions was worth considering. They thought "Diaz-X" might fill the bill if it was whipped into shape. They taught me how to revise the story into acceptable form and gave it the prize, $50. It was printed with the title, "The Broken Axiom." They continued their professional guidance and I've never stopped being grateful to them.

Recently, doing an interview for *Publishers Weekly* on my old friend and hero, Robert Heinlein (he prefers "Robert" to "Bob"), I asked him how he got started in science fiction.

"In '39. I started writing and I was hooked. I wrote everything I learned anywhere; navy, army, anywhere. My first science fiction story was 'Lifeline.' I saw an ad in *Thrilling Wonder* offering a prize of $50 for the best amateur story, but then I found out that *Astounding* was paying a cent a word and my story ran to 7,000 words. So I submitted it to them first and they bought it."

"You sonofabitch," I said between my teeth. "I won that *Thrilling Wonder* contest, and you beat me by twenty dollars.

We both laughed but despite our mutual admiration I suspect that we both knew that twenty dollars wasn't the only way Robert has always bettered me in science fiction.

I think I wrote perhaps a dozen acceptable science fiction stories in the next two years, all of them rotten, for I was without craft and experience and had to learn by trial and error. I've never been one to save things, I don't even save my mss., but I did hold on to the first four magazine covers on which my name appeared. *Thrilling Wonder Stories* (15¢). On the lower left-hand comer is printed "Slaves of the Life Ray, a startling novelet by Alfred Bester." The feature story was "Trouble on Titan, A Gerry Carlyle Novel by Arthur K. Barnes." Another issue had me down in the same bullpen, "The Voyage to Nowhere by Alfred Bester." The most delightful item is my first cover story in *Astonishing Stories* (10¢), "The Pet Nebula by Alfred Bester." The cover shows an amazed young scientist in his laboratory being confronted by a sort of gigantic radioactive seahorse. Damned if I can remember what the story was about.

Some other authors on the covers were Neil R. Jones, J. Harvey Haggard, Ray Cummings (I remember that name), Harry Bates (his, too), Kelvin Kent (sounds like a house name to me), E. E. Smith, Ph.D. (but of course) and Henry Kuttner with better billing than mine. He was in the left-hand upper comer.

Mort Weisinger introduced me to the informal

luncheon gatherings of the working science fiction authors of the late thirties. I met Henry Kuttner, who later became Lewis Padgett, Ed Hamilton, and Otto Binder, the writing half of Eando Binder. Eando was a sort of acronym of the brothers Ed and Otto Binder. E and O. Ed was a self-taught science fiction illustrator and not very good. Malcolm Jameson, author of navy-oriented space stories, was there, tall, gaunt, prematurely grey, speaking in slow, heavy tones. Now and then he brought along his pretty daughter, who turned everybody's head.

The vivacious *compère* of those luncheons was Manley Wade Wellman, a professional Southerner full of regional anecdotes. It's my recollection that one of his hands was slightly shriveled, which may have been why he came on so strong for the Confederate cause. We were all very patient with that; after all, our side won the war. Wellman was quite the man-of-the-world for the innocent thirties; he always ordered wine with his lunch.

Henry Kuttner and Otto Binder were medium-sized young men, very quiet and courteous, and entirely without outstanding features. Once I broke Kuttner up quite unintentionally. I said to Weisinger, "I've just finished a wild story that takes place in a spaceless, timeless locale where there's no objective reality. It's awfully long, 20,000 words, but I can cut the first 5,000." Kuttner burst out laughing. I do, too, when I think of the dumb kid I was. Once I said most earnestly to Jameson, "I've discovered a remarkable thing. If you combine two story-lines into one, the result can be tremendously exciting." He stared at me with incredulity. "Haven't you ever heard of plot and counterplot?" he growled. I hadn't. I discovered it all by myself.

Being brash and the worst kind of intellectual snob, I said privately to Weisinger that I wasn't much impressed by these writers who were supplying most of the science fiction for the magazines, and asked him why they received so many assignments. He explained, "They may never write a great story, but they never write a bad one. We know we can depend on them." Having recently served my time as a magazine editor, I now understand exactly what he meant.

When the comic book explosion burst, my two magi were lured away from Standard Magazines by the *Superman* Group. There was a desperate need for writers to provide scenarios (Wellman nicknamed them "Squinkas") for the artists, so Weisinger and Schiff drafted me as one of their writers. I hadn't the faintest idea of how to write a comic book script, but one rainy Saturday afternoon Bill Finger, the star comics writer of the time, took me in hand and gave me, a potential rival, an incisive, illuminating lecture on the craft. I still regard that as a high point in the generosity of one colleague to another.

I wrote comics for three or four years with increasing expertise and success. Those were wonderful days for a novice. Squinkas were expanding and there was a constant demand for stories. You could write three and four a week and experiment while learning your craft. The scripts were usually an odd combination of science fiction and "Gangbusters." To give you some idea of what they were like, here's a typical script conference with an editor I'll call Chuck Migg, dealing with a feature I'll call "Captain Hero." Naturally, both are fictitious. The dialogue isn't.

"Now, listen," Migg says, "I called you down because we got to do something about Captain Hero."

"What's your problem?"

"The book is closing next week, and we're thirteen pages short. That's a whole lead story. We got to work one out now."

"Any particular slant?"

"Nothing special, except maybe two things. We got to be original and we got to be realistic. No more fantasy."

"Right."

"So give."

"Wait a minute, for Christ's sake. Who d'you think I am, Saroyan?"

Two minutes of intense concentration. Then Migg says, "How about this? A mad scientist invents a machine for making people go fast. So crooks steal it and hop themselves up. Get it? They move so fast they can rob a bank in a split second."

"No."

"We open with a splash panel showing money and jewelry disappearing with wiggly lines and—Why no?"

"It's a steal from H. G. Wells."

"But it's still original."

"Anyway, it's too fantastic. I thought you said we were going to be realistic."

"Sure I said realistic, but that don't mean we can't be imaginative. What we have to—"

"Wait a minute. Hold the phone."

"Got a flash?"

"Maybe. Suppose we begin with a guy making some

kind of experiment. He's a scientist, but not mad. This is a straight, sincere guy."

"Gotcha. He's making an experiment for the good of humanity. Different narrative hook."

"We'll have to use some kind of rare earth metal; cerium, maybe, or—"

"No, let's go back to radium. We ain't used it in the last three issues."

"All right, radium. The experiment is a success. He brings a dead dog back to life with his radium serum."

"I'm waiting for the twist."

"The serum gets into his blood. From a lovable scientist, he turns into a fiend."

At this point Migg takes fire. "I got it! I got it! We'll make like King Midas. This doc is a sweet guy. He's just finished an experiment that's gonna bring eternal life to mankind. So he takes a walk in his garden and smells a rose. Blooie! The rose dies. He feeds the birds. Wham! The birds plotz. So how does Captain Hero come in?"

"Well, maybe we can make it Jekyll and Hyde here. The doctor doesn't want to be a walking killer. He knows there's a rare medicine that'll neutralize the radium in him. He has to steal it from hospitals, and that brings Captain Hero around to investigate."

"Nice human interest."

"But here's the next twist. The doctor takes a shot of the medicine and thinks he's safe. Then his daughter walks into the lab, and when he kisses her, she dies. The medicine won't cure him any more."

By now Migg is in orbit. "I got it! I got it! First we run a caption: IN THE LONELY LABORATORY A DREADFUL CHANGE TORTURES DR.—whatever his name is—HE IS NOW DR. RADIUM!!! Nice name, huh?"

"Okay."

"Then we run a few panels showing him turning green and smashing stuff and he screams: THE MEDICINE CAN NO LONGER SAVE ME! THE RADIUM IS EATING INTO MY BRAIN!! I'M GOING MAD, HA-HA-HA!!! How's that for real drama?"

"Great."

"Okay. That takes care of the first three pages. What happens with Dr. Radium in the next ten?"

"Straight action finish. Captain Hero tracks him down. He traps Captain Hero in something lethal. Captain Hero escapes and traps Dr. Radium and knocks him off a cliff or something."

"No. Knock him into a volcano."

"Why?"

"So we can bring Dr. Radium back for a sequel. He really packs a wallop. We could have him walking through walls and stuff on account of the radium in him."

"Sure."

"This is gonna be a great character, so don't rush the writing. Can you start today? Good. I'll send a messenger up for it tomorrow."

The great George Burns, bemoaning the death of vaudeville, once said, "There just ain't no place for kids to be lousy any more." The comics gave me an ample opportunity to get a lot of lousy writing out of my system.

The line "...knocks him off a cliff or something" has particular significance. We had very strict self-imposed rules about death and violence. The Good Guys never deliberately killed. They fought, but only with their fists. Only villains used deadly weapons. We could show death coming—a character falling off the top of a high building "Aiggghhh!"—and we could show the result of death—a body, but always face down. We could never show the moment of death; never a wound, never a rictus, no blood, at the most a knife protruding from the back. I remember the shock that ran through the *Superman* office when Chet Gould drew a bullet piercing the forehead of a villain in "Dick Tracy."

We had other strict rules. No cop could be crooked. They could be dumb, but they had to be honest. We disapproved of Raymond Chandler's corrupt police. No mechanical or scientific device could be used unless it had a firm foundation in fact. We used to laugh at the outlandish gadgets Bob Kane invented (he wrote his own squinkas as a rule) for "Batman and Robin" which, among ourselves, we called Batman and Rabinowitz. Sadism was absolutely taboo; no torture scenes, no pain scenes. And, of course, sex was completely out.

Holiday tells a great story about George Horace Lorrimer, the awesome editor-in-chief of *The Saturday Evening Post*, our sister magazine. He did a very daring thing for his time. He ran a novel in two parts and the first installment end with the girl bringing the boy back to her apartment midnight for coffee and eggs. The second installment opened with them having breakfast together in her apartment following morning. Thousands of indignant letters came and Lorrimer had a form reply printed: "*The Saturday Evening Post* is not responsible for the behavior of its character between installments." Presumably our comic book heroes lived normal lives between issues; Batman getting bombed and chasing ladies into bed, Rabinowitz burning down his school library in protest against something.

I was married by then, and my wife was an actress. One day she told me that the radio show, "Nick Carter," was looking for scripts. I took one of my best comic book stories, translated it into a radio script, and it was accepted. Then my wife told me that a new show, "Charlie Chan," was having script problems. I did the same thing with the same result. By the end of the year I was the regular writer on those two shows and branching out to "The Shadow" and others. The comic book days were over, but the splendid training I received in visualization, attack, dialogue, and economy stayed with me forever. The imagination must come from within; no one can teach you that. The ideas must come from without, and I'd better explain that.

Usually, ideas don't just come to you out of nowhere; they require a compost heap of germination, and the compost is diligent preparation. I spent many hours a week in the reading rooms of the New York Public Library at 42nd Street and Fifth Avenue. I read everything and anything with magpie attention for a possible story idea; art frauds, police methods, smuggling, psychiatry, scientific research, color dictionaries, music, demography, biography, plays...the list is endless. I'd been forced to develop a speed-reading technique in law school and averaged a dozen books per session. I thought that one potential idea per book was a reasonable return. All that material went into my Commonplace Book for future use. I'm still using it and still adding to it.

And so for the next five or six years I forgot comics, forgot science fiction and immersed myself in the entertainment business. It was new, colorful, challenging and—I must be honest—far more profitable. I wrote mystery, adventure, fantasy, variety, anything that was a challenge, a new experience, something I'd never done before. I even became the director on one of the shows, and that was another fascinating challenge.

But very slowly an insidious poison began to diminish my pleasure; it was the constraints of network censorship and client control. There were too many ideas which I was not permitted to explore. Management said they were too different; the public would never understand them. Accounting said they were too expensive to do; the budget couldn't stand it. One Chicago client wrote an angry letter to the producer of one of my shows, "Tell Bester to stop trying to be original. All I want is ordinary scripts." That really hurt. Originality is the essence of what the artist has to offer. One way or another, we must produce a new sound.

But I must admit that the originality-compulsion can often be a nuisance to myself as well as others. When a concept for a story develops, a half-dozen ideas for the working-out come to mind. These are examined and dismissed. If they came that easily, they can't be worthwhile. "Do it the hard way," I say to myself, and so I search for the hard way, driving myself and everybody around me quite mad in the process. I pace interminably, mumbling to myself, I go for long walks. I sit in bars and drink, hoping that an overheard fragment of conversation may give me a clue. It never happens but all the same, for reasons which I don't understand, I do get ideas in saloons.

Here's an example. Recently I was struggling with the pheromone phenomenon. A pheromone is an external hormone secreted by an insect—an ant, say—when it finds a good food source. The other members of the colony are impelled to follow the pheromone trail, and they find the food, too. I wanted to extrapolate that to a man and I had to do it the hard way. So I paced and I walked and at last I went to a bar where I was nailed by a dumb announcer I knew who drilled my ear with his boring monologue. As I was gazing moodily into my drink and wondering how to escape, the hard way came to me. "He doesn't *leave* a trail," I burst out. "He's impelled to *follow* a trail." While the announcer looked at me in astonishment, I whipped out my notebook and wrote, "Death left a pheromone trail for him; death in fact, death in the making, death in the planning."

So, out of frustration, I went back to science fiction in order to keep my cool. It was a safety valve, an escape hatch, therapy for me. The ideas which no show would touch could be written as science fiction stories, and I could have the satisfaction of seeing them come to life. (You must have an audience for that.) I wrote perhaps a dozen and a half stories, most of them for *Fantasy & Science Fiction* whose editors, Tony Boucher and Mick McComas, were unfailingly kind and appreciative.

I wrote a few stories for *Astounding*, and out of that came my one demented meeting with the great John W. Campbell, Jr. I needn't preface this account with the reminder that I worshiped Campbell from afar. I had never met him; all my stories had been submitted by mail. I hadn't the faintest idea of what he was like, but I imagined that he was a combination of Bertrand Russell and Ernest Rutherford. So I sent off another story to Campbell, one which no show would let me tackle. The title was "Oddy and Id" and the concept was Freudian, that a man is not governed by his conscious mind but rather by his unconscious compulsions. Campbell telephoned me a few weeks later to say that he liked the story but wanted to discuss a few changes with me. Would I come to his office? I was delighted to accept the invitation despite the fact that the editorial offices of *Astounding* were then the hell and gone out in the boondocks of New Jersey.

The editorial offices were in a grim factory that looked like and probably was a printing plant. The "offices" turned out to be one small office, cramped, dingy, occupied not only by Campbell but by his assistant, Miss Tarrant. My only yardstick for comparison was the glamorous network and advertising agency offices. I was dismayed.

Campbell arose from his desk and shook hands. I'm a fairly big guy, but he looked enormous to me—about the size of a defensive tackle. He was dour and seemed preoccupied by matters of great moment. He sat down behind his desk. I sat down on the visitor's chair.

"You don't know it," Campbell said. "You can't have any way of knowing it, but Freud is finished."

I stared. "If you mean the rival schools of psychiatry, Mr. Campbell, I think—"

"No I don't. Psychiatry, as we know it, is dead."

"Oh, come now, Mr. Campbell. Surely you're joking."

"I have never been more serious in my life. Freud

has been destroyed by one of the greatest discoveries of our time."

"What's that?"

"Dianetics."

"I never heard of it."

"It was discovered by L. Ron Hubbard, and he will win the Nobel Peace Prize for it," Campbell said solemnly.

"The Peace Prize? What for?"

"Wouldn't the man who wiped out war win the Nobel Peace Prize?"

"I suppose so, but how?"

"Through Dianetics."

"I honestly don't know what you're talking about, Mr. Campbell."

"Read this," he said and handed me a sheaf of long galley proofs. They were, I discovered later, the galleys of the very first Dianetics piece to appear in *Astounding*.

"Read them here and now? This is an awful lot of copy."

He nodded, shuffled some papers, spoke to Miss Tarrant, and went about his business, ignoring me. I read the first galley carefully, the second not so carefully, as I became bored by the Dianetics mishmash. Finally I was just letting my eyes wander along, but was very careful to allow enough time for each galley so Campbell wouldn't know I was faking. He looked very shrewd and observant to me. After a sufficient time, I stacked the galleys neatly and returned them to Campbell's desk.

"Well?" he demanded. "Will Hubbard win the Peace Prize?"

"It's difficult to say. Dianetics is a most original and

imaginative idea, but I've only been able to read through the piece once. If I could take a set of galleys home and—"

"No," Campbell said. "There's only this one set. I'm rescheduling and pushing the article into the very next issue. It's that important." He handed the galleys to Miss Tarrant. "You're blocking it," he told me. "That's all right. Most people do that when a new idea threatens to overturn their thinking."

"That may well be," I said, "but I don't think it's true of myself. I'm a hyperthyroid, an intellectual monkey, curious about everything."

"No," Campbell said, with the assurance of a diagnostician, "you're a hyp-O-thyroid. But it's not a question of intellect, it's one of emotion. We conceal our emotional history from ourselves although Dianetics can trace our history all the way back to the womb."

"To the womb!"

"Yes. The fetus remembers. Come and have lunch."

Remember, I was fresh from Madison Avenue and expense-account luncheons. We didn't go to the Jersey equivalent of Sardi's, "21," even P.J. Clarke's. He led me downstairs and we entered a tacky little lunchroom crowded with printers and file clerks; an interior room with blank walls that made every sound reverberate. I got myself a liverwurst on white, no mustard, and a Coke. I can't remember what Campbell ate.

We sat down at a small table while he continued to discourse on Dianetics, the great salvation of the future when the world would at last be cleared of its emotional wounds. Suddenly he stood up and towered over me. "You can drive your memory back to the womb," he said. "You can do it if you release every block, clear yourself and remember. Try it."

"Now?"

"Now. Think. Think back. Clear yourself. Remember! You can remember when your mother tried to abort you with a buttonhook. You've never stopped hating her for it."

Around me there were cries of, "BLT down, hold the mayo. Eighty-six on the English. Combo rye, relish. Coffee shake, pick up." And here was this grim tackle standing over me, practicing Dianetics without a license. The scene was so lunatic that I began to tremble with suppressed laughter. I prayed. "Help me out of this, please. Don't let me laugh in his face. Show me a way out." God showed me. I looked up at Campbell and said, "You're absolutely right, Mr. Campbell, but the emotional wounds are too much to bear. I can't go on with this."

He was completely satisfied. "Yes, I could see you were shaking." He sat down again, and we finished our lunch and returned to his office. It developed that the only changes he wanted in my story was the removal of all Freudian terms which Dianetics had now made obsolete. I agreed, of course; they were minor, and it was a great honor to appear in *Astounding* no matter what the price. I escaped at last and returned to civilization where I had three double gibsons and don't be stingy with the onions.

That was my one and only meeting with John Campbell, and certainly my only story conference with him. I've had some wild ones in the entertainment business, but nothing to equal that. It reinforced my private opinion that a majority of the science fiction crowd, despite their brilliance, were missing their marbles. Perhaps that's the price that must be paid for brilliance.

One day, out of the clear sky, Horace Gold telephoned to ask me to write for *Galaxy*, which he had launched with tremendous success. It filled an open space in the field; *Astounding* was hard science; *Fantasy & Science Fiction* was wit and sophistication; *Galaxy* was psychiatry-oriented. I was flattered but begged off, explaining that I didn't think I was much of a science fiction author compared to the genuine greats. "Why me?" I asked. "You can have Sturgeon, Leiber, Asimov, Heinlein."

"I've got them," he said, "and I want you."

"Horace, you're an old scriptwriter, so you'll understand. I'm tied up with a bitch of a show starring a no-talent. I've got to write continuity for him, quiz sections for him to M. C. and dramatic sketches for him to mutilate. He's driving me up the wall. His agent is driving me up the wall. I really haven't got the time."

Horace didn't give up. He would call every so often to chat about the latest science fiction, new concepts, what authors had failed and how they'd failed. In the course of these gossips, he contrived to argue that I was a better writer than I thought, and to ask if I didn't have any ideas that I might be interested in working out.

All this was on the phone because Horace was trapped in his apartment. He'd had shattering experiences in both the European and Pacific theaters during World War II and had been released from the service with complete agoraphobia. Everybody had to come to his apartment to see him, including his psychiatrist. Horace was most entertaining on the phone; witty, ironic, perceptive, making shrewd criticisms of science fiction.

I enjoyed these professional gossips with Horace so much that I began to feel beholden to him; after all, I was more or less trapped in my workshop, too. At last I submitted perhaps a dozen ideas for his judgment. Horace discussed them all, very sensibly and realistically, and at last suggested combining two different ideas into what ultimately became *The Demolished Man.* I remember one of the ideas only vaguely; it had something to do with extrasensory perception, but I've forgotten the gimmick. The other I remember quite well. I wanted to write a mystery about a future in which the police are armed with time machines so that if a crime is committed

They could trace it back to its origin. This would make crime impossible. How then, in an open story, could a clever criminal outwit the police?

I'd better explain "open story." The classic mystery is the closed story, or whodunit. It's a puzzle in which everything is concealed except the clues carefully scattered through the story. It's up to the audience to piece them together and solve the puzzle. I had become quite expert at that. However, I was carrying too many mystery shows and often fell behind in my deadlines, a heinous crime, so occasionally I would commit the lesser crime of stealing one of my scripts from Show A and adapting it for Show B.

I was reading a three-year-old Show A script for possible theft when it dawned on me that I had written all the wrong scenes. It was a solid story, but in the attempt to keep it a closed puzzle, I had been forced to omit the real drama in order to present the perplexing results of the behind-the-scenes action. So

I developed for myself a style of action mystery writing in which everything is open and known to the audience, every move and countermove, with only the final resolution coming as a surprise. This is an extremely difficult form of writing; it requires you to make your antagonists outwit each other continually with ingenuity and resourcefulness. It was a novel style back then.

Horace suggested that instead of using time machines as the obstacle for the criminal, I use ESP. Time travel, he said, was a pretty worn-out theme, and I had to agree. ESP, Horace said, would be an even tougher obstacle to cope with, and I had to agree.

"But I don't like the idea of a mind-reading detective," I said. "It makes him too special."

"No, no," Horace said. "You've got to create an entire ESP society."

And so the creation began. We discussed it on the phone almost daily, each making suggestions, dismissing suggestions, adapting and revising suggestions. Horace was, at least for me, the ideal editor, always helpful, always encouraging, never losing his enthusiasm. He was opinionated, God, knows, but so was I, perhaps even more than he. What saved the relationship was the fact that we both knew we respected each other; that, and our professional concentration on the job. For professionals the job is the boss.

The writing began in New York. When my show went off for the summer, I took the ms. out to our summer cottage on Fire Island and continued there. I remember a few amusing incidents. For a while I typed on the front porch. Wolcott Gibbs, the *New Yorker* drama critic, lived up the street and every time he passed our cottage and saw me working he would denounce me. Wolcott had promised to write a biography of Harold Ross that summer and hadn't done a lick of work yet. I. F. (Izzy) Stone dropped in once and found himself in the midst of an animated discussion of political thought as reflected by science fiction. Izzy became so fascinated that he asked us to take five while he ran home to put a fresh battery in his hearing aid.

I used to go surf-fishing every dawn and dusk. One evening I was minding my own business, busy casting and thinking of nothing in particular when the idea of using typeface symbols in names dropped into my mind. I reeled in so quickly that I fouled my line, rushed to the cottage and experimented on the typewriter. Then I went back through the ms. and changed all the names. I remember quitting work one morning to watch an eclipse and it turned cloudy. Obviously somebody up there didn't approve of eclipse-breaks. And so, by the end of the summer, the novel was finished. My working title had been *Demolition*. Horace changed it to *The Demolished Man*. Much better, I think.

The book was received with considerable enthusiasm by the *Galaxy* readers, which was gratifying but surprising. I hadn't had any conscious intention of breaking new trails; I was just trying to do a craftsmanlike job. Some of the fans' remarks bemused me. "Oh, Mr. Bester! How well you understand women." I never thought I understood women. "Who were the models for your characters?" They're surprised when I tell them that the model for one of the protagonists was a bronze statue of a Roman emperor in the Metropolitan Museum. It's haunted me ever since I was a child. I read the emperor's character into the face and when it came time to write this particular fictional character, I used my emperor for the mold.

The *réclame* of the novel turned me into a science fiction somebody, and people were curious about me. I was invited to gatherings of the science fiction Hydra Club where I met the people I was curious about: Ted Sturgeon, Jim Blish, Tony Boucher, Ike Asimov, Avram Davidson, then a professional Jew wearing a yarmulka, and many others. They were all lunatic (So am I. It takes one to spot one.) and convinced me again that most science fiction authors have marbles missing. I can remember listening to an argument about the correct design for a robot, which became so heated that for a moment I thought Judy Merrill was going to punch Lester del Rey in the nose. Or maybe it was vice versa.

I was particularly attracted to Blish and Sturgeon. Both were soft-spoken and charming conversationalists. Jim and I would take walks in Central Park during his lunch hour (he was then working as a public relations officer for a pharmaceutical house) and we would talk shop. Although I was an admirer of his work, I felt that it lacked the hard drive to which I'd been trained, and I constantly urged him to attack his stories with more vigor. He never seemed to resent it, or at least was too courteous to show it. His basic problem was how to hold down a PR writing job and yet do creative writing on the side. I had no advice for that. It's a problem which very few people have solved.

Sturgeon and I used to meet occasionally in bars for drinks and talk. Ted's writing exactly suited my taste, which is why I thought he was the finest of us all. But he had a quality which amused and exasperated me. Like Mort Sahl and a few other celebrities I've interviewed—Tony Quinn is another Ted lived on crisis, and if he wasn't in a crisis, he'd create one for himself. His life was completely disorganized, so it was impossible for him to do his best work consistently. What a waste!

In all fairness I should do a description of myself. I will, but I'm going to save it for the end.

I'd written a contemporary novel based on my TV experiences and it had a fairly decent reprint sale and at last sold to the movies. My wife and I decided to blow the loot on a few years abroad. We put everything into storage, contracted for a little English car, stripped our luggage down to the bare minimum and took off. The only writing materials I brought with me were a portable, my Commonplace Book, a thesaurus, and an idea for another science fiction novel.

For some time I'd been toying with the notion of using the *Count of Monte Cristo* pattern for a story. The reason is simple; I'd always preferred the anti-hero, and I'd always found high drama in compulsive types. It remained a notion until we bought our cottage on Fire Island and I found a pile of old *National Geographics*. Naturally I read them and came across a most interesting piece on the survival of torpedoed sailors at sea. The record was held by a Philippine cook's helper who lasted for something like four months on an open raft. Then came the detail that racked me up. He'd been sighted several times by passing ships which refused to change course to rescue him because it was a Nazi submarine trick to put out decoys like this. The magpie mind darted down, picked it up, and the notion was transformed into a developing story with a strong attack.

The Stars My Destination (I've forgotten what my working title was) began in a romantic white cottage down in Surrey. This accounts for the fact that so many of the names are English. When I start a story, I spend days reading through telephone directories for help in putting together character names—I'm very fussy about names—and in this case I used English directories. I'm compelled to find or invent names with varying syllables. One, two, three, and four. I'm extremely sensitive to tempo. I'm also extremely sensitive to word color and context. For me there is no such thing as a synonym.

The book got under way very slowly and by the time we left Surrey for a flat in London, I had lost momentum. I went back, took it from the top and started all over again, hoping to generate steam pressure. I write out of hysteria. I bogged down again and I didn't know why. Everything seemed to go wrong. I couldn't use a portable, but the only standard machines I could rent had English keyboards. That threw me off. English ms. paper was smaller than the American, and that threw me off. And I was cold, cold, cold. So in November we packed and drove to the car ferry at Dover, with the fog snapping at our ass all the way, crossed the Channel and drove south to Rome.

After many adventures we finally settled into a penthouse apartment on the *Piazza della Muse*. My wife went to work in Italian films. I located the one (1) standard typewriter in all Rome with an American keyboard and started in again, once more taking it from the top. This time I began to build up momentum, very slowly, and was waiting for the hysteria to set in. I remember the day that it came vividly.

I was talking shop with a young Italian film director for whom my wife was working, both of us beefing about the experimental things we'd never been permitted to do. I told him about a note on synesthesia which I'd been dying to write as a TV script for years. I had to explain synesthesia—this was years before the exploration of psychedelic drugs—and while I was describing the phenomenon I suddenly thought, "Jesus Christ! This is for the novel. It leads me into the climax." And I realized that what had been holding me up for so many months was the fact that I didn't have a fiery finish in mind. I must have an attack and a finale. I'm like the old Hollywood gag, "Start with an earthquake and build to a climax."

The work went well despite many agonies. Rome is no place for a writer who needs quiet. The Italians *fa rumore* (make noise) passionately. The pilot of a Piper Cub was enchanted by a girl who sunbathed on the roof of a mansion across the road and buzzed her, and me, every morning from seven to nine. There were frequent informal motorcycle rallies in our piazza and the Italians always remove the mufflers from their vehicles; it makes them feel like Tazio Nuvolare. On the other side of our penthouse a building was in construction, and you haven't heard *rumore* until you've heard stonemasons talking politics.

I also had research problems. The official U.S. library was woefully inadequate. The British Consulate library was a love, and I used it regularly, but none of their books was dated later than 1930, no help for a science fiction writer needing data about radiation belts. In desperation, I plagued Tony Boucher and Willy Ley with letters asking for information. They always came through, bless them, Tony on the humanities—"Dear Tony, what the hell is the name of that Russian sect that practiced self-castration? Slotsky? Something like that."—Willy on the disciplines—"Dear Willy, how long could an unprotected man last in naked space? Ten minutes? Five minutes? How would he die?"

The book was completed about three months after the third start in Rome; the first draft of a novel usually takes me about three months. Then there's the pleasant period of revision and rewriting; I always enjoy polishing. What can I say about the material? I've told you about the attack and the climax. I've told you about the years of preparation stored in my mind and my Commonplace Book. If you want the empiric equation for my science fiction writing—for all my writing, in fact, it's:

Discipline
Experiment
Experience
Pattern sense
Concept + Drama sense = Story ↔ Statement
Preparation
Imagination
Extrapolation
Hysteria

I must enlarge on this just a little. The mature science fiction author doesn't merely tell a story about Brick Malloy vs. The Giant Yeastmen from Gethsemane. He makes a statement through his story. What is the statement? Himself, the dimension and depth of the man. His statement is seeing what everybody else sees but thinking what no one else has thought, and having the courage to say it. The hell of it is that only time will tell whether it was worth saying.

Back in London the next year, I was able to meet the young English science fiction authors through Ted Camell and my London publisher. They gathered in a pub somewhere off the Strand. They were an entertaining crowd, speaking with a rapidity and intensity that reminded me of a debating team from the Oxford Union. And they raised a question which I've never been able to answer: Why is it that the English science fiction writers, so brilliant socially, too often turn out rather dull and predictable stories? There are notable exceptions, of course, but I have the sneaky suspicion that they had American mothers.

John Wyndham and Arthur Clarke came to those gatherings. I thought Arthur rather strange, very much like John Campbell, utterly devoid of a sense of humor, and I'm always ill at ease with humorless people. Once he pledged us all to come to the meeting the following week; he would show slides of some amazing underwater photographs he had taken. He did indeed bring a projector and slides and show them. After looking at a few I called, "Damn it, Arthur, these aren't underwater shots. You took them in an aquarium. I can see the reflections in the plate glass." And it degenerated into an argument about whether the photographer and his camera had to be underwater, too.

It was around this time that an event took place which will answer a question often asked me: Why did I drop science fiction after my first two novels? I'll have to use a flashback, a device I despise, but I can't see any other way put. A month before I left the States, my agent called me in to meet a distinguished gentleman, senior editor of *Holiday* magazine, who was in search of a feature on television. He told me that he'd tried two professional magazine writers without success, and as a last resort wanted to try me on the basis of the novel I'd written about the business.

It was an intriguing challenge. I knew television, but I knew absolutely nothing about magazine piece-writing. So once again I explored, experimented and taught myself. *Holiday* liked the piece so much that they asked me to do pieces on Italian, French and English TV while I was abroad, which I did. Just when my wife and I had decided to settle in London permanently, word came from *Holiday* that they wanted me to come back to the States. They were starting a new feature called "The Antic Arts" and wanted me to become a regular monthly contributor. Another challenge. I returned to New York.

An exciting new writing life began for me. I was no longer immured in my workshop; I was getting out and interviewing interesting people in interesting professions. Reality had become so colorful for me that I no longer needed the therapy of science fiction. And since the magazine imposed no constraints on me, outside of the practical requirements of professional magazine technique, I no longer needed a safety valve.

I wrote scores of pieces, and I confess that they were much easier than fiction, so perhaps I was lazy. But try to visualize the joy of being sent back to your old university to do a feature on it, going to Detroit to test-drive their new cars, taking the very first flight of the Boeing 747, interviewing Sophia Loren in Pisa, De Sica in Rome, Peter Ustinov, Sir Laurence Olivier (they called him Sir Larry in Hollywood), Mike Todd and Elizabeth Taylor, George Balanchine. I interviewed and wrote, and wrote, and wrote, until it became cheaper for *Holiday* to hire me as senior editor, and here was a brand-new challenge.

I didn't altogether lose touch with science fiction; I did book reviews for *Fantasy & Science Fiction* under Bob Mills's editorship and later Avram Davidson's. Unfortunately, my standards had become so high that I seemed to infuriate the fans who wanted special treatment for science fiction. My attitude was that science fiction was merely one of many forms of fiction and should be judged by the standards which apply to all. A silly story is a silly story whether written by Robert Heinlein or Norman Mailer. One enraged fan wrote in to say that I was obviously going through change of life.

Alas, all things must come to an end. *Holiday* failed after a robust twenty-five years; my eyes failed, like poor Congreve's; and here I am, here I am, back in my workshop again, immured and alone, and so turning to my first love, my original love, science fiction. I hope it's not too late to rekindle the affair. Ike Asimov once said to me, "Alfie, we broke new trails in our time but we have to face the fact that we're over the hill now." I hope not, but if it's true, I'll go down fighting for a fresh challenge.

What am I like? Here's as honest a description of myself as possible. You come to my workshop, a three-room apartment, which is a mess, filled with books, mss., typewriters, telescopes, microscopes, reams of typing paper, chemical glassware. We live in the apartment upstairs, and my wife uses my kitchen for a storeroom. This annoys me; I used to use it as a laboratory. Here's an interesting sidelight. Although I'm a powerful drinker I won't permit liquor to be stored there; I won't have booze in my workshop.

You find me on a high stool at a large drafting table editing some of my pages. I'm probably wearing flimsy pajama bottoms, an old shirt and am barefoot; my customary at-home clothes. You see a biggish guy with dark brown hair going grey, a tight beard nearly all white and the dark brown eyes of a sad spaniel. I shake hands, seat you, hoist myself on the stool again and light a cigarette, always chatting cordially about anything and everything to put you at your ease. However, it's possible that I like to sit higher than you because it gives me a psychological edge—I don't think so, but I've been accused of it.

My voice is a light tenor (except when I'm angry; then it turns harsh and strident) and is curiously inflected. In one sentence I can run up and down an octave. I have a tendency to drawl my vowels. I've spent so much time abroad that my speech pattern may seem affected, for certain European pronunciations cling to me. I don't know why. GA-rahj for garage, the French "r" in the back of the throat, and if there's a knock on the door I automatically holler, "*Avanti*!" a habit I picked up in Italy.

On the other hand my speech is larded with the customary profanity of the entertainment business, as well as Yiddish words and professional phrases. I corrupted the WASP *Holiday* office. It was camp to have a blond junior editor from Yale come into my office and say, "Alfie, we're having a *tsimmis* with the theater piece. That *goniff* won't rewrite." What you don't know is that I always adapt my speech pattern to that of my *vis-à-vis* in an attempt to put him at his ease. It can vary anywhere from burley (burlesque) to Phi Beta Kappa.

I try to warm you by relating to you, showing interest in you, listening to you. Once I sense that you're at your ease I shut up and listen. Occasionally I'll break in to put a question, argue a point, or ask you to enlarge on one of your ideas. Now and then I'll say, "Wait a minute, you're going too fast. I have to think about that." Then I stare into nowhere and think hard. Frankly, I'm not lightning, but a novel idea can always launch me into outer space. Then I pace excitedly, exploring it out loud.

What I don't reveal is the emotional storm that rages within me. I have my fair share of frustrations and despairs, but I was raised to show a cheerful countenance to the world and suffer in private. Most people are too preoccupied with their own troubles to be much interested in yours. Do you remember Viola's lovely line in *Twelfth Night*? "And, with a green and yellow melancholy, she sat like Patience on a monument, smiling at grief."

I have some odd mannerisms. I use the accusing finger of a prosecuting attorney as an exclamation point to express appreciation for an idea or a witticism. I'm a "toucher," hugging and kissing men and women alike, and giving them a hard pat on the behind to show approval. Once I embarrassed my boss, the *Holiday* editor-in-chief, terribly. He'd just returned from a junket to India and, as usual, I breezed into his office and gave him a huge welcoming hug and kiss. Then I noticed he had visitors there. My boss turned red and told them, "Alfie Bester is the most affectionate straight in the world."

I'm a faker, often forced to play the scene. In my time I've been mistaken for a fag, a hardhat, a psychiatrist, an artist, a dirty old man, a dirty young man, and I always respond in character and play the scene. Sometimes I'm compelled to play opposites—my fast to your slow, my slow to your fast—all this to the amusement and annoyance of my wife. When we get home she berates me for being a liar and all I can do is laugh helplessly while she swears she'll never trust me again.

I do laugh a lot, with you and at myself, and my laughter is loud and uninhibited. I'm a kind of noisy guy. But don't ever be fooled by me even when I'm clowning. That magpie mind is always looking to pick up something.

Hell's Cartographers, 1975

Introduction to the Interviews

Editor's Note: Bester provided written introductions for the stories and articles that made up the 1976 omnibus anthology Starlight. *This one originally appeared as a preface to the Isaac Asimov interview that appears here. In a slightly altered form, it provides a good introduction to his collected interviews* in toto.

The question most often asked by fans is: Why did I stop writing science fiction? The answer is difficult because I'm a complex man with tangled motivations. However, I can try oversimplifying. Many times I've been driven off a bus by a child nagging its mother with "I wan' ice cream,"—over and over again. I can't endure repetition; I enjoy only new things. I'm the exact opposite to Gustave Lebair, a famous bibliomaniac, who read the same book *St. Apollonius of Tyana* in the Bibliothéque Nationale every day for sixty years. A perceptive friend once said, "Alfie Bester believes that the entire world was made for his entertainment." I really don't go quite that far in my selfish egotism, but I come damned close to it.

When I was serving my apprenticeship and trying to become a master craftsman in my profession, science fiction was merely one of many fields that I attacked. There were also comics, slick fiction, mainstream novels, radio and television scripts. As soon as I mastered a field and became successful, I'd be driven off the bus and have to catch another one in my search for the entertainment of a fresh challenge. I don't mean to imply that I was successful in everything I tried. I had my fair share of grim failures, and I'm saving them up to have another go.

My two successful science fiction novels of many years ago brought me dangerously close to boredom with the field. Brian Aldiss is much kinder than I am to myself. He says, "No. You stopped writing science fiction because you realized that you'd said all you had to say. I wish more writers would have that good sense." That may be true, but the fact is it was my association with *Holiday* magazine that cut me off from other forms of writing.

Holiday was a godsend to a man of my temperament. As a regular contributor and ultimately a senior editor, my professional life was filled with variety, fresh challenges, and constant entertainment. As an interviewer and feature writer, I had to master a new and difficult craft. Once mastered, there was no danger of boredom because I was meeting and spending time with hundreds of fascinating people in hundreds of different professions. With the cachet of a then-important magazine backing me, no door was ever closed; ideal for an incurably curious man.

I enjoyed interviewing the most and want to show you the sort of thing I was doing issue after issue. You may ask what interviews are doing in a story collection. Well, it isn't a story collection, it's a Bester collection, and there's no reason why there can't be variety. I'll trouble you not to object. It will only remind me of Whistler's libel action against John Ruskin. On cross-examination, Ruskin's barrister asked Whistler how he could call one of his paintings "A Study in Blue" when there were so many other colors in it. Whistler shot back, "Idiot! Does a symphony in F consist of nothing but F, F, F?"

Colorful man, Whistler. Deadly opponent. I'd love to have interviewed him.

Starlight, 1976

John Huston's Unsentimental Journey

When I was a kid, I knew all about movie directors. The movie director was an extravagant genius with an exotic name like Sandor Von Satyr, and his private life was scandalous. He wore boots and riding breeches on the set and shouted at actors through a megaphone. If his leading lady did not play her romantic scenes convincingly, he made love to her (after hours) to get a realistic performance. When the film was finished, he coldly cast her aside, breaking her heart. He ended up a has-been, either chauffering for a new star who never heard of him, or swimming out into the Pacific until he drowned.

Now I keep telling myself that all this is absurd. The movie director is usually an ordinary guy with an ordinary name; a combination of artist and businessman. He is talented but not scandalous; he may break hearts but he does not swim out into the Pacific; certainly he does not behave like an 18th Century rake. Or so I keep telling myself. And then along comes the last of the Regency bucks, a Corinthian, elegant, charming and seemingly cold hearted: the extraordinary John Huston.

Mr. Huston is one of the most colorful and successful of the Hollywood directors. His most recent films are *The Roots of Heaven* (which he admires) and *The Barbarian and the Geisha* (which he loathes). *The Roots of Heaven* was unfairly scorned by many critics for those obscure reasons which critics seem to devise in the dark. Most of the public agreed with Huston and found the picture admirable; nature lovers found it inspirational.

Huston admits that he loathes *The Barbarian and the Geisha* because he quarreled with his producers and washed his hands of the entire affair before the film was completed. He swears that this will not happen with the two pictures he's making this year: *The Unforgiven* for Hecht-Hill-Lancaster, and Arthur Miller's *The Misfits*, starring Marilyn Monroe. Other Huston credits of the past are: *The Maltese Falcon, The Treasure of the Sierra Madre, Moby Dick, Asphalt Jungle, Beat the Devil, Red Badge of Courage, Moulin Rouge* and *The African Queen*.

In these days of disaster, with movie companies retrenching and slashing staffs, with top stars turning to TV Westerns and TV commercials, when even lordly producers are reduced to writing plays, Huston is more in demand than ever. He can write his own ticket and even thumb his nose at the tycoons, which indeed he did in the case of *A Farewell to Arms*. What sort of natural selection has made him fittest to survive in this catastrophic environment?

In a Packaging Age when all women look as though they have the same mother, and all men conform to the Ivy League denominator, John Huston is uncompromisingly an original. He is as tall and lean as a basketball player and co-ordinated like a cavalryman. He dresses like a horseman in narrow twills, hacking jackets and Tattersail waistcoats. His thin grooved face, brown as teakwood, looks Chinese; his iron-gray hair is cut in no discernible fashion-say, halfway between Buster Brown and Boris Pasternak. He is an attentive listener and a courteous disputant.

His father, the beloved star Walter Huston, was a vaudeville actor when John was born in 1906, and the boy grew up touring the circuits With his father. Bred in the same sort of environment that produced such rake-hell Corinthians as Wilson Mizner, wit and con man, and John Barrymore, young Huston lived the lunatic Bohemian life.

He trained as a prize fighter, switched to horses, studied singing, got a commission in the Mexican cavalry, turned writer and sold a few stories to *The American Mercury* and *Atlantic Monthly*; went to Paris to study art, got a job with Gaumont-British as a script writer, returned to America as an actor, and finally landed a job as a writer with Warner Bros., where he collaborated on *Jezebel, Juarez, High Sierra* and *Sergeant York*. Then Huston got his big break.

Warner Bros. had a story on their shelf which they'd tried twice—once starring Bebe Daniels and Ricardo Cortez, and again starring Bette Davis and Warren William. Both pictures were abysmal flops, so Warner Bros. decided to use the story a third time. After their top stars, James Cagney, Edward G. Robinson and George Raft, turned it down in disgust, tile head brain decided to do it as a low-budget picture with second-string actors. He asked Huston to write the script. Huston wanted no part of this turkey, but agreed to write it if he could direct it. Warners wearily gave in and that was the big break. The picture was *The Maltese Falcon*, which revived the fading careers of Humphrey Bogart, Sidney Greenstreet and Mary Astor.

"In *The Unforgiven*, the picture I'm working on now," Huston said, "the gross salary of any of the stars—Audrey Hepburn, Tony Curtis, Burt Lancaster—is more than the entire cost of *The Maltese Falcon*. It was made for less than $300,000."

The phenomenal success of *The Maltese Falcon* started the ascent of the Huston rocket. Since that film Huston has, in rapid succession, directed a dozen more, served as a major with an Army film unit making war documentaries, married a fourth wife, Ricki Soma, a former ballet dancer (actress Evelyn Keyes was his third), bought a castle in County Galway for the riding and racing, and moved his family to Ireland. He joins them between pictures.

Gangling in a chair between a bottle of whisky and a box of black cigars, Huston said in a nicely managed voice: "The physiology of picturemaking is a fascinating study. I'll give you an example. Look at the left corner of the room."

I looked.

"Now look at the right corner."

I looked.

"Did you notice what you did? You blinked your eyes when you looked from left to right. That's a picture cut. Now here's something else. What do you do when you've got something emphatic to say?" Huston heaved to his feet and advanced on me, waggling his cigar. "You move closer to the person you're talking to. That's a truck shot and close-up. But if there are three or four of us in a room, all talking, we automatically spread out. That's a full shot. This is the technical art of picture making. It must correspond to what we unconsciously know to be the physiological truth." He laughed hesitantly, almost self-consciously.

"Is that how you first think as a director?"

"No. First I think in terms of story, just my own interest in a story atmosphere. Not coconut palms, but the mood in which the author has set the story."

"For example?"

"Almost any of the pictures I've done. I quit *A Farewell to Arms* because Selznick and I couldn't agree on the mood I wanted."

"What did you want that Mr. Selznick didn't want?"

"Well, in the book do you remember the billiard game in the hotel with the old nobleman—just before the lovers escape across the lake to Switzerland? That sort of mood. And the atmosphere in the officers' mess."

"Do you ever disagree with authors about the mood?"

"I've rarely worked with contemporary authors. Never with Tennessee Williams, for instance. I'm about to work on a script by Arthur Miller from a short story he wrote. He told me about it while Marilyn was in the hospital having her miscarriage and we were in the waiting room together. Every day we'd meet in the waiting room and he'd develop the idea instead of reading a magazine. A couple of months later he sent me the script."

"Anything about it you disagreed with?"

"No. It was a hell of a script and I'm going to do it with Marilyn. Now, when the director has a script, he's got to find people who'll reflect its qualities, and then look for a way of doing it that's unlike any other picture that's been made. You have to find the thing that makes this story like no other story, and tell it in its own way."

"Are there any particular problems in casting?"

Huston winced and gave his little laugh. "When you cast, there's the ever-present danger—one steels oneself because the threat is always there—to use someone whose name is thought to be box-office. I think big box-office names have ruined as many pictures as they've made successful. The temptation to use box-office names can lead to disaster."

"After you've cast a picture do you ever have trouble directing your actors to get the quality you want?"

"I never direct my actors," Huston said. "The work is all done in the casting."

He insisted this was no exaggeration, but I was suspicious. I checked with Miss Juliette Greco, star of *The Roots of Heaven*. Miss Greco, exotic in bronze slacks and black sweater, her beautiful mouth pale, her sloe eyes Egyptian, was volatile about her experiences with Huston.

"We live in little huts on location in Africa. I was the only woman. I had the filling at night I was in a military house. All dose men snoring.

"You learn very much when you wek up, and you learn so much when you see others wekking up. Some men are wekking up very nicely. Like Trevor [Trevor Howard]. Always happee and alive. Mr. Huston—all depends. Not always in a good mood in the morning. You have the same thing in the middle of the day. As though he just wek up. In a dream. Always he is in a dream. He had a very friendly way to us. He say: 'And now, kids, show me.' And he sit like this..."

Miss Greco slumped back in her chair with her knees up. She wrapped her right arm across the top of her head, with fingers over mouth; her left hand took hold of her right toe. "He sit like this and say: 'Now, kids, show me.' Other times he sit like this."

Miss Greco spread her knees and leaned forward between them with her hands drooping on the floor, like a gibbon. "He never tell us when we are good or bad. That drove me mad the first day. I was crying. I said: 'He does not like me. I take the plane back to Paris.' But sometime he look at you like a snake and say: 'Fine, fine' through his teeth. 'Fine, honey,' is the most he can say. 'Fine, honey.'"

"Didn't he ever direct you? Tell you what to do?"

"I tell you how he work. You remember the scene where I take Paul [Paul Lukas] to my bedroom? Well, it was a new set. We never see it before. We come on the set, Paul and I, and we are looking around, trying to find a way to do the scene, and Paul was grumbling. He has a very bad temper. And Mr. Huston, he sit like this...."

Miss Greco went into posture Number One.

"And he say through his teeth: 'And now, kids, what do you fill? Tell me. Show me. Show me what you are filling. Do what you want to do.' And we did. And he never say a word. He never tell good or bad. He say: 'All right. All right. Put camera here. Put camera there. Lights like so.' And we did what we wanted and he followed us with cameras."

This is Huston as the actors know him, controlled and reticent, looking like a snake and talking through his teeth; but there's another Huston—the drinking, riding, Corinthian Huston, loving the small hours in Jimmy Glennon's Third Avenue saloon, where he will sit and drink sometimes moderately, sometimes for broke, and gab with strangers, get bets down on races, argue with jockeys, and tell stories about stag hunts with the Ward Union near Dublin.

It was this Huston that made Katharine Hepburn regard him as a ruffian when she first started work on *The African Queen*.

"But Katie's a little bit high-tone anyway," Huston grinned. "I noticed she was acting suspicious so I sat down with her one night and had a little talk. Now we're the best of friends."

"Yeah," an old friend of Hus grunted. "He gave her the Huston Treatment."

The Huston Treatment, hypnotic, coolly applied with 18th Century elegance, ranges from discourses on Japanese metaphysics to practical jokes. When Huston was on location in Africa, money-man Sam Spiegel became impatient with some unavoidable delays and flew from Hollywood to Africa to straighten things out. Mr. Spiegel has the reputation of being a scourge, and the entire company quailed. "I'll take care of this," Huston promised.

When Mr. Spiegel arrived at the airport, he was met by one hundred African natives hired by Huston. They banged their drums and chanted: "Wel-kum Sam! Wel-kum Sam! Wel-kum Sam!" The serenaders followed the bewildered Mr. Spiegel wherever he went, deafening him with their chant.

"It's no use, Sam," Huston said. 'You're too popular here. We'll never be able to talk business and you'll never get anything done. You might as well go home."

Money-man Spiegel departed without scourging anybody, and the picture got under way again.

Again flanked by a bottle and cigars, but this time sitting in the gibbon pose, sketching quick caricatures of me on paper napkins on a coffee table, Mr. Huston said: "The pressure in movies comes from the men who put up the money. They were the dictators of taste before the war. They are no longer."

"Why? What's happened?"

"They were engaged in turning out a mass product. They aren't now."

"What about the question of public taste? We hear so many stories about studios' trying to make good pictures but being forced to make bad ones because that's the only kind the public will buy. Is that true?"

Huston arose like a derrick and strolled for a moment. "I'll have to answer that with a story with which I console myself rather often. There was an old man sitting in a doorway with his old hound-dog." Huston sat in a doorway with his old hound-dog. "And another old man came tottering up the street carrying a paper bag full of candy." Huston tottered up the street with a paper bag full of candy. "He stopped, looked at the dog, and said: 'That's a mighty nice dog you got there. You think he might like some candy?' And the man in the door said: 'Well, he eats garbage, so he ought to be crazy about candy.'

"Unfortunately, the taste for garbage can be developed like a taste for olives. Does the public really want it? They do now. The point is, there are many directors and producers who like it too. Not to mention any names. Cecil B. DeMille didn't lower his standards for the public, and who's to say he was wrong? Because a large segment of the public agrees with him."

"Can a director fight this?"

"Those who try, and try to put quality on the screen, have a special obligation. The canvas of the motion-picturemaker and his palette are enormously expensive.'" Huston grinned. "Permanent Green: $300,000. Flake White: $275,000. Ivory Black: $150,000.

"When these costs are tied up in a movie, it must be with some judgment or high hopes that it will be accepted. And if it isn't, not only will you not be permitted to make candy the next time but other directors too. They'll all say 'Look at *The Red Badge of Courage.*'"

"Was that a disaster?"

"It was a bomb. And that makes it harder for directors like Billy Wilder and George Stevens to do anything they want to that comes under the heading of candy."

Huston's father-in-law, the famous Tony Soma, proprietor of New York's Tony's Wife Restaurant, does not believe his son-in-law's talk about the gamble of costs and the risks of expense.

"He has no respect for money," Mr. Soma says. "He is not sensitive. With me, love and money are sacred. They should never be abused. But he has no respect for women. He uses them for a picture and then ignores them. And he has no respect for money."

"He has supreme confidence in his ability," Mrs. Soma objected.

"No. He is reckless. He has no consideration for others."

"He has faith in himself, so he can afford to be reckless," Mrs. Soma persisted.

"He's accustomed to going his own way," Mr. Soma said angrily. "All co-operation must come from the other person."

It was evident that Mr. Soma was annoyed with

Huston for having kidnaped his daughter to Ireland, three thousand miles away from her adoring parents.

He showed me some photographs of Ricki (short for Erica), and I mourned the loss too. She is beautiful. She studied ballet with George Balanchine who said of her: "Ricki will never become a ballerina. She is too intelligent."

"You say Huston has no respect for women, Mr. Soma. Is that why he married four times?"

"No," said Mr. Soma. "Because the first three did not give him children. But Ricki has two. Tony—eight. Anjelica—seven," he counted proudly. Then he relented toward the kidnaper. "John is an egoist, but not an egotist. He is very objective. He has taste and immense patience with people. He never loses his temper. But he is a dual personality."

"How do you mean?"

"I will show you." Mr. Soma produced a framed linen napkin. "He was sitting here at this table and I was bawling him out; and he was answering very sweetly, but all the while he was drawing this picture of me. An evil one. Look." Mr. Soma showed me a pencil drawing on the framed napkin. It made his chubby face look somewhat cruel and Mephistophelean.

"You see? He is two people. He's a mystery to himself. He doesn't want to be analyzed. He has no self-criticism. He likes sincerity and is sincere himself. If he lies, he's unaware of it. But it's only the sincerity of the moment because he has so many things on his mind."

Mr. Soma, who is a vegetarian and studies yoga, suddenly pulled his foot up into his crotch and stroked his toe. "If he could do this, he would be a better man."

But there is a cool, pervading sincerity in Huston that is perhaps best demonstrated by his reverence for the late Robert Flaherty, first and greatest maker of documentary films.

"He was a great man," Huston said. "He was a man who really believed that mankind at his source was good, and that he was only corrupted by civilization. And that the hope of man was to took at his original image."

"Do you agree?"

"I'm inclined to agree with him. I think the best art was the original art."

"How can that apply to anything that is as complex as the making of a movie?"

Huston emitted his little laugh. "Let's see if we can reconcile this. When Cézanne came along there was a history of painting concerned with flesh tones, lacy trees, sugary clouds, a sentimentality that misted painting and was pretty artificial and corrupt. Then this great revolutionist appeared, rediscovered the angle, and started using color not to make effects but to describe form. This I call going back to original principles. It's the power of perception piercing through the artifices of life."

Huston pointed to the lamps around us.

"For instance, there are four lights in this room. There's a cacophony of light. If we turned them all out except one, there'd be an order in the shadows. Bob Flaherty went back to one light, and order in shadows."

"And this is what you try to do?"

"Yes. It's a search for purity."

And this, I think, is why Huston is fittest to survive in the schmaltz-land of Hollywood. This elegant and charming Corinthian isn't really cold-hearted; he's simply unsentimental.

Holiday, May 1959

Rex Stout

"Excellent!" I (Dr. Watson) cried.
"Elementary," said he (Holmes).

Edgar Allan Poe started it all with Auguste Dupin, who solved The Murders in the Rue Morgue and located The Purloined Letter. The mystery story was born and, more importantly, the detective hero was invented. Mystery writers discovered that although puzzles intrigued readers, the people who solved them were the main attraction.

Hundreds of popular detective characters have been created: Nick Carter, Philo Vance, Charlie Chan, Miss Marple, Philip Marlowe, Sam Spade, Hercule Poirot, Ellery Queen, Inspector Maigret. And please no arguments. I admit that there are many others equally popular But two alone tower over all the rest: the immortal Sherlock Holmes and the all-too-mortal Nero Wolfe.

Readers around the world know Wolfe and his obstinate habits as intimately as The Baker Street Irregulars know Holmes. One seventh of a ton of intransigence, tart and thorny, a confirmed misogynist, immured (except on extraordinary occasions) in his old brownstone house on West 35th Street in New York City, a thousand rare orchids in the greenhouse on his roof, a thousand books in his office, a *chef extraordinaire* in his kitchen, and Archie Goodwin for his confidential assistant.

It's Archie who narrates the stories in a typical New York style, even though he was born and raised in Ohio: hip, tough, witty, cocky and yet often as perceptive and intuitive as a woman. And he can be a perfect bitch with Wolfe. In *And Be A Villain* there is an exchange between Wolfe and Archie that typifies them and their colorful relationship. Archie becomes exasperated with Wolfe as usual, glares at him and says, "I resign as of now. You are simply too conceited, too eccentric and too fat to work for."

"Archie, sit down."

"No."

"Yes. I am no fatter than I was five years ago. I am considerably more conceited, but so are you, and why the devil shouldn't we be? Some day there will be a crisis; either you'll get insufferable and I'll fire you, or I'll get insufferable and you'll quit. But this isn't the day and you know it."

Thirty five years have passed since the first Nero Wolfe mystery, *Fer-de-Lance*, appeared in 1934, and though they have bickered and feuded through forty-two books, that day has never come. Like Huck Finn and Miss Watson's Jim, down the Mississippi in a perpetual summer, Nero Wolfe and Archie Goodwin live their independent bachelor lives in a perpetual youth: ageless, fearless, assured, poised, fixed in amber forever by their author, Rex Stout.

Readers often wonder how much of the author goes into his characters. Much of Stout goes into his novels, but his characters do not reflect him. There is absolutely no resemblance between him and Wolfe, either in appearance or character, though both have the identical broad cultural background. Archie Goodwin's poise and sophistication are the author's, but it's doubtful whether Mr. Stout (5'9"-139 lbs.) ever delivered a right hook to the kidney, which is Archie's best punch. Actually, it's the ambience of the books that is pure Stout—humor, experience, energy and a robust love of life.

It's always a delight to meet him at authors' meetings in New York and chat with him afterwards. He has a massive calm, is dedicated to his craft and fellow craftsmen, is cool toward publishers and agents, and quietly angry with the U.S.S.R., which has pirated him and so many of his colleagues.

He dislikes coming to Manhattan and prefers to stay home in Brewster, New York, where he owns a hill overlooking miles of countryside. He makes a quaint sight pacing slowly through the elaborate gardens, rake or hoe in hand, amusedly surveying his flowers, arbors and fruit trees, wondering what to do with the old swimming pool that has been dry since his two daughters married and left home. He told me, rather proudly, that he'd just become a grandfather for the fifth time.

He sits in a deep chair in the old-fashioned *avant garde* modern home that he designed and built himself in the 1930s. There is a sunken living room, with an off-center fireplace, Rockwell Kent paintings on the walls, and large windows overlooking the countryside. There's a good working kitchen but nothing elaborate. Upstairs the house is a mishmash of corridors and bedrooms and studies (a large one for his wife, a small one for himself). The exterior is painted a rather unpleasant blue-green.

Mr. Stout smokes thick cigars placidly, often letting

them go out. During the day he drinks a horrendous mixture of Earl Grey tea and grapefruit juice, half and half, unsweetened. He's a slight man with a big head and cherubic face decorated with a curious white fluff under his chin. His voice is a beautiful bass. He's a little hard of hearing.

"I built this house in 1930. I worked fifteen hours a day for seven months, with some outside help, but no experts because experts always disagree with each other. Somehow I can't visualize drawings or blueprints, so I made seven plywood models of the house before I was satisfied. The general layout is a copy of the palace of a Bey which I saw in Tunis, with one exception; he had a eunuch well and we don't have any eunuchs around here."

"What on earth is a eunuch well?"

"They didn't like eunuchs to come too close to the house, so they used a well to mark the point in the courtyard beyond which eunuchs couldn't approach. I have fifty-eight acres here, just enough so I'll never have to put up window curtains because, goddam it, windows are made to see out of.

"Once Frank Lloyd Wright came out here to spend a weekend a couple of years after it was built, and naturally I was anxious for his opinion. After a few hours of walking around and looking, he stood out there on the front terrace and made his only comment. 'Very nice. Very nice. I would have liked to have built a house here.' Oh boy! Did that put me in my place."

Stout smiled and shook his head. "But here's a funny thing. The first time my wife, Pola—you know she's Polish—saw the place, she stood out on the terrace on the very same spot and said, 'Very nice. Very nice. Of course copied after Poland.'" He laughed and re-lit his cigar. "But that's better than the opinion of the people around here. When I was building the place they called me 'the guy that's building the Monkey House.' Have you been reading those underground newspapers?"

"Yes, with a sort of horror and disgust."

"That's very interesting." He contemplated me. You're a writer and a reporter. Nothing should horrify you."

"It's visualizing the kind of people who read and enjoy them that sickens me."

"Well, it's like the story about the two psychiatrists who pass in a corridor and one gooses the other. The guy who's been goosed turns around indignantly. Then he shrugs and says, 'What the hell, it's his problem.'"

Stout has always been an independent, an original, a man who knew his own mind. In a way it's sad to converse with him because he reflects the best of a 19th Century which no longer exists, which, indeed, is unjustly scorned today. He is all interest and tolerance. Once during an intense discussion of the Vietnam war, a neighborhood boy who was present became angry with Stout because he felt he wasn't being included in the debate. "I don't see why you can't discuss it with me," he said. Stout smiled. "Because I know what I was like at your age, but you don't know what you'll be like at mine."

He was born Rex Todhunter Stout in Noblesville, Indiana on December 1, 1886, one of four brothers and five sisters. He is the third in three solid generations of Quakers. "I went to public schools in Topeka, and then went to the University of Kansas at Lawrence, Kansas. I stayed two weeks, decided I knew more than the whole damn faculty, quit and joined the Navy because I wanted to see the real color of the ocean.

"I was assigned to Teddy Roosevelt's yacht, *Mayflower*, as pay-yeoman. I saw a lot of the Caribbean and became a good whist player. I was promoted to warrant officer because there were seven commissioned officers on board and they needed an eighth for two tables of whist. I earned $26.20 a month in salary and made up to $400 a month playing whist."

After he left the Navy, Stout spent five years roaming around the country. "I saw every goddam state and must have had at least 150 jobs in 150 different cities. I never had any adventures but I had a lot of episodes. It was not only a good preparation for a writer, but also for life.

"I began writing in 1912. I wrote fiction and sold it to *Argosy, Munsey's* and a few others. Edgar Rice Burroughs was doing his Tarzan stories for *Argosy* then. I never had any trouble selling what I wrote, but I saw after four years that I'd never get anywhere that way."

"Why not?"

"I'd write a 20,000-word story and then spend the money taking girls to concerts and the opera and the theater. I wouldn't write again until I needed money to get my shirts out of the laundry for another date. Then I'd dash off 8,000 words and run up to *Argosy* for the check. I decided to make enough money in business to support myself and then write. So I invented a new accounting system."

"You invented an accounting system?"

Stout smiled. "I just love figures. That's why I do my own books and act as my own agent. When I was a kid they used to stand me with my back to a blackboard. Then someone would write random numbers, eight across, four tiers of them. They'd turn me around and I could get the total in a minute."

"That's fantastic."

"No, it's just a kink, the same thing that makes a chess player or a Willie Mays or a Joe DiMaggio, which is a shame because he was a goddam Yankee. They can hear the crack of the bat and move at once to where the ball will be."

"What have you got against the Yankees?"

"I've been a Giants fan for so many years. I still see their games; baseball's the only thing I use television for. I used to go quail-hunting with Christy Mathewson. Once we took Chief Bender along...I don't suppose you know who he was."

"I do. He was a great Giants catcher."

"Right. Bender had never been quail-hunting before, and when we sighted a covey on the ground he raised his gun and took aim. Matty said, 'You aren't going to shoot them while they're running on the ground, are you?' And the Chief said, 'Hell, no! I'm going to wait until they stop.' How about another drink? Help yourself."

"What happened with the accounting system?"

"It was quite a success. By 1928 I'd made half a million dollars and retired to write."

"Marvelous!"

"Bushwah! I got expert advice, invested everything, and by 1930 I was broke, so I went back to 'serious' fiction and wrote five novels. They got some recognition but didn't make enough money to live on comfortably. I realized that I was a good story-teller but would never make a great novelist, so I decided to write detective stories. You just tell stories and you don't have to worry about making new comments on life and human beings. That's when I started Nero Wolfe for *American Magazine*."

He doesn't remember how he came up with the idea for Wolfe and Archie; it's too long ago. His working technique is interesting and rather unusual. "I write afternoons and evenings. My mornings are just God-awful, I'm not miserable and unhappy; I'm just not alive yet. I'm in a fog."

"That seems to have a familiar sound."

"Yes, it does sound like Archie Goodwin, doesn't it? I'm a one-job man. No matter what I'm doing, by God that's what I'm doing and nothing else. When I'm writing a story I don't do anything else. I don't go out for dinner; I don't have anyone to dinner; if a leg falls off a piece of furniture I don't give a damn. I will after the story's finished, but not while I'm writing."

"How do you outline your stories?"

"I never outline a story. Sometimes the idea will come from a *milieu*. Once I wanted to get Wolfe connected with ababy, and that turned into *The Mother Hunt*, In my latest, *Death of a Dude*, I wanted to get Wolfe out of New York again, so I took him to Montana, naturally." (Fans will understand the "naturally." Lily Rowan, Archie Goodwin's extra-special girl, is a high-spirited, wealthy young lady who owns, among other things, a ranch in Montana.)

"When I start at the typewriter I have a slip of paper with the names of the people, their ages and what they do, and that's all the outline I have. You see, in my life I've done maybe a thousand interesting things, and I think that nine hundred and thirty-seven of them happened in my subconscious. I remember when I was writing *How Like a God* I had a scene where the hero's son comes into his office and talks to him for two or three pages. Suddenly I pushed back from the typewriter, jumped up and said, 'Jesus Christ! I didn't know he had a son!'"

I was incredulous. "But Mr. Stout, if you sit down at the typewriter without an outline, what happens?"

"You know very well what happens. First you hit one key and then you hit another, and as far as I'm concerned that's all that happens. The things that people say and do in the stories I write, I make up one-third of them, but the rest I have nothing to do with.

"I have two categories for Writers; Supremely Great and Great. I think what makes a Supremely Great writer is the assurance of knowing all about your characters, of being sure of them. Balzac had that. Shakespeare did. Tolstoi did. The most important goal for a writer is to get and keep a firm, unalterable conviction, and that's what all the great writers had. The uncertainties of a writer come from a lack of this conviction, and that's why so many writers today are unwilling to make a statement and unwilling to tell a story.

"I don't know what John Updike thinks he's doing. Does he like words? Yes. Does he think he's using words? Yes. But he's not telling a story. Does he think he's revealing something about psychology and human nature? I don't know. I don't know what he's doing. I know what Balzac and Homer and Norman Mailer are doing. I know what Malamud is doing. But I don't know what Updike is doing.

"Take Hemingway. He wanted to prove that if a

man thinks he's strong he is strong. To me this is nonsense, and I think Hemingway knew it was nonsense, which is why he kept writing the same thing over and over again to convince himself. He was a good writer, at times a great writer, but this is why *Across the River and Into the Trees* is so sad. It was a kind of half-assed admission that he was wrong."

Stout grinned. "I kind of insulted Philip Roth the other day. I told him he gave the wrong title to *Portnoy's Complaint*. I told him he should have called it *Penrod Revisited*. He got mad. He didn't think it was funny. Have you read it?"

"Not yet. My wife says it's very witty."

"I'm thinking of writing a book; not a mystery, not a great novel, a trilogy similar in treatment to *Portnoy's Complaint*. Portnoy had a lot of trouble getting into women. Well, my trilogy will be about a man's trouble with a catheter."

He arose suddenly and came over to my chair so purposefully that I was alarmed.

"Have I done anything wrong, Mr. Stout?"

"No, no. I just wanted to see how you were taking your notes. Shorthand?"

"Longhand."

"May I see? Oh, yes. When you write do you write in longhand?"

"No, I've learned to think at the machine, except when the going gets tough. Then I revert to pen and ink."

"Yes. Anything to keep the story going."

"Is it the fact that mysteries are story-telling that makes them so popular?"

"You know goddam well why, of all kinds of stories, the detective story is the most popular. It supports, more than any other kind of story, man's favorite myth, that he's Homo sapiens, the rational animal. And of course the poor son-of-a-bitch isn't a rational animal at all. I think the most important function of the brain is thinking up reasons for the decisions his emotions have made. Detective stories support that myth. That accounts for the fact that that fantastic bloodhound, Sherlock Holmes, is known to more people around the world than any other character created in fiction."

"Were you ever a fan of Sherlock Holmes?"

"As a small boy I was impressed by Holmes, but even more impressed by Nick Carter...and Frank Merriwell. God! I thought Frank was a wonderful person."

"What about Poe?"

"He wasn't a story-teller at all. He was a manipulator and thinker and a wonderful user of words. The development of occurrences in a detective story should happen with as little contrivance as possible. The writer should not move the pieces around, but that goes for all writing. In the work of what writer does the least amount of contrivance take place?"

"I couldn't answer that."

"I would say Chekhov." He paused.

"But it's silly of me to make a statement like that about any writer you read in translation. You've got to read a writer in the language he wrote But about Poe; he never created a character or a human being. He invented a technique that has been used by—how many thousands? He did for the detective story what Petrarch did for the sonnet."

"Mr. Stout, why aren't good detective stories being written today?"

"The answer is simple: they're too goddam hard to write. Let's assume that you're a pretty good story-teller. Then you think of a difficult situation that arises among six people. The situation becomes so bad that the conflict forces one to kill another. Now, if you're a story-teller it isn't too difficult. You establish your characters, prepare the conflict, develop it, and in time build to the climax.

"But for a detective story writer it's much more difficult. The murder must come soon. The focus must not be on the people and their conflicts, but on an outside person, the detective who is finding it out. And the reader must not find out what the detective is finding out while he's finding it out. This is damned hard to do.

"Technically, *The Maltese Falcon* is the best detective story ever written. Do you remember that wonderful moment in the last chapter when Sam Spade says to Brigid O'Shaughnessy, 'Why did you shoot him?' My God! Those five words explain the whole thing. You say to yourself, 'Of course! That's it!' Have you read Josephine Tey? If you haven't read her you haven't read a detective story at all. Her *Daughter of Time* is superb."

"Yes, I've read it. That's the one about the murder of the young princes in the Tower."

"But what a magnificent device; to have a detective stuck in bed with a broken leg solving a five-hundred-year-old mystery. Didn't you like it?"

"It was all right, but it didn't fracture me. To tell the truth, I don't care much for women writers."

"I would have agreed with you until I read Jane Austen. If I were asked of all the dead women in the world who I'd rather have dinner with this evening, it would be Jane Austen. No, goddamit, first would have to be Sappho."

"And what about the male writers?"

"I've known a lot of them in the States and in Paris. I met Oscar Wilde a couple of times. I was very young and I remember I had the *shootspa* (sic.) to argue about his use of words. He was an enormous man and very flabby then, but his voice was beautiful, like low silk. But the most interesting talk I ever had was with Joseph Conrad, when I spent a week at his home. He didn't talk a lot but in a curious way the things he said were more intense and interesting than I'd heard from any other writer. And he was a hell of a good listener. He had an interest in anything anyone would say."

"You sound like you're describing yourself."

"Me?"

"Yes. You're an extraordinary man."

"Not at all. I know that in all aspects of life I'm really a very ordinary person. That's the way I feel. I'm not extraordinary; I'm very usual. Take flowers, for instance. Edward Steichen has specialized in delphiniums for years. He grows the most beautiful delphiniums in the world. Now *he's* extraordinary. I'm not. I just like to grow flowers.

"Take arguing. I like to argue, but in a perfectly ordinary way. Max Eastman was here one evening-in the most comfortable chair, as usual—and suddenly he jumped up and said to his wife, 'Come home, I won't stay in the same room with anyone who talks like that about Plato.' Now that was extraordinary. I'd never do a thing like that; get out of a comfortable chair and leave a house for that reason.

"I'm a very usual person. Am I pleased with myself?

Yes, but anyone who lives long enough must be pleased with himself. I can't remember any five minutes of my life when I've been bored. I can't understand people who get bored. If you're alive, you can't be bored.

"I can't understand guilt, either. Can you? I learned this at an early age; never ask the question, Why? Especially of yourself. You can waste more goddam time. The silliest question a man can ask is, Does life have a meaning? And if there is an answer it's no good because it's like fingerprints; no two answers are alike."

Holiday, November 1967

Conversation With Woody Allen

"Basically everybody is a loser," Woody Allen, high priest of the cult of the loser, says, "but it's only now that people are beginning to admit it. People feel their shortcomings more than their attributes. That's why Marilyn Monroe killed herself, and that why people can't understand it.

"I'm a loser, and that's been one of the appeals of my stage career. I'm a complainer. I'm more acutely aware of the negative side of life. That's why I don't like sunny weather. I like gloomy winter days. I like gloomy weather, period. I'd like to spend a winter in Copenhagen.

"Look at San Francisco. It has the highest suicide rate in the United States. It has perfect weather, around sixty-five degrees all year 'round, and the city is lovely—and everybody jumps off the Golden Gate Bridge."

In his latest hit, *Play It Again, Sam*, Woody has written and stars in the role of the popular modern loser. Allan Felix is a mousey movie reviewer for an obscure magazine. He's a mass of fears, repressions, and hang-ups not yet healed by years of pyschoanalysis. His wife has divorced him because he's a dullard, and he is currently flailing around trying to make a connection to a girl—and failing at every opportunity. He is obsessed by his idolatry of

Humphrey Bogart (hence the title, from a famous line in *Casablanca*) soley because of Bogey's masterful way with women, at least in the films Allan Felix has seen, and he once sat through *Casablanca* twelve times in succession.

In his earlier hit, *Don't Drink The Water*, he wrote about another loser, an American *schnook* with a *yenta* wife on tour abroad, who involves himself in serious trouble with an Iron Curtain country because he innocently takes pictures of top-secret military installations. In his albums, Woody turns losing into a kind of comedy that evokes sympathy and wry laughter, almost precisely the reaction one has when a broken-spirited dog rolls over on its back in surrender.

He's a red-headed, skinny kid from Brooklyn (5' 6"—120 pounds), born December 1, 1935, the son of an obscurity who worked at such odd jobs as hack driving and in a jewelry store. Woody went to P.S. 99 and Midwood High School in Flatbush—"They were gruesome experiences."—and was thrown out of New York University and City College "for bum grades and being a non-student." But he had already started professional comedy writing in his last term in high school. "I wrote for the Peter Lind Hayes radio show, one-liners mostly. I had a contract, twenty-five dollars a week. I was sixteen years old."

Then he moved on to the Herb Shriner show, *Two for the Money*, and continued gag writing for the next eight or nine years. His first big break was a TV special he wrote in collaboration with Larry Gelbart (author of *A Funny Thing Happened on the Way to the Forum*) for Sid Caesar, Art Carney, and Shirley MacLaine. That was in the mid-1950s, and the show won several awards. "We were nominated for an Emmy, but we got beaten out by Fred Astaire."

"I wrote more specials for Sid and Art, but I had no real interest in TV writing after I got over the glamour. I wanted to be a playwright. I kept going to theater and reading books. Then a funny thing happened; I began to come up with comedy ideas that could only be expressed in monologues. So I started to do the monologues in a place in the Village called Upstairs at the Duplex. They worked very well and I began to get a lot of bookings in clubs. It turned out to be a ride I couldn't get off. Then came *Don't Drink the Water* in 1966, which ran for a year and a half, and now *Play it Again, Sam*, which is a solid hit.

"Last summer I wrote, directed and starred in a movie that hasn't been released yet, *Take the Money and Run*. It's a frivolous little comedy about a pathological criminal; strictly an exercise for laughs. This year I'm spending a couple of months writing comic prose pieces. Then I'm going to write a play, a political satire, not for myself, and them I'll prepare another film script. I'm going to do all this before October first when I leave the play."

When he does leave *Play it Again, Sam* to mount his new play and shoot his new film, he will not yet be thirty-four years old.

Woody isn't a very funny man in real life—very few professional comics are. He saves his one-liners for his writing. He's quiet and serious and rarely laughs. After a prelude of shyness, he reveals a warm ability to relate to people and touching consideration. Yet for a star, which indeed he is, he displays disconcerting insecurity. The first time we had dinner together he was afraid that his clothes (he usually wears a tatty sweater, wrinkled chinos and battered sneakers) might prevent him from getting into a restaurant, and a Broadway restaurant at that.

There is nothing about himself he will not reveal and discuss, openly and frankly. He keeps only one secret in the world, his real name, although he will tell you in confidence. His explanation makes sense; he has spent his entire life building up the reputation of his professional name, and he doesn't want it endangered by any confusion. Everybody in the entertainment business understands that your one essential asset is your credit line.

Asked if his poise and quiet adjustment were the result of his psychoanalysis, Woody said, "No. Psychoanalysis is not as fulfilling as I hoped it would be. It's like when you have your clarinet repaired. When you get it home and play it it sounds good, but not as good as you had hoped. But then, I've only been in analysis eleven years.

"Psychoanalysis helps my work quantitatively because I'm liberated; I can get more done. Qualitatively it's helped because it's broadened my point of view. It's made my work more commercial because I no longer have a limited focus. I'm appealing to more people."

"Do people think the Allan Felix in *Play it Again, Sam* is really you, a neurotic twitch?"

"Everybody unequivocably confuses the real Woody Allen with the onstage character. Sure it's me, just like my act is me, but greatly exaggerated. It's a question of selectivity. I select only those things in myself that make for the best comedy—my most embarrassing moments, my worst fears."

This was in his dressing room backstage. The most prominent objects on his make-up table were a blender, a can of chocolate syrup, a jar of malted milk and a jar of honey. He swallows honey by the spoonful to soothe his raw throat. The truth is, Woody as an actor is a complete amateur, unequipped for projection across the footlights, and his throat suffers from the strain.

There were a couple of paperbacks on the make-up table: *Selections from Kierkegaard* and *Basic Teachings of Great Philosophers*, exactly the sort of thing you'd expect to see a young intellectual reading on a bus. We discussed books. "I don't enjoy reading," Woody said. "It's strictly a secondary experience. If I can do anything else, I'll duck it. Maybe it's because I'm a very slow reader. But it's necessary for a writer, so I have to do it, but I don't really enjoy it. The thing in itself is boring.

"The only thing I find interesting today is sporting events. They have everything that great theater should have; all the thunderous excitement and you don't know the outcome. And when the outcome happens, you have to believe it because it happened. I need something crammed with excitement. I like things larger than life."

He believes that Stendhal's *The Red and the Black* is one of the great fathers of modern novels. He says that he hates Terry Southern and had to struggle through Phillip Roth's new novel. "I felt there were many passages that could have been done better. In the masturbation scenes Roth was reaching for wild effects; in fact, I feel that Roth was pandering to the public. His attitude was: 'All right, I'll give you what you want.' Salinger didn't do that in *Catcher in the Rye*. His whole book was on a much higher level."

Woody is hip on the subject of pandering. "I feel the same way about Lennie Bruce as I do about, Roth. Bruce was not particularly brilliant. He pandered. He was and is idolized by the kind of people who must invent an idol for themselves. Nichols and May didn't do that. Mort Sahl doesn't do that; he doesn't pander."

The name of another prominent comic came up. I said, "Now there's a no-talent for you."

"He's very successful," Woody said quietly.

"And that's what amazes me; the number of no-talents who are successful."

"You don't understand," he said. "These days everybody's successful, talent and no-talent."

He lives in a high-ceilinged duplex apartment in a converted mansion just off Park Avenue. "Before I take you around I have to explain," he said apologetically. "I stopped decorating when I was only half-finished. I've decided it's too much rent and I want to get more for the money—he's paying close to $900 a month—so I'm looking to buy a co-op apartment or a townhouse."

"You can get some wonderful places on Central Park West."

"No, I couldn't live on the West Side. I have to be on the East Side in the mid-seventies, just about ten blocks away from the mainstream. What do you think about living in the country?"

"Forget it, Woody. You're a city boy. Not for you."

"Yes, but I often fantasize about a house or a farm in the country. When I visited Mt. Vernon, with its back porch on the Potomac, it made me imagine that it might be wonderful to live like that. But then I think of the bugs and the mosquitoes and how Washington must have sweltered in the summer, and I get realistic.

"Another one of my fantasies is that I can always move to rustic surroundings, in the south of France, live like a Tolstoi and write what I like. But I guess you're right. I'm a metropolitan boy, so I always want to go to a big city when I travel. I want a big city where you know it's all there. You may not go for six months, but you know it's there, twenty-four hours a day."

There's no doubt that the duplex is under furnished. One example should be enough. The living room on the main floor is beautifully paneled with, I thought, rosewood, but Woody said oak. There was no way of telling because, when I flipped the light switch, the only thing that turned on was a jukebox in the far corner. "My gift to my wife," Woody said. There was a magnificent Aubusson rug on the floor. There was an organ in the near corner. "My wife's gift to me," Woody said. There was an air conditioner lying in a wicker clothes hamper. There was a movie projector and a screen. Nothing more.

We had dinner in the formal dining room, sparsely furnished with a few expensive pieces, the ceiling pierced with pin-spots to illuminate pictures, but there were no pictures on the walls. We were served vitamin capsules, salad, scrod, peas and a choice of cherry pie, blueberry pie, pudding or cake for dessert. "I can't handle these decisions," Woody said. We discussed the problem and he settled for cake. He confessed that he eats fish most of the time, but didn't say why.

His present wife, his second, is Louise Lasser, a talented young comedienne, pretty and petite. "I like pretty little blond girls," Woody said. You've seen Miss Lasser in half a dozen prime-time TV commercials. They were married on Groundhog Day in 1966. He married his first wife when he was nineteen and she was a sixteen-year-old high-school kid. They split up amicably enough, but Woody says the much publicized million-dollar suit she's bringing against him for telling ex-wife jokes is not a stunt; it's for real.

"But that's nothing," Woody said. "I was sued once by a woman who claimed I was her husband. She said he'd been a garage mechanic who deserted her, but he made exactly the same kind of jokes I did, and when she saw me on television she knew I was her husband.

"We had a confrontation in my lawyer's office and she said, 'Yes, that's my husband,' even though her father-in-law was there and said he'd never seen me before. She was around ten years older than me, so if we'd been married when she said, I would have been thirteen years old. All the same she hauled me into court twice."

We discussed his writing regimen. "I get up around 10:30, shower, have a light breakfast, and work for about six hours. Then I knock off and play the clarinet for a while." He loves jazz, has a traditional knowledge of it, and owns a clarinet and a soprano saxophone. He says the only real satisfaction he ever had was when he was on the coast and played clarinet with an old-style band.

"After the theater," Woody went on, "I work from midnight to 3:00 A.M. When I'm writing a play or anything to be spoken, I work at the typewriter, but I write prose in longhand in bed." He bent over with his nose close to the table. "It's like working with a finer tool. Your concentration is focused.

"The difference between an Arthur Miller and a comedy writer is that the latter must obey all the structural rules that Miller does and also must keep the audience laughing for two and a half hours. It's an additional burden.

"But the frivolity attached to laughter prevents people from respecting it and taking it seriously. Laughter undermines respect. People will laugh at Neil Simon, but they won't respect him like Tennessee Williams and Edward Albee. It's an easy thing for people to slip into; if a thing doesn't have obvious importance, like dope addiction or Negro problems, they won't respect it.

"I've been trying to stay in both fields, literature and the stage, because what's funny to the eye is not funny to the ear, so I'm trying to diversify, and that keeps me interested. I'm looking for the middle line between reportage and humor. Truman Capote achieved that in *In Cold Blood*."

Walking downtown on Madison Avenue for a visit to his throat specialist, we discussed the walks that writers have to take when they're hung up on a story. Woody insisted that he was never stuck, and on those rare occasions when he was, a mere change of scene—moving from one room to another—was enough to get him going again. He said that when he did take walks he preferred Park Avenue because it was so completely dull that it didn't distract him from his thoughts.

Suddenly he said, "You said once that only a writer can understand a writer."

"I think that's true."

"Then what about that shameful flash of pleasure that comes to me when I hear about someone else's failure?"

"Oh, sure," I said. "The Germans call it *Schadenfreude*. We all suffer from that."

"Schaden? Freude? What's that?"

"The joy you feel at someone else's misfortune."

"At least I can control it consciously, but I only have contempt for my friends who call me up and gleefully report other people's failures. The nightclub people aren't like that, maybe because they're too dumb. Nightclubs are great. All the people are very nice. Those stories about nasty houses and drunks are exaggerated; it happens maybe once a year. The nightclub people—they sit out there and root for you. If you're sick they go on for you. And they all sing *There's No Business Like Show Business*.

"I have great contempt for the theater—for the presumption of the theater. TV is idiot stuff, designed by idiots for idiots, which is why you have *The Beverly Hillbillies*. But the theater puts on such airs-the producers, the directors, the critics—that's why it's dying today. And it should."

We went to the Broadhurst Theater, just across the street from Sardi's, and Woody began warming up for the evening performance, skipping imaginary ropes and shooting imaginary baskets. He exhorted the cast: "Okay, we're going to kill 'em tonight. We killed 'em at the matinee and we're going to kill 'em tonight." He jogged offstage and said to me, "We should do research on how often a laugh should come, every minute? Every half minute? I don't know. Did you clock our laughs the other night?"

"Yes."

"How many?"

"Sixty-nine in the first act. Sixty in the second..."

"That runs five minutes shorter," he interposed quickly.

"Twenty-six in the last act. Total: a hundred and fifty-five."

"Not bad. Not bad at all, but you never know. My club act has forty-five minutes of unrelenting jokes. Some nights some jokes get the laughs, other nights, others. You can never tell about laughs. The phenomenon of getting and losing laughs can't be understood. It's a delicate chemistry."

The stage manager called "Places, please."

"You know, I didn't prepare for this show," Woody said: "Not one jot. And I haven't taped my club act at all, outside of failing with women and psychoanalysis and being short."

He jogged to his position onstage in his tatty sweater, chinos and sneakers, his raggedy red hair disheveled, and sat down to watch the TV presentation of a Bogart film that opens the show: The curtain went up with a creak, and the world's most successful loser was on.

The name of this game is Masochism For Fun and Profit.

Holiday, May 1969

Isaac Asimov

There's no doubt that Isaac Asimov is the finest popular science writer working today, and in my opinion Ike is the finest who has ever written; prolific, encyclopedic, witty, a gift for colorful and illuminating examples and explanations. What makes him unique is the fact that he's a bonafide scientist—associate professor of biochemistry at Boston University School of Medicine—and scientists are often rotten writers. Read the novels of C. P. Snow and the short stories of Bertrand Russell if you want proof. But our scientist professor, Asimov, is not only a great popular science author but an eminent science fiction author as well. He comes close to the ideal of the Renaissance Man.

His latest (120th) book, *Asimov's Guide to Science* (Basic Books), is a must for science-oriented and/or science-terrified readers. Many people have the frightened feeling, "What are they up to now?" Asimov tells us with clarity, charm, with calm. His new *Guide* will fascinate the layman, and if the layman gives it to his kids to read they may very well wind up on university faculties with tenure. Ike makes everyone want to turn into a scientist.

Asimov's Guide to Science is the new and third edition of *The Intelligent Man's Guide to Science*, first published in 1960 by Basic Books. Asked why the change in title, he said, "Well, there's a whole slew of *Asimov's Guides* and *Asimov's Treasuries*, so we decided to go along with it. I presume the fourth edition will be *Asimov's New Guide to Science*. What the fifth will be, I don't know."

The encyclopedia has been revised and updated, of course. Much has happened since the 1960s. Asked about his changes, Ike rattled off, "Pulsars, black holes, the surface of Mars, landings on the moon. Then there's seafloor spreading and the shifting of continents, which I dismissed with a sneer in the first edition. You see, at the time of the first edition the space satellites were just being flown and hadn't done their research yet. I thought the earth's crust was too solid and hard for the continents to drift. I was wrong. Now we know that the continents aren't floating; they're being pushed apart by the upflow of magma from the seafloor. Then I've covered quarks and—"

"Wait a minute. What are quarks?"

"They're hypothetical particles which may make up all the subatomic particles, but first we have to isolate one. In other words, you can think that ten dimes make a dollar, but you have to take a dollar apart first and find a dime." This is the Asimov style.

He also discusses why enough neutrinos have not yet been detected coming from the sun, the biological clocks in animals, tachyons—a fascinating hypothesis about subatomic particles which travel faster than the speed of light—and cloning.

"What's so special about clone cultures, Ike? They're simply families raised from a single individual. I raised many clone cultures from a single paramecium or amoeba when I was a biology student."

"No, no. Now we're talking about despecializing specialized cells. You can take an abdominal cell from a frog, fertilize it with an ovum and get a whole frog.

There may come a time when they can cut off your little toe when you're born, fertilize it and end up with a whole race of Alfie Besters."

"What a horrible thought."

"Yes, but they wouldn't know it at the time."

He's a powerful man, 5'9"—180 pounds, with thick hair going grey, steel-blue eyes, beautiful strong hands, and rather blunt features. He was born in Russia in 1920 and was brought to the States in 1923 by his family, which wasn't exactly well-to-do. Nevertheless he managed to put himself through Columbia University to his doctorate which he won for a thesis on enzyme chemistry.

He was married in 1942, has two kids, and is recently separated from his wife. He now lives in a comfortable suite in a residential hotel just off Central Park West. The living room is his workshop; jammed with shelves of reference texts, files and piles of scientific journals. He works from nine to five, seven days a week without a break.

"No, I'm lying. Sometimes I goof off on part of Sunday."

"Do you think at the typewriter, Ike?"

"Yes. I type at professional speed. Ninety words a minute."

"Great, but do you think at ninety words a minute?"

"Yes, I do. The two work together neatly."

He receives an enormous amount of mail from his fiction fans and his science fans, which he answers. Small boys ask him to settle disputes they're having with their science teachers. Asimov winces when he recalls a terrible boner which he perpetrated in the first edition of his *Guide*. A student got into an argument with his teacher over it and said, "Asimov is always right." Asimov was forced to write "Sometimes Isaac Asimov is a damned fool."

He gets a few crank letters. "One guy was mad because I wouldn't say that Nikola Tesla was the greatest scientist who lived. I've only had one anti-Semitic letter. This was a kook who thought I gave too much space to Einstein. He said Einstein was all wrong, and anyway he stole everything from a Gentile. Naturally I didn't bother to answer that."

He's rather amused by what he calls his steel-trap memory. "I have a tight grip on things in inverse proportion to their importance. The trouble is, I can't throw anything out. The day a friend mentioned an old song, 'The Boulevard of Broken Dreams,' and I sang it for him."

Damned if he didn't start singing it for me, miserably. "You see?" he grinned. "Another five brain cells wasted."

Publishers Weekly, 1973

Robert Heinlein

The one author who has raised science fiction from the gutter status of pulp space opera (still practiced by Hollywood) to the altitude of original and breathtaking concepts is Robert A. Heinlein. And there is no doubt that his latest novel, *Time Enough for Love* (Putnam), an enormous work covering the next 24 centuries, played on nine planets, with several hundred vivid characters, will evoke the same reaction that his 30-odd previous books have: a curious combination of admiration, awe, shock, hatred and fascination.

For Heinlein is a delightful paradox, and the contrasts of his character show in his splendid, challenging and sometimes infuriating writing. One thing is certain: Heinlein (the name is pronounced "Heinlein" and he prefers being called Robert to Bob) will never bore you, in life or on the page.

The layman's image of the science fiction author is of a frail, skinny intellectual wearing huge spectacles and subscribing to publications like *Space Symbiosis*. Heinlein is a big, tough ex-Navy lieutenant (6'-170 lbs), a graduate of Annapolis and a guy you would hate to get into a fight with. The public also thinks of the science fiction author as a cold-blooded logician, a sort of walking computer. What, then, do you say to a hard-headed gunnery officer who is yet so warm, courteous and empathetic to the needs of others that he verges on the sentimental? He has a dry, hard voice; he is witty (but tells the worst jokes in the world), he knows his own mind and can never be deflected; he is a hard-hat patriot, which is why some members of the intellectual community accuse him of fascism.

But let him speak for himself, in his Navy way: "Born 7-7-07—which makes me very lucky at craps—in Butler, Missouri. The family moved to Kansas City when I was four and I was raised there. The family is German and homesteaded in Bucks County, Pennsylvania, in 1756, but I'm more Irish than anything else. Some Cherokee Indian in the family, too, and a trace of African."

"How big a family, Robert?"

"I have three brothers and three sisters. I'm No. 3. I had no older sister so I had the privilege of being an honorary sister, with the right to wash dishes. I went to Greenwood Grammar School, with Sally Rand, then Horace Mann and Kansas City Junior College."

"How did you end up at Annapolis? Were you queer for the sea like another Kansas boy I know, Rex Stout?"

"I got a political appointment. Our family was always in politics. I worked two years writing letters and applications and finally got the appointment through a Boss Pendergast man, Jim Reed. I would have taken West Point as readily, but the only opening was the Academy. I was always honored by Reed because I was the first of his appointees that ever graduated."

Heinlein graduated 20th in a class of six hundred from the Academy in 1929 and swears he would have been fifth if he hadn't acquired three "Black N Stars" which are demotions in rank for malefactions. "I got caught off-limits too many times when I was out chasing girls." He went to the carrier *Lexington*, shifted to destroyers as a gunnery officer, and was retired from the Navy when it was discovered that he was suffering from TB.

"So how did the science fiction start, Robert?"

"In '39 I started writing and I was hooked. I wrote everything I learned anywhere—Navy, Army—anywhere. My first science fiction story was 'Lifeline.' I saw an ad in *Thrilling Wonder* offering a prize of $50 for the best amateur story. But then I found out that *Astounding* was paying a cent a word, and my story ran to 7,000 words, so I submitted it to them and they bought it."

"You son of a bitch," the *PW* interviewer said between his teeth. "I won that *Thrilling Wonder* contest and you beat me by $20."

He burst out laughing. Then he continued, "I asked myself how long had this been going on? I kept on writing science fiction. I never served an apprenticeship. I never rewrote. Nobody ever told me. I still never rewrite."

"Then how do you work?"

"I write three or four months out of the year and then Ginny [his wife] and I take off and travel. Then I get the twitches and have to start writing again."

"How fast do you work?"

"Well the fastest was—I'll have to explain. When we were living in Colorado there was snowfall. Our cat—I'm a cat man—wanted to get out of the house so I opened a door for him but he wouldn't leave. Just kept on crying. He'd seen snow before and I couldn't understand it. I kept opening other doors for him and he still wouldn't leave. Then Ginny said, 'Oh, he's looking for a door into summer.' I threw up my hands, told her not to say another word, and wrote the novel *The Door Into Summer* in 13 days."

"What's your technique?"

"I start out with some characters and get them into trouble and when they get themselves out of trouble the story's over. By the time I can hear their voices they usually get themselves out of trouble."

"Robert, I have to bring up a very sensitive issue. You're often accused of being a hard-hat fascist in your writing, justifying and sympathizing with villainous hawk types."

"Alfie, have you ever seen a villain in any of my stories? I don't really believe in villains. No man is a villain unto himself. Once or twice I've used cardboard villains, but that's all. One thing runs all through my stories. I believe in freedom. I believe in a man's total responsibility for his own acts. I'm downright reactionary about that.

"Patriotism is a nice long polysyllabic abstract word of Latin derivation, which translates into Anglo-Saxon as Women and Children First. And every culture that has ever lasted is based on Women and Children First or it doesn't last very long. But there's no way to force patriotism on anyone. Passing a law will not create it, nor can we buy it by appropriating billions of dollars."

At this point he actually began to break down. *PW* could not endure the sight of a colleague on the verge of tears, so I changed the subject. "Forget it, Robert. It's the politicians who've given patriotism a bad name. Let's get back to science fiction. What's your definition of it?"

"Well, it's not prophecy, despite the endless list of things which have appeared in science fiction before they were physical realities. Nor is it fantasy, even though critics ignorant of science have trouble telling them apart. I'm not running down fantasy; I enjoy it and sometimes write it, but fantasy is not science fiction."

"Then what is science fiction?"

"Science fiction is realistic fiction. A serious science fiction writer must attempt to start with the real world and ask, 'What if—?' He must do it alone, then turn his scenario into a story that will entertain a reader—thousands of readers—or he has failed, no matter how logically he has extrapolated the present into the future."

"And how do you make sure that you don't fail?"

He grinned. "First you've got to pull 'em in off the sidewalk. Then you hang on to their lapels—don't let 'em get away—then pass 'em along from paragraph to paragraph and finish with music."

Publishers Weekly, 1973

Introduction to *The Demolished Man:* The Deleted Prologue

This section includes the original prologue to *The Demolished Man*, as published in *Galaxy* in 1952. It's a centuries-spanning recap of the events that led to the Esper society and the Esper League, the formation of the Reich—D'Courtney dynasties, and details about the conquest of space through the discovery of antigravity (Nulgee) and the provenance of the knife-pistol-knuckleduster that comes into deadly play in the novel.

Bester obviously loved this form of intense storytelling, for he used it again four years later in *The Stars My Destination*. Why then, does the latter novel retain the prologue, while the former had it stripped in 1953?

The answer lies in *The Demolished Man*'s popularity. After its run as a serial in *Galaxy*, it was picked up by the small publishing house Shasta for a hardback reprint (which went on to win the first Hugo award for best SF novel in 1953). Paper shortages were common in post-WWII, and the cut was made as the book was assembled for printing. Shasta also apparently made Bester clean the novel up a bit—a careful reader will notice that Ben Reich's company is called *Sacrament* here, and not *Monarch*—and some small cuts were made. Future editions followed the Shasta edition, and the prologue was lost. Here it comes again, almost a half-century since its last appearance.

This section also includes Bester's illuminating essay, "Writing and the Demolished Man," published in 1972.

The Demolished Man: The Deleted Prologue

Rich and powerful, Ben Reich was a criminal who couldn't possibly fail in a society where telepaths made it unlikely for criminals to succeed!

On Sol Double-3 (for the Cosmic Eye sees Earth and her moon as a planetary binary) in January of 2103, Edward Turnbul of Coates Teachers College decided to explore the Hysterisis Enigma for his research thesis. The Reamur Variations on the Einstein Post-mortem Equations had suggested a paradox which no one had bothered to explore. Atomic research had bypassed it; and what are the dead ends of science for if not to provide harmless occupation for graduate students? Turnbul studied the original research, ran a few duplications and then tinkered with the apparatus.

Get the picture: A serious young man, fat, sallow, a genuine bore. A Phi Beta Kappa anesthetising his frustrations in a laboratory. A magnet is his sweetheart, caulds of X-27 Duplexor are his conjugal embraces. He tinkers at midnight and sublimates his maladjustments in the excitement and suspense of the experiment. Will it work? Can he really develop a commercial process, earn a million dollars and overpower women with this uncontestable proof of his virility?

Turnbul unwraps a sandwich, aping the dashing insouciance of fictional heroes, then pulls the switch. The experiment works. Thirty-two pounds of apparatus and a liter of methylene dimethyl ether loft up from the bench and smash against the ceiling. Turnbul has stumbled on something they just missed a century ago...anti-gravity. Unique? No. Inevitable. In the infinity of a universe crawling with searching, inquiring, experimenting creatures, this had happened, was happening and would happen beyond the count of simple integers. Statistics made it inevitable.

Forget Turnbul. He is not your protagonist. If you identify with him, you will be lost in this story, as Turnbul himself is lost in the shifting pattern that produced *The Demolished Man*. Turnbul patented; he was sued. He fought in courts for fifteen years with inadequate counsel and the patent was broken. Turnbul was notorious enough by that time to receive a full professorship at the Institute. He married a librarian, raised children, taught miserably, and jealously inspected each new textbook, content if credit for Nulgee was paid him in footnote or appendix.

On September of 2110, Galen Gart's wife died. She was a tall, lustrous, remote woman, and he had loved her deeply for thirty years. They had been a devoted couple, and in the course of their marriage had grown to resemble each other, as couples often do. It was hard to distinguish their handwriting, their voices, their jokes.

"We even think alike," Gart used to say. "Half the time I answer her before I realize she hasn't had a chance to speak her thoughts." And after her death he said: "What's the use of going on? We were part of each other. We didn't need words. How can anyone else give me the same intimacy?"

But Galen Gart, fifty, desolate, prematurely aging, met a pungent child of twenty with an exciting poitrine, a satin skin, and the infantile nickname of Duffy, and they were married six months after the funeral.

"You're not so old in the dark."

"Why, Duffy!" exclaimed Mr. Gart. "What a nice thing to say."

"But I didn't say anything." Nor had she.

It was a year before Mr. Gart realized that it was he who didn't need words. It became his joke, his little parlor trick, a quaint trait.

"So this is the famous Galen Gart. Mind reader? Imposs. Tricks. Can't fool me. Can't read my mind."

"But I can, dear lady. I can."

"You ca—But I didn't say it. I—"

"Hey! Everybody! Gart's done it again."

"Look at her blush."

"What's she thinking, Gart?"

"Why's she blushing?"

"The lady," Mr. Gart smiled, "is thinking that I'm laughing at her. She's blushing because I'm telling her I admire her. She has one of the loveliest minds I have ever met."

Laughter.

Oh yes; laughter at the quaint trait when gentle, tactful, courteous Mr. Gart performed his parlor trick. But the trait was an extracted recessive that appeared in his son.

There was no more laughter when the amoral animal that a child is discovered it had inherited Extra Sensory Perception and used it brutally. Galen Gart,

Jr. turned laughter to tears, and many texts were written about his lurid criminal career that ended with his murder. And Galen Gart, Jr., Esper blackmailer, confidence trickster and thief, helped produce *The Demolished Man*.

The vacant lot across the way from Sheridan Place was finally sold, and Space Clubs, Inc., was forced to move its Raffle Office and prizes to Brooklyn. Their funds barometer, a miniature explosive rocket hanging, halfway up an illuminated column calibrated in thousands of dollars, was abandoned. The lot was turned into a block of experimental al fresco stores, without walls or roof, protected from the elements and casual theft by the new Donaldson Resistance Hedge, an invisible bubble of radiation that scintillated in wet weather with the prismatic glitter of oil on water.

The center shop, alongside the entrance to the Pneumatique Station, was taken in 99 year lease by Wilson Winter, an ambivalent artist turned bookseller, who purchased one lot of odds and ends for the benefit of literature, and conducted a thriving trade in pornography for the benefit of his purse. Among. the worthless items in the odds & ends was *Let's Play Party* by Nita Noyes. It collected dust on the shelf until it was bought by *The Demolished Man*.

REALISM IS 4TH DIMENSION

PLATON QUINN, brilliant young producer of Pantys, attributes his phenomenal success to close attention to detail. In an exclusive interview with yr recorder he said: "People forget that 'Panty' is slang for Emotional Pantograph. When you get five thousand people into a theatre to see a Panty performance, you can't make them feel love, hate, horror.... You can't Gestalt *them unless you put authentic detail on the Passion tape.*"

Quinn, lithe and enthusiastic, waved his hands creatively. "Too many producers think that Pantys are a three-dimensional medium...sight, sound & sensation. To me, Pantys are four dimensional and my fourth dimension is realism. Every prop, every costume, every bit of cloth, metal, china, plastic and so on in my productions is authentic. And the public feels it; Here, look at this..."

The brilliant young producer showed us a glittering bit of steel. "You won't recognize it," he smiled, "until you've seen Murder's Memory Bank. *This is the only one of its kind in existence. A rare French folding pistol. Watch."*

He pressed the gadget. There was a vicious click. The steel unfolded like a flower. A stiletto point appeared, an explosive muzzle, and four heavy steel rings which, Quinn explained, were knuckledusters.

"A fistful of murder," Platon said enthusiastically. "Wait until you're in your seat at the preview. You feel the knife. You feel the bullet tear into your heart. You feel all the pain and horror of peril and passion. It's sensational. It's all in my new Panty, Murder's Memory Bank."

Platon Quinn refolded the pistol, replaced it in the desk and forgot it. He forgot it when he left the hotel. It remained forgotten until it was used by The Demolished Man.

Anti-Gravity or Nulgee was explored, developed and exploited. It smashed one industrial world and created five others. Among a million entrepreneurs scrabbling

Phoenixlike in the ruins, it was adopted by "The 7 Sacrament Brothers," a single-truck moving firm owned and operated by a lone brother named Reich. Reich was a thin young man, equipped with a fishy eye, cannibal ambitions and a minimum of social responsibility.

Nulgee was also adopted by Space Clubs, Inc., who were having difficulty raising funds. Industry shrugged, preferring to leave the wild pioneering to fools. Who wants to speculate on probabilities? What commercial advantage can there be in reaching the arid Moon or the icy methanated planets? Who sponsored Cayley, Henson, Stringfellow, Chanute, Santos-Dumont, the Wrights? Also, there were several wars pending, and the armies were fighting to stifle Nulgee for insecure reasons of security.

Meanwhile, there was Alan Courtney. After divorcing his twelfth wife, Courtney started looking around for a new kind of hyper-thyroid release. He had enough money to bore him, and that was enough to start building a starship. His statement to the press announced that he was off to search the stars for an ideal wife. The press was indifferent to Mr. Courtney and he was piqued. Out of spite he finished the ship, and out of drunkenness he took off.

He never returned. No one believed he'd left. Five years later, most people were asking: "What ever happened to marrying Alan Courtney?" And people were answering: "He's living in Santa Fe, isn't he? Married again, probably."

There was also Glen Tuttle, a renegade psychotic who fleeced his wife and in-laws, bilked his creditors, defrauded his friends, and, in a final attempt to jump out of the frying pan, constructed a flimsy starship on credit and lofted to space unknown. Tuttle also never returned. His escape was never believed. Space Clubs was still talking about funds for the first ship to carry men to the Moon.

There were, in addition, Atmedo Zigerra, Joan Turnbul, Fritz Wonchalk, Speeman Van Tuerk and a few others...maladjusted, incapable of social compromise, escapists all...which is to say, pioneers all. They left Earth one by one with varying publicity, little recognition, and never returned. Space Clubs Inc. cheered the donation of $100,000 by a transportation magnate named Reich, and predicted that man would soon leave Earth for his first journey into space. It had already taken place. It had already produced The Demolished Man.

She came through the door into the quiet consultation room and looked around. She was a drab woman, forty, faded, frightened. She saw the man behind the desk, a young man with black hair, black eyes, and Duffy's white satin skin.

"Come in, madam. Be seated."

His voice was low, slightly harsh, as though it contained conflicts under compression.

"Thank you." She lowered herself painfully. "*Looks too slick. Thief-type. Hannerly said the guy might be legitimate. Not a chance. My recorder on? Right.*"

"Your name, madam?"

"My name? *Rhoda Rennsaeler, buster, when you read it in the byline*. I'm Mrs. Thomas Nolles. Elvira is my given name."

"And your problem, Mrs. Nolles?"

"Well, I keep hearing those voices in my ear all the time talking to me. So I thought a doctor could—"

"I'm not a doctor, madam. Understand that. I do

not practice medicine. I merely advise my friends. You may call me mister. Mr. Lorry Gart."

"Cautious, aren't you? But I'll get you, buster, don't ever imagine I won't."

"Your problem, Mrs. Nolles?" Gart repeated.

"It's these voices. I hear them telling me I'm God. *And if you can resist that come-on, you're a smarter crook than I think.* I can pay for the treatment. *I've got a roll of bills you'll drool for, you cheap quack.*"

"Provided by Mr. Hannerly?"

"Oh, no. It's my savings. I—" She stopped short.

Gart nodded and smiled. "Beginning to understand, Mrs. Rennsaeler?"

"I never said it. Never!"

"No, of course you didn't. Nor your name. You do understand, don't you? Now let's be practical, Mrs. Rennsaeler. I'm not a quack. You won't expose me. You'll forget all about this episode."

"But what in God's name are you?"

"A mind-reader...telepath...esper. I have Extra Sensory Perception, Mrs. Rennsaeler—ESP. I still haven't decided what to call myself." He looked at her quizzically. "I'd welcome a suggestion from an experienced reporter."

"The louse! Reading everything in my mind. Stop thinking! Why can't I stop thinking? He's listening. Like a Peeping Tom. Peeping. He—"

"Mrs. Rennsaeler, stop that!" Gart spoke sharply. He arose from his chair and stepped around the desk to her. "Listen to me. Don't be afraid. You feel the privacy of your shame is being invaded. That makes you hostile. But you have nothing to be ashamed of, Mrs. Rennsaeler. We're all alike inside our minds. *All* of us. I know. I've found that out."

She stared up at him in terror.

"Believe me." He nodded and grinned painfully. "Shall I tell you my shames, my secret fears and vices, my terrors? Shall we be brothers below the conscious threshold? My father was a criminal...Galen Gart Jr., a telepathic blackmailer, a cheat, a man who read minds to destroy people. He was murdered. I have in me the same extra sense, the ability to read minds...not deeply, but deeply enough. It's an ability tempted by greed, vicious hatred of society, compulsions to shock and destroy people...compulsions to destroy myself."

"I don't understand." She shook her head. "I don't understand at all."

"I'm stripping myself psychologically naked for you, Mrs. Rennsaeler. It's my defense against your hostility. I'm hoping that you can help me become something more than a backstreet conjurer. You're experienced in public relations."

"No," she said. "No. I came here to expose a quack. I—"

"Listen to me. I use my ability to help confused people. They come to me...the poor sick ones...so sick they can't discover their problems. I do only one thing for them. I help them recognize their problems. While they talk, I listen to their broken thoughts. While they wander and flounder in confusion, I pick out the pieces, the artifacts...I tell them what their crisis is. I make them see it. I wrap up their problem in a neat parcel and place it in their hands. They can carry it to the nearest analyst for solution though that's generally not necessary."

"Then you're no quack."

"No. Mrs. Rennsaeler. I'm not. And you believe

me. That much I can read in your mind. You believe me and you want to help me. Isn't that true?"

After a long pause she said: "Yes, you damned peeper. I believe you and I want to help you."

Gart took her hand. "You've started helping me already. You've given me my name."

The *Geoffrey Reich*, first manned ship to reach the Moon, discovered Glen Tuttle's ship and body in the center of a seventy-mile bed of Haines' Stellite valued at $6.83 a pound. The airlock of Tuttle's ship was open and the body sprawled at the entrance. Poor Tuttle was so ignorant that he never knew the Moon was airless. He had had time for one quick glance at Mare Imbrium before he suffocated. His body was riddled with machine-gun perforations from the meteoric pellets that bombard the unprotected Moon at 30 miles per second.

MR. ASJ: Counsel may cross-examine the witness.

MR. LECKY: If it please the court, at this time I would like to introduce Dr. Walter Clark, E.M.D., as Esper Medical Expert to conduct the crossexamination of this hostile witness.

MR. ASJ: Objection.

THE COURT: What is your argument, Mr. Lecky?

MR. LECKY: I submit, your honor, that in this Matter of the Estate of Alan Courtney, a sum exceeding twenty-five million dollars is at stake. Although I do not impugn the conscious honesty of my opponent's witnesses, I suggest that their recollection has been colored by dollar signs.

MR. ASJ: Is counsel making an argument or writing a Panty scenario?

MR. LECKY: It is an established fact that men remember what they want to remember, and forget what they want to forget. They do this in all sincerity. Objective truth does not exist in the psychoanalytic sense and our courts have affirmed and reaffirmed the psychoanalytic principle in a long line of cases.

THE COURT: This court is acquainted with the precedents, Mr. Lecky, but the present course of action does not lie with them.

MR. ASJ: There never yet has been a case where a peeper was admitted to give evidence, and if counsel imagines he's going to ring in a—

MR. LECKY: What are you afraid of? If your witnesses are telling the truth, my man will peep them and confirm it, But if they're lying as I suggest—

THE COURT: Gentlemen! Gentlemen! Such exchanges cannot be countenanced. The court is cognizant of the fact that Extra Sensory Experts perform valuable services for society in many walks of life...the Esper Medical Doctor, the Esper Attorney, the Esper Educator, the Esper Criminologist...to mention only a few; yet the Esper Expert cannot properly be admitted to any court to give Esper evidence for the record.

MR. LECKY: It cannot be ruled an invasion of privacy your honor, any more than a snapshot of a nude sunbather can be ruled an invasion of modesty. Three hundred years ago the human body was imagined to be a thing of shame. Concealment was the strange custom of the day. Two hundred years ago the human mind was imagined to be a thing of shame. Concealment was the strange custom of that time. But we have progressed far beyond such medieval concepts.

THE COURT: Very true, Mr. Lecky, but human justice has not yet abandoned the established principle that a man cannot be used as a hostile witness against himself. A man cannot be forced to convict himself of subconscious mendacity. Justice must always remain on the objective level. If it does not, what would become of the deluded innocents who falsely believe in their own guilt? How would the courts reconcile their subjective confessions with their objective innocence? The objection is sustained.

In 2300, the *Sacrament III* carefully quartering the East Quadrant of Mars for **FO** (fissionable ore) discovered the remains of marrying Alan Courtney. He had survived his landing some two years, eking out his dwindling supplies with lichens and the dew that formed on the surface of his starship. There were scars and rust particles on his tongue.

Evidently he had gone insane, for they found his dessicated body genuflected before a rock on which the symbol of the Order of Python had been cut.

The symbol, a serpent coiled in an infinity sign was ignored in the reports, but they named a city after him.

In honor of Alan Courtney, his great-grandnephew, Samuel Dus, took his name, took his twenty-five million dollars and took up residence in Courtney City on Mars.

There were other reasons. Samuel Dus-Courtney had been mauled in a financial scrimmage with old Geoffrey Reich III, and was retiring to lick his wounded bank account.

Joan Turnbul's ship, a converted Empire submarine,

fell into the Three Body Problem, and follows Jupiter in his eternal course as one of the Trojans. Passing Sacrament Liners sometimes waste enough fuel to give their passengers a glimpse of her staring skeletal face framed in a crystal port. Sentimental virgins often weep pretty tears at the sad fate of the lovely (she was ugly as sin) daughter of the discoverer of Nulgee.

Van Tuerk smashed on Titan. A D'Courtney tanker found him inside his little spacecan, lying broken on the deck on which he'd chalked: *Die Kunst ist lang, das Leben kurz, die Gelegenheit flùchtig*. The D'Courtney ship also found a forty billion dollar crater of radiant magma.

"Magma Cum Laude," snorted Ben Reich when he received the news from Relations in Sacrament Tower, but he was not amused.

For Ben Reich is The Demolished Man.

Galaxy, January 1952

Writing And *The Demolished Man*

Many years ago, when my wife and I returned from a trip to Europe, a friend of ours was quite indignant with our account of our travels and said with great anger that he felt that I felt that the entire world was created for my amusement and my entertainment. And he was pretty sore about it. He was only half right. Later on, a lady, a very perceptive lady, said to me after we had been discussing things, "I understand you. You are in love with the world." And I said, "Yes, that is perfectly true!"

And it is also true that when I write science fiction, I write out of love. I must fall in love with a story or a novel and once having fallen in love with it consummate the affair right through to the end. My wife is rather amused by this. I've heard her say more than once, "He doesn't love me anymore, he has fallen in love with a book...." And this does happen. But, of course, the interesting problem is: how does one fall in love with a story, or with a book?

It is easy to fall in love with a short story because this is a quick thing. It is more or less like the situation when you are driving your car and stop for a traffic light; you glance to the right or the left and you see a lady in the car next to you. You fall instantly in love with her and, in your mind of course, you leave your car and leap into her car and for a half-hour you have this wild thing going for you. This is, in a sense, what one does with a short story. An idea comes along, some sort of a bit of dialogue which you've heard at a bar, or some sort of research that you have done—because, indeed, the writer does not sit at home in an ivory tower waiting for inspiration to come. He gets out and digs, he shuffles around, he listens to people, he talks to people, he is like a giant dragnet; he is dragging up for future use anything that he can hear, that he can see, that he can possibly use.

Some of the stuff is stored away in one's notebook, but occasionally there is one of these lucky moments when something comes out of the blue and hits you between the eyes and you say: Ah, I'm in love, here is the idea, here is the story. And off you go to work up the steam for your half hour affair with this short story.

But with a novel it is a different proposition. The novel is not jumping from one car to another. The novel is a long-term love affair. Now, don't hold me too closely to this analogy because it does not work all the way down the line. But it is in a sense a kind of affair, a long-enjoying affair with the novel, or the lady, however you will. And it usually starts of course with that first meeting with an idea, which very often you think is a short story idea; and then you start it and suddenly discover there is this long perspective reaching into space, and you realize that you will not have enough room within 3,000 or 6,000 words to handle this and you suddenly realize that you are stuck with a novel. As in an affair with a lady, you are afraid in the beginning. And steps which lead into the genuine love affair are, at least for me, rather interesting.

Let us take, for example, a book written many years ago by me, *The Demolished Man*. It is old now but since so many people seem to be still interested in it, I will explain what the emotions were in putting this book together. In the first place you should all understand (not my colleagues, because they all know about this) that I am a working writer, I am a working stiff, I am not an entirely science fiction writer—I am *an everything* writer as indeed we all are.

So, when I was first approached by Horace Gold who was then editor of *Galaxy Magazine*, and when he asked me if I would write something for him, I was a little surprised. I was rather busy writing radio scripts at the moment. We discussed various ideas and I submitted several proposals to him. I can recall that two of the proposals were:

1. Would it be possible to do an interesting story about a time and a future in which the people will have time-scanners which can scan back into the past so that it will be impossible for a criminal to commit a crime and get off, because with the time-scanners they could go back to the origin of the crime to find out who the guilty parties are, and of course arrest them? I thought this would make an interesting conflict.

2. Another suggestion I had, in a half dozen of them, was that I thought: could there be a time in the future when people who are trading agents should be perhaps more versed in psychiatry, in the understanding of other areas, or perhaps even capable of extrasensory perception, so that they can help train them

in the races with whom the people of the world really have no sympathetical understanding?

There were five other ideas, one of which Horace kicked out; and then he said, "Why not do a story about a crime committed in the future in which there is extra sensory perception? Let us combine two of these ideas. What will extra sensory perception do? These are the law enforcements against crime: what will telepathy do?" And we discussed it on the phone (Horace at the time was in bed in his apartment; he was suffering from frightful agoraphobias as a result of his war experiences—so we were on the telephone very often). I was quasi-interested in it, because quite frankly the idea of writing a science fiction novel terrified me. But, as we discussed the idea of a telepathic society, or a semi-telepathic society and what influences it might have on life as we knew it, I became more and more interested; and then I did something which writers often do: I wrote a "bubble" number 1. [I'd better explain that: in the old days when an act came on it was introduced with what was called a D-Board No. 1, which was a high upbeat exciting introduction to the act to follow.] I did that with what subsequently became *The Demolished Man*. I also did it with another novel which followed it, and submitted it to Horace Gold who was enthusiastic enough about it to get me started on the writing.

Now, I had not yet fallen in love with the book. I remember the moment when I fell in love with the book quite well. It was the moment when I was attempting to describe the sort of evening party, the evening events which we had all week long, but exclusively in terms of telepaths. And I tried very hard to think of what special quality this party might have, and I thought of the many parties which I had given or attended (since I come essentially from the entertainment business). I thought of parties given for entertainment people, all of whom speak the same slang, who all know the same jokes, and who are very quick and very hip and up-to-the-moment on everything—and I thought: how could I translate that into telepathy? At the same time I suddenly recalled embarrassing experiences when a square, a civilian from the middle west, would by accident come to one of these parties and be completely out of place. Every line of dialogue would be a source of embarrassment; we would all blush, and try to cover up. And it was from all that, that I more or less extrapolated into the telepathic party which I tried to describe; and then, of course, came this great notion of doing it in a typographical pattern, in geometrical forms. I spent about two days in my workshop working it out and I was so pleased with it, so delighted with the entire dimensions that all the various visual effects that one could achieve in writing could do to this story, that at this moment I fell in love with it.

Now, at the moment I fell in love with it I began to drive down very, very hard; as hard as I could. I was in constant discussion with Horace Gold; we discussed many ideas; we dismissed many ideas, we adopted many, but always the central theme was: the open-mystery story. I must explain that I had been until then, in radio, a mystery writer. And there were in those days two forms of writing: there was that of the English mystery in which Body A is found and Body X is found, and Body Y, and so forth and so on, when no one knows what the hell is going on until the last scene, the explaining scene to which the whole thing is tied up. These long and interminable expositions of where, when, you know: Joe got into Max's taxi-cab and he didn't know that Max was keeping Bubbles le Grand who was really financing the entire Mafiosa organization, but he did know that the Mafia was double-crossing him. You go mad with this thing and then where are you? It is endless. Many of you, I am sure, have been forced to go through that.

The other form of mystery which we wrote was the open-mystery, in which you play the events, the conflicts and the acts of violence, as they occur. You keep no secrets from your audience except one secret. The secret either of motivation—why the killer has killed—or, secondly, the gimmick: how he or she killed. These little things you hold back for that additional suspense. It occurred to me that this *Demolished Man* was a marvelous opportunity to do a new form of open-murder mystery. That is, to do a chase in which we lay out the events, event by event; in which we give the motivation, but actually we are cheating on that because the protagonist—who is the killer—does not really know his own motivation. It is concealed within himself and we are now deeply involved in psychiatry. And if any follower of Freud's objects to what I say, I apologize, but this is the thing that really grabbed me.

Now, the three critical points in writing a novel for me—and I am speaking for all of us—are these: First, the attack. There must be a tremendous attack on a story. In fact, I have always believed that the first-rate writer starts a story at the point where a fifth-rate writer stops it. You start at the peak of the action and then you move on. This is, for me, the first big problem.

The second problem is, of course, the mid-point, because at this point you suffer from fatigue. You have been re-reading your manuscript over and over again to get the flow and the tempo, to see if you are headed in the right direction. After you have read it for about 479 times, it begins to occur to you that it is a little bit boring. You get a little tired of it and you say to yourself, "The hell with it! This thing is no good; let's forget it!" It is at this point that you must have the courage to say, "Look, if I liked it enough to start it, it must still be good. I will finish it." But if you are lucky—and indeed I was lucky—you can find a new gimmick at the mid-point which will recharge you with enthusiasm. I found mine in a very curious way. I was writing the book at a cottage we have at a Fire Island beach; I was fishing one afternoon, without luck, and once I was minding my own business casting for fish, suddenly the idea of typography jumped into my mind and suddenly I thought: Good God, it could be possible in the future that people's names could be spelled instead of with letters—they could be spelled typographically. I grabbed my fishing rod, I rushed back to the cottage, spent an entire afternoon next day working out all sorts of typographical gimmicks; this was enough to charge me through the midpoint to get on towards the finishing.

Thirdly, now. The 3/4-mark in a novel is also very dangerous because you start with an earthquake and build to a climax. Well, this is the problem in novel-writing: you start with an earthquake and you try to build to a climax, and at the 3/4-mark you say, "My God, where is my climax? What I have planned seems too flat, what can I do?" If you are courageous and faithful you will say, "The original climax that I planned must be good and I will go through with it." If you are lucky a new idea will come to you which locks in with everything you have done before and this, indeed, did happen to me. A new idea came to me—a new idea which was actually not a new idea but was a put-down of an old idea. The old paranoic idea of philosophy in which "I am truly the only reality and the rest of the universe is false" occurred to me: why not take this and put it down? Take a man, whom I am going to break to pieces, and let him suffer from this rather common concept which most young men in college are playing with off and on. But we'll take it and instead of merely putting it down we will turn it into the novelist's typographical device to achieve a tempo and a finale to the story which will really rack everybody up—because, after all, we are all professional writers and we have only one intent, which is to tell a story to entertain, to grab them, to rack them up, to knock them around. And when we are finished with them, to leave them gasping.

I am not putting down the philosophy of science fiction or the meaning of it, or what great contributions it makes to philosophy. All I am saying is what we professional writers are trying most to do is to draw from within ourselves. Every bit of color, every bit of experience, every gimmick we have used, or seen, we steal (just as much as everybody else) we will take, we will transpose. We will do anything in the world to leave our readers gasping.

But here I am, not describing science fiction writing—I am describing writing itself.

Nowadays science fiction writers seem to be rather jealous because they feel—and perhaps rightly—that the contemporary novel receives a lot more attention and a lot more respect than the science fiction novels which very often are much better than contemporary novels. The science fiction authors feel a little jealous, a little hurt, and a little irritated by this. Which brings me to my point, and it is this: Science fiction is iconoclastic; science fiction is stimulating. I do not care what its pretenses are to philosophy, or to science, or to anything like that. The important thing is that it is mind-stretching, it stretches the imagination, it stretches the mind, and for this reason it is adored by young people, particularly, or by older people who still have young minds, who enjoy having their minds stretched.

The contemporary novel does not stretch the mind. The contemporary novel nowadays, has a tendency to more or less report on the social scene to people who would like to sit comfortably at home and read a report without any sense of responsibility, without any response whatsoever.

But science fiction demands response, and By God! we get it; we kill ourselves to get it!

Which brings us, of course, to the last point about good and bad science fiction. Since science fiction is mind-stretching and since its purpose is to really grab people, shake them, and make them think, it implies that the science fiction author must himself be capable of thought, must have had experience, must indeed have something to say in his book. In other words, science fiction, I think, is the supreme test of the career of the author. There is no other form, (no other form of art) that tests the artist as science fiction does—which is why I would like, in the Russian manner, to applaud my colleagues.

Algol, May 1972

In Memoriam: Alfred Bester (1913-1987)

Isaac Asimov

introduction by Gregory S. Benford

Editor's Note: The Science Fiction Writers of America's annual Nebula Awards volume for 1987 included a memorial on Bester from Gregory S. Benford and Isaac Asimov. It's a fitting end to this collection.

Isaac Asimov, designated the eighth Grand Master of the Science Fiction Writers of America in 1986, here memorializes the ninth, Alfred Bester. Asimov is the indefatigable author of nearly four hundred books, including a clutch of classic science-fiction titles and a number of nonfiction guides to the sciences, the Bible, the plays of Shakespeare, and so on. For most readers of these Nebula Award volumes, he genuinely requires no introduction.

Therefore, let me write briefly of Alfred Bester.

Bester's reputation today owes its enviable sheen to two witty, colorful, and pyrotechnic novels, *The*

Demolished Man (1953) and *The Stars My Destination* (1956), as well as to a dozen or more indescribably dazzling and original pieces of short fiction, among them my own favorite, "Fondly Fahrenheit" (1954), which deservedly appeared in the anthology *Science Fiction Hall of Fame*, published in 1970 to showcase landmark stories that had appeared before the founding of SFWA (the Science Fiction Writers of America) and the inception of the Nebula Awards in 1965. "Fondly Fahrenheit" seems a pizzazzingly paced, far-future riff on Faulkner's "Dry September"—but it isn't. It's that, and an interplanetary psychological thriller about confused identities, the master-slave relationship, and lots more besides. Whatever the story is, its elements mesh in kaleidoscopic ways that propel and unsettle. "The thermometer in the power plant registered 100.9° murderously Fahrenheit. All reet! All reet!" No way to explain. You'll have to read this one for yourself.

My first encounter with Bester's work came with a reading of *The Stars My Destination*, a vivid, space-age recension of Victor Hugo's *The Count of Monte Cristo* and a kind of prose forerunner—if not the actual inspiration—of the psychedelic "through-the-stargate" sequence in the Kubrick/Clarke film *2001: A Space Odyssey*. I have wanted to jaunte ever since, and I can never think of Bester without thinking of imaginative flash, intellectual nimbleness, and an inborn feel for character that always alchemized these first two gifts from mere gimmicks into powerful reflections of distinctive genius.

Two later novels, *The Computer Connection* (1974) and *Golem*^{100} (1980) were disappointing fallings-away from the apex of Bester's early achievement, and we must forgive Bester if he did in fact—according to Charles Platt in a recent reminiscence in the British magazine *Interzone*—come to view *Golem*^{100} as "beyond any doubt" his "best book." Writers always want to think their latest novel is their most nearly perfect, and, both proverbially and provably, they are often self-deluding judges of their own output.

So it apparently was with Bester, that outgoing gadfly with the omnivorous "magpie mind." His last years were reportedly not the happiest, but his knowledge that he had won the Grand Master Award may have afforded some solace. And, too, he had to have realized that his influence on the field has been not only far-reaching but revivifying. Indeed, his work seems to have had a strong impact on the new wave Samuel R. Delany avatar who wrote *Nova* (1968) as well as on the William Gibson computer demon who hard-copied *Neuromancer* (1984) into the annals of the Mirrorshades Mob.

Not long ago, in fact, K. W. Jeter, who has himself been touted as a cyberpunk on the basis of his novels *Dr. Adder* and *The Glass Hammer*, told an interviewer, "What's being labeled as cyberpunk is just the usual rediscovery of Alfred Bester that happens every two or three years in the SF field. Almost everything labeled as cyberpunk, just as with almost any supposedly new thing in SF, really resembles nothing so much as Alfred Bester's closet. Or his wastebasket."

Jeter here indulges in hyperbole, of course, but by no means gross or indefensible hyperbole—for the simple reason that Alfred Bester was an original. Unquestionably, he was the most energetic, vivid, and imitation-inspiring stylistic and structural pathfinder among the nine fine writers upon whom

SFWA has so far bestowed its Grand Master Award. His innovations will necessarily continue to crop up in the work of new writers. Ironically, however, some of these new writers may have only the dimmest notion from whom—at several diluted removes—they are cribbing.

As Peter Nicholls observed in *The Science Fiction Encyclopedia* (1979) "[Alfred Bester] is one of the very few genre SF-writers to have bridged, unconsciously, the chasm between the old and the new wave, by becoming a hero figure for both; perhaps because in his images he conjures up, almost in one breath, both outer and inner space."

—Gregory Benford

Alfred Bester died on September 30, 1987, aged seventy-three. He did not receive an obituary in *The New York Times*.

I know that because I have reached the age where I read the obituary page carefully. I am a quasi-celebrity myself and therefore have accumulated, with the years, a number of friends who are worthy of obituaries and who have also reached the age where such sad bottom lines become increasingly likely. I read the pages, wincing with apprehension, but I dare not miss the smallest notice.

Yet I did not know of Alfred Bester's death till I phoned Harlan Ellison on another subject entirely, and he told me of the event several days after the fact. "Another good guy gone," he said.

Alfie (I never heard him referred to by his friends in any other way) was an old-timer, of course. His first story, "The Broken Axiom," appeared only three months after my first story, and that's old-timish enough for anyone.

He was never what I would call prolific, but prolific just means a lot. It has nothing to say about quality, and as far as Alfie was concerned, the word was quality. He published such early classics as "Adam and No Eve" and "Fondly Fahrenheit." He published a fantasy novella, "Hell Is Forever." He worked with comic magazines and travel magazines; he wrote radio scripts and sat in an editor's chair.

Most of all, he wrote a few great novels. His best (and one that knocked me for a loop when it appeared—a loop which, I realized even at the time, had a strong component of envy in it) was *The Demolished Man*, which appeared in 1953, and which had the well-deserved honor of being the first novel to win a Hugo. It is, with scarcely any argument, I imagine, the best novel about a telepathic society ever written. It is the only one I could thoroughly believe. It seemed to me that if a telepathic society existed it would have to be as Alfie described it. *The Stars My Destination* published three years later was even more flamboyant and scarcely lagged in quality.

But *The New York Times* did not give him an obituary. He was mentioned only in the "ad department" at the bottom of the page for which people pay.

Frankly, I was furious. Any two-bit writer who did not write science fiction would have been memorialized. Any musician, serious, popular, or jazz, would have made it. Any vice-president of any obscure business firm would have been favored with a headline. Upon what meat does a great science fiction writer feed that he is grown so ignorable?

It is a source of great satisfaction to me that the

Science Fiction Writers of America (we guys!) did *not* ignore him. He was chosen to receive the Grand Master Award in 1988 (the ninth), and he knew about it. He was told. Nor will his death abrogate the decision, for it makes him no less worthy. At the next Nebula Awards banquet, the Grand Master Award will be given him posthumously.

And it means, sadly, that in the dozen-year history (so far) of the awards, he will have been the first Grand Master to break ranks and pass on to the Grand Perpetual Convention in the Sky.

Alf a was always a cheerful and amazingly extroverted fellow. He made me seem shy and bashful. Of course, he used to take an occasional drink, whereas I remained a teetotaling sobersides. That may well have made a difference.

In any case, he always gave me the biggest hello it was possible to hand out. I use the term figuratively, because what he gave me more than once (lots more than once, especially if he saw me before I saw him) was more than a verbal greeting. He enclosed me in a bear hug and kissed me on the cheek. And, occasionally, if I had my back to him, he did not hesitate to goose me.

This discomfited me in two ways. First, it was a direct physical discomfiture. I am not used to being immobilized by a hug and then kissed, and I am certainly not used to being goosed.

A more indirect discomfiture and a much worse one was my realization that just as I approached Alfie very warily when I saw him before he saw me, it might be possible that young women approached me just as warily, for I will not deny to you that I have long acted on the supposition that hugging, kissing, and goosing was a male prerogative, provided young women (not aging males) were the target. You have no idea how it spoiled things to me when I couldn't manage to forget that the young women might be edging away.

I wonder if Alfie did it on purpose in order to widen my understanding of human nature and to reform me. No, I don't think so. It was just his natural ebullience.

He was a lot more serious when he called me up. Of all my friends, he and Harlan were most likely to call me up to ask me questions for which they needed answers they couldn't readily find in what reference books were available. I must say that Alfie's questions were hard ones and I could rarely come up with satisfactory answers. Generally, I would be reduced to saying, "Just make something up, Alfie. That's what I do." However, whereas a prolific writer such as myself is forced to make something up as otherwise the steady patter of the typewriter keys is interrupted, Alfie, whose hallmark was quality, could not manage that escape. He had to keep worrying the Universe till he got his answer.

Alfie had a queer and highly lopsided view of the Universe even when he wasn't writing science fiction. He interviewed me for *Publishers Weekly* about fifteen years ago. We spent a couple of hours together, while he managed to maneuver me into odd corners of my life. It finally turned out that I was very fond of soppy old ballads I had heard when I was quite young and that I would occasionally sing them. He encouraged me (I am quite a naive fellow) and so I sang for him, with a wealth of emotion, "The Boulevard of Broken Dreams."

The interview was published, and there on the printed page of the super respectable *Publishers Weekly* was a description of me singing:

I walk along the street of sorrow,
The Boulevard of Broken Dreams,
Where gigolo and gigolette
Wake up to find their cheeks are wet
With tears that come of shattered schemes
(and so on)

It's the only place and the only time where this foul secret addiction of mine was uncovered.

Farewell, Alfie, my friend, with your gaiety and your gooses, your madness and your genius, until I come to join you in that Grand Perpetual Convention—if they let me in.

—Isaac Asimov
Nebula Awards #23, 1987

RICHARD RAUCCI is the author of *Personal Robotics: Real Robots to Construct, Program and Explore the World (1999)*. A former editor for McGraw-Hill and IDG computer technology magazines, Richard also was a Chesterfield Writers Project semi-finalist in 1998.